Copyright © 2023 by Jayne May
All rights reserved.

No part of this book publication may be reproduced, distributed or transmitted in any form without the prior written permission from the author.

This book is a work of fiction. Names, places, names of businesses, characters, events and incidents in this book are from the authors' imagination, or they are used fictitiously. Any similarities or resemblance to real events or real persons either living or dead is entirely coincidental.

Chapter 1

I rest my head against the window of the plane, that familiar scent of reheated aeroplane food lingering in the air. Closing my eyes, I at last drift off into a much needed deep sleep but it doesn't take long…I'm back there, I'm reliving it.

The darkness of the outside feels heavy and oppressive…my heart pounds loudly in my chest. I feel as though the world is closing in around me. I lean against the lamp post next to me, desperately trying to steady my breathing. I feel disorientated as ringing begins in my ears.

I concentrate on my breathing, slowly taking a deep breath in as I count to five before releasing as I count to five.

I hear her footsteps as she slowly reaches my side. "Nic are you okay, are you having a panic attack?" She reaches out toward me but I push her arm away, concentrating on my breathing.

Who is this woman? I thought I knew her better than anyone but why do I get the feeling that this is the first time in 29 years I'm seeing her for who she really is? The sense of dread washes over me again and again. I feel dizzy, like I can't control my body or anything around me…

I wake with a jolt, quickly realising my surroundings and looking cautiously around me, trying to catch my breath.

"Are you okay, dear?" The lady in the seat beside me asks, her hand on my arm in concern.

I exhale waiting for my breathing to steady back to normal, that familiar clammy feel on my skin.

"I'm okay thanks, bit of a bad dream…" I smile nervously as she turns her attention back to her magazine.

It's less than 24 hours since that happened to me and every time I close my eyes it's like I'm back there, finding out all over again.

I look out the window of the plane and focus on the positives of this situation. I'm almost there, my dream is in touching distance.

The view as I come in to land at Madrid Barajas Airport isn't how I expected it to be. Views of field after field, I wonder if it could be a national park, or maybe just farmland? There's certainly more greenery than I was expecting which is lovely to see.

The huge expanses of green grass with the roads running in between remind me of veins as they stretch up and around, connecting everything together. There's a lake or maybe a reservoir, the water looks so still and peaceful almost like a pane of glass, the sun reflecting its' rays against it.

The closer to the airport we get, the more built up it becomes, which is more in line with the image I'd painted in my head. Motorways with the cars driving along appearing tiny from our altitude and huge apartment blocks. I see another tower which looks as though it's made of crystal as it protrudes up into the skyline sitting amongst three other towers. They make me think of trophies sitting on display in their grandeur.

We come into land and as the plane comes to a halt I feel some relief already, relief at being far away from her.

Once I'm off the plane, I follow the signs and reach the luggage carousel. Waiting for my enormous overloaded suitcase, I text my parents to let them know I've arrived safely and that I'll call them in a couple of days. I can't face any more questions at the moment. Judging by my Dad's attitude before I left this morning, he can't accept my decision to be here. If only he knew...

When the luggage carousel starts to move, my suitcase is surprisingly and to my relief one of the first to be off-loaded. I heave the weight of my case onto the floor and exhale, feeling liberated. I'm here and better still, without a return ticket and that's a great feeling.

So many people are scared of flying but believe it or not it's actually one of the few things I'm not afraid of. If I'm on a flight and turbulence starts I'm fine at first, I know it's to be expected. As long as the captain speaks to us to reassure us, I'm back to enjoying the flight. If it lasts too long, and the captain doesn't speak to us, I start to get horrible images.

I imagine the pilot panicking in the flight deck pushing all of those buttons and I have to do something to distract myself, so out comes the book. I do love flying though because, for me, flying always means I'm on my way to a time where I know that I'll feel safer, more settled and calm. More in control of my mind. Whenever I go on holiday my anxiety eases off, I don't worry about every single thing and my mind is just focused on the here and now, not three weeks into the future, not two months away but all on the present moment and those times are so few and far between.

When I'm on holiday or travelling I feel like I'm a completely different person, like I'm the person that I should always be and I feel like I'm the same as everybody else and I fit in.

Getting here today didn't exactly happen according to a carefully laid out plan which is usually more my style. Things happened in rather a rush, which is something that would normally cause me a massive amount of anxiety but in the end, I felt like this was the only option. I just had to get away from there, away from her. I know I've made the right decision.

I follow the crowds out into the busy arrivals hall. There, people stand waiting for friends and family to arrive. I see drivers holding signs as they wait for their clients. I spot a sign for Doctor Rosá and who looks like a Chauffeur waiting for her in his smart grey suit and hat. A casual looking driver holds a sign for Mr and Mrs Corbett, another for Mark Palmer…I wonder what their stories are, why they're here?

I make my way through the noise of echoed excited chatter from the people around me and outside to the taxi rank.

The heat hits me as I step outdoors, the bright sunshine reminds of where I am and what I've been missing since I was last here, in Spain. I get that feeling as though I've just opened a steaming hot oven door and it's wonderful. I can't help but take a deep breath, needing to let some fresh air into my lungs.

Armed with Laura's address written on a scrap of paper I approach a taxi driver, feeling nervous as the palms of my hands begin to sweat. I attempt my first conversation.

"Hola, necesito ir a este dirección por favor."

I show him the piece of paper, keeping my fingers crossed he can read my writing as well as understand me. My heart pounds loudly in my chest as I nervously await his response. He glances down at the paper, seems to do a double take at the size of my suitcase before finally he replies.

"Sí, por supuesto." He reaches down to take the handle of my suitcase from my grasp and taking that as a good sign, I climb into the back of the taxi.

As I sit down, the leather seats feel scalding hot from the intense heat of the day, even through my jeans. The shock of the temperature makes me move my hand sharply away from the seat beside me.

I type out a short text letting Laura know I'm on my way.

Laura - my best friend, lives and works here in Madrid teaching English as a Foreign Language. She made the move out here just a couple of months ago and promises me it's the best thing she ever did and now here I am, suitcase in tow following in her footsteps, only I'll be sleeping in her spare room.

Leaving the airport and heading for the city, the traffic is heavy. Cars, taxis, vans and buses are backed up bumper to bumper along the street as motorbikes do their best to cut through the lanes. Drivers are getting irate, horns are being blasted, people are shouting out of their windows. It's quite a shock to the system.

The taxi driver puts his window further down, muttering away, apparently rather annoyed as he leans his head out of the window. A couple of minutes later we begin to move forward again at a slow pace, passing shops I know from back home, banks, restaurants and bars. I notice to my left on the other side of the road, the Gran Via metro station where we seem to come to a standstill once more. I know this is the nearest station to Laura's apartment and so feeling brave, I tell the driver that I can walk from here.

"*¿Aqui?*" He asks me, pointing to the kerb. He indicates to pull over. When the driver lifts my case from the boot of the taxi I start to have second thoughts. Dragging my luggage around in this heat along with my huge handbag may not be the best idea I've ever had, but it's time to start living now, not panicking. Heaven knows I've done enough of that over the years. This is my new life. MY new life.

I move away from the edge of the kerb and into the shade of a shop awning to check where I am on the map on my phone. Apparently it's a five-minute walk from here, but 10 minutes later I'm completely lost and really regretting wearing jeans to travel, I feel like my legs are suffocating. I take another breather and after catching sight of myself in a shop window, I smooth my hair down. It's starting to frizz slightly already. I rest my sunglasses on my head and it's then that I notice how red and puffy my eyes seem to look. I'm reminded all over again of what happened.

A sudden yapping at my feet snaps me out of my thoughts and I can't help but smile as I bend down to pet the adorable Yorkshire Terrier sitting beside my feet. Her owner rounds the corner holding an empty lead looking rather flustered and muttering his apologies. Noticing the grin that's now appeared on my face, I could do with a distraction like that every time I start to dwell on things.

I look back down at my phone map before scanning my surroundings, looking for street names, anything that can help me. What I wasn't expecting was to see two policemen walking towards me, one of which catches my eye and I think I actually make a tiny gasp under my breath.

They're both dressed in the uniform of navy blue short-sleeved shirts with navy blue trousers, cap and black boots. They have a gun held in a holster on their belts and a silver whistle which the sun reflects off. They walk with such authority but the slightly taller one of the two, I can't take my eyes off him. They're chatting between themselves but I can't stop looking. It's like there's a magnet between us, some kind of force that pulls me in his direction. I feel like I need to make contact somehow, but obviously I don't.

As they draw closer to me I notice his dark brown eyes, his smattering of stubble clearly defining his jaw and that's when it happens, we lock eyes. I hold my breath for a split second, excitement filling my body. As they get closer still I can feel the heat radiating from him. Moments later, they've passed me, they've carried on and so I look back to my phone, only I can't help myself. I have to look over my shoulder and as I do so, I see him doing the same. Dare I think he could be looking at me?

I feel embarrassed and turn my attention back to directions, trying to steady my breathing down back to normal and then suddenly he appears at my side. I'm so shocked that I appear to have forgotten how to speak at first, but I certainly haven't forgotten how to blush and I do so, profusely.

"¿Hola, estás perdido?" He asks me, as he points to my map, his alluring voice in that beautiful language. Think Nicole think, *'perdido'* he said, *perdido*…lost?

"Hola, sí, necesito…erm…ayudarme?"

"You are *Inglés*? English?" he asks.

I smile, feeling partly pleased because now the pressure will be off as I can get directions in English, but also annoyed because I should be speaking Spanish.

"Yes, I'm lost… I think."

I show him where I need to get to, and as he moves his fingers on my phone screen to show me how far away I am on the map, I can't stop looking at his beautiful hands. My eyes travel along to his arms. A silver watch sits on his left wrist, I notice how the watch face is rather scratched. His very well-toned arms, his biceps hiding underneath the sleeves of his shirt, the sleeves rolled up slightly higher.

He gestures that I need to take the next left and walk just a few minutes down the street, at least I think that's what he's saying. I'm struggling to take it in as I can't help but study him some more. His skin has that lovely olive tone which comes from walking around in the sun protecting the public and fighting crime. I bet he's no stranger to admiring glances.

Fully equipped with my directions, I smile my thanks to him. It must be so obvious that I'm attracted to him, but I'm making the most of every second being in close proximity to this man.

"I hope that you enjoy Madrid, how long you stay?" He asks me, the scent of whatever he's wearing filling the air between us. He smells very masculine yet not overpowering. His stance as he talks to me tells me he's confident and completely comfortable in his own skin. He turns the volume down on his radio as it sits against his shirt pocket, the rapid Spanish now becoming just a background hum.

"Well...I've sort of just moved here today..." I take my sunglasses from my head as I talk and attempt to self-consciously tidy up my hair, hoping that it's behaving itself. If anytime I need it to, it's now.

He seems surprised at my response. "Well....enjoy."

On that, he seems to cast his eyes over me once more as he pulls his sunglasses from his shirt pocket and slides them on. He gives me a cheeky smile and off he jogs to catch up with his colleague. Welcome to Madrid, Nicole....

I'm brought out of my trancelike state by the sound of my mobile ringing. It's Laura.

"Hi, I was completely lost, but I think I know where I am now..."

I start to push my case along, pressing my bodyweight against it.

Laura laughs. "I guessed that. Are you sure you know where you are?"

I turn around and stare up at the shop behind me.

"I'm on a corner standing outside a make up shop I think..." I lean back, struggling to see the name with the glare of the sun "...a policeman just gave me directions from here."

"Did he?" She giggles. "I'll wait outside the restaurant called Mio's, it has a green sign you should see it and we're two floors up from there."

"Right okay..."

"If you're not here in five minutes, I'll call you again. I know what you're like with directions and I also know how flustered you get around a good looking man."

Surprisingly, a few minutes later I take the next corner and I see the restaurant a few metres away. I walk past a chemist and a couple of shops that look like they've recently gone out of business. The metal shutters are pulled down and some have graffiti on them. I recognise some of the Spanish slang words sprayed across the shutters. A couple of taxis are parked on one side of the street and a driver stands on the pavement, leaning through into one of the cars impatiently pressing his horn as he stares up at the apartments next to him. I get closer to the restaurant and I see Laura.

She's wearing cut-off denim shorts and a black vest top, her dark hair pulled up into a high ponytail. She chats away with an elderly man with an apron tied around his waist. Seeing me walking towards her she grins with excitement, running towards me. She grabs me so tightly I feel like she'll leave me distorted.

"It's so good to see you."

"Laura….." I sigh, returning her embrace.

Emotion takes over as we continue to hug and I try my hardest to stay strong. She releases me, holding both of my hands in hers and looks at me solemnly, tilting her head like she's trying to look into my soul.

"You're here now Nic…" She tries compose herself, looking emotional. "…put her out of your mind…"

I nod my head, pressing my lips together to stop me from crying yet again. I take a breath as she leads me towards the elderly man who stands hands on hips, outside the restaurant next to us.

"Nic, Nicole, I'd like you to meet Mio."

She motions proudly towards the man. I reach out my hand to shake his.

"*Encantada...*" I tell him I'm pleased to meet him, to which he grins as he shakes my hand placing his other hand on top of mine.

"Guapa...Encantado. I have heard a lot about you, I feel that I...I know you already."

He speaks in a rather husky voice with a very strong accent. Mio has a familiar quality about him, maybe it's because Laura talks about him so much.

Laura gestures proudly. "Mio's the owner of this restaurant, it's one of the best restaurants around." She gives his arm a friendly squeeze.

Mio nods. "This is true…" Which makes the three of us laugh.

Laura turns to me. "Right, I'll take you upstairs get you unpacked and maybe later we could eat here?"

"Sounds good."

We slowly edge away from the restaurant towards the door to the side, which leads up to the apartments above.

"Hasta Luego Mio." Laura calls as we walk away.

Mio waves to us, as he greets some diners into his restaurant. We walk up the two flights of stairs, both of us attempting to haul my case behind us.

"Mio's lovely." Laura starts. "…Diego has known him for years and I call him our 'surrogate Uncle'. He's almost 70 but he still insists on working…." She pauses to catch her breath. "He used to do all the cooking but he's started to slow down a little now, just serving drinks and mostly chats to the customers, they're all regulars."

We reach the top of the stairs, both out of breath from the lugging of my suitcase and Laura opens the seemingly traditional brown Spanish front door and leads me inside. A compact living room houses a burgundy sofa and armchair. Behind the sofa is a dining table, which is home to Laura's laptop. There's a large open window behind the table which a soothing breeze floats through, the people and the sound of the outside on the street now barely audible.

The scene of the window with the laptop on the table is so familiar to me from our numerous video calls. I recognise the wooden blinds as they sit partially pulled up against the window. It feels strange to be here for the first time and yet in some ways, I feel like it isn't the first time because I've seen that image before so often.

A comforting arm is thrown around my shoulders and I look at Laura.

"I can't face talking about it anymore yet…" I tell her.

"Let's get you settled in tonight and relaxed and then tomorrow…we'll talk properly if you feel like you want to. I want your first night in Madrid to be a happy one."

"I like the sound of that." Trying to forget about things for a few hours certainly sounds good.

Laura knows exactly what happened. She found out in the early hours of this morning when I called her in hysterics from the back of the taxi on my way home. I told her I'd booked a flight and she immediately agreed it was the right thing. She even told me that she'd pull a sickie from work to meet me at the airport but I told her no, that I'd find my way…and I will find my way - through this…wont I?

A small open plan kitchen is nestled in the corner and I see three brown doors leading off the living area. I don't feel like I'm really here, it's like I'm in a daze. I wasn't prepared for this and yet, I've wanted it for so long. So much has happened over the last 24 hours that I think I'm still trying to process it all.

Laura takes me through the first door and into her and Diego's bedroom, the scent of Laura's familiar perfume hits me straight away, making me feel at home. The walls are painted a lemon yellow and there's ample space for the double bed with its large wicker headboard and a double wardrobe to the side.

A pine dressing table sits in the corner of the room and I see dozens of necklaces, a few rings and bracelets on display. I have to have a closer look.

"Laura...did you make all of these?" I ask.

"Yeah, I ended up bringing everything with me that I've made so I can carry on out here. I think maybe you had the right idea when you said I should be selling them so, I thought why not see how I go?"

There are dainty silver bracelets with beautiful orange stones, statement necklaces in a variety of colours, but it's a silver ring with tiny turquoise stones in the shape of flowers that catches my eye and I find myself trying it on. I knew Laura had started to make jewellery just before she moved out here and she's sent me a couple of photos of bracelets recently. I asked her why she wasn't putting them out there to sell but wow, these are fantastic. Seeing them for myself I can see exactly how good they are.

The ring I've slipped on is made to look as though the flowers are growing up and around the finger, it's really very delicate looking. I love it.

"These are amazing, you could definitely sell these. Have you had any luck yet?"

She giggles. "Truth be told I haven't even tried yet. A couple of people at work have asked me about pieces I've been wearing so that's a start…"

We continue on with the tour. The next room is the bathroom with a suite in gleaming white complete with toilet, walk-in shower and a bidet.

"I know what you're thinking when you look at that…" Laura points to the bidet and breaks out into a fit of giggles, to which I join in.

Just before Laura moved to Madrid, we stayed one night in a rather posh hotel in Bristol. After dinner that night which consisted of very little food and two bottles of wine, we staggered back to the hotel and she just made it through the bathroom door before being sick in the bidet. In my rather intoxicated state I proudly proclaimed to finally know what a bidet is used for.

We pass back through the living room and I stop to admire a painting on the wall. It's instantly recognisable as the Puerta de Alcalá.

"That's one of Diego's paintings." She tells me. "He went out one night with his camera to capture the image he was looking for and spent the next few days turning the picture into a painting."

"Really? It's fantastic."

I love how he's really captured the feeling of dusk, as the beam from street lights line the road towards it. The sky a subtle shade of inky blue, with a few floating clouds off to the side.

"He displayed that one at his last exhibition, but I knew we had to have it here, so I made him put a sold sign on it straight away." She giggles.

Through the third door we go, into another bedroom.

"I know it's small, but this is your room."

A single bed with a decent sized double wardrobe with mirrors on the front awaits me, which will hopefully store all my clothes I've brought with me. I see a guitar perched in the corner which momentarily transports me back to where Laura and I met, on our Spanish course.

Birmingham - June 2019 – Three months ago…

I sit listening to the soothing rhythm of the Spanish guitar at an evening class not far from home. Maybe the tutor has this music on to hide the awkward silence that would otherwise fill the room whilst he waits for his students to arrive. I like to think perhaps it's to set the scene, to get people ready to start speaking Spanish.

Nervously glancing around I see a couple of people engrossed in their phones, as is the usual distraction nowadays. Gradually more students enter the room and the sound of chatter starts to pick up.

"Can I sit here?"

I turn to see a friendly face.

"Sure, carry on."

"Thanks. I'm Laura." She smiles as she retrieves her notebook and various pens from her bag.

"I'm Nicole...ever studied Spanish before?"

She pauses in thought. "Hmmm, not really. I always fancied giving it a try and I saw an advert for this taster course so I thought, why not. Have you?"

"Not since school, although I always regretted not continuing with it." *Another thing anxiety has stopped me from pursuing.*

"Well it's never too late, you're here now." And she was right.

That's the thing that I noticed straight away with Laura, her positive attitude and by the end of the class Laura and I had clicked. As we were packing away our books, I felt lifted at the fact I'd started the course, fully inspired that someday this could help me to live out my dream of living in Spain. At least it's one small step to getting me there...

Heading outside, Laura nods in the direction of the pub across the street.

"Fancy a drink, or do you need to head off?"

"A drink sounds great."

A few minutes later we're settled in the corner of the pub sharing a bottle of white wine. I can't help but notice as she talks that she occasionally has a slight lilt to her voice and as I listen to her, I do my best to place where the hint of an accent is from.

"Are you local? Only you sort of sound like you have an accent with some words but..."

Laura raises her eyebrows as she takes a drink.

"Not many people notice anymore. I'm Irish, born in Cork. My parents moved us over here when I was eight."

She goes onto tell me that she comes from a huge family. She has two sisters, two brothers and her Mom is one of seven children and her Dad is one of four. Now that's a big family. Especially now that some of her siblings have started to produce their own children too.

"Wow. That's a lot of people in one house when you were growing up."

"Mmm, it was. Still is truth be told, although there's only me and two of my brothers at home now, I really should move out soon but it's just easier staying at home…" She tops up our glasses. "..what about you, do you live with your parents?"

"I moved back home with them four months ago."

She looks surprised. "Oh…" She grimaces slightly "Did you have a break up?"

It feels like I'm opening old wounds but Laura is so easy to talk to.

"James and I were together for seven years, we even got engaged last year. Luckily we never did get around to wedding planning…" I joke, feeling the need to break eye contact just for a second to compose myself.

She listens, nodding her head sympathetically as I tell her about the demise of my relationship with James.

It didn't feel sudden when it happened. The day we moved out - him back to his parents, and me back to mine. It felt almost a relief as things had been so strained between us. There was something not right for the last five months or so of our relationship but I couldn't understand what it was. I even worried that James had depression for a while, but he assured me that he didn't. He just wasn't the same with me anymore. He refused to do anything together, even crying off on my Dads birthday party earlier this year with some excuse or another.

Living together day after day with that feeling was intense. It really knocked my confidence again if I'm honest, and that was a downward spiral for me. I spent hours talking to my sister Annie about my concern of him finally having had enough. Did he tire of me and my anxieties and the way it impacted not just my life but his too?

Annie told me I was better off without him as he was clearly more selfish than we thought if he gave up on us at any sign of trouble…the trouble here being my mental health.

Eventually we decided to call it a day but we should've made that decision a lot earlier, maybe it would've been easier that way.

It's hard even now to adjust to being single again especially when I thought I'd be spending my life with him. I'm not in love with him anymore, but it's still strange without him in my life. We went through a lot together. When I think of how bad my OCD was when we first moved in together all of those years ago, the rituals I had to do every night before bed to check that the flat was secure, the constant seeking of reassurance that we were safe. James was really good to me…at least he was at first. He helped me through one of the most difficult periods of my life and I will be forever grateful to him for his help, love and patience but even patience runs out sometimes it would seem.

"Do you feel ready to meet someone else?" Laura asks.

"I feel like I've slowly started to turn the corner." I think this is the first time I've realised that.

"That's good news. It will take time but you're on the right track now." We clink glasses.

"My sister tried to set me up with someone a couple of months ago but it was just too soon but now…hmmm." I think to myself. "We'll see…"

I play with the beer mat that sits on the table, running my fingers around the edges, feeling uncomfortable. Laura drinks back her wine, her glass now empty.

"How about you?" I ask.

"I can't seem to meet the right man, maybe I'm too fussy?" She laughs. "Nicole, you and I should holiday in Spain someday, to practice Spanish of course."

That became our usual thing every week after our Summer Spanish taster class. Usually on the pretence of talking about what we'd learnt, off we'd go for a drink but inevitably, it turned into just non-stop talking about anything and everything. We started going shopping together at weekends and generally being each other's allies with both still living with our parents in our late twenties, that became our 'thing' that we laughed about. I never imagined then that Laura would feel more like a sister to me than my own twin sister.

Present Day September 2019 - Madrid

"Thanks so much for letting me stay with you, are you sure Diego doesn't mind?"

I follow Laura back out to the kitchen. Laura chuckles to herself as she pours me a glass of bottled water, before sitting down on the sofa. I sit down next to her.

"Don't be stupid, of course he doesn't mind." She nudges me to tell me off. "So, come on tell me about this policeman…" She smirks excitedly, pulling her feet up underneath her on the sofa.

"Oh Laura he was…" Just as I begin to recollect and tell her about him, the front door opens and in walks Diego.

"Ah, *hola* Nicole." He drops his bag down on the floor whilst simultaneously throwing his keys onto the top of the bookcase next to the door. He walks towards me, holding his hand out right, and as he approaches the sofa I stand up to greet him. He takes my hand and kisses me on each cheek.

Again, this is so strange because even though this is the first time we've met in person, we've spoken before when I've been chatting to Laura so we've already done the introductions.

Diego is 10 years older than Laura at 38. His dark brown hair is swept back from his face and is slightly longer at the back.

"Nic's worried about outstaying her welcome already." Laura tells him to which I shoot her a look of embarrassment.

"Nicole…" He pronounces my name Nic-ol-eh. "…You are welcome to stay with us for as long as you want. I hope Madrid is everything you are looking for."

Chapter 2

A short time later I head off to my room to unpack my case and once I've unpacked, wedging as much as possible inside my wardrobe, I suddenly feel really sleepy. I lie down on the bed and rest my eyes just for a few minutes. The next thing I'm aware of is Laura standing next to my bed, waking me up.

"How long was I asleep?" I wonder out loud, the humidity of the room quickly noticeable.

"Not that long really. It's gone nine so get yourself ready and come and meet me and Diego downstairs at the restaurant."

I take a quick shower and snatch my maxi dress from the hanger and pull it on. Topping up my make-up I notice three unread messages on my phone. Two of them are from Annie.

*

"That food was absolutely delicious, *Muy deliciosa…*" I tell the waitress as she removes our plates that night at Mio's.

The three of us have just eaten a selection of tapas including jamon de serrano, manchego cheese, tortilla de español and croquestas mixtas, all washed down with a bottle of vino tinto. I don't normally drink red wine I'm not keen on the taste, but Laura was very insistent that I'd like this one.

Mio's Restaurant is larger inside than I expected. The bar runs for the full length of one side, and I see a typical Spanish fireplace at the rear. All of the tables and chairs are a mismatch other than the booth tables in the windows, but that's part of the charm. The walls are painted a warm terracotta, which meets wooden panelling on the bottom half of the wall, giving the whole place a kind of traditional and loved effect.

Locals are here for tapas or just a few drinks, the atmosphere is really relaxed and the radio plays quietly in the background. Mio employs just a handful of staff to keep the place running smoothly including his 50 year old Nephew, Juan, who Mio trained himself to be his Chef.

I relax back in my seat and look out of the window next to me. Our street is still busy, even though it's getting late. As I people watch, it seems that there's no constant wondering of what the time is, of rushing to the next place, the next meeting. It's a much better pace of life here and I'm so envious.

Laura and Diego sit next to each other on the opposite side of the table from me. Diego sits back in his seat with his arm draped around her and every now and again Laura snuggles into his body, resting her head on his shoulder.

Diego drinks the last of his glass of wine, kisses Laura on the lips and stands up, thanking us for our company.

"Ladies, gracias por su compañía. I have some preparation for the exhibition to do, but enjoy the rest of your night together."

Laura watches him leave with an infatuated smile on her lips. I study her for a couple of seconds, noticing how happy she is.

"You two make such a good couple."

"He's lovely, isn't he?" She smirks. "I'm so glad you've met him in person now. I know it might have seemed a bit sudden me moving in with him, but…."

"You're happy, anyone can see that and that's all that matters at the end of the day."

The two of them met the day Laura went to the Education Centre for her job interview. She had actually finished the interview and as she left the office and stepped out onto the corridor, she walked straight into Diego. She said it was love at first sight, despite the fact he spilt his hot coffee all over her white blouse. He ushered her in the direction of the toilets so she could clean herself up and when she came out about 20 minutes later, she was shocked to see him standing waiting for her and he insisted on taking her to lunch as an apology. A month later, they were smitten and Diego asked her to move in with him.

I knock back my drink. "I don't have red wine lips do I?"

Laura giggles. "Yes, here you go…" She throws a clean napkin in my direction from the holder on the table. "…how about I show you another couple of bars in the area, what do you think?"

"Yeah that would be great but are you sure you don't mind? It's getting late."

She stands up. "Its fine, I don't have lessons until the afternoon tomorrow. It'll be grand."

*

The next bar we go to is back towards the Gran Via Metro station. It has a younger crowd and music playing loudly, enticing people to the dance floor but it still has that care free laid-back atmosphere.

We take a seat in one of the bright red booths and begin to look at the drinks menu when one of the Spanish Songs that I play back at home starts to play and everyone seems to head to the dance floor.

"I love this song…" I drag Laura to dance. The beat of the song, mixed with the red wine I'm not used to drinking makes me sing at the top of my voice along with the music. I feel full of life…and alcohol, as we dance with a handful of people all enjoying a Wednesday night drink in wonderful Madrid. To think I'd just be watching TV right now if I were at home.

The song finishes and I tell Laura to sit down whilst I buy the drinks. I wait to be served at the bar and as I do so, I notice a man about a metre away from me, sipping from a bottle of beer and staring in my direction. The wine I've drank means I have the confidence to make eye contact with him and as I do, he smiles at me. He has closely shaven brown hair, is quite slender and looks to be around the same age as me. The barman edges in my direction.

"¿Dos vinos tintos por favor?" I ask.

Whilst he's busy pouring our wines, I can still feel the stare coming from the guy next to me. As I go to pay for our drinks, suddenly he appears at my side.

"Compraré estos…" I will buy these, he utters confidently.

Before I can argue his €10 note has been accepted by the barman.

"Gracias, estas muy amable." I thank him, unsure of what to do next. Do I stay and speak to him? I suddenly feel quite self-conscious.

He begins to speak to me in Spanish, some of which I understand some of it I don't.

"Lo siento, I understood your name is Luís and that you come here every Wednesday after football, but…"

A look of realisation appears on his face. "I am sorry, I thought you were Spanish. You are right, my name is Luís."

He holds out his hand and as I take it, rather surprisingly he takes it to his lips and kisses the back of my hand. My mouth opens in shock as I look across to Laura who has the biggest smile on her face as she gestures for me to look away from her and back to him.

"Nicole."

"I am with friends." He beckons behind him towards a booth, the next one down from where Laura is sitting.

About five lads some of them still wearing their football kits, sit around the table surrounding a silver bucket filled with bottles of beer. One of them facing our direction raises his bottle towards us in greeting to which I awkwardly smile back at him.

Struggling to make myself heard with the music still pounding in the background, I lean in towards Luís.

"I'm with my friend over there, she's English too."

He nods to Laura, who is half texting on her phone and half watching us. I start to feel nervous, I feel totally out of practice with this kind of thing and my confidence has recently taken a further battering. I don't know whether I should ask him to join us or just thank him for the drink and go back to Laura. It seems he reads my mind as he leans into me.

"I know that you need to get back to your friend but how long are you here on holidays? I would love to take you out, to show you our city."

I feel on edge. "I actually, I sort of live here too. I only arrived today." It seems so surreal saying that and for the second time in one day, but it feels amazing.

His smile reaches his eyes; I notice he has really kind looking eyes which stand out more because of his closely cropped hair. He takes his mobile from the back pocket of his jeans.

"Can I have your number?"

"Erm…yeah sure. I'm hoping to change to a local number…"

He taps away on his screen before passing his mobile over to me.

"Put your number in here…" He touches my arm lightly with his other hand which catches me off guard. "…You must remember to tell me your new number also."

Luís returns to his friends as I take a seat beside Laura in the booth.

"Mmm, he seemed nice." She smirks as she watches him join his group of friends.

I feel myself blush slightly, as I pass Laura her long awaited glass of wine.

"I can't quite believe that just happened."

Laura checks her watch. "You've been here, what five hours? And you've already been approached twice."

"Twice?"

"Don't tell me you've already forgotten the policeman?" She giggles, throwing her wine around her glass as though she's stirring it, just like she's trying to stir me now.

"He hardly approached me in that sense of the word, he could see I was completely lost, even with a map in my hand." I lean back against the comfortable high backed booth seat as I picture his face. "…although I wish he had Laura…I'm not kidding, he was absolutely gorgeous. I can still smell his aftershave when I picture him, it must have ingrained itself into my senses."

Laura leans her head back, copying my position against the seat as she's seemingly trying to imagine what he looks like, before we both roar with laughter. Luís and his friends look in our direction and so, we do our best to turn the volume down, which is more than can be said for the DJ who plays another great song and this time, it's Laura's turn to drag me to dance.

Chapter 3

The next day, stepping back outside from the cool, air-conditioned mobile phone shop the scorching temperature kisses my skin once again.

For me, you can't beat that natural feeling of heat from the sun. I was beginning to get goose bumps for a minute being indoors. Back to the pleasure of outside and with Laura's help, I've managed to buy a new sim card for a local network, which will make things easier and cheaper to keep in touch with my parents back home.

We stroll down the busy Calle Gran Via, passing those dressed smartly in suits, with an air of professionalism about them clearly being on their way to work. There's tourists with their maps and cameras, stopping to take pictures of anything and everything. People bumping into each other as they reach the pavement from crossing the road, the next set of people attempting to cross the street before the lights change again.

The Calle Gran Via is one of the main streets of Madrid and is home to some of my favourite clothes shops, dozens of hotels and commercial buildings, perfume shops and places to eat. We attempt to cross the road as the lights change in our favour and the street feels huge with the four lanes of traffic. I think the sheer amount of cars, taxis and buses makes it seem even bigger but with it not being a confined space and with the fresh air around me, I don't feel too enclosed.

"So what shall we do next?" Laura asks. "Please don't say the *Mejores* football Stadium…"

"There's so much I want to see that I don't know where to start, but listen don't feel like you have to be with me all the time. I'm perfectly happy to stroll around on my own."

"I know you are, but I just want to make sure you're settled in." She links my arm as we continue, turning off to the left in the direction of the Puerta de Alcalá. "Don't forget it's a novelty for me having someone here from back home."

I loose myself in thought for a couple of seconds before Laura continues.

"If you want to talk about it Nic, you know you can. I just don't want to bring things up if you'd rather forget for a while…"

I gesture towards a table outside a café. "I don't think I can quite believe it Laura, it's the shock of it." I sit down before moving myself closer toward the table as she takes the seat beside me.

Laura grabs the drinks menu before resting her chin on her hand in expectation.

"Shall we get coffees?" She signals the waiter.

"Sure."

I rest back into my chair as I finally feel able to speak about it some more.

"I know she was upset when I left but even after all that, after she told me what she did, it's like she couldn't understand why I had to leave, why I had to get away from her." I give up trying to hold in my tears.

Laura rubs my hand in support. "Now you're away from her you'll have time to try and get your head around things. Just try and let yourself work things through, take your time. Remember the things you've learnt over the years with Gill. I know it's difficult to see the positives in the situation directly with Annie but, the positives of here, of what you're doing now."

I think back to the numerous conversations over the years with my counsellor, Gill and how we talked about my relationship with my sister.

"I don't think me or my head will be able to understand any of this, ever. What about Amelia? How could she let Pete think that…" I subtly wipe my eyes as our coffees are placed in front of us. I take a breath before I carry on.

"It's like she has always been this constant in my life, not just as my sister but as my friend. But she always has to be better than me at everything. I always remember my Mom saying 'Nicole's the dreamer, the over thinker and the worrier, but Annie just goes for it' and she was right. Annie goes for whatever she wants and who cares who gets hurt along the way. Everything always had to be about her and it still is, even now. " I can hear my voice getting louder. "I hate the fact it took her doing this to me to get me out here."

Laura shakes her head. "Nicole I think that's the only good thing to come out of it. You…finally following your heart and coming here to start anew."

"It's a shame it took my sister breaking my heart to do it though."

April 2005 – Aged 15.

It's Saturday afternoon and Annie is desperately trying to persuade me to go with her to watch the local football team play, which is mostly made up of boys from our year at school.

She's had a crush on Ben Jacobs in our year for a while now and he's been picked to play today and she's desperate to get his attention, although I'm sure she already has it. I don't know what it is with Annie it's like she walks into a room and every boy there sits up and dusts himself off, pleading with her to look their way and who can blame them? I know we're twins but I should probably point out that we're unidentical and we couldn't have more different personalities if we tried.

Annie is the oldest by just seven minutes, we have the same shade of brown hair, although Annie's currently trails halfway down her back and she has a fringe, whereas mine is just below shoulder length and never seems to do what I want it to do. The slightest bit of moisture in the air and bam, my hair is a ball of frizz. I never really do anything different to my hair, I rarely even wear it up. I feel like if my hair's down and around my face, I can hide behind it to some extent, maybe it's my way of protecting myself and stopping people seeing the real me, the anxious me who is trapped inside her own torturous mind.

A couple of years ago I used to be more adventurous with my hair, trying out styles occasionally even just a simple ponytail, but I'll never forget one time in geography class one of the girls kept staring at me and nudging the girl next to her and they were giggling. A few minutes later one of them shouted so everyone could hear *"did you style your hair this morning whilst hanging out the window?"* I felt humiliated as the whole of the class burst out laughing. After that day I always felt safer with my hair down, I can hide behind it and conceal how I'm feeling inside.

I'm organised, honest and loyal. I like to think that I'm confident at times, but that's something that I've always struggled with. Anxiety is a problem I've had ever since I can remember. Annie on the other hand, I would say has more of a hippy persona. She's almost always late, is laid back and even she herself would say she's scatty. She's quite often the loudest person in the room and she's got that 'go out and get it attitude' that I've secretly always desired but somehow never really managed to adopt. We get on well which is why I find it hard to say no to her and so, she drags me along to the football club close to home.

The chill in the early April morning air makes the plastic seats feel freezing as we sit down on the front row. I pull my black woollen coat further underneath my legs for protection against the cold temperature, that simple act alone stirs up my restless mind. I'm wearing a black coat, black…that reminds me of funerals does that mean something bad will happen? Horrible images start to invade my mind making me start to panic.

"There he is…" She grabs hold of my arm in excitement, snapping me out of my solitary unwanted thoughts.

I look ahead of us on to the pitch. "So what's the plan? Are we sitting here and he'll spot you and come running over to celebrate with you if he scores?"

"Oh if only…no, he'll see me sitting here and then after the game we'll go to the clubhouse and get talking and he'll say 'I didn't know you liked football'…"

"…but you don't." I interrupt.

"Ssssh, he doesn't have to know that does he?" We laugh loudly, a few of the players actually look in our direction. One of them holds eye contact with me and I feel myself begin to blush.

In fairness Annie does seem to be at least attempting to watch the match. I find myself watching the players trying to see who I recognise and who I don't. That same player keeps looking in our direction, maybe he's looking at me, but how can I tell? I smile shyly and he smiles back, oh okay, that's how. My confidence goes up a notch.

Annie looks at me "Are you and Liam Scott checking each other out?"

"What? Noooo..." I feel my heartbeat begin to pound louder.

She laughs. "Yes you are...I saw that."

I can't hide the look on my face. "We were only smiling Annie."

"That's how it staaaarrrrtss..." she sings happily.

"He *is* fit..." I admit.

"So are you, Nicole."

After the game we stand at the bar in the clubhouse with a lemonade each, and we share a bag of ready salted as the lads walk out from the changing room. Ben looks directly at us and I think Annie holds her breath...well, that is until he walks to the opposite side of the room to sit with a group in the year above us at school.

"I can't believe that." She shakes her head in disbelief.

I turn away, taking the last couple of crisps and as I greedily eat them, I see Liam walking in our direction. I freeze.

"It's Nicole isn't it?"

Annie flinches next to me.

"Erm, yeah h-h-hi Liam."

"I'm Annie…"

Liam glances at her. "Annie." He nods his head before looking back at me.

"You two don't normally come here do you?"

I laugh. "No, not really…but…"

"I persuaded her, it was my idea." Annie jumps in.

I smile meekly.

The three of us spend the next ten minutes making small talk. He asks me if I plan on coming to the game next week. But I'm desperate to use the loo, even though I don't want to go whilst I'm talking to Liam and it seems to be going well. I head off for the fastest pee in history. A few minutes later as I leave the ladies toilets I can hardly believe what I'm seeing.

Annie stands close to Liam, she tosses her hair over her shoulder which is a move I've seen her do so many times before when she's flirting and wants to get attention. She's holding onto his arm and every couple of seconds she moves in closer still. Liam doesn't look like he's pushing her away. I stand frozen on the spot. My heartbeat quickens, I feel such an idiot. It's not me he likes it's her, and Annie…well she could see I liked him yet she's throwing herself at him.

Moments later, Liam is walking away and out of the door. I don't know what to say to her. I take a deep breath, tentatively walking back over to my sister.

"Oh, where did he go?"

"He had to go, his Dad was waiting outside in the car…how embarrassing." She cringes.

Disappointment fills me.

She starts to grin. "He gave me his number though…" She clasps her mobile triumphantly.

I look down at the ground, feeling humiliated. For a second though, I do wonder if she means he gave her his number for me. Maybe she was working her magic on him to get his number for me?

"Really? Well I should text him later and…"

"Ssssorry Nic, I mean he gave ME his number, he said we should go out sometime."

"Ugh, well thanks Annie, that's…thank you." I stand shell shocked.

"Oh don't be like that sis…you were only looking at him, it's not like you really fancied him or something."

She looked so proud of herself and that look on her face stayed with me for weeks. I knew I should've confronted her about what I saw her doing, so why didn't I?

Present Day

We continue walking, passing the well-known Metropolis Building and through an area of the street with more greenery. Lush green trees sparingly line the curb as we approach the Plaza de Ciebles. The noise of the engines of a group of motorbikes flying past startle us both for a second, as they increase their speed to make it through the lights before they change to red.

The plaza is a square which is home to beautiful cream marble buildings, including the Bank of Spain. As we get closer to the Ciebles

Palace it's really impressive, it reminds me of a beautiful white castle jutting out from the cloudless blue sky.

Sitting just across from the buildings with the traffic flowing by in between is the Ciebles Fountain. There are Spanish flags being proudly displayed on flagpoles, the flags waft very gently in the breeze. Even the flags are relaxed here it would seem.

I lean next to the main building feeling really contented whilst Laura takes my photo. I see to my left hand side a couple of policemen and my heart flutters. It's obviously not him there's thousands of policemen in Madrid, but it's nice to be reminded of him all the same.

Laura snaps me out of my daydream. "Are you going to get in touch with Luís later to give him your new number?"
We walk slowly, still admiring the pristine buildings.

"I already have…"

"You see this is just what you need, keep yourself busy and enjoy yourself…" Laura nudges me.

She certainly has a point, and just putting some distance between me and Annie feels in some way better already.

"Luís asked me to meet him tonight…"

"Oooh. You're going aren't you?"

"I think so…" I tell her nervously which is met by a look of annoyance.

"No, let me tell you instead. You. Are. Going."

I roll my eyes.

"Just think of it as making new friends in your new country, after all, it's exactly what you need."

"I know I know." Laura does make sense. "Anyway, I need to work out how far away the *Los Mejores* Stadium is…"

"Nic, you know you're my best mate, but you also know that I find football boring…"

"I know, but I've always enjoyed watching *Mejores* even when I was a kid, my Dad used to watch them sometimes and there's just something about that team that I love…"

Laura exhales. "Okay, you've won me over. But whatever you do, don't tell Diego. I've always refused point-blank to go to any games with him, so if he finds out…"

I mimic zipping my lips. "My lips are sealed. We'll go later this week."

*

We head back to the apartment via the *supermercado* for some water and then Laura goes out to work. I charge my mobile in readiness to take the hundreds of photos that I'll no doubt be taking.

I feel a bit lost, unsure of what to do with myself. I need to keep busy so I make myself a late lunch of a cheese sandwich, saying the names out loud in Spanish of the items that I'm using. Every little bit of practice helps.

I use pan (bread), queso de manchego (manchego cheese) no mantequilla (no butter) and I cut my sandwich with a cuchillo (a knife).

I relax down onto the sofa and hear the sounds of the birds chirping outside, the vague sound of chatter and occasional roar of a car engine. It's good to just enjoy the sounds around me as I eat my sandwich. Next,

I reply to Luís agreeing to meet him later tonight at the Mercado de San Miguel, that's assuming I can find it with my sense of direction.

Now I'm here in Madrid, I need to make sure I make the most of every minute. I want to see all the sights, experience the culture, the food and I want to practice as much as Spanish as possible. I sit down at the table and look at the leaflets Diego gave me this morning on Spanish courses at the Adult Education Centre where both he and Laura work.

There's lots to choose from, but the first to catch my eye is one full day per week, including a salsa lesson. Another option of two evenings per week works out slightly cheaper, but I think I'll go for the first choice with the salsa dancing thrown in. Something else I've always fancied trying but never have.

The course runs on either Saturday or Monday, so I make the decision to enrol tomorrow to start this coming Saturday. This course along with speaking more Spanish on a daily basis should really help me to not only improve, but to also pick up the language quicker. This feels better doing something proactive, keeping my mind occupied. But it doesn't take long for the self-doubt to creep in. Can I do it? I picture myself sitting in a class of people, the teacher asking me a question…my face burning with embarrassment as everyone turns to look at me. I feel annoyed, pushing those thoughts away. Yes I CAN do it is the answer. I know I'll be nervous on my first day, but once I'm there and see everyone else is in the same situation, I'll be fine.

A short while later, I'm woken by the sound of a video call coming through on my laptop. I feel confused at first, wondering where I am for a second. I dash over to the table to my computer, pressing one of the keys to wake the screen up.

I see my Mom's face appear on the monitor and I note, from the background of our childhood photos on the wall that she's in the living room.

"There she is...oh, Clive look, isn't it wonderful that we can see Nicole, even though she's 839 miles away in a different country."

It seems my Mom has been doing her Internet research as she continues to fuss.

"Are you okay love? You haven't burnt have you? Only you look little pink." She starts moving around on the screen as though she's trying to examine me.

"No, stop worrying. I've just woken up and it's really hot in here."

"Did you hear that Clive? Nicole's just woken up from a siesta it's what they do in Spain, isn't it? How lovely."

My Dad appears on screen beside Mom. I can tell that she's actually really excited for me, which makes me feel even more certain that this experience is going to be brilliant.

I watch my Dad on the screen for a moment. "You're quiet, Dad. How's things?"

My Dad seems awkward and clears his throat. "Things are fine, it's just I don't understand why you left the way you did."

"It was rather sudden, Nicole." Mom adds.

"I...I, you know me if I didn't do it then I'd talk myself out of it for some reason or other." I fake a laugh, doing my best to cover up the real reason. Why am I covering for her?

"You didn't even say bye to Amelia. Have you and your sister had a falling out?"

"I don't want to talk about it Mom." I feel myself tensing up.

"Don't be silly, you two haven't fallen out in years, it's all rather dramatic isn't it? Dramatic is more like Annie not you. You're sensible, careful…"

"Yes I am aren't I? Maybe it's time that changed!" I bite.

It seems that the upset that my sister caused the night before I came here and the huge secret that I'm stupidly keeping for her is starting to grind on me.

Chapter 4

Ready to leave the apartment, I'm dressed in my navy blue midi dress with my hair pulled into a bun. I set out with the maps on my phone to find the Mercado de San Miguel. Nerves almost get the better of me, I feel shaky but I pull myself together, telling myself how I'll be experiencing somewhere new tonight. I picture how beautiful the *mercado* looks from the images online.

As soon as I step onto the street outside, I start to feel better. The humidity of the evening slaps me in the face but I'm not complaining, it's great to step outside without having to have a cardigan, a jacket, a scarf and whatever else is needed to keep the English weather from freezing you. I can hear the happy sounds of the relaxed chatter of friends and families alike as they sip their drinks outside Mio's. I can even smell the warmth, if that makes sense? It's consuming every single one of my senses. I see Mio just finishing his cigarette as I approach the restaurant.

"¿Guapa, Buenas tardes. Cerveza, vino? You would like drink?" He looks tired, but I get the feeling he's one of those people who is only happy when he's chatting and serving others.

"Buenas tardes Mio. No gracias. Voy a Mercado de San Miguel. ¿Puedes ayudarme por favor?"

I point to my map on the screen asking him to help me with directions. His finger hovers over the screen, seemingly unsure of what to do and then he grunts something under his breath about technology.

He locates our street. "Ah, *aqui*..." He declares.

Mio tells me it's around a ten minute walk to the market. He gives me directions in Spanish, which I then repeat to him in English, just to be sure.

I start the gentle stroll, turning left and following the road along, people watching as I go. There's a calm feel in the air as I round the corner on to the Calle Mayor, oh how I could get used to this pace of life. Everyone is taking it easy and it's so refreshing. Despite Madrid being the capital city and it obviously being busy, life just seems so much simpler here and it's because of the wonderful laid back atmosphere.

I love strolling down the street and hearing Spanish spoken at the turn of every corner. I just feel that this is where I'm meant to be, I have such a passion for this country.

A quick check of the watch tells me I have five minutes until I'm due to meet Luís…I feel nervous suddenly so I slow my walk down even more, taking some deep breaths.

According to Mio's directions, Calle Mayor will turn off to the left at any minute. There it is, I can see the glass fronted market ahead of me. It's not really what I was expecting, it is so much more than that.

Darkness is beginning to set in now and the lights from inside the markets shine warmly out onto the street, making the area feel cosy as I approach the front. There's no sign of Luís yet and that's when I begin to wonder if he'll arrive late with that cool laid back Spanish trait he no doubt has but, as long as he actually turns up, that's fine by me.

I give myself a minute to take a couple of pictures of the front of the market. Fresh fruit stalls sit near the front. The stand out colours of the green water melons and the juicy yellow lemons make a great photo. I can almost taste the red apples they look so good.

"I would like to taste your watermelons."

I turn around with a start to see Luis smiling at me with his hands in his pockets.

"Sorry?" I ask, trying to supress a laugh.

He kisses me on each cheek. "You would like to taste some watermelons?"

"Ohhh, sorry I thought you said something else…never mind." I wave the thought away.

"What do you think of the market?"

"Very inviting."

He puts his hand on the small of my back as we walk up the steps into the market. Luís is dressed smart but casual in a burgundy and black short-sleeved chequered shirt, which he wears with black jeans.

"You are looking very beautiful tonight." He tells me as we reach the glass doors.

"Oh…thank you." I just about manage to say between blushes. He's very sweet.

Inside the *mercado*, people are talking animatedly, some are eating, some are drinking and others appear to be simply watching and absorbing, deciding which stall deserves their attention the most. Again I'm struck at how vivid everything seems. The aroma of delicious meat cooking makes my stomach growl.

"You would like to walk around first, or…" He asks.

I nod. "Lead the way."

We begin to walk through, passing stalls selling different varieties of cakes that ooze with Spanish tradition. Luís pauses at the next stand which sells a selection of red wines that appear full of rich flavour. He takes a small sample cup to taste, gesturing to me to take one but I decline. It's the bread stall that catches my eye and the mouth-watering aroma reminds me of a safe and homely kitchen with the oven full of delicious crusty bread baking. I could quite happily live here in the *mercado*.

"Is there anything you would like to try?"

I'm practically salivating at all of these different foods on offer.

"Erm…yeah everything." I giggle.

"How about some tapas?" He nods towards a stall in front of us. The stall we stop at has many different types of tapas, wines and I even spy churros.

"I know I probably should have these last but, it is going to have to be churros for me."

Luís smirks playfully. "You must try something else first… these are delicious." He motions to some fresh bread topped with goat's cheese and onion chutney.

"The thing is, that's goat's cheese…I can't eat goats cheese." I grimace.

He tilts his head and looks at me realising I won't be defeated, he gives in easily.

"Okay, that is fine. Is there anything else that you do not want? Are you happy for me to choose for you? I am your expert."

"Erm….squid." I tell him.

He nods his head in agreement and looks deep in thought. "Leave it to me I will show you some delicious food."

He places his hand on my shoulder and steers me over to some high stools at a table just behind us. I take a seat, and place my bag on the table, whilst I wait eagerly for his choice of foods.

As yet, I still don't know much about Luís, other than he considers himself to be a food expert. I do find him attractive and quite charming, so I'm looking forward to finding out more about him.

A few minutes later he returns just about managing to carry two plates loaded with different foods and two small glasses of red wine.

"I remember you were drinking red wine when we met so..." He places the glasses down on the table.

"You remembered well." I smile, trying to hide the fact that it's really not my drink of choice. I don't want to seem rude.

He takes the seat opposite me and pushes the two plates into the middle of the table filled with bite size pieces of bread with different toppings.

"Obviously you know that is goat's cheese - that one is for me. Here we have scrambled egg on a bed of tomato." He looks up at me. "Trust me it is better than it sounds. With the correct seasoning, the taste is *fantastico*. This is manchego cheese with pepper and chorizo, then lastly this one is spinach croquetas."

"Wow, where do you suggest I start?"

"Nicole, I am sorry. I should be speaking Spanish for you to practice?"

I laugh. "It's fine, don't worry."

On that note, he repeats the names of all of the foods in Spanish.

Luís and I get to know each other more as we eat the beautiful food in front of us. I learn that Luís is a couple of years younger than me at 27, is an only child and has lived in Madrid all his life. His parents own and run a *panadería*, a bakery, in the northern area of the city.

"When I was younger after school, I would help my mother to serve customers. My father and his brother would make the most wonderful breads and cakes."

I swallow my last bite of manchego and chorizo.

"I think I could quite happily live on bread alone..." I laugh. "...fresh bread, olive loaves..."

Luís smiles. "You have the good taste."

"So do you work at the bakery?" I ask.

"My parents wanted me to work there full-time when I finished school, to be in the family business but I wanted to be outside, to work outdoors." He sips his wine gently.

"Who could blame you for that...what do you do now?"

"I am a builder..." He opens his hands in front of me to reveal very tired and dry looking hands.

I wouldn't have pictured him to be a builder really. I lean towards him. "Ah, so I see."

Without even thinking, I rub my finger lightly over the dry skin on the fleshy part of his thumb to see him revert his eye contact back to my own. Feeling a little unsure of the situation, I take drink to distract me.

"Also I love to make furniture, this is my hobby."

"What sort of thing do you make?"

"I have made furniture for the garden, tables and benches. My dream, it is to someday open a shop to sell furniture that I have made with wood that I have recycled."

Luís shows me several photos of furniture he's made on his phone, it seems he's very creative.

"Wow Luís, these are brilliant. Honestly."

The carving he's made on the back of the beautiful bench he shows me, the care he's clearly taken with this, it's so delicate.

He begins to ask more about me. I tell him about being made redundant last year and the fact that I've stuck to temping jobs ever since whilst I tried to decide what I wanted to do, but still being unable to figure it out. I decide not to bring up the subject of James.

I tell him how much I love his country and how I met Laura just a few months ago, although it feels longer. He looks completely absorbed as I tell him about my life back home. But then I see his expression change slightly, an air of sadness shows on his face.

"I work just three days each week now, there is not many building opportunities at the moment, so my hours they have been made less."

I sympathise with Luís. "That's awful, and then you get me coming out here hoping to get a job."

Luís laughs. "Believe me we are glad that people like you think so much of our country and tourism is very important for us. As for you looking for work here, that happens all over the world. I hope you will find work."

He raises his wine glass towards me, albeit his almost empty glass. "To finding a job. *Trabajar...*"

"*Trabajar.*"

I can't believe how quickly the time has gone tonight as Luís suggests moving on to a bar at the Plaza Mayor which is just a stone's throw from here.

As we head out into the night, I can feel the after effects from the strong red wine. I touch my hair, hoping that it isn't starting to go bushy. Again, Luís puts his hand on to the small of my back as though to steady me as we walk from the market through the walkway into the square.

The Plaza Mayor houses several bars that all share the same outdoor seating area, that being the square itself. Much like the market, the buildings which surround us have the golden lighting jutting out from underneath every archway that faces the *plaza*. Although it's close to eleven, the square is still bustling with people as they walk through. Some of them stop for a drink in one of the bars or take a seat underneath one of the elegant lamp posts, the glow from the lights providing their ambience.

Luís leads me to a table outside of one of the bars over on the left-hand side. The tables are adorned with red tablecloths and the glimmer from a small candle in the middle of the table. I make myself comfortable on one of the white metal bistro style chairs and begin to glance through the menu. As I do so, the waiter appears at our side and before I have the chance to object, Luís orders us more red wine. It's probably a good thing I know, as mixing my drinks certainly hasn't ended well for me in the past.

"It's lovely here." I declare. I momentarily stand to angle my chair slightly to face the view which also means I'm now sitting slightly closer to him.

Luís relaxes back in his seat and I catch him looking at me for a moment before he responds.

"It is very nice, especially at Christmas time when we have the markets here."

I start to picture that scene in my mind. "I can imagine…"

The waiter brings our wine and we both take a drink as I continue to take in my surroundings. Luís leans forward and points in the direction of the statue across from us in the middle of the square, which is that of someone riding a horse.

"The statue is of Felipe III…the building directly behind it is the Casa de la Panadería."

The said building has two small towers protruding from the roof..

"Oh, the house of the bakery?"

Luís nods in agreement. "Inside, if you need it is a tourist office and you can also get tours around the building."

"I'll remember that, thanks."

Well our first awkward silence is here. I continue to people watch whilst intermittently sipping my wine. A busker sits at the opposite side of the square, playing a soft rhythm on his guitar…it's blissfully soothing and I can feel goose bumps on my arms as I let myself be taken in by the music. I've always loved to hear the sound of acoustic guitar, the strum of the strings. It must be wonderful to be able to play an instrument.

"You said that you are a twin?" Luís asks.

I pause mid drink. I have to answer. I swallow heavily.

"Yes I have a twin sister, Annie." I feel aggravated just talking about her. I almost have to grit my teeth.

He seems genuinely fascinated. "I have a friend who is a twin. You are youngest?"

"How did you guess?" I look away for a second wondering how to subtly change the subject.

We continue chatting about our respective families but I manage to steer the conversation more towards his family, luckily without any more silences before the evening comes to an end.

We take a slow stroll together back onto the main street of Calle Mayor to get a taxi home. As we live in different directions, he insists I take the first taxi that arrives. As the now familiar sight of the white taxi with its green light on parks next to us, Luís opens the door for me.

"Thanks for a lovely evening." I kiss him on each cheek. (You see I'm a natural with the etiquette already). He takes hold of my left hand as simultaneously he kisses me in return.

"I have enjoyed it. Would you like to go out again?"

"Sure, you've got my number." I smile. Then slightly unexpectedly, he gently touches his lips to mine, which then turns into a full-blown kiss. I'm not going to lie it's actually really nice and when it's over I climb into the back of the taxi and he closes the door behind me.

Chapter 5

I arrive at the Adult Education centre in the Salamanca area mid-morning the next day. It doesn't take long to enrol on the course and I even get to meet my tutor, Inés.

Inés looks to be in her early 50's with long black curly hair, and is immaculately dressed in a grey pencil skirt which shows off her curves, and a black blouse. She's really friendly and reassuring about the course.

"Trust me it will not take long, you will pick up the language…" She clicks her fingers. "…just like that." Her encouragement gives my confidence a welcome boost.

"That's good to hear."

I see Laura emerging from a classroom with her arms full of paperwork as she attempts to wave hello, without dropping anything. She has the biggest smile on her face.

I walk through the reception area towards Laura who looks as though she might burst at any second, it's like she can't keep still.

"*Hola*… everything okay?" I laugh to myself wondering what's going on.

"I'm fine, just…..well, never mind…" she gestures her hand dismissively "…Are you all signed up then?"

"Yep, all enrolled and ready to start tomorrow."

Laura uses her free hand to check my watch. "That's good news, but the even better news is I now have an hour before my next class so that gives you just enough time to buy me a coffee and tell me all about last night."

"...and I think you'd better start talking too." I tell her.

I buy two café con leches and two slices of orange and almond cake from the cafeteria outside and join Laura at her table on the patio area. She looks more relaxed now with her sandals kicked off, her legs outstretched and the sunglasses on.

"Here we are..."

I place the tray down in front of her and take my seat in the chair Laura has readily positioned for me so I'm facing the sun. It's another beautiful day, in fact, I can't imagine there being any other kind of day here as I see another cloudless sky.

I take a bite of the cake, tasting the fresh light sponge and the subtle flavour of the orange.

Laura prompts. "Come on then, I take it last night went well?"

I swallow my mouthful of cake, watching her. "You first...out with it..."

She starts giggling. "Well, I might be getting excited prematurely but...one of the students in my class last week commented on some of my jewellery I was wearing and she seemed shocked when I told her I made it myself. This morning she did it again and she asked me if I'd be willing to make her one of these bracelets..." She gestures toward her wrist.

Today Laura wears a very simple rose gold bracelet with stones in two different shades of pink. It's simple, but the colours she's put together are so effective.

"That's brilliant Laura…"

She takes a sip of her coffee. "Thanks…I feel really excited I know it's only one bracelet but…have to start somewhere…"

"Exactly." I have a really good feeling about this.

She nudges me. "So….last night was a late-night."

"Oh no, I didn't wake you and Diego did I?" I've only been staying with them for two days, I was hoping they'd barely know I was there.

"Don't be daft, I went straight back to sleep. Diego didn't even stir…all this work he's doing for the exhibition is exhausting him."

"When's that?"

"The exhibition? It's early January here at the centre, just some of his paintings, sketches and another of the art lecturers….stop changing the subject." She laughs.

"No…I'm interested."

"Hmmm…interested enough to come to the show then?"

"I'll be there, definitely." I take another bite of cake.

Laura holds her hand out toward me. "So….last night?

"It went well, I think. He's really nice, very easy to talk to, but…" I drink some coffee. The suspense is almost killing her.

"…But what?"

"Erm… I'm not sure, I don't know if we have much in common and I just, well…do I like him in that way?" I ask myself out loud.

Laura thinks for a moment. "How did you leave things, are you going out again?"

"Yeah I'll see him again I think. As I said he's nice, and at the end of the night…" I feel myself blush.

"You didn't? You went back to his?" Laura's almost jumping out of her seat with excitement.

"Of course I didn't…"

She laughs. "Okay… So?"

"We kissed."

"Aww, who made the first move?"

"Well, we did the usual kiss on each cheek thing and then he sort of gave me a long kiss on the lips, which turned into a proper kiss, so it was both of us really I guess."

"So you must like him a little then to kiss him?"

"Well I think I do. I feel out of practice to be honest but it's just….I woke up this morning feeling unsure if I like him in that way, maybe I'm just thinking about it too much? Anyway we'll see how it goes."

*

After our coffee and cake, I make my way to the nearest metro station of Serrano, and I find myself wondering how busy it will be on the train and that unease does its best to claw its way into my system.

Six months ago – The train to work

I see the train pulling in to the platform and that recognisable knot appears in my stomach and I feel myself begin to get warmer. I hover at the door of the nearest carriage waiting for the usual beeping sound before pushing the button for the doors to open.

I tentatively step up into the carriage and to my relief there are a few seats free. Taking an aisle seat next to the guy I see every morning who I always think looks like he should be a rock guitarist, I take off my scarf in an attempt to make myself feel cooler and try to relax. I hear the gentle hum of chatter in the background. *'This is okay, I'm sitting down and everyone looks the same as me - they're off to work'* I tell myself. It's early and at this time of day people are usually quieter, they're still waking up. There's always one person though who talks louder than everyone else as I hear a woman talking non-stop further down the carriage. I have no idea how anyone can be so loud before 7 a.m.

A few minutes later we stop at the next station and what feels like 100 people get on the train. In reality, it's probably about 30 people but the unease that floods my system as they pile on, some of them heading in my direction makes it feel like a stampede. Only a few of them get a seat meaning the rest of them are standing in the aisle and I feel like I'm surrounded. I look next to me, towards 'said guitarist' and see that he's editing photos on his laptop so rather nosily I try to distract myself by sneakily looking at the pictures.

On the screen sits a close up picture of a robin as he takes a drink from a cream bird bath. I focus on the redness of his breast as it meets the grey underside feathers. The picture looks so crisp and clear, almost like I could feel the softness of the bird's skin.

I look away resting my head back on the seat and take a deep breath. I see a blonde guy looking up and down the carriage continuously. I watch him for a minute, he looks suspicious and I manage to convince myself that he looks very shifty when in reality, he's probably just looking for a seat. I know this happens most days on the train, and I spend the rest of the journey hoping that I'm just imagining things, but yet again those awful images invade my mind. Will I get off this train in one piece? In my head the list of concerns is endless. I try my hardest to ignore the images, but by the time my train pulls in to Birmingham I'm absolutely exhausted.

As this is how I feel every day on my journey, over the years I've become used to it. There's been a couple of times in the past where I've got off my train early, the feeling of dread being so strong that I just had to get outside in the fresh air. It doesn't matter whether I get the train or the bus to work whenever it's busy, the feeling of apprehension is there until finally I have space around me, and then I do it all again on the way home.

Every day on the train I say a little prayer in my head, asking for us to be kept safe and if I don't say it in the exact same way every day I have to start again until it feels 'right' or something bad will happen. It's not nice feeling like this. Sometimes I feel like a prisoner in my own mind, the thoughts that go round and round in my head, the things that I feel like I have to do to keep myself and my family safe.

Present day

I catch the metro from Serrano down to the stop for Alonso Martinez, where I change lines to get the next metro to Gran Via. The metro is fairly busy but there's no one standing. The difference that I feel here is worlds apart from how I would feel back at home going to work. My mind is quieter, the torturous mental chatter isn't as loud. I feel better able to function and just concentrate on the here and now and what is actually going on around me and not what's going on in my mind or what my mind wants me to believe is going on.

All in all the journey takes just over 20 minutes. I also feel quite proud of myself for navigating through the tricky metro system considering I'm not the best with directions, even if I do have a map.

Coming out of Gran Via station I amble along Calle de la Montera down towards the Puerta del Sol. I know I've arrived at the Puerta del Sol straight away as it's so busy and I remember reading in my guidebook that this area is one of the busiest in Madrid. I see the famous clock that marks the Spanish tradition of eating of twelve grapes at midnight on New Year's Eve, shops, bars, and restaurants. I enjoy people watching for a few minutes, taking a few photos before continuing up onto Calle de Carretas where I stumble upon a stationery shop.

Realising as I browse the shop that I'll need paper and pens for my course, I buy a notebook and various pens without exchanging a single word of English with the shopkeeper and I'm chuffed. Just as I'm paying for my goods I hear a message arrive on my mobile, its Luís. The whole text is in Spanish but I can understand it. He's asking me if I'd like to go for a drink with him tomorrow night and immediately after, I get the same message from him again translated into English.

I stand outside the shop to text my reply. I'm really not sure if he's my type, but it can't hurt to see him again to find out. A few messages later and we've arranged to meet here, at the Puerta del Sol tomorrow night.

I go to put my phone away into my bag and it starts to ring. Annie.

I take a deep breath my thumb hovers over the screen. Should I swipe and cut her off, or answer her call?

I answer, holding the phone against my ear but feeling unable to speak.

"Nicole? Please don't put the phone down…"

Hearing her voice makes me feel so angry. "What do you want Annie?"

"Nicole I need to speak to you, please I need to know what you're going to do. Please don't tell Pete."

"You're unbelievable. All you care about is yourself, what about the lies you've told me and Pete for months? And Amelia…"

"Nicole, Amelia is one month old she's…"

"What does that have to do with it? I'm well aware how old my niece is, especially now." I yell before realising where I am and lowering my voice. "All you care about is me keeping your secrets for you, you don't care about the people you've hurt. All you care about is yourself…" I stifle a sob. I purse my lips together. "…Do not call me again!"

I hang up and burst into tears, turning my back to the world whilst I compose myself enough to make the rest of the journey home.

Chapter 6

Two hours into my course and the first day nerves are long gone. We've recapped general greetings, numbers and the like before moving onto present tense verbs.

The class size is quite small, there are just eight of us. Eva, Greg, Leon and myself from the UK, Hans and Nadia are from Germany and Klaudia and Tymek are from Poland. Everyone is really friendly and speaks good English so it's easy to communicate.

Eva is from Bridgnorth so she's quite local to me back home. She tells me she's come to Spain for six months and has left her boyfriend at home and she's missing him so much that he's flying out next weekend to see her, despite her having only been here for two weeks.

Aged 23, Eva has just finished training to be a nurse but she wanted to have the experience of living abroad for a short time before starting her career. I get the impression from what she's told me that leaving the country for six months hasn't gone down too well with her parents.

Now we have a 30 minute break before the next session begins so I head outside, taking a seat on the wall in the sunshine to the front of the building. The road the Education Centre's on is fairly quiet, just the gentle ebb and flow of the occasional car driving by. I look up at the sky, tilting my head back and closing my eyes, letting the heat sink into my skin. It feels so medicinal to me being outside, particularly in the sun with the peacefulness that it can bring.

We spend the next hour working with a partner practising talking about different scenarios that happened in the past so I get to talk to more of the group. Firstly working with Nadia and then afterward, I'm partnered with Tymek. Now we talk about our daily routines in the past, what we did yesterday, what time we got up etc etc. As the practising goes on, in between each scenario when we chat amongst ourselves back into English it feels really strange not speaking Spanish, which is no doubt a good thing.

I'm absolutely ravenous, so when Inés announces it to be lunchtime I'm more than ready to eat.

"After lunch, we will have one hour of recapping what we have learnt today before Gael arrives for the salsa lesson." She tells us.

She smoothes down her pencil skirt as she stands to walk out of the room. Even though I love pencil skirts and the way that they show off your shape, I personally could never wear those when I was working in offices. I always felt like I was walking like a penguin, but somehow she manages to look so elegant and sophisticated.

At the mention of the salsa lesson my stomach begins to do somersaults with nerves. I'm looking forward to it as it's something I've never done before, but I can't help but feel a little dubious and wonder what I'm letting myself in for.

I check my phone as I leave the classroom to see a message from Annie asking me to text her when I'm free so she can call me. That sinking feeling returns. I decide to head for a walk and pick up some lunch, I won't be texting Annie. A few of my classmates are heading their own way at lunch time so at least I won't be the only one not sticking with the group. I don't want to look unsociable.

As I reach the street I hear someone calling my name and I turn around to see Eva walking towards me.

"Do you fancy some company?" She asks.

"Yeah sure, why not."

We walk towards the few shops that sit to the side of the Education Centre, chatting about our first morning on the course. A table becomes free outside the tapas bar just as we approach. One of the waiters clears it for us and we take a seat, both ordering salads as we don't want to feel too full to salsa this afternoon. We sit back and enjoy our ice teas.

Eva asks me about where I was working back at home so I fill her in on the redundancy and the temping jobs and she in turn, tells me about her studies in nursing over the past three years.

"So have you and your boyfriend been together a long time as you're missing him as much as you are?"

"Two years but, he still hasn't met my family, can you believe it?"

"What's stopped you?" I ask.

Our salads are delivered and we each take our knives and forks from the napkin.

"He's a musician, he's in a band…they're really good and he's so talented but I just know he isn't the sort of guy that my parents would choose for me…I think they saw me settling down with some kind of entrepreneur who wears a suit every day…but what does it matter? I'm happy and he loves his job."

She goes on to tell me that her parents run their own business selling exercise equipment to high end spa's and gym's. She worries they'll think that Connor doesn't have a 'proper job' because he relies on gigging up and down the country.

"Does it matter to you if they don't agree with what Connor does for work?" I ask.

She takes a drink from her glass. "Well, I guess not, but I want them to see how lovely he is. But put it this way, they really didn't want me to come here after studying but I didn't let that stop me. They've always been so cool and laid back but when I told them I wanted to come here for six months after my training before I started work…"

"Maybe your parents will surprise you?"

Hearing her talk like this, even though we hardly know each other makes me realise that at times, we all just need someone to talk to, someone to hear us. Even just to voice our feelings out loud to try to make sense of everything. I start to realise even more how important talking is to all of us.

Chapter 7

As soon as the music starts it makes you want to get up and dance without even knowing any of the steps, it's infectious.

Gael our salsa teacher, is Puerto Rican and has lived here in Spain for three years where he teaches several types of dancing and he even works as a DJ two nights per week. He's tall, well-built and boy can he move those hips, there's something about a man who can dance.

We stand in a line as Gael takes us through the basic steps. Firstly explaining to us about the timing of salsa being 1, 2, 3, and 5, 6, 7, and encourages us to count out loud in Spanish.

The first step we do with our left foot is on the count of 1, where we step forwards moving our hips in time with the music, returning the foot back and holding after 3, before stepping back with the right, returning and holding after 7. It's not actually a difficult as it sounds I'm pleased to say and I really relax into it.

After the first five minutes, everyone seems to have got the hang of the steps so Gael restarts the music, and we practice it properly. We're all laughing as we go to the sound of trumpets, drums and maracas. Inés chooses this moment to walk back into the room, shimmying as she goes to this vibrant up-beat music making us all laugh once again, before she takes a seat behind Gael to watch.

Next we practice the same step, but moving out from side to side, left and right. This is the point where some people get toes trodden on which only helps to fuel the laughter even more. After various rounds of practice, we are paired up, boy-girl and I get partnered with Hans.

Hans is really tall, making me feel tiny as I stand next to him. He seems to be pretty muscular from what I can see and he wears his blonde hair tied back into a short ponytail.

Gael entices Inés to be his partner as he shows us the next round of steps, although in that skirt I don't know how she manages it, but she does and they dance so well together.

Now we're instructed to stand opposite our partner loosely holding hands as we practice those same basic steps which actually works quite well.

I see Eva dancing with Leon with a huge smile on her face, despite the fact that she will have two heavily bruised feet after this lesson the way Leon is treading on them. All's going well until Gael introduces some intricate salsa arms. After the first basic step us girls turn to our right, still holding our partner's hands, and as we return back to face our partners, he's then also mid-turn as he throws his partner's right arm around his shoulder allowing him to still move whilst holding on. Phew, it's hard work but so much fun.

Just as I'm leaving the building after class, I hear Diego shouting my name.

"How was your first day?" He asks as he reaches my side.

I have the biggest smile on my face as I tell him in Spanish it's been brilliant. As Diego's also off home, we head back into *el centro* together on the metro.

Diego works as an art lecturer at the Education Centre and he tells me all about some evening art classes he's going to start in January, with a taster class in a few weeks' time.

"You should come to the taster class, artistry is very good for the mind…" He says.

"I have heard that, but, I can't even draw let alone paint." I laugh.

He shakes his head. "It does not matter, it is good to just…let go and paint or to draw, even if it is just colours on a page, it is very therapeutic…" Maybe I'll think about giving it a try.

He continues on. "…the first lesson will be about sketching so you can start off slowly."

After our journey on the metro we're almost home, and as we approach Mio's, we can see he's having a delivery of bottles of water and various wines. As I am learning to be typical of Mio, he's attempting to help the delivery driver.

Immediately Diego throws his bag to the ground and takes the bottles from Mio's grasp, chuntering in Spanish as he does so. I can make out that he's telling Mio he needs to be more careful, which is met by the rolling of eyes and more profanities. I take a few bottles from the back of the van myself to help Diego and the driver to which Mio seems very grateful for. Diego and I then continue on inside and up the stairs.

"He needs to be more careful, he will be 70 next month but…" Diego shakes his head as I follow him.

"People at his age are set in their ways."

Diego agrees and its then that I realise I don't know how they met, so I ask him.

"Mio and his wife Sofia lived on the same street as us when I was growing up in Gran Canaria. They became very close with my family, Mio even more so after Sofia passed away. He spent a lot of time with us and he became part of my family."

We stop for a second before climbing the second set of stairs as he continues.

"Mio decided to move to Madrid, his nephew was already here and he felt like he needed a change, so he brought the restaurant. I loved hearing about Madrid so much that I came here a couple of years later, I stayed with him for a while before I found this place."

Diego clearly thinks so much of Mio and that's lovely to see.

We leave the dimly lit staircase and open the front door to see Laura tidying away some paperwork from the table, her expression brightens as we walk through the door.

"Good timing…my marking is done and I was just thinking about heading down stairs for a drink." Diego reaches her side, slips his arm around her waist as they greet each other properly with a kiss on the lips.

"Nic, you fancy a drink? I want to hear all about your course." She looks at me expectantly.

I relax down onto the sofa and turn to face them.

"To be honest today's been brilliant but all I want to do is lie down before tonight, I didn't really sleep much last night."

"Ahhhh yes, the second date is tonight…" Laura breaks away from Diego and joins me on the sofa, eager to boost my enthusiasm for my date with Luís. She nudges me playfully and I mimic the action back to her in an attempt to quell her excitement.

Diego reappears from their bedroom in a fresh shirt.

"You should join us for a drink, it will relax you…" Diego says.

I stand up and walk towards my bedroom door, stopping momentarily in the doorway.

"Seriously, the only relaxing I want to do is a *siesta*, so enjoy your drink and I'll see you later."

*

Leaving the quiet sanctuary of 'Bar Verde', Luís takes me onto another bar just off the Puerta del Sol.

It's really busy but we get lucky, managing to bag ourselves two stools at the bar. I do my best to climb onto the stool in my best ladylike manner by smoothing down my green dress as I go.

So far the conversation has flowed fairly well and we've spoken as much as possible in Spanish tonight but having said that, there's still something I just can't put my finger on. Luís is lovely, but there doesn't seem to be an attraction there for me other than as friends. I'm not sure that seeing him again after tonight in a romantic sense would be right.

"*Salud*." Luís holds his bottle of beer toward me.

I raise my wine glass to his bottle. "*Salud*."

I tuck a stray strand of hair behind my ear as I study my surroundings. There is an "L" shaped bar with soft lighting and grey tables and chairs that lead to a small dance floor. I can hear both English and Spanish being spoken, making me think that the bar is popular with tourists as well as locals and expats.

I lean a little closer to Luís, to make myself heard.

"Is this one of your regular bars?" I feel reverting to English might be best owing to the music levels.

"*Sí*, I come here with friends sometimes."

Our knees are almost touching as we sit closer to continue conversation and just then he rests his hand on my crossed leg as he continues to talk, making me feel awkward. Now would be a good time for a couple of minutes break to use the toilet.

Reaching the ladies, I pass the girls touching up their make up in the mirrors and find myself a cubicle. I begin to wonder how the night will end. What's the best way to tell him I'd just like to be friends? It's a long time since I was single. Maybe I wouldn't be single now though if......I stop myself, remembering the tricks I've learnt over the last few years when my mind goes into those negative thoughts. I shake my head in annoyance and leave the cubicle.

I wash and dry my hands and run my fingers through my hair before heading back out to the bar. As I approach Luís I see a group of about four men have gathered at his side. Luís is laughing and joking along with them, patting them on the back jovially.

I stand next to him for a moment before quietly clearing my throat unsure of how else to tell him I'm back without feeling stupid in front of his, I'm assuming, his friends.

"Ah Nicole…" Luís starts before introducing me, I'm relieved to hear as his '*amiga*'.

They talk quickly in Spanish and I do my best to interact with them the best that I can. They then divert their attention over to the bar where it seems another of their friends has just brought a round of drinks. I turn around to say hello and as I do so, my stomach jolts and my breath catches in my throat. It can't be, surely? But I know it's him, I'd know those eyes anywhere. It's the policeman that I met the day I arrived.

He places the tray loaded with drinks down on the bar next to the lads and immediately his eyes flit back to mine and I mean it, I feel short of breath.

I reach for my almost empty wine glass from the bar and take a much-needed drink as Luís introduces us.

"This is another of my friends, Jesé."

Jesé reaches out to shake my hand and as our skin comes into contact, I've never felt anything like it in my life. My face immediately flushes and the chemistry between us is unreal, and judging by the way he's looking at me he can feel it too.

"Nicole…" I love how he says my name. "It is a pleasure to meet you properly."

His name suits him perfectly. As a 'J 'is pronounced as a 'H' in Spanish, I pronounce his name several times in my head as Hesé. Jesé. It seems so rugged, so manly, so him.

Thankfully the others are talking and drinking amongst themselves because I swear if they were paying attention to the situation here, they would definitely sense something between us. It seems no one has picked up on the fact that he said 'pleasure to meet you properly' too.

We mingle in with the others and as Jesé takes a drink from his beer my eyes are drawn to his toned arms again, lightly skimmed by the short sleeves on his white shirt. He notices me watching him and I take another drink from my glass to hide my awkwardness. With my glass now empty, I'm about to ask Luís if he wants another drink when Jesé appears next to me.

"White wine?" He motions towards my glass, retrieving his wallet from his back pocket.

"Oh no I'm fine, thanks. I was actually just about to ask Luís if he wanted another."

Jesé looks over my shoulder. "I think he is enjoying himself…he's forgotten about you?"

I glance at Luís to see him in hysterics with his friends and as I look back to Jesé, I see that he's no longer next to me and is ordering a drink at the bar. I nervously stand next to him and see him paying for a glass of wine and two shots of something.

He returns his wallet to his back pocket and turns to me, handing me one of the shot glasses.

"This is for me?" I ask.

"Yes, I think you need to relax more, you seem to be…a little nervous…" He places the glass onto the bar.

Just hearing him say that makes me more nervous. I watch him for a moment as he leans one arm on the bar next to us as he faces me. He simply oozes confidence. I glance again over my shoulder to Luís, to see him still chatting with his friends. I'm not sure he's even noticed I'm not standing with them anymore.

Jesé slides a shot glass towards me before picking up the other and waiting.

"What is it?" I ask, staring at the pink liquid which reminds me of the mouthwash used in a dentist's chair.

He places his hand lightly on my hip and leans into my ear. "Try it, you will find out."

His mouth is so close to my ear as he speaks that I feel his stubble brush against my cheek, which sets my nerve endings on high alert. My hip is on fire from his touch even after he's removed his hand.

I take my shot glass from the bar and knock the drink back in one swift movement. The liquid warms the back of my throat and chest, making me cough out loud and I see Jesé smile, before throwing his shot back too. Next, he slides the glass of wine towards me.

I begin to feel giddy from the alcohol and from the chemistry between us.

"The wine is for me too, are you trying to get me drunk?" I smirk, whilst quietly shocked to hear the confidence in my voice.

"Would I need to?" He asks as he takes another drink from his bottle of beer, his eyes never leaving mine for a second. *Is it hot in here?*

"You are on a date with Luís?" Jesé asks.

"Technically yes, but…"

"You don't like him?"

I stutter with my words for a moment. "I… I think I should tell him that first, don't you?"

He laughs. "I don't think you very well suited…"

"How can you say that? You don't know anything about me." I smile, somewhat puzzled.

"Just a feeling I have…"

I 'come to' when Luís reappears at my side.

"Nicole, there you are…" In that moment, I feel as though I've been caught smoking behind the bike sheds by my Dad.

"Sorry, I got talking to my friends and I forgot…"he continues.

"Don't worry Luís, its fine." I tell him, sneaking another glimpse at Jesé.

Jesé, Luís and I re-join the rest of the group and continue chatting for a while longer until it starts to get late and I decide to call it a night.

I pull Luís to one side. "I think I'm going to make a move Luís, you stay with your friends, I can get a taxi it's no bother."

He tells me in Spanish that he wants to get me to a taxi safely.

"Honestly, it's fine."

"Just let me tell my friends…" He insists, as he proceeds to tell the others I'm leaving.

Jesé strolls back over to me, my heartbeat speeding up as he does so.

"*Mucho gusto* Nicole. Nice to meet you." He kisses me on each cheek but, rightly or wrongly of me I wish it could be more than that, as well he knows. I do my best but I just can't fight the urge to look back as we leave the bar and there he is, watching me leave.

Luís escorts me outside into the muggy, now early morning air and we wait on the Calle Preciados for a taxi.

"I'm sorry that I didn't get to speak to you much once my friends arrived, it had been a while since I had seen them and…"

I brush his apologies away. "Don't be silly I understand, they're your friends." I glance up and down the street searching for a taxi.

"Did you like them?" He asks and for a minute, I wonder if he noticed my attraction to Jesé.

"Erm…yeah, they were great." I answer self-consciously.

I see a taxi approaching us as Luís lifts his arm to hail.

"I'm glad you said that because tomorrow night a few of our friends, we will meet for Raul's birthday. Just as we left I don't know if you heard, but they told me to bring you along."

Just as we left, it was probably when I was saying goodbye to Jesé, I immediately feel guilty.

If I say yes to this I'm agreeing to a third date, which is something I really should not be doing. As the taxi pulls up next to us and the thought comes into my head that Jesé might be there tomorrow night, I find myself agreeing to go. I feel like complete cow.

I open the taxi door and see Luís take a step towards me and so, I quickly peck him on the cheek before climbing into the back of the taxi.

Chapter 8

Laura and I leave the Metro Station and there it is right in front of us, the *Gran* Stadium, home to *Los Mejores* football team. I look at the huge grey building - I've only ever seen this on TV and I'm so excited.

"I can't believe you've managed to get me here." Laura jokes as we head towards the ticket office to begin our tour.

I pay for both our entrance tickets which was part of the deal to get Laura here with me in the first place. We walk up numerous flights of stairs which lead us back inside before finally our first stop on the tour, which is outside to the panoramic view.

The first thing that hits me is the sheer size of the stadium. It's a brilliant view from up here and it makes me realise just how big it actually is. There's people mowing the grass on one half the pitch and on the other half, there are dozens of lights on wheels, I wonder what they're for?

The fellow *Mejores* fans around us are just as excited as me taking photos of the different views. The couple next to me ask me in Spanish to take a picture of them which I do so, and then I ask them to take one of me and Laura together. Laura does her best fake smile but I think she's secretly enjoying it.

Next we go back indoors into a room named 'the trophy room' which houses shiny silver trophies, ex-player football shirts, boots and television screens showing different clips of games. This team has a heck of a lot of history and I won't even pretend that I know much of it, but I enjoy reading and learning more about them.

I begin to read a team list from the year 2005 just as Laura brings up the subject of last night again. I told her the full story about Luís and how I just want to be friends and of course all about Jesé and how it felt to see him again.

"So tonight what are you going to do? Tell Luís you don't feel anything for him but you actually fancy the pants off his friend?"

I feel annoyed. "Don't say it like that Laura, I feel bad enough as it is." She moves next to me, obviously thinking about my situation.

"I didn't mean that how it sounded. It's not like anything has really happened between you and Luís but the way I see it, you've really got to tell him tonight how things are."

I take a sharp intake of breath before blowing it out again with frustration. "I know, you're right, and I will."

"Do you really think something could happen between you and Jesé?"

The mere thought of something happening between us makes my legs feel like jelly, I don't know what it is but there seems to be something there between us. Am I kidding myself that someone like him could be interested in me?

Welcoming the distraction I look around at all the photos of the teams over the years. It feels unreal being here. Later on the tour we go out near to the pitch itself. Certain sections are blocked off with white tape but we get closer and closer to the pitch. We're now at a different angle than when we were at the panoramic view area so I snap away happily with my phone, looking forward to sending these pictures to my Dad. Maybe I could even bring my Dad here when he and Mom come to visit which could help to win him round.

We briefly go into one of the boxes used for entertaining, before going onto the changing rooms. Next it's out through the players tunnel, which obviously leads outside to the players dug out and we see those famous seats where the substitutes sit. We take the opportunity to sit on one of the seats as I grab the chance to absorb my surroundings a little more.

I try to imagine what the atmosphere would be like on a match day with thousands of chanting fans, I'd be so excited. I wonder if I could get Laura to agree to come to a game with me whilst I'm here…I'll have to work on her.

We each take a turn to stand as close to the pitch as the barriers will allow for another couple of pictures, before heading inside to the Press Conference Room.

"How are things at work now?" I ask Laura.

"Oh, it's fine, as busy as ever. Can you believe that Diego and I have been together for almost two months? That's a record for me."

"Ah, that's lovely."

Laura looks so in love. Her face lights up when she talks about him, I'm really happy for her.

"What'll you do to celebrate?"

"He's taking me to my favourite restaurant, it's not too far from work actually its run by two brothers from Valencia. I'm not joking Nic, the food is the best I've ever tasted."

We continue through to the hustle and bustle of the Official Shop. There are football shirts, full kits, mugs, key rings, you name it and it seems to be here in this shop. I can't resist buying myself a *Mejores* team Shirt.

Sadly we then leave the Stadium and begin what Laura assures me is a five minute walk to her clothes shop.

"Did Diego tell you that Mio will be 70 soon?" Laura checks as she retrieves her sunglasses from her bag.

"Yeah he did mention. Does Mio have any family, other than his Juan, his Nephew?"

"Mio's wife passed away a long time ago. Everyone keeps telling him he shouldn't be working anymore. I think he's finally realised."

We pause to cross over the road, passing some huge glass fronted buildings that look like very up market office blocks. A small garden area filled with trees and grass sits in front of them, almost encouraging people to stop and switch off to take a seat on the bench as a welcome respite to the busy city. I like how Madrid has these small pockets of greenery dotted around.

"I suppose he's worried who will look after the business if he retires?" I ask.

"He's already said that Juan will be in charge but what he doesn't want to lose is the experience that his customers get when they arrive at the restaurant with Mio being the host."

I open the door to the huge store and we're met by the scent of dozens of different perfumes and the chill of the air conditioning. Clearly an expert, Laura leads the way to the women's clothing.

There are so many beautiful clothes, shoes and boots in every direction I turn that I'm not quite sure where to look first. Laura gets stuck right in and tries on a pair of brown ankle boots.

"I just can't imagine needing to wear anything like that here." I sit myself down next to her. "I mean, I know it does obviously get cooler in the winter but when it's so warm like this…"

Laura laughs as she zips up the second boot and stands to look at them in the mirror.

"Well that's one of the many beauties of Spain isn't it, the weather is always better than the UK."

On the way home we stop off at Mio's for a well-earned café con leche. We take a seat at one of the small tables outside on the pavement and sure enough, here comes Mio.

"Buenas tardes…" He calls as he places a basket of beautiful fresh bread and a plate of sun-dried tomatoes and olives in front of us. He goes on to ask us in Spanish about our day to which Laura stays silent for me to reply to him to practice.

Moments later, one of the waitresses delivers our coffees and it's so delicious I almost drink it all in one. I feel like I could sit here all day in the wonderful warm sunshine and decide that yes, that's just what I'll do for the rest of the afternoon at least.

Laura and I head back upstairs to the apartment and whilst Laura makes herself comfortable on the sofa, I grab my books from my course and head back down stairs to the haven of the little table in the sun.

I go through my notes from yesterday and make a start on my first assignment, talking about my typical daily routine. I have a couple of minutes break to send a couple of messages to my Mom.

Hearing my phone beep again, I assume it will be her replying but I feel a little nervous to see that it's Luís. He's telling me where we're going tonight with the others and asking if I want to meet at the restaurant, or if I'd like to meet for a drink first.

Could I meet him for a drink and tell him the truth before we meet the others I wonder, but that would be really awkward at the meal then. If I even felt comfortable enough to still go to the meal. I find myself wondering what my sister would do in this kind of situation. Damn it, why do I do that?

Knowing Annie, she'd tell Luís straight about how she felt about just being friends and probably even drop some hints about Jesé. That would be so brazen, I couldn't bring myself to do that.

My nervous excitement in the pit of my stomach about seeing Jesé again only serves to make me feel guiltier, and I don't even know if he'll definitely be there tonight. I really hope he will be.

Mio appears at my table to ask if I want anything else to drink and we get talking about my time in Madrid so far.

"I'm having the time of my life Mio, I wish I'd done it sooner."
He sits himself down opposite me and asks if I mind him smoking. I tell him to go ahead.

"I am glad you love it here, how could you not? That is what life is all about Nicole, you must do... things you want, life is there to be lived." He lights his cigarette and looks at me curiously.

"*Chica*, you have a-a sadness in your eyes..."

"A sadness? I'm okay Mio... a little tired but..." I shift a little awkwardly in my seat at his observation.

"Here…" he motions around with his hands. "Here it will be good for you, yes? You need something new…"

I look at the floor before holding his gaze again. "Yes, something like that."

A car drives past us playing loud music which is a welcome diversion and gives me a chance to change the subject.

"I hear someone has a special birthday soon…"

"My nephew, he is throwing me a party here on the…condition that I do not work and that I just… to enjoy myself."

I laugh. "That's what you should be doing every day, just enjoying the sun and this beautiful city."

"You must come to the party with Laura and Diego they have been very good to me. I have known Diego since he was this high…" He motions with his hand the height of a child.

"I'd love to come, thank you."

"I will need someone after my birthday. I know I need to…to slow down."

I begin to wonder what he's trying to say.

"Would you like to work for me, meet customers and chat to them, a little waitressing?"

I'm stunned for a moment, I don't quite know what to say it's so unexpected. I do need to get a job, I need some money coming in so this could be perfect.

"Are you serious?" My hand flies to my mouth in surprise.

Mio nods his head. "I need someone who is easy to talk to who is welcoming to my customers and you need a job and another way to practice speaking the Spanish…"

"That would be brilliant, I can't thank you enough." I stand up and lean across the table, giving him a gentle hug and I'm surprised to see that he looks quite emotional.

I think I just got a job in Madrid…

Chapter 9

As my taxi pulls up on the same street as Roma - the Italian restaurant, my anxiety begins to take its hold. I pay the taxi driver and after purposely asking him to drop me a few minutes' up the street, I begin the slow walk to the red fronted restaurant.

I open the door and I'm met by the delicious aromas of garlic and herbs and I have to remind myself for a second I'm in Spain and not Italy. Even that isn't enough to stir any hunger pangs tonight, I'm so on edge. The restaurant is bigger than it seems from the outside and is lit with candles on each table and lanterns that hang from the walls.

I see Luís, the birthday boy Raul and a couple of girls that I haven't met before at a long table on the left-hand side of the restaurant. Immediately Luís raises his hand to wave to me and I apprehensively make my way over to them.

"¿Nicole, qué tal?" Luís asks me how I am as he kisses me on each cheek.

"Bien, bien." I reply.

I wish Raul a happy birthday before taking a seat next to Luís and next to Raul's girlfriend Isabel. We all chat amongst ourselves and I can tell that Luís is making a real effort to ensure I don't feel left out or uncomfortable.

More people begin to arrive which means more introductions and I notice that it seems to be mostly couples tonight, which makes me feel a little uneasy. A waiter arrives at the table to take our drinks orders and I decide to drink rosé for a change. My heart is almost leaping out of my chest in anticipation every time the door opens until finally, in walks Jesé.

He's wearing a smart black short-sleeved shirt with jeans and the darkness of his shirt, along with his heavy stubble adds to his striking good looks. He greets Raul to wish him *"felicidades."*

As Jesé hugs Raul, his eyes find mine bringing back that familiar feeling from last night, the sudden pang of nervous excitement mixed with electricity.

He moves around the table behind me to greet Isabel, who sits to my left before he moves on to me. As his lips meet my right cheek and then my left, the heat that touches my skin is incredible and the look in his eyes tells me everything that I need to know. I already feel like I've had a bottle of wine and I'm still completely sober.

Jesé sits on the other side of the table from me and a couple of seats down. We make eye contact several times throughout the meal and it's so distracting. I somehow manage to eat my lasagne and drink two glasses of wine, but I have to refuse dessert.

I chat with Luís throughout the meal but every time I do, I can see Jesé from the corner of my eye watching us as he eats and I begin to feel uncomfortable. I try my best not to look in his direction.

After we've eaten, people begin to move around the table talking to each other. Luís goes to chat with one of the lads from last night and his girlfriend and I chat with Isabel. She tells me she works as a general manager in one of the large hotels in *el centro*.

"It's where I have picked up this…how you say…habit?" she asks me, holding up a packet of cigarettes. "Work can be stressful…do you smoke Nicole?"

"No, I don't. I tried it when I was younger but…"

"Good, do not start…" She looks to Raul. "I keep promising him that I will stop, and I will but, when you have done this for many years…"

"Hard habit to break?" I ask.

She heads off outside to smoke, leaving the seat free beside me. Jesé stands as he picks up his glass of red wine and before I know it, he's sitting next to me.

"I take it you have not spoken to Luís yet?" I know exactly what he means.

I look around us, wondering if anyone has heard what he said to me but they all seem engrossed in various conversations.

"Why are you so bothered?" I hear myself say, yet again with an air of confidence that sounds really quite unlike me.

I fidget in my seat, crossing my legs towards him. I can't help it there's something about him that makes me feel so different, despite only having met him twice.

He shrugs his shoulders. "Maybe I am just nosy."

He pulls his seat forward slightly, meaning that our legs are now touching. The chemistry I can feel between us is palpable. I need to change the subject.

"You're not patrolling the streets tonight?" I smile before taking another sip of my wine.

He laughs. "Luckily for you, I have two nights off in a row."

I smile. "Luckily for me?" I shake my head as I continue to grin. I wonder if he really is this big headed or, if it's just for show.

"What about you, what has Nicole's day been like?" He asks.

I see Isabel return to the table and sit on Raul's knee despite Jesé gesturing to get up for her, she refuses.

"Well, today I actually did something I've wanted to do for so long. I did the *Los Mejores* stadium tour, then I went shopping…."

He interrupts me. "You did this? The stadium tour?" He looks shocked.

"Yeah…"

He leans back in his seat smiling as he does so, and just watches me.

"I am huge fan, I have season ticket."

My smile gets bigger by the second. "You're so lucky, I would love to go to a game."

"You must go if you are a fan, you have to…"

We continue to talk about what I thought of the stadium which leads onto him telling me how he's been a fan for as long as he can remember and how he and his twin brother never miss a home game.

Now it's my turn to be shocked. "You're a twin?"

He nods in agreement as he fills his wine glass from the bottle of red on the table.

"I have a twin sister." I tell him half-heartedly. "She's seven minutes older than me…"

"This is…" He seems to be searching for the right word to use. "…strange, my brother is seven minutes older than me."

We hold each other's gaze for a moment before I laugh awkwardly and have to look away. All of a sudden, the rest of the party begin to stand up and Luís returns to the chair next to me to retrieve his jacket from the seat.

"We are going to a bar a few streets away, you are coming?"

I think for a moment and am aware of Jesé still standing next to me.

"Okay, sounds good."

We leave the restaurant and a few minutes later, we arrive at a bar that puts me in mind of an old traditional style Spanish inn, honed with bare brickwork and a dark mahogany wood bar. There's no music playing in the bar just the loud sound of people chatting and laughing which is actually quite overpowering and makes me feel on edge at first. I try to distract myself by concentrating on the details of the things that I can see in the room.

All of the bar staff are decked out in a white shirt, black bow tie and a red waistcoat. Legs of *jamon* hang high above the bar maturing as people drink their beverages beneath them.

Our party gather in small groups around the bar and I continue to chat with Luís, Jesé, Raul and Isabel, feeling my mind begin to calm. I tell them how pleased I am to get a job working at Mio's, and I learn Isabel's father is an old friend of Mio's.

I'm finding it so enjoyable talking to more Spanish people. They do talk English around me when they remember out of politeness, but I tell them not to. If I can't understand what they're saying, I ask or if I look confused, they repeat in English so they're really helpful.

As Luís doesn't attempt to get closer to me or to even talk to me that much, I really think he feels the same way that I do, in that we won't be anything more than friends which is certainly easier.

The heat is still there between Jesé and I. There are still copious amounts of stolen glances between us, I just can't seem to help myself. Sometimes when he looks at me, I feel like I've known him before, which is crazy I know, but now that I've found out how much we have in common too, I can't help but think that perhaps we were meant to meet.

The fact that it's Sunday night clearly doesn't bother anyone in this bar which is slightly alien to me. Back home on the odd occasion I went out on a Sunday night, I had a rule of two drinks maximum. Monday mornings are bad enough without the added annoyance of a hangover. But no Sunday night feeling for me, I have no work tomorrow and I'm out with new friends so I'm going to enjoy myself.

It's my turn to buy a round of drinks, and as I move closer to the bar I find myself standing closer to Jesé. There's hardly any space around the bar area and as I battle my way to get served, Jesé gently places his hand on the small of my back, to steer me into a space. Once I'm in that space, his hand remains there, sending all sorts of signals up and down my spine. I'm scared to look at him because I know the look on my face will tell him more than I want him to know.

I'm just recovering from the shock of the sensations from his hand when a woman with cat like eyes and brown hair almost to her waist appears next to Jesé. He snatches his hand away from my back, making me feel suddenly bereft. She kisses him on the cheek and speaks in rapid Spanish. I only catch a few words, but I hear her telling him that she's sorry she's late.

Isabel and Raul greet her rather frostily I notice which seems quite out of character for them because they seem such warm and friendly people. I'm wondering what's going on but, I'm distracted as the barman arrives in front of me. I order the drinks trying my best to keep one ear on the conversation behind me, which is still seeming awkward to me.

I pass the drinks out to their rightful owners and Isabel looks at me with concern. I make eye contact with this mystery woman for the first time. She's wearing an extremely tight white skirt and a navy and white striped top which is struggling to cover her chest. She looks me up and down with a look of scorn on her face.

I hear her ask Jesé who I am and he tells her that I'm a friend of Luís, to which her expression softens. Jesé looks at me with an expression I find difficult to read. At a push I'd say it's a look of embarrassment, and it's then I realise who she must be as Jesé introduces us.

"Nicole, this is Lolita…"

She holds out her cold hand towards me. "*Llamarme* Lola…" She tells me to call her Lola before going on to confirm my fears that she's Jesé's girlfriend.

'*Llamarme Lola…*' Right now I can think of a few things I'd rather call her. I extend my hand towards hers, hoping my facial expression isn't that of shock, which is what I'm feeling at this moment.

The group continue to chat and I feel completely deflated. Despite his girlfriend now standing next to him, I can still feel him looking at me. Eventually I manage to look at him, but when I do, it's a far cry from the looks we were exchanging not long ago. I think it's still sinking in, and what a fool I feel.

For the rest of the night, I do my best not to watch as Lola drapes her arms around Jesé one minute and throws dirty looks to everyone else the next.

By this point I've had far too much to drink and so I decide to call it a night. I say goodnight to everyone, wondering if this will be the last time I see them considering how things are with Luís and I, and I certainly won't be seeing Jesé again. I can't even look at him as I leave the bar.

Luís walks me out. Why can't I fall for someone like him? He's so genuine and gentle and just loves to look after people. It's time we had that talk.

There's definitely a chill in the air tonight outside, and the air has that smell of rain mixed with the earlier evening warmth. The ground looks damp from an earlier shower.

"Thanks for tonight, Luís." We walk to the nearby taxi rank.

"I am glad you came…" There's an awkward silence for a moment. "…Am I right that Jesé didn't tell you he had a girlfriend?"

Shocked by what he's asked, I get a jolt of guilt in my stomach as I look at him. I'm unsure of what to say, as I stammer in my response. "I'm…I…don't know what to say."

He laughs. "Do not worry Nicole, it is fine. I could see that there would be nothing between me and you and that there was definitely something…in the air between you and Jesé."

I'm taken aback to hear this. "I'm sorry…"

"You do not need to be sorry, I hope we can remain friends?" He asks. We reach the taxi rank and I breathe a sigh of relief. "I'd like that, I hope we can too."

Luís pulls me into a friendly hug, which is really nice. I feel my shoulders relax in relief.

"And to answer your question, no he never mentioned Lola." Luís shakes his head. "I was not sure whether I should say anything when after the restaurant, but I thought it best to stay out of things."

"It shouldn't be up to you to tell me, its fine don't worry about it. Honestly."

Luís smiles sadly as I feel the need to tell him more.

"I think that I just got caught up in…." I wonder what word to use. "…in the moment." I laugh nervously. Even I don't believe a word of that.

"If it helps, Lola is…. not a very nice person."

I giggle half-heartedly. "Thanks, Luís."

Chapter 10

I sit up in bed the following morning as Laura perches next to me, cup of tea in hand. I tell her the whole sorry tale of last night.

"I feel such a fool." I complain.

"It's hardly your fault, how were you to know the fella had a girlfriend? He was giving you plenty of signs he was interested, so how would you know?" She takes a drink from her mug.

I sigh. "I know but, I just can't believe it. The flirting, the looks and then bam…he's got a girlfriend. I just never thought for a minute…"

"Look on the bright side, at least the situation with Luís is sorted out now so you can stop fretting about that."

I put my head back against the wall. "I suppose so…I just feel so…so disappointed. Jesé, and I… there was such an attraction there and we had so much in common. I let myself start to be taken in by him and…"

"No, don't you dare do that…"

"Do what?" I ask.

"Don't let how James turned out to be make you think that every guy will let you down or can't be trusted."

Is that what I'm doing? I wonder.

"I…I don't know how to think anymore, Laura." I try my best to laugh at myself.

Seven Days ago - Birmingham

In a bar not far from home, all I can hear is ferocious laughter from behind me as I slip my change into my purse at the bar. This can only mean one thing - my sister has arrived. As I turn around, vodka and tonic in one hand, lager and lime in the other, sure enough there she is walking towards me finishing a phone call on her mobile. I raise the drinks in her direction and gesture to an empty table on my right hand side.

"Hiiii" she chirps, as she slides her phone back into the safety of her bag. "Not late am I?"

"Annie, if you weren't late, I think I'd be worried."

I taste my drink for the first time and as I swallow, I immediately feel myself begin to relax, with the drink giving me a tingling sensation down my arms. My tensions begin to ease away and boy do I need to feel that.

"How's Pete?" I ask.

Annie takes a drink from her lager and lime and shrugs off her jacket. Pete is her boyfriend of five years and he's at home looking after their one month old daughter, my niece Amelia. This is Annie's first night out since Amelia came along.

"Erm… Pete's okay."

"Not another argument?" I ask.

Annie adopts a thinking expression. "You know us Nic, we're never happy unless we're arguing. I just look forward to making up later…"

I almost choke on my drink. "Hmmm, I can imagine. So how does it feel to be on your first night out in…."I wonder how long it's been.

"Too long is how long it's been, Nicole. You know I love Amelia to pieces but it's good to get out with you, just like the old days."

"Old days, you make it sound like it's been about twenty years."

"Well to be honest it feels like it's been that long sis." She takes a drink. "Mmmm...I'm so glad I decided against breast feeding."

I snigger as she adjusts her enormous post pregnancy boobs.

"So, come on..." she continues, "...How's things at Mom and Dads?"

I shrug my shoulders. "They're okay, it's still weird being back there. Sometimes I wonder if I should've stayed on at the flat on my own."

"With the memories of James all around you? No, you did the right thing...it's only temporary after all being with Mom and Dad isn't it. Anyway, you could've gone with Laura to Spain...that would've been amazing."

I exhale. "I know, I know, I should've gone but...I..."

"But what?"

"You know it's not that easy for me Annie, I can't just make huge changes like that, I'm not like you."

"Nicole, you need to have more confidence in doing the things you want to do. Now that you and James are over especially..." She changes the subject "It's my round. Same again?"

I glance down at my almost full glass. "Erm...Yeah, okay."

"Don't give me that look, this is my first night out in a while don't forget."

I watch as Annie saunters towards the bar, purposely slotting herself in between a load of rugby lads as they turn to admire the view. She turns to wink at me which, makes the lads look in the direction of her stare, at me as I hear her utter the words...

"That's my sister over there..."

I shake my head with embarrassment.

"Who wants to buy her a drink?" I'm absolutely mortified as she returns to the table with three of the lads. She really has no shame.

Annie places a heavily drink laden tray down on the table in front of us. Shots and a vodka and tonic are passed in my direction.

This always used to happen. One drink in the pub with Annie, always lead to several more in a nightclub. Annie now, just like when we were younger always attracts the male attention. One of the lads next to her can't take his eyes off her, well can't take his eyes off her chest to be more precise but she's loving the attention. Annie has never cheated on Pete and she wouldn't, she's always been a flirt but tonight, she seems worse than usual. Maybe it's because she hasn't been out for a long time, she'll calm down.

As I get talking to one of the lads sitting with us, Richard, it turns out that we went to school with him. I really can't remember him, but it seems he remembers us.

"I remember you, you're Nicole…" I nod my head. He looks to Annie. "…and she's Annie."

I see Annie look over at the mention of her name.

"At school you were always the quiet one and she was always the loose one."

The lads all burst out laughing. Annie looks momentarily furious before regaining her smile.

"I wasn't loose, I just always got the attention, that's all." She flutters her eyelashes.

In that split second I'm back at school, I'm back at being second best.

Richard leans in to my ear. "I always did prefer classy, not trashy."

I don't know what to say. I glance in Annie's direction who looks rather put out but then she turns her attention to the guy next to her who's been talking to her cleavage for the last ten minutes.

About an hour and four shots later, I'm not quite sure how I'm still standing but the five of us head off to a local nightclub.

The music's great and it feels so good to dance and let loose. Richard hasn't left my side all night which is quite flattering and he's a really good dancer. If I'm honest it's nice to be noticed, it feels like it's been a long time.

"You have to give me your number Nicole…" He mumbles into my ear between songs.

I laugh. "We'll see." Feeling awkward, I lean over in my sister's direction. "Annie, I'm going to the ladies…"
She's checking her phone as she sways on the spot. I think it might be time to get her home.

"You carry onnnn, I'm j-j-just checking that Amelia's okay…"

I go on the search for the toilets and when I return a few minutes later I feel like I've gone back in time again. It's like it's that Saturday afternoon and I'm back in the clubhouse after the football match.

Annie stands next to Richard whispering into his ear and giggling. She's trying her best to put her arms around him but he brushes her away. Richard sees me coming towards them and nods his head in Annie's direction. I reach her side.

"Annie I think I'd better get you home."

"Do you need a hand?" Richard offers.

"Thanks but I'll get her into a taxi and take her home."

Annie starts laughing hysterically. "Nicole he wants to come home with yoouuu…take the hint."

I shake my head in apology to Richard as I support Annie around her waist to get her to the door as she carries on with her drunken ramblings.

"Sorry Richard, Nicole's the boring sister….it's meee you should've gone for if you wanted a good time."

Richard and I look at each other as I try my best to block out Annie's slurs and the hurt that hit me as I heard those words. But it seems she hasn't finished yet.

"…Plus s-s-she's living with our parents…" She staggers. "…Not sure what Dad would say if you turn up there with her. What do you think Nicole?"

Richard looks furious. "Hey, don't speak to your sister like that."

I look to Richard, surprised to have heard him stick up for me like that, surprised but grateful…not that it will do much good when she's this drunk.

"..Nicole you need to live a little…you're always soooo…dull so…" she stumbles. "…so predictable…"

She's right I think to myself….I can't look her in the eye.

Richard shakes his head as my sister continues to make me feel like I have the personality of a dishcloth.

"That isn't all I want Nicole. Look, let me help you get her outside." The two of us take her out to the street where I tell him I can manage from here. The truth is I'm embarrassed of what she might come out with next and I'd rather he wasn't around to hear it.

"Annie you need to try and sober up or we won't get a taxi." I snap.

She looks at me. "Why didn't you get his number?"

"Will you stop?"

"Have I upset you, Nicole?"

"Actually you have …but I know you're drunk so we'll talk about this tomorrow."

She laughs. "I know I've upset you…I have and I'm sorry, I shouldn't have done it…"

She sinks down onto the wall outside of the nightclub, holding her head in her hands.

I walk closer to the kerb checking up and down the street but there's no sign of a taxi. I fumble in my bag for my phone in the hope I can order one and thankfully, there's just a few minutes wait.

I start to think about the cruel words she used just seconds ago to describe me. Dull, boring, predictable…I have to get us home, I can't stand being around her when she's like this.

"No, you don't understand Nic, you s-s-see it was just once and it was so s-s-stupid but I couldn't help myself.…"

"What are you talking about?" I put my phone away.

She stands up from the wall and gingerly walks towards me.

"I just couldn't stop…I…" Tears fill her eyes. I've never seen her this drunk before.

"I slept with James, I.. I'm…I'm s-sorry…"

I feel like someone has punched me in the stomach.

"What did you just say?"

She puts her hand on my shoulder. "Please, please don't hate me…"

"You…you slept with my fiancé?"

In that split second, I feel like my whole world has crashed down around me. My heart starts to pound loudly in my chest.

Annie starts to cry as she looks down at the ground before looking back up at me. I throw her hand off me and take a step back trying to register what she's telling me. I walk away from her, feeling lightheaded and my immediate thought is that I need to find somewhere to sit down. Annie starts to follow me.

"Please wait….it was just once…it w-was…"

"When?" I yell, spinning round to look at her.

She looks shocked. "What?"

"When?" I need to sit down…

"Erm…in…in N-November it was just once Nicole I-I-I swear…"She's sobering up.

I feel my bottom lip start to tremble. "How could you? Why would you…?"

That would've been around the time that James started to change and things started to go downhill for us. I remember it being November as it was just after his birthday. Then it hits me.

"November…" I wipe my eyes and try to catch my breath as I work it all out in my head. "…10 months ago…"

Annie stops crying for a second and looks terrified.

"Amelia is one month old….." I can't believe what I've just realised.

"She's James' daughter isn't she?"

She panics. "Nicole, please, she could be Pete's she…she is Pete's…"

I think I'm going to be sick and sure enough, I rush further down the street away from the night club and am sick right there in the gutter. I must look drunk. I wish I was then maybe this wouldn't be so painful. I lean against the lamp post next to me, desperately trying to steady my breathing. I feel disorientated as ringing begins in my ears. I know what this is, I've been through this feeling of panic so many times.

I concentrate on my breathing, slowly taking a deep breath in as I count to five before releasing and for the count of five.

I hear Annie's footsteps as she slowly reaches my side. "Nic are you okay, are you having a panic attack?" She reaches out toward me as I push her arm away, concentrating on my breathing.

We stand next to each other in silence. She's too scared to speak and I'm too scared to listen, afraid of what more I might found out about this person, my sister, that through everything, I trusted the most in the world.

"How the hell could you do that to me?" I scream.

She tries to creep closer to me with the colour now drained from her face, but I take a further step backwards.

"Nicole, I'm sorry…I know it was wrong…"

I'm in shock. How could my sister do this? But now, as I stand here on the street with the truth sinking in I think back to our childhood. The constant feeling of second best, Annie desperate for the attention always. I feel such anger building up inside of me as I stand up to her.

"It's worked out well for you hasn't it, me having these issues…you could push me into anything and walk all over me. Even when I reached out to you when we were teenagers and I needed help but I was too afraid…you shot me down, you made your flippant comments and at one point, you even called me crazy…"

"Nicole p-please…I'm s-sorry…"

I start to cry, I can't help it, I'm just so angry and I can't quite believe what she's done.

"You even let me believe that all of this was my fault…that I drove James away because of the way that I am… You know how ill I was after that… Mom and Dad thought I was close to a breakdown."

Annie runs her hands through her hair in desperation. "Pl-please…I'm sorry…"

Does she really think that saying sorry is enough? I think if I hear her say that one more time I'll scream but I go on… I tell her exactly what I think of her.

"I don't know why I'm surprised that this has happened. Ever since we were kids you had to be the best, be better than me…you always wanted what I had and if I wouldn't give it then you'd just take it from me. You took my toys, my homework, you even managed to take most of my confidence over the years but now, you even took my fiancé…"

I see the bouncers outside of the nightclub start to look in our direction as I continue Annie's character assassination in the street.

"You've made it your lifelong mission to make me feel inferior to you…well you know what Annie, you've done it, you really have this time…but you've screwed up your own life in the process. I just hope it was worth it!"

My throat stinging from shouting and my whole body shaking, I speed off into the night as far away from her as I can get but she follows me, bawling as she does. I need to get away from her but on that, the taxi that I ordered flies past us and pulls up outside of the night club. I march back towards the club as a black cab also pulls up. Annie climbs into the mini cab and moves across to the other side for me to sit beside her.

"Nicole will you please get in…."

I hold the door open as I go to climb in and as I look at her sitting there, for the first time in my life I feel like I see her for who she really is. Who is this person? She's supposed to be my sister yet look how it's always been between us. I glance at the black cab behind and slam the door on her, jumping in the other cab.

"Where to love?" the driver asks.

I start to cry, tears of anger and hurt. "Home…" I tell him before I realise that he doesn't know where that is. I don't think that I do anymore either. I mumble my address to him and we're on our way. That's when it hits me. Home. My home is with my parents. I have a temping job which is coming to an end in two weeks' time. What am I doing with my life? I could stay here waiting for my life to start, where I'll always feel like this around my sister with anxiety ruling my life, or I could go where I should've gone two months ago, with Laura – to Spain and not allow my worries to dictate my life anymore.

I look out the window as we move through the streets, it's almost like I'm having an out of body experience. Passing through the streets in the taxi, places that have been in my life ever since I can remember and I just know I want more for myself. Out comes my phone again, but this time I load up the "Fly out" Website. A few minutes later I'm booked onto a flight to Madrid the following afternoon.

Chapter 11 - *Present Day*

Tuesday brings an early start to do some more work on my assignment. Feeling happy with the notes I made on Sunday, I add some more before reading it aloud several times to check it flows properly, using my dictionary to check the words I'm not sure on. Then feeling satisfied with my work, I type out an email to my Dad.

With my Dad an avid football fan, he might appreciate the *Los Mejores* stadium photos but then again, he might not…it's worth a try. Things have been a little strained with my Dad the last couple of times I've spoken to him, but as I attach the best twelve shots of our stadium tour to an email and press send, I feel confident these will win him around.

Jesé pops momentarily into my head as I let my imagination go picturing him sitting in the stadium amongst the crowds of people watching a game, lost in the moment. What a let-down he turned out to be.

I make my way downstairs to Mio's to work a few hours with him to begin to learn what's what in the world of waitressing. The first thing he does when I arrive, is give me my white polo t-shirt to wear with the restaurant logo. That, teamed with my black apron over my denim skirt makes me feel ready to start.

I meet the staff properly - Juan, Clara and Eduardo. Despite having seen them here dozens of times already, it's good to be working alongside them. Mio explains to me how he wants me to greet the customers and make them feel welcome before showing them to a table.

"That is one of the things that brings me the most joy, meeting people and making them feel welcome, like family." He tells me. "It will help you to pick up our language even faster."

Mio talks about his business with such pride and enthusiasm as he ushers me behind the bar, showing me where the menus are kept.

I'm lost in thought for a couple of seconds as I begin to picture the many, many hours that he's put in over the years as he's built up his restaurant.

"You are worried?" He asks me.

"No…I'm fine, I'm really looking forward to working here…" Well maybe I have just a tinge of nerves, but anyone would be starting a new job.

He puts his arm around me for encouragement. "I think you will be a….a natural with customers."

Just then, two women enter the restaurant and Mio hands me two menus and urges me to greet them at the door.

I stride over to greet the women wishing them a good afternoon. As I begin speaking to them my nerves completely disappear.

I show them to a table in front of the window and take their order, scribbling this down onto my pad. I tear the page with the food order and take it to the kitchen, hanging it up on one of the hooks for Juan, the chef. The next task is mastering the coffee machine.

"If you are making drinks and more customers come just shout a greeting to them, tell them to make themselves at home and you will be with them shortly." Mio advises me as he demonstrates how to use the coffee machine.

He's so relaxed, it's clear that nothing intimidates or concerns him and that's a great way to be. I get the feeling that spending more time around Mio will be good for me, maybe his carefree attitude might transfer onto me.

I spend the next few hours meeting and greeting, making drinks and taking a couple of food orders to the tables when it gets busier. When Mio tells me I can finish for the day, I decide to relax outside at one of the pavement tables to enjoy the late afternoon sun with a glass of homemade sangria. Mio even joins me for a while.

*

That night, Diego has prepared some tapas for the three of us which we relax on the sofa to eat. I enjoy delicious mouthfuls of perfectly cooked asparagus drizzled in olive oil with creamy manchego cheese. Next, there's jamon with fresh crusty bread and a dish I haven't tried before called flamenco eggs which is baked eggs with tomato, spicy chorizo and delicate green beans.

Laura mops up the leftover juices of her food with the fresh bread. "So you've been living in Madrid for just over a week. Already you have a job, you've started a course and not to mention catching the eye of two men."

I laugh along with her shaking my head almost in disbelief at what I've achieved so far with my new job and my course.

"I can hardly believe it myself." I swallow a mouthful of food and take a swig of ice cold water, returning the glass to the coffee table in front of me.

Diego scrapes the last of the Flamenco eggs from his plate onto his fork.

"What has been your highlight so far?" He asks.

I know the answer to this hands down, it has to be the stadium tour but I promised Laura I wouldn't mention this in front of Diego so I choose my answer carefully.

"Erm…. I can't pick out just one thing to be honest."

My answer is met by a knowing wink from Laura, to which I almost burst out laughing but manage to stifle it, just about.

I see Diego look at me and then at Laura as he swallows his last mouthful of food and puts his plate on the table. He rests back, draping his arm across the back of the sofa as he does so.

"You two…." He laughs. "How can you think I do not know…"

Laura looks at me guiltily. "Know what?" I can see she's trying desperately to keep her face straight.

"….But just remember now that you have been there, you have to come with me…"

Laura throws me a look of blame, which makes me crease up with laughter and once Diego sees the look on Laura's face he joins in.

The three of us get chatting about what we love about Madrid. Laura mentions the Puerta de Alcalá and how lovely it looks at night. I glance up again at Diego's painting on the wall and we decide to take the 15 minute walk to see it.

Leaving the apartment we turn onto the Calle Gran Via, which is just as busy at night as it is in the day. Cars and taxis continue to zoom up and down the street with the gentle paced buses following behind them. Many of the buildings, shop and restaurant signage are lit at night which makes me feel that the city is so alive.

We bear left onto the Calle de Alcalá, passing the Metropolis Building which is an office block, but it looks striking as it glows. It has a dome with beautiful statues around it, all of which are lit by a golden colour and just underneath, the building name of Metropolis pops out. I stop to take a couple of photos before we continue on what seems like an extremely long street and it's then that Diego tells me this street is the longest in Madrid. It certainly feels it too, but not in a bad way. It gives you a sense of just how big the city is.

When we reach the Puerta de Alcalá, it looks so beautiful. Even the cars driving around it don't ruin the effect that the building has as it sits in front of the night sky, illuminated in glory.

Lights are nestled underneath the archways making the arches glow and the street lights behind and to the sides on the streets make the whole area exhilarating. The white of the structure itself stands out all the more against the dark night sky and you can clearly see the statues as they sit proudly in place at the top.

Laura and Diego wait patiently whilst I take photos. As the traffic lights change and the traffic stops around the monument, a couple of people in cars begin to wave at us. Amused, I wave back to them as I move to different positions to catch the monument at different angles. I turn around to see Laura and Diego in an embrace and I can't resist taking a sneaky picture of them too.

Chapter 12

I wipe away the sweat from my brow following our second salsa lesson after our morning of Spanish the next day. Gael has taught us more moves to use when dancing with a partner and even though mine and Tymec's arms almost got tangled at one point, I had so much fun I couldn't stop laughing for the remainder of the lesson.

Gael tells us that each month, one of the clubs that he DJs at hosts a salsa party and he hopes we'll all go along to one of the events. It sounds brilliant in theory, but on the night who knows who you could end up 'getting your arms knotted with'.

On my way home, I round the corner onto the Calle de la Salud and I'm almost home, rummaging in my bag for my keys when I hear the sound of a man's voice talking rapid Spanish rather loudly. It sounds like it's coming from a radio, and when I look up, I'm shocked to see Jesé leaving Mio's with two takeaway cups.

My walking slows down, but my heart rate speeds up as I take in the sight of him in his police uniform once again. Why did I have to run into him? Especially when I've been sweating for the past couple of hours, it can't be a good look. I'm just deciding whether I should speak to him or carry on when he sees me.

"Nicole…"

Ahhh, the way he says my name. Just hearing his voice is enough to turn my legs to jelly.

"… I was hoping I would see you, I have just been to a call at the end of the street and thought I would get coffee from here." He takes off his sunglasses, meaning I can now see his striking brown eyes clearly and the butterflies return in my stomach. I leave my sunglasses on, almost like a shield to protect myself from him.

"See me? Why?" I move my hair to let it drape around on to one shoulder allowing some air to my neck.

He shifts from one foot to the other, watching me for a couple of seconds before he replies.

"*Mejores* will play tonight and I have spare ticket, I wanted to give it to you."

"Oh…" For a minute I thought maybe he'd come to apologise to me, obviously I was wrong.

"… Thanks but no thanks." I could kick myself for refusing but I feel it's the right thing to do.

He looks stunned at my response. "No? I thought you would love to see a game, you told me…"

"I would love to see a game, but…"

"Come with me." His enthusiasm is almost contagious. "My brother has to work, only two of my friends are fans and they cannot go."

I think for a moment. "Take Lola."

He starts laughing, stopping when he sees the look on my face. I think the penny may have dropped.

He rolls his eyes. "She hates football."

There's a lull of silence between us until his police radio pipes up again briefly and he turns the volume down.

"You are mad at me about her…"

"Well, yes I am."

"Why?" He asks.

"Why?"

His response is to stare at me until I can feel myself begin to blush.

"Look, thanks for the offer but…"

"I'm sorry, I know it was not fair of me… but we can be friends. Do you really want to miss a game?"

The answer is no I don't, and he knows that. The question is could I be just friends with him?

I think for a second and the truth is I'm willing to give it a go.

"Okay, I'll come. Thanks."

He looks relieved, which does nothing to crush the excitement I feel of being near to him again.

He checks his watch. "I will meet you here at six thirty…"

"I can meet you there, I know where I'm going now." I tell him, feeling that might be best.

"I will meet you here and we can travel together. I only live two streets away." This, I did not know.

"I'll see you soon, I have to get back to the station to finish my shift." He touches my arm fleetingly before walking off towards the main road.

I make my way inside as I see him passing the other cup over to his shift partner as he waits for him down the street. The tingling on my arm, where his hand touched me lasts until I reach the inside apartment door.

"Hi…"

Laura's in the kitchen when I open the door, sitting at the worktop making some necklaces. There's beads and stones in every colour imaginable strewn all over the worktop. She's currently fixing some clasps onto necklaces with her pliers. After selling another couple of pieces of her jewellery to people at work she's been working on some new designs.

I'm really pleased for her, as is Diego – other than when he flew across the kitchen floor a few days ago after treading barefoot on some of her beads. At least I've now learnt some new Spanish swearwords thanks to him.

"Hi Nic. How was salsaaaa?" Laura shimmies playfully.

I fill her in on my unexpected chat with Jesé.

A huge smirk appears on Laura's face as she ushers me to start getting ready for the game.

I take a shower and decide to dress in my jeans and newly purchased football shirt, black sandals and I leave my hair down.

"Does this look okay?" I ask Laura.

"Wit-woo" she whistles. "Those jeans look like they've been painted on."

I roll my eyes. "Laura, I'm being serious."

She puts her pliers down, giving me her full attention. "So am I. I don't know what you're worried about, you're only going to watch a football match." She smirks.

"Yeah, but I can still look nice, can't I?"

*

I reach the bottom of the communal stairs and take a breath before opening the door that leads out onto the street. There he is just a few metres away, hands in the pockets of his dark blue jeans as he stares up the street. As I slowly approach him I see that he's wearing his white *Mejores* training polo shirt and his arms protrude very pleasantly from the sleeves, his team scarf hangs loosely around his shoulders.

I almost reach his side before he turns around and straight away, there's that spark again. I see him look me up and down, which makes me feel slightly warm to say the least.

He nods his head and smirks. "That is…" He clears his throat before continuing. "…good shirt."

I laugh. "Yeah, yours too."

We walk to the Gran Via Metro Station making small talk as we go. As soon as we're waiting for the metro, it's obvious how many people are on their way to the game. I look around us and the amount of people waiting awakens the nerves inside of me. I distract myself by concentrating on what I can see around me in the positive sense. There are team T-shirt's, scarfs and jackets everywhere and once we board the metro, I exhale a huge breath that I didn't realise I'd been holding on to as thankfully we manage to get a seat next to each other, but the train is really starting to fill up.

"I bet your brother is gutted to be missing this tonight?"

I note the look of confusion on his face and rethink what I have said. "Erm…gutted, disappointed?"

Jesé laughs. "Ah…yes. Ramon is a *Conductor*, a driver of lorries. Sometimes but not very often, he cannot change his shift."

The next station is announced and we make our way off the train. The platform is really busy as we follow the crowds to get the next train to the *Gran* Stadium. This is the busiest environment I have been in for a while. As we get to the next platform, there's a train already there and what seems like about 100 people charge towards the doors before they close. We just manage to squeeze on and as Jesé is in front of me, he turns and reaches out his hand towards me to pull me on and make sure we don't lose each other. The warmth as his hand finds mine spreads like wild fire through my hand and straight up my arm.

My heart pounds loudly in my chest and my throat feels dry but I concentrate on what I'm doing, concentrate on my breathing. I look to Jesé. I like that he's looking out for me, the way he took hold of me so that we don't get separated. As innocent a gesture as it may seem, it feels magnified when it's him.

As we stand in the middle of the carriage holding on to the overhead bars squashed in like sardines, we're standing so close to each other that the whole of my body feels alight. At first, I feel like I can't look at him because the feeling is so intense but I can feel his gaze on me. As we start to move the train jolts slightly at first, meaning everyone loses their balance a little which makes my vision shoot up to him.

With Jesé being just a few inches taller than me, I feel so excruciatingly close to him that my temperature begins to rise again with the heat rapidly spreading up my neck and into my cheeks. My heartbeat begins to quicken, seemingly louder as the whole world seems to fall away around us. I hear his breathing becoming almost ragged and then just like that, we reach our stop and everyone begins to pile off the train.

Outside of the stadium are rows of stalls selling every snack you could think of. A strong sweet smell lingers in the air, almost like that smell of candy floss and doughnuts mixed together that you always seem to get at fair grounds. Jesé stops to buy some snacks.

"You like these?" He asks as he buys a bag of seeds.

"I've never tried them."

He pays for the huge bag and wastes no time in opening them, offering them to me.

"They are sunflower seeds that have been oven baked with salt. Try them, they are very tasty."

I take a few from the bag and I have to admit, they are pretty good.

Stalls selling different flags, hats and other souvenirs are just as popular as the food stands. I glance at what's on offer as we head towards the entrance closest to our seats, where my bag is searched and I'm told that I can't take the lid from my bottle of water inside, which I find a little strange at first.

Jesé smirks at me. "They must think you are...what would you call it? A thug?" He laughs.

I smile sweetly at him. "Of course, there's nothing I like more than starting a fight at a football match."

There's chanting and shouting to be heard inside the stadium which adds to the atmosphere. It's getting really exciting now as kick off creeps closer. I follow Jesé through the gate and as we reach the top of the steps and he shows the steward our tickets, I get my first glimpse of the ground from our seats as the teams warmup. I'm shocked at how close we are and at how much we can see but the first thought that enters my head is how can I get out?

Why do I think like this? I feel my breathing start to change as I feel fully surrounded. It's only because I'm around so many people that my mind starts to play its tricks on me, it sends me into a panic. I try to push those thoughts aside. *Concentrate on the positives Nicole*, I tell myself. I look up at the sky, still visible above the stadium and take a deep breath.

"You are okay?" Jesé asks me, to which I nod my head.

No sooner have we sat down Jesé is tucking into his snacks, whereas I'm throwing myself into taking photos of the view before me, partly as a distraction and partly because I'm in awe.

Now that the *Gran* stadium is heaving with fans, it feels even bigger. Even though I was only here a few days ago with Laura, I marvel again at how huge this place is, feeling rather different than I did just a few minutes ago now that I have settled in and concentrated on the positives.

The more we chat, Jesé and I seem to be more relaxed around each other again just as we were before I found out about Lola. The unease that was between us has definitely disappeared again.

Twenty minutes into the game, *Mejores* score their first goal and everyone seems to go crazy, it's fantastic. Five minutes later, they score another. People around me are shouting and chanting. The other thing I notice is how much people seem to eat as they watch the game. I see that Jesé has already finished his seeds and has now moved on to a bag of chocolate covered peanuts. Quite frankly I feel too excited to eat anything, maybe everyone's eating out of nervous excitement? Jesé's really into the game. I take a sneaky glance to my right and once again, I realise how ridiculously handsome he is.

His biceps…how they tense each time he throws a handful of chocolate into his mouth. He has a girlfriend for goodness sake, I need to stop this.

As the game reaches half time, Jesé breathes a sigh of relief, as though he's been holding his breath the entire time.

"What do you think so far? It is a great game?" He asks.

I laugh, sensing his excitement. "It's brilliant…I'm so glad I came."

He nods his head. "So am I…"

I smile awkwardly just as we are interrupted by the people sitting the other side of him as they ask us to move so that they can no doubt, buy more snacks. We sit back down before Jesé retrieves his phone from his jeans pocket and mumbling something I can't understand.

I ask him in Spanish if everything is okay. He makes eye contact with me and seems to think about his answer for a second.

"Nothing important."

After the second half and after securing a win of 4-1, I feel absolutely on top of the world. I realise that my mind is being completely consumed by what we're doing here and now which is exactly what I needed. Jesé suggests we wait for the crowds to disappear and then he 'has a surprise for me' apparently. He's beaming as he tells me this news, making me feel quite nervous all of a sudden.

As the crowds disperse we make our way down to the very front row where Jesé insists on taking a photo of me close to the pitch. As he does so, a woman walking past stops him and offers to take one of the two of us together. He thanks her and makes his way over to me. Feeling slightly hesitant, I lean in towards him as he puts his arm around my waist and he rests his hand on my hip. I'm sure I must be blushing but I do my best to look comfortable and smile, all the while enjoying being closer to him.

Jesé retrieves my phone from the woman and we both thank her. As he looks at the image on the screen, he smiles and passes it back to me. I'm sure I detect just a hint of awkwardness, or maybe it's guilt on his part.

"Okay follow me, we cannot leave it much longer." He insists.

"Where are we going exactly?"

I follow him up the steps back inside, before we leave the stadium completely and begin to follow the road around to our left. I suddenly realise its dark now, the floodlights made it seem like daylight in the stadium. I check my watch to see that it's just after 10 p.m.

The whole area around the ground is still pretty busy with satisfied fans leaving the ground in good spirits, making their way home or to bars for celebratory drinks. We reach what seems to be a small driveway coming out from the side. As he leads me, he's almost sprinting down the driveway, I see what's going on.

"Oh my God, do you think we will see some of the players?" I can't hide my excitement and I really don't care.

He watches me for a moment and he begins to laugh as he puts his arm around my shoulders and rubs the top of my back lightly, just for a second.

"You are pleased?"

"Pleased? This is the best idea I think you've probably ever had."

Various metal barriers have been placed around the edge of the pavement next to the driveway and around 20 or so people are hanging around desperate to see the famous faces.

The closest we can get to the back exit is about 15 metres away. Jesé manages to get to the front of the barriers and he pulls me in just in front of him. People around us are chatting impatiently and each time a car pulls out from the car park just to the side of the barriers, the expectation and suspense rides higher and higher.

Suddenly we see a couple of players emerge from inside the building. They pause on the steps next to some fans as they have their photo taken.

"How did those people manage to get inside there with them?"

"They were most likely in the…what would you call it VP area?" He asks.

I stop taking photos. "Oh, VIP?" I'm so jealous…

We stand for a while longer but no one we recognise appears so we head off on a slow walk towards the metro station.

"That was a brilliant idea, thank you." I'm genuinely so glad he took me to do that after the game.

Jesé' slips his hands into his jeans pockets. "You are welcome."

We make eye contact and for some reason, we can't help but start to laugh. We're laughing so much that I actually have to stop and stand still for a second. Maybe it's the tension that I was holding earlier in the day or the fact that we've had such a good couple of hours together I don't know, but I like it.

We're lucky in that as we arrive on the platform a metro is just pulling in so we climb aboard and begin the first leg of the journey back towards home. When we sit down next to each other, our legs are almost touching and after a couple of minutes I can feel his phone begin to vibrate in his pocket. I instinctively look at him but he makes no effort to retrieve his phone at all. I wonder if it's Lola.

Chapter 13

We arrive our metro stop and head up the stairs to a different platform before catching another metro. We aren't as lucky this time in getting a seat so we hold on for dear life next to the door, squashed in closely to each other. I feel like I can hardly breathe, but then something really strange happens. Everyone around us is buzzing with the excitement of a Saturday night, talking, laughing and joking, but we're just still and in complete silence as we can't take our eyes off each other.

I feel Jesé's hand reach the side of my thigh and he caresses it lightly with his fingertips. It's as though he's asking for my go-ahead that this is okay. I have to look away as I feel my insides melt and because I want him to carry on, but I know it's wrong. Maybe I feel like if I'm not looking at him, then it's innocent in some way. His fingers reach my hand as it hangs loosely at my side and I let him entwine his fingers with mine. I feel electricity flowing up my arm, enjoying the sensation of what us loosely holding hands gives me.

Arriving at the station jolts us out of our moment and we head back outside. As we reach the outdoors, I do a double take when I see the name of the station.

"We got off at the wrong stop?" I ask in confusion.
He smirks and in that moment, as I look at his smirking mouth I feel desperate to kiss him, wondering how his lips would feel against mine.

"It is okay, it is a nice night we can walk." He insists.
We begin to walk side by side along the street and the chemistry between us is clear. Jesé suddenly pauses beside me and so, I stop and turn around.

"What?"

He tilts his head. "You are hungry?" He asks me, repeating it again in Spanish.

"A little." I tell him as I nod my head. "I'm surprised you are though, given the endless amount of snacks you ate."

"That must have been almost two hours ago. Come, we can get coffee whilst we decide what to do."

He places his hand on my back again as he steers me gently down the busy street. When he moves his hand away literally seconds later, I desperately want him to return it.

We reach a café and Jesé leads me inside. When we get to the front of the queue, the fact that Jesé's wearing his football scarf starts a conversation with the assistant behind the counter, as they discuss today's score.

After ordering two coffees to take away, we set off in search of somewhere for food that isn't too busy given it's a Saturday night

We walk beside one another casually drinking our coffees and my head drifts back to that feeling on the metro when he was holding my hand. As our hands came together I felt desired and I shamefully ached for more.

"You are okay? You are quiet." He asks.
I take another sip of my coffee whilst I contemplate my answer.

"Erm…yes I'm erm…fine." I stutter.

I try to get the conversation flowing again

"So tell me more about your brother, are you alike or…"

He laughs. "Oh, so because my brother looks like me because we are twins, you want to know if he is single?"

"Ha ha very funny…it's hardly a good thing if he looks like you is it?"

He stops momentarily, placing his hand on his heart in mock pain.

"Nicole, you hurt me…"

I light-heartedly push him and we carry on walking.

"… So is he single?"

"No actually, he is married with one son."

"You're an uncle?"

We turn right along the Calle de Carmen which isn't as open as the streets we have just walked along. The buildings and shops feel as though they stand taller because the road is narrower. A shoe shop which is still open attracts my attention, they have some beautiful stilettos on display outside but it's the pair of black knee high boots that really draw my attention.

"Yes, Jorge is two years old… I think. I still cannot get used to Ramon being a *Papá*, it seems like yesterday that we were growing up together, but we are 33 next March…"

"I'm 30 in March…" I interrupt.

"You are in March also?"

I tell him in Spanish that my birthday is 14 March and he looks at me in disbelief.

"¿Cómo? ¿De Verdad? You are joking? This is very…what is the word… spooky?"

I'm confused for a moment before I realise what he's telling me.

"You mean that your birthday's the same day?"

He nods his head, the look of bewilderment is clear on his face and it's obvious that we are both really taken aback by this. It's really weird but straight away all I can think once again is that somehow we were meant to meet. It's just too odd to be a coincidence. We both howl with laughter and for a minute as our eyes connect again I wonder if he's thinking the same as me, is this some kind of fate bringing us together?

I realise I'm almost back at Laura and Diego's apartment and feel disappointed, so I decide to try to prolong the evening.

"We never did get food tonight." I look down at the floor, feeling cautious that I said that.

He looks at me knowingly. "We can't go home yet, we should talk some more. I live just a couple of streets away, you could come for drink?"

I bite my lip as I wonder whether I should go.

"....I have food..." he teases.

I have to go home with him, I need to find out more. I need to know if there's something between us other than just a physical attraction or lust or whatever it is. I can't just forget about him, or about the way he makes me feel. I've never felt this...how do I explain it? This...'right' around a man before, not even with James.

Five minutes later we arrive at Jesé's apartment. We enter through the door into a short hallway which then gives way to a compact lounge area, decorated in cream and grey with two black very comfortable looking leather sofas. It's really modern inside, very tastefully decorated.

Jesé gestures towards the sofa. "Sit down..." He walks away into what I can only assume is the kitchen, judging by the clanging of bottles that I can hear.

I sit down, taking a deep breath in a bid to quell the nerves that I'm feeling. I take off my jacket and relax back into my seat as he presents me with a small bottle of cerveza. The mere sight of him re-entering the room creates flurries of excitement inside of me.

He flicks on his music system on with a controller, which begins to play a gentle guitar rhythm.

"*Salud...*" He clinks his bottle to mine as he looks endearingly into my eyes. He sits next to me.

"*Salud.*" I sip the cool cerveza, savouring the taste on my tongue. "You've got a really nice place here."

"I have to tell truth, it belongs to my parents. Me and my brother, we were brought up here in Madrid but a few years ago, our parents decided to move to Denia, to be at the coast."

Jesé twists his body on the sofa, facing himself towards me and relaxes his arm across the back of the sofa.

"They sold our family house in Tetuan maybe 10 years ago… but they still wanted somewhere in *el centro*, so…..this apartment makes sense for them." He shrugs.

The air feels fraught once again and after taking another drink from my bottle I become very aware that he's looking at me, watching me. I feel the tension building between us as I look at him. Slowly, he places his bottle on the coffee table in front of us before relieving me of mine. Could this really be about to happen?

He drops his voice to an intense whisper.

"Nicole…." And then suddenly he kisses me.

As our lips meet for the first time, it's so powerful that I immediately feel completely gripped with the intensity.

His hands are in my hair before falling down onto my arms then to my thigh as I drag my hands underneath his T-shirt and up his back. We lie back onto the sofa and continue to desperately explore each other as his hand slides up underneath my shirt and his kisses travel down to my neck, his five o'clock shadow gently grazing my skin.

He stops abruptly to peel away his T-shirt and I have a flash back to that moment on the street when I couldn't stop looking at his arms. It seems that his arms aren't the only part of him to be toned. He brings himself back down to me, tugging at my T-shirt as he does so, that is until the sound of his ringing mobile phone makes me grasp exactly what I'm doing. This man has a girlfriend and despite the way I feel about him, because of that fact, what we're doing now is wrong.

"Jesé, stop…" I tell him, pushing him away. "No…"

"Stop? Now?" He asks, his face flushed.

He returns back to his original position sitting next to me on the sofa.

"Nicole, I think you know how I feel about you…" He caresses my leg.

"Your phone…Lola….this is wrong." I rest my head in my hands as he clambers closer to me, placing his arms around my shoulders and I shrug him away to which he looks taken aback. Am I like her, am I like Annie? Is this as bad as what she did to me?

He takes his phone from his pocket, unlocking the screen to see the missed call is from Lola. He casually throws his phone onto the coffee table in front of us before turning himself back in toward me.

"Nicole, I am sorry. I will tell Lola, I will finish things with her."

"Really?" I ask, surprised to hear him say that.

He takes a hold of my hand in my lap, gently circling the back of my hand with his thumb.

"Yes, of course…Lola, she is not erm… not an easy person to be with."

"Yet you are with her…"

".. only because of habit.

I stand up, pulling my jacket on and take a deep breath as he stands beside me.

"You don't have to go, stay…"

"Jesé, believe me I really don't want to go."

He moves closer to me again, placing his hands on my hips.

"Then don't…" He pulls me towards his still shirtless chest, consuming me once again. Despite that, I need to be sensible so I pull away for a second time.

"When you've spoken to Lola…"

"… I will call you." He takes his phone from the table. "I don't have your number…" He hands his phone to me and I type in my number before I walk to the door. As he follows me, I pause before I open it and turn back towards him.

"Jesé, thanks for a great time tonight."

"I have loved every minute." He says, squeezing my hand.

Taking another deep breath, I kiss him on the cheek and leave his apartment.

When the fresh air of outside hits me, I can't believe what just happened and I have no idea how I managed to drag myself away. I touch my fingers to my lips as they continue to tingle, almost as though to check that it actually happened. Just then, my phone beeps and it's him. The text reads just one word. *"Mañana."*

Excitement fills me at the thought that next time I see him, he'll be single, yet part of me feels mortified that I let what just happened happen, knowing he has a girlfriend. I'll make sure it doesn't happen again, well, not until he's broken things off with Lola that's for sure.

Chapter 14

"Noooo…" Laura gasps, making me feel as though the whole of Mio's Restaurant just heard every word.

"Ssssh…" I clutch her arm nervously looking around us not wanting anyone to hear.

Laura glances over at the bar where Diego stands chatting to Mio as I continue to tell her about last night over Coffee.

"I wonder how Lola will take the news?"

"Well we'll see…" I sip my coffee. "I'm determined not to keep checking my phone every five minutes to see if he's done it, which is why I've left it back at yours."

Diego returns to the table, clearing his throat conveniently loudly to signal his return which is met by the rolling of Laura's eyes.

"It's okay…we've finished the catch up now." She rubs his arm reassuringly.

"I can always stand at the bar for more time?" He jokes as he sits down. We tuck into our light breakfasts of churros with hot chocolate for Diego and freshly baked bread rolls to go with mine and Laura's coffees.

"Diego and I are heading to Retiro Park today if you fancy joining us?"

I swallow a mouthful of food. "Thanks but today I'm going to do some more studying." And try my best not to agonise about what might or what might not be going on with Jesé and Lola.

*

It's Saturday night once again and as I reach Laura's apartment on my way back from class, I reminisce at how this time last week Jesé was waiting to invite me to the *Mejores* game. One week ago since that perfect evening and those steamy kisses, and yet there's still no word from him. *Nada*.

I recall the memory of him telling me he'd speak to Lola the next day, that he'd finish with her and call me but in spite of that a week has passed by and I haven't heard a single thing. I've remained strong, I'm actually quite proud of myself for managing to restrain and not even drop him a casual message. Maybe he's changed his mind about me? It's probably for the best.

When I told Eva on my course the tale of Jesé today she told me the best thing to do is 'get myself out there and get him out of my system' maybe I should take her advice?

Connor her boyfriend from the UK arrives next week and she's invited me out to eat with them one night so I can meet him which is nice. It feels good to be surrounded by positive people, people who even after knowing them for such a short period of time I feel I can trust.

Over the years I've struggled to keep a hold of any real friendships - they couldn't understand my mind-set some of them even lost patience and just stopped bothering with me. That's why it's mostly just been me and Annie over the years, until I met Laura a few months ago.

The thing with anxiety is that no matter how many people you talk to about it, anxiety can be a very lonely place. The amount of time spent living inside your head, being unable to make your friends and family understand the situations that you fear, especially when there is no logic to them is difficult. Only you can hear the absolute chaos of your mind but without sharing and getting the help that I've had in the past I know that things could have been a lot worse.

After spending the week playing out different scenarios in my head of Jesé arriving at my door to tell me the news in person he was now single. Or, me bumping into him on the street whilst he was working and him giving me the good news were suddenly, in an instant replaced by Jesé and Lola smooching on the sofa. That same sofa he was kissing me on last week. My thoughts turn to Lola.

Although I didn't get the best first impression of her with the poisonous looks she was throwing me and how Luís had told me that she wasn't a very nice person I wonder if Jesé regularly cheats on her? No one deserves that, as I've certainly come to realise even more so recently.

Meeting up with Luís before my course this morning wasn't strange in the slightest. After our first date just after I arrived in Madrid I think I knew we'd only ever be friends and when Luís told me he'd like to stay in touch, I didn't think for a minute I'd hear from him again. The odd message here and there led to us catching up for coffee this morning which led to him putting me out of my misery of the waiting game with Jesé.

It was Luís who eventually brought up the subject of him. I told him we'd been to a game together but I left out the part about what happened back at his apartment, obviously. I wasn't about to start slating him to one of his friends. However, when he told me he'd seen Jesé and Lola together shopping the previous day, unbeknown to him he'd told me all I needed to know.

I recall Luís explaining…. *"They looked happy enough. I had never pictured Jesé as a father before and I was shocked, but I guess they are both excited about the baby…"*

That hit me like a hammer to the heart. I did my best not to react to the news, not until I left Luís anyway. He asked me if Jesé had told me about the baby, assuming we were friends, but I told him no. I did my best to change the subject.

I have to admit I cried tears of frustration on my walk to the metro station, as I was hit with the realisation that he clearly had no intention of finishing with Lola. Did he know then, that night with me that Lola was pregnant with his baby? I'm such an idiot.

*

I walk into the apartment after a long day on my course as Diego and Laura are preparing a meal of paella.

"Your timing is *perfecto*." Diego calls as he plates up the food.

Laura pours three glasses of wine. "How was school today?"

"Ha ha…it was okay thanks. I think I needed to keep my mind busy…" Even I can detect the miserable tone of my voice.

Diego mumbles. "Pffft, *mujeres*…" Women. Laura shoots him a look of annoyance.

The three of us take a seat at the table and begin to eat the delicious tender seafood, cooked with saffron, rice and green beans.

"Okay Diego…" Laura begins. "You're a man…you tell us, what was going on in Jesé's mind that night?"

With what I found out today I feel like it's neither here nor there now but nevertheless, I'm interested to hear his opinion.

"I think you know the answer to your question…he thought of sex that is all."

"Exactly." I swallow my food. "The thing is I found out today that Lola…his girlfriend, she's pregnant."

Laura freezes with her fork full paella midway to her mouth. Diego passes a look of concern before shaking his head.

After tonight I'm determined to draw a line under things with Jesé, it's time to concentrate on my job, my course and on building my new life here.

*

"Morning." I call to Diego a few days later as he closes their bedroom door behind him. "Coffee?" I pour myself a cup.

"*Gracias*, Nicole."

He takes a seat at one of the stools at the kitchen worktop and I pass him a fresh cup of coffee, of which he takes a sip. I watch him warily.

"You look like you needed that this morning."

He nods his head, outwardly still half asleep. I start to wonder if it's me being here, maybe it's getting to be too much. After all this is his place.

"¿Todo bien?" I check that everything is okay.

He sits up straight and takes a deep breath, glancing towards the bedroom door before finally speaking.

"There is something…" He clears his throat and leans in closer. "I have a plan, to ask Laura if she will marry me…"

Unfortunately Diego's brilliant news is interrupted by a horrendous squealing sound which I'm quite sure could be heard in Australia…that would be me, shrieking with excitement before quick thinking Diego jumps up in a bid to quieten me down.

"I'm sorry but I'm so excited for you both…"

Diego's huge smile tells me just how excited he is too. "Please…it is surprise."

"Of course, of course…" I watch him pacing around the kitchen. "You're nervous, Diego?"

He grins. "Not of the asking her no, I am so certain that it is right but I hope she does not think this is too soon?"

I shake my head. "She won't, trust me she knows you two are perfect for each other…as do I."

"Thank you, Nicole."

"Are you buying a ring…or?"

"I am to pick this up today…I know exactly the sort of thing she would want. She was telling me about a ring that her Mother had when Laura was younger…she will now know that I also listen to her, yes?" he laughs.

We hear the movement of Laura around the bedroom and so we need to wrap it up quickly.

"…I would like to ask her tonight on our anniversary. I am taking her to her favourite restaurant."

"What was that squeaking noise?" Laura asks whilst sleepily rubbing her head as she emerges from the bedroom. Diego and I look to each other for an explanation.

"Nicole thought that she saw a mouse, but it was just a…." He searches for a word.

"… It was just a wire." I laugh heartily, pulling a 'sorry' face at Diego.

*

That evening, Laura and I decide to go for a drink to Mercado de San Miguel. Tonight's proposal night for her, not that she knows that of course. Diego's coming to pick her up from here as it's on the way to the restaurant.

It's just as busy at the *mercado* as when I visited that first time with Luís. As I follow Laura to a stall, I remember just how much I love the atmosphere in here. Everyone seems so cheerful as I look around. Even the sheer colour of all of the different foods on offer seem to act as mood boosters. The pinks of the jamon, the pistachio greens and bright yellow of the macarons. Even the cheesecakes with the bright red strawberry topping. Everything around us just seems to be so uplifting.

All of these people, and every single one of them is enjoying the great selection of different foods, the wines and the company of friends or family. It feels a million miles away from my old life back in the UK which is exactly what I needed.

We manage to bag one stool which Laura takes and I collect the food.

I return with a couple of plates which Laura takes from the tops of the two small glasses of wine as she sees me attempting to balance them.

"Have you spoken to Annie?" Laura asks.

"Not since she called me last week and I told her not to call me again." I take a bite of some stuffed peppers, allowing the smoky chorizo flavouring to keep me in the moment.

"Do your parents not know what's going on?"

I shake my head. "They know that we've fallen out, which of course is 'me being dramatic about something' because it couldn't possibly be anything Annie has done wrong…"

I feel like I'm on the outside talking about someone else's family dramas, not my own.

"They will find out, this can't stay a secret surely?" Laura peels a slice of jamon drizzled in olive oil from the plate and pops it into her mouth.

"I know all Annie's worried about is if I tell Pete what she's done, or if I tell my parents, what will happen for her and how her life will change. I'm not even sure she's actually bothered about what she's done."

"How could she not be bothered about what she's done to her own sister and the relationship with her boyfriend?"

I shrug my shoulders. "Pete needs to know. He can't go on believing his daughter is his if there's a chance she isn't."

"You're going to tell him?"

"Now there's a question. I really don't know…I was thinking about it last night. Maybe I'll give her the chance to tell him herself and if she doesn't then…I don't think I have much choice. I can't leave him to think he has a daughter if… " I get teary and have to stop.

Laura squeezes my hand. "I think that's the best way Nic. It has to come from her and if she has anything about her, any ounce of remorse at all about what she's done she'll know what she has to do."

I see Diego heading in our direction. He's certainly scrubbed up well in a light blue open collar shirt and navy blue blazer jacket with smart jeans.

"It must be my lucky night, two beautiful women…" He slides his arm around Laura, and kisses her cheek to which she looks absolutely smitten.

Laura looks stunning tonight in a simple navy blue shift dress and her black hair pinned up loosely, with light waves of hair framing her face.

"You are ready to go?" Diego asks checking his watch. Laura gives a concerned glance in my direction, to which I interrupt her before she even starts.

"Don't worry about me, go and enjoy your meal."

She smiles sadly at me. "Are you okay?"

"I'm fine honestly, now go and enjoy your anniversary."

Diego spies the plates in front of us. "I hope you have saved room for your meal…"

"Relax, do you really think I'd risk ruining dinner?"

Diego winks at me as they stand to leave and Laura pulls me in for a hug. As I'm facing his direction I mouth "good luck" to him, to which he pats his hand on his pocket with a confident smile. To think, the next time I see Laura she'll be engaged…

I sit down on the stool and see my phone on the table and consider texting my sister. I begin to type a message, telling her she needs to tell Pete the truth if she ever wants to rebuild our relationship but the thing is, do I really think that we can rebuild it after something this huge? I delete the message and drink the rest of my wine slowly, relishing the fact that I'm sitting drinking alone in a foreign country and to my amazement, I don't feel the slightest bit awkward about it.

Chapter 15

The week passes by quickly in a blur of Mio's birthday party discussions, another couple of shifts at the restaurant and wedding chats with the newly engaged Laura. She had absolutely no idea of Diego's plans to propose but she was overwhelmed by his proposal and his choice of ring.

I brought them a bottle of their favourite fizz to celebrate but I think we've actually celebrated almost every night this week which has been a very welcome distraction.

Annie tried to call me yesterday but I just couldn't face speaking to her. She did text me to tell me she was going to tell Pete the truth, whether she will or not is a different story.

I feel so upset that we're not speaking but I'm beyond hurt at what she's done. The last couple of days I've even started to consider emailing James. We haven't spoken in quite some time but I feel like I want to have it out with him too. It takes two for that to happen after all.

Laura pops her head around my bedroom door. "You ready Nic?" She looks lovely in her black and red chequered short-sleeved dress and tights.

"Yep, ready to go". I stand up smoothing down my black flowery shift dress.

I jokingly adopt a superior voice. "May I just say how well your enormous engagement ring suits your dress, Madam?" To which we both laugh as she examines her ring once again.

"Oh I know dharrrrling…" She playfully scratches her nose with her ring finger and we giggle again.

"I might have to head home for a few days with Diego, the family are pacing the floor at not even meeting Diego yet and now we're engaged to be married…" She rolls her eyes to which I laugh.

"Come with us?" she pleads.

"Haha, nice try but even I'm shell shocked when all of your family is in one room, Lau."

Birmingham – June – Three months ago

It's Saturday night and as Laura and I leave the local pub at closing time we consider our options.

"Okay so there's pizza, chips or…"

"… Or." Laura interrupts. "… You could come back to mine? My parents have a few people around which is usually quite entertaining and there's more than enough food and drink."

"Sounds good to me."

We make the short taxi journey to Laura's parents' huge detached house. As we walk through the front door it feels much more like a party than Laura had described.

Music plays loudly, people are singing and dancing and this is just her immediate family so I'm told. I think I'm in shock and it must be written all over my face judging by the amount of people who look genuinely concerned as they ask me if I'm okay as Laura introduces me.

Everyone is so welcoming and within an hour of me arriving I feel like I known these people for years. I don't think I've ever been kissed by so many people in such a short space of time as I meet the family. It's certainly a surprise walking into the house and seeing this many people who are so genuinely pleased to meet you.

Laura's eldest sister, Colleen starts Irish dancing with a couple of her cousins and they attempt to teach me a few steps.

It's so impressive when you watch them and it's a lot harder than it looks. I definitely prefer watching them rather than attempting it myself. The fast yet precise leg movements, the way the upper body is kept straight with perfect posture. It really does take some skill.

The thing that strikes me the most, the more time I spend with them is that I feel like I somehow fit with these people, despite them being more or less strangers. Not that I don't feel like I fit with my own family but it's just that tonight, I'm just me. With my family I've always been one of two people, one of the twins…the one that isn't always on a pedestal to other people. I feel lighter, I feel brighter, and it's a strange feeling, but I like it.

After lots of dancing and laughing, I spend the night on Laura's sofa. In all honestly it's hardly 'the night' as its gone 4 a.m. by the time I lie down and loose myself in some sleep. Sometimes the best nights really are the ones that aren't planned.

Present Day

Mio's is hardly recognisable tonight. It's decked out in stunning fairy lights hung over the bar, the tables have been pushed to the sides of the room and '70' banners are displayed as music plays gently in the background.

When the three of us arrive, Mio is working the room receiving hugs and kisses from everyone. I recognise Isabel from the night at the Italian restaurant and remember her telling me Mio is a friend of her Dad's.

The birthday boy spots us and bounds straight over, looking very dapper a grey suit. He greets us excitedly in Spanish taking another look at Laura's ring and pinching her cheeks, telling her she's like family to him. He's clearly delighted for them.

"My parents are so sorry to be missing your night..." Diego tells him.

Mio nods his head. "I spoke to them earlier today... we will tell them all about the party tomorrow."

"Mio is there anything I can do to help?" I ask.

He takes my hand. "Drink, drink and drink some more." He laughs. "No one is working tonight. The food is prepared, we have drink I want everyone to dance esta noche..."

I see Isabel filling her glass at the bar and head over to say hi.

"Nicole, it seems such a long time since we saw you."

My head flies back to memories of that night at the restaurant and to Jesé and the chemistry we had.

"How are things?" She asks.

I take a sip of my wine. "Good thanks. I'm still enjoying working here, the course is going good..."

"You have seen Luís?"

"Last weekend, we had breakfast." I tell her to which she raises her eyebrows and smiles.

I laugh. "It's not like that, he's really lovely but we're just friends." Raul joins us, slipping his arm around Isabel's waist as she continues.

"I know it was a shame, but you would be so much better suited to Jesé..."

Just at the mention of his name a pang of nerves begin in my stomach.

Raul nudges Isabel and shakes his head in jest. "Ignore her she just loves to....how do you say? Get people together?"

I laugh nervously. "Don't worry I'm kind of like that myself, but I think we all know that Jesé is a no-go."

I see Isabel is surprised, then a look of confusion appears on her face. She looks to Raul, who shakes his head. Juan then chooses that moment to whistle loudly to get everyone's attention and we see him in the centre of the room with his arm proudly around his uncle Mio, as he begins his speech.

"Well what can I say about my uncle that you do not already know?" He gestures towards him.

"You are the most hard-working, warmest and friendliest man I think most people in this room have ever met. You have touched so many people's lives every day, serving drinks, making them laugh and generally being you. You trained me to be your chef, and now you are trusting me with your restaurant as you take your very long overdue retirement on your 70th birthday. I know you will still be in here most days because as everybody knows, you hate to miss out..." The room fills with laughter.

"...But I will do you proud, I promise." Juan raises his glass.

"Everyone, please raise your glass to Mio…"

"To Mio…"

"*Salud.*"

Mio wipes a stray tear from his face before kissing his nephew and hugging him tightly. Even Juan is choked up but then again so am I and looking around the room, I can see that there is barely a dry eye.

Once he composes himself, it's Mio's turn.

"I cannot thank you all enough. Since my beautiful Sofia left my side 20 years ago, my restaurant has been my life. You are all…" He motions his an arm towards everyone in the room "…like family to me. Some of you, I've watched you grow from a child…" He looks around and spies Diego and nods to him. "…. You make me so proud."

Now it's Diego's turn to get emotional.

Mio continues "… Tonight I want to celebrate my birthday, my retirement and my wonderful family and friends."

Various people head in his direction to offer him hugs and kisses, signalling the end of his speech. The music is turned back on and is now more upbeat at Mio's request as people begin to dance.

Sometime later, the music is turned off and the sound of flamenco guitar begins. Everyone turns around, following the sound of the traditional music to see Mio's oldest friend, Sebastián sitting down strumming away in front of the bar. He's completely immersed in the guitar, the look of concentration clear on his face.

Gradually a few people begin to clap along, making the tempo of the music stronger. Diego tells me as he claps along that the handclapping is called *palmas*. Gradually Diego moves in the direction of the guitarist and begins to sing along loudly. I look to Laura next to me who has the biggest smile on her face.

"I didn't know Diego could sing…" I'm shocked.

She laughs. "Only on special occasions…"

Everyone is completely taken in by the infectious music and I really want to clap along to the rhythm but I have no idea how.

A couple of women come forwards next to the guitarist and begin some impromptu flamenco dancing, it's fantastic. I watch in complete amazement as they dance along making some beautiful shapes with their hands and stamping their feet, completely immersing themselves in the music which is gradually getting faster and faster as it is played with such passion.

Following a rapturous applause, Mio takes the guitar from his friend and begins another song, nodding to Diego who signals in agreement as they start. I gaze around the room and it's clear to see how much love there is for Mio here tonight. Just then, I jolt, no it can't be. But it is. Just in front of the doorway, staring in my direction is Jesé.

I feel myself begin to heat up. This is the first time I've seen him since that night, after the *Mejores* game. The night we almost went too far. The very same night that he promised me he would finish with Lola and get in touch. He never did. But then I know why now don't I, Lola is expecting his child.

I can still hear the flamenco music but it's like someone has hit a pause button in some way. I try and break away from my thoughts and concentrate on the music but my eyes keep returning to his. Ignore him, ignore him, I tell myself.

The music finishes and there follows another round of applause and masses of cheering before the music behind the bar is back, the party now in full swing.

Diego re-joins us, receiving a long kiss from Laura. "You were amazing..." She tells him. They stand with their arms around each other, yet turned to face me.

"Diego she's right, that's one hell of a voice you have there."

He raises his glass toward me. "*Gracias.*"

I subtly try to scour the room to see where he is, but there's no sign. I'm annoyed with myself for feeling disappointed.

"Why don't I get some more drinks?" I offer but Laura stops me.

"No you don't, it's our turn." They start to walk towards the bar but just then, she turns back towards me. "... plus I think it's best that you don't have anything you could use as a weapon in your hand considering who's heading in your direction." She gestures her head to the right as I see Jesé walking towards me.

I panic slightly, not sure what to do with myself. As he reaches my side the scent of his aftershave brings a feeling of familiarity.... and longing.

"Well, I wasn't expecting to see you here..." I start.

I note the awkwardness in his stance which seems quite out of character. I'm used to seeing him so confident and even quite cocky at times.

He gives me a half smile. "I know this, but.... Nicole I want to speak with you..."

He's completely shameless. I can't help but interrupt.

"It's a shame you didn't want to speak to me a couple of weeks ago."

He looks at the floor before meeting my eyes again. *Oh those eyes...*

"Please Nicole I am sorry I did not get in touch..."

"That's okay I expect you didn't have time, I'd imagine you've had lots to do. Baby clothes shopping…"

He looks surprised that I know as he interrupts me. "It has been very difficult."

"I have no doubt about that. It's bad enough that you conveniently forgot to tell me that you had a girlfriend"…I look around us, suddenly realising that we're in public and lower my voice before I carry on. "…but a pregnant girlfriend, that's something else."

He takes a step closer towards me, breathing a sigh of frustration as he places his hand on my elbow. "No… No it is not like that please, Lola is not…" He takes a look around us. "Can we step outside?"

"I don't think so Jesé…"

He gives me a pleading look. "Nicole please I just want five minutes. I only came because I knew you would be here."

I wonder for a second before I soften slightly. "Look Jesé, I think it's best we just leave it there."

He looks infuriated. "Five minutes then I will go, please?"

I make eye contact with Laura at the other side of the room before agreeing.

"Two minutes."

We walk through the now very busy party, dodging people's arms flailing around as they dance, and we step out onto the pavement. There's people outside smoking and chatting, so we move away from the restaurant for some privacy. We're actually now outside Laura's apartment and given that it's quite cold, I'm tempted to just ask him up there, but I think better of it.

I lean against the wall and he stands in front of me. It's then that I notice his hair is slightly more tousled than normal, I think it's the first time I've seen him that little more natural looking. He looks so good, not that I'm noticing of course.

"After that night, I went to see Lola the next day to break up. She told me she was pregnant, how could I do this now?"

This really isn't making me feel any better.

"I know I should have got in touch but what could I say?"

"How about the truth?"

He rolls his eyes. "Please…"

I shrug my shoulders.

"… I felt I should do the right thing even though I felt trapped. Lola is very manipulative. This week I found out she lied, it was not true. I felt relief."

You feel relief? "That's terrible, how did you find out?"

"Things just didn't seem right, a few things did not add up. I confronted her and she admitted she made the whole thing up as she knew I wanted to finish."

"So that's that?"

He gives me a sad smile and nods his head. "Yes. That is that."

A moment of silence passes between us as I think of all the things I've been thinking of him the last couple of weeks.

"I'm sorry she did that to you. Maybe you could have got in touch…"

"I know, but I wanted to tell you to your face, to see you…" He steps closer to me, placing his hand on my cheek. My stomach does somersaults and I close my eyes briefly to allow myself to think straight, although with him touching me that's not easy. I open my eyes and put my hand on his and move it away, keeping hold of it just for a second between us before letting it go.

I swallow, my mouth now feeling dry. "I'm sorry, I…"

"Nicole you know how I feel about you." He takes my hand back into his, and I let him.

I take a deep breath. "I'm not sure I do." I shake my head. "I don't know if I can trust you Jesé. I don't even know you, not really."

He looks disheartened. "Then you will get to know me, properly this time. Can we start again?"

Oh I want to. I need to tread carefully until I know I can trust him.

"You will see you can trust me, Nicole, we have started off wrongly…that is all."

"I have to get back to the party." I glance in the direction of the restaurant.

"I only came here to see you, I knew you would be here. I do not really know the owner but I had to see you."

I can feel myself warming to his advances, to his words and this feels dangerous.

"Look let's just be friends for now."

"…. For now…" He winks which makes me laugh. "So friend, we can meet to watch the game in the bar tomorrow?"

He really isn't giving up. Sensing my thoughts he reassures me.

"It will not just be me and you, other friends too. We are friends now, yes?"

"I don't know…tomorrow…"

"Friends… for now." He kisses me on each cheek, making the temptation in me fire up again before he walks slowly away.

I stare up at the night sky. For whatever reason, it looks really soothing, navy blue with beautiful scattered stars sparkling brightly. It's not very often stars are so noticeable in the sky but they are tonight. Maybe it's a sign, or a reminder? A reminder that no matter how you're feeling, there are always good things there for you to see if you stop and look for them.

Annie springs into my head, I wonder if Pete knows yet? I'm surprised Mom and Dad haven't picked up on the fact that this fall out that we've had is serious.

I emailed James earlier today, as I don't have his number anymore since he moved away to Chester for his new job. It was my attempt to have it out with him, I just had to do it. He needs to know his secret has come out, so I told him exactly what I thought of him. Did he really have a new job that took him up there or did he just need to get away from Annie, and from me? He knew she was pregnant, he must've realised the baby could've been his.

I guess I just wanted him to know I knew exactly what had happened. Whether or not he'll reply is a different story but I thought maybe it would help me in some way.

Back inside at the party, I see Laura talking to two women who I don't recognise but I can see they're admiring her necklace. One of the women takes the pendant in her hand as it hangs around Laura's neck. She gently runs her thumb over the emerald green stone pendant, by the look on the ladies face I'd say she's completely fascinated.

Chapter 16

I deliver two coffees to Laura and Diego's table at the restaurant the next morning. Laura sits head in hands groaning dramatically with her hangover as Diego shakes his head in jest.

I hold the menu out. "No food Laura?"

She looks up as the colour drains from her face.

I continue to taunt her "Not even any toast?"

She puts her hand to her mouth and swallows carefully.

Diego sniggers next to her, taking a sip of hot coffee as Laura dashes in the direction of the toilet. I sit down opposite Diego.

"Oops maybe that was too much?" I ask, resting the empty tray down next to me.

"She will be fine." He assures me. "After Laura was introduced to Mariella, the celebratory drinks were too many." He laughs.

Last night, I found out that the two women Laura was talking to, one of them was Elisa who is the student of Laura's who brought one of her bracelets. She was introducing her to her Aunt – Mariella, who owns her own boutique clothing shop here in Madrid.

Mariella had already seen the bracelet she made for Elisa a few weeks ago and she also fell in love with it. They were at Mio's party last night purely by coincidence as she has also known Mio for years. They got talking about Laura's jewellery and she's interested in selling it in her shop. They still need to discuss the details fully, but Laura was understandably ecstatic at the offer and celebrated a little too heavily it seems.

Diego leans across the table toward me. "You are okay today?"

"I'm okay, I only had a couple of glasses really."

He sits back in his seat. "I meant after talking to Jesé? Laura said you were quiet afterward."

I begin to play with a napkin on the table awkwardly.

"She did? I think it sobered me up I really wasn't expecting to see him that's for sure."

"You have spoken to your sister?" He picks up the menu from the other end of the table.

"Not really no…" I smile miserably.

Sensing my unease, Diego attempts to broach the subject carefully.

"In the December holidays we will go for a few days to visit my parents in Gran Canaria. Maybe you ask Annie to come and stay with you to give you a chance to talk?"

The thought of that fills me with dread. I listen to Diego.

"…December seems a long way, but it is almost November already."

I groan. "Thanks, but I just don't know how I can at the moment."

I feel my eyes begin to water and I purse my lips together in an attempt to stop the tears that I feel are about to make an appearance. Diego looks on, unsure of what to say.

Taking a deep breath I attempt to change the subject.

"Last night was definitely a hit, everyone seemed to have a great time."

"It was *perfecto.*" He smiles, gesturing with the 'perfect' sign with his fingers. "…although I feel that some people drank too much." He nods his head in the direction of Laura as she returns to the table looking brighter.

"Sorry about that, I won't give you the gory details…"

Diego and I grimace.

*

That afternoon once my shift is finished, I meet Luís outside the Plaza de Espana Metro station.

"Nicole it is good to see you." He greets me with a hug.

"You too Luís." It is lovely to see him, I'm really glad we've stayed friends.

"So I'm intrigued, what is the Temple of Debod exactly?"

We walk at a slow pace along the street that leads to the Temple. I notice there seems to be more coaches around than I usually see. Luís clears his throat jokingly before using his best 'Tour Guide' voice.

"The temple was donated to our country many years ago by the Government of Egypt. It is very beautiful."

"Oh wow, so it's still used as a temple now?"

"No. You cannot go inside the temple but it is in a park, Parque del Oeste, you will see…"

We cross over the Calle de Bailén and walk a little further until we are met with the scene of coaches with hordes of people getting back on, about to leave the park (luckily for us). It feels quite cool today so I'm glad I wore my faux leather jacket. Luís looks stylish in blue jeans, a white T-shirt and a navy blue bomber jacket.

The outside of the park area has a type of evergreen tree that reminds me of a scarecrow. It looks somehow like it has arms and a hat— just a branch on each side obviously, and one around the top but the way it moves delicately in the slight breeze of the day just conjures up that image for me. Luís thinks it's hilarious when I tell him.

I'm surprised how close to the road the temple seems to be, I was expecting it to be quite far into the park and not even visible from the road. We walk along the pathway and there's three stone built 'gateways' before the temple itself sitting behind them.

Surrounding the gateways seems to be some kind of shallow moat and I can see the brickwork reflecting in the water as the sun shines down. The air feels really crisp and the autumn leaves are scattered around, mostly at the bottom of the water. We walk further on, as I marvel at the structures and then as I stand still a little further along there's an air of calmness. It's almost as though you can really feel the history in the air and in the gateways and picture the people that built them all of those years ago.

People are sitting around on the low walls next to the temple itself, just lounging back and letting the world continue around them, lazing in the late October sunshine.

Luís has carried on ahead, leaving me to my own devices as I slowly follow him whilst taking in the setting. I walk further into the park to catch up with him, where he sits relaxing on a wall in front of the water feature. It seems a really nice place to just sit and think or to really clear your mind. I sit next to him.

Luis grins. "Well, you like it here I think?"
I take a deep breath, even the air feels clearer here. "Mmmm, I do."

Just behind us on the other side of the water, a couple sit beside each other on the wall, arms around each other and giggling quietly. I see two women power walking, both dressed in pink and grey gym gear. But, I think what sums this place up the most is the guy lying down just a few feet away from us on the wall, his eyes closed in complete relaxation, or even in sleep.

I can fully appreciate how he's feeling. The relaxed sensation that consumes me by being here....I feel like I could curl up and drift off into an undisturbed sleep and it's been quite some time since I had one of those.

Looking at the beautiful colours around us, the autumnal orange and brassy reds show through. The trees standing tall and proud, gently dancing in the breeze with the water feature behind. It's nice that Luís and I can have this comfortable silence between us as we admire the nature that surrounds us.

It's been a long time since I've managed to feel completely immersed in the moment like this. There's been so many times when I've gone for a walk or even been doing something but it's like my mind is somewhere else completely. Quite often when I go for a walk I feel like I can't really 'be' there mentally no matter how hard I try. I just can't get my mind to cooperate because it always seems to be thinking of something else that I need to do tomorrow or next week but today, here and now, I feel so grounded and present.

He snaps me out of my thoughts. "Jesé told me he had seen you last night. I take it that you know about Lola?" He asks.

I shift my seating position, pulling my right leg up onto the wall in front of me and hugging it towards me.

"I can't believe she did that to him, to lie like that."

He frowns. "I can. I think that she thinks she can have whatever she wants. She had a difficult start in life, she was in foster homes for most of her childhood I think. Even she herself says she was so lonely as a child that she does not want to be lonely as an adult."

"That's awful that she feels like that. So lying about being pregnant with someone's baby to get someone to stay with you. Wouldn't she rather be with someone who wants to be with her? Easy for us to say I guess, if she's feeling like that…."

"She has been nothing but problems for him for a long time."

I'm intrigued. "You make her sound terrible, I mean I know that this was but…"

"That is for Jesé to tell you if he wants to, but she is bad news. I hope that she will stay away now. I know that Jesé isn't perfect but he is a good friend of mine and a good man."

Luís glances around us before returning his gaze to me.

"Perhaps now you can get to know each other better?" He nudges me playfully.

I smirk. "I don't know, maybe. We'll see…" I nudge him back to which we both smile.

I tell him briefly about what happened with Annie and James and he listens intently, seeming to fully understand my reservations about becoming involved with anyone at the moment, my trust issues feeling very raw.

"How about you? Any *señoritas* on the horizon?" I ask him.

He throws his head back with laughter. "I do have a date on Saturday…so ask me again on Sunday."

He stands up, holding his hand out towards me.

"*Venga*, come on, if we walk through the other side of the park, I know a great café."

I take his hand as I get up, letting it go again as we start to walk.

*

Time is getting on when I start back to Laura's after spending a lovely afternoon with Luís. I'm still torn over whether I should meet Jesé tonight at the bar with him and his friends. I know Luís will be there as he was heading straight over when I left him but I told him to carry on without me as I wasn't going. I didn't want him to know too much about the turmoil running through my mind over whether to go or not, I want to decide for myself.

As I walk past the cinema, I stop to see which films are showing. Seeing a film could be a good idea to keep the Spanish flowing through my head, maybe they even show English films with Spanish subtitles which would help even more. On that, my mobile starts to ring. I move back towards the cinema next to the door as I find my phone so I'm out of the way of the Sunday evening hordes. Finding my phone, I'm shocked to see it's Pete.

I stare at the screen for a second unsure of whether to answer.

"Hi Pete."

"Nicole, hi. I hope you don't mind me calling?"

I instantly know she's told him. I can feel it, I can hear the emotion in his voice

I walk through the crowds and around the corner into the quieter side street that leads back to Laura's and slow down to a gentle stroll.

"Erm...no of course not. Is everything okay?"

He sighs. "Not really Nic, I know....Annie's told me. Now I know why you left so suddenly." His voice begins to break. I don't know what to say.

Five minutes later, I end the call feeling horrendous. I miss Annie and the friendship that we had like you wouldn't believe but this, this goes to a whole new level. It's as though she's a different person to me now. Gone is my confidant and my friend, she's been replaced by someone who I hardly know. I need a drink.

I take a deep breath and check my watch, its coming up to eight thirty so I've missed most of the first half. I open the maps on my phone to refresh my memory to see how far away I am from 'Bar Cómodo'. It's a four minute walk, so off I go.

As I reach the bar I feel so nervous that I have to slow down. It looks busy inside which puts me on edge. I can hear the match from out on the street and as I glance through the window as I approach even though it's busy, my eyes immediately find him, Jesé. He stands in front of the huge TV with Luís, Raul and a couple of others I don't recognise. I hover on the doorstep. I really do want to go inside, to have a drink with him and hang out with him and his friends and watch the game, but something stops me. I know I can't trust him and I also know myself - in that I could really fall for him, what happens then when he lets me down? Which could well happen when he gets to know 'the real me' I pull my jacket around me, and dart off back in the direction that I came from.

My mobile rings again. I consider ignoring it but as I look at the screen, I see that it's Eva.

"Eva, Hi"

"Hi Nicole, Connor and I are just off out for some drinks, I wondered if you're around, do you fancy joining us? I'd love for him to meet some of my friends."

I think this is exactly what I need, a distraction and some time with friends and of course I get to have that drink.

*

I see Eva standing at the bar and as I reach her side she holds her arms out towards me.

"Nicole, I'm so glad you came..." She releases my hug. "This is Connor."

"Hi Connor good to meet you." I tell him.

Connor is petite like Eva and as he kisses me hello I note that I'm taller than him in my heels.

Not having been to this bar before, I take a look around at the casual bench seating and the jugs of beer that most people seem to have on their tables. We see a table becoming free next to the bar so we decide to take a seat. Conner carries over one of the jugs of beer and I note, four glasses. He pours the three of us a drink.

Connor asks where about in Birmingham I'm from and as we begin to chat, Eva keeps looking around us and in particular at the door. I glance a few times at her line of sight before diverting my attention back to Connor who's telling me about his band and what sort of music they play.

Just a few minutes later Eva suddenly perks up and I turn to see Hans walking in our direction. I think it's the first time I've seen him with his hair down.

She does the introductions between the guys before Hans leans my way to kiss me on the cheek before sliding in beside me on the bench. I catch Eva looking pleased with herself and my suspicions of this being a set up are confirmed when she winks at me. I'm not sure how I feel about that.

The four of us actually have a lot to chat about as the night goes on and I find myself having a really great time. Eva and I pop to the ladies and once we are safely out of earshot, she links my arm in excitement.

"Soooooo…" Eva starts.

"Soooooo…?"

"Oh come on Nicole, Hans is gorgeous and he likes you."

I raise my eyebrows as I smirk. "I knew it, I knew this was a set up…"

She grins. "It's like I said you need to get you know who, out of your system and I thought tonight could be the perfect opportunity for you and Hans to spend some time together."

Back at the table, Hans moves over to let me sit down and Connor decides we need another round of drinks.

"I'll help you." Eva offers, therefore leaving Hans and I alone.

He turns in my direction. "You did not know I would be here tonight?"

"Ah, well to be honest, no."

He looks like he's been let down.

"Not that I mind you being here or anything…" I quickly add.

He smiles. "I am glad to hear this."

We both laugh at the awkwardness of the situation.

"A friend of mine, he works here." He nods towards the bar. I look over in that general direction but as it's so busy, I can't make out who he means exactly.

"I knew you would be here tonight, it is why I came."

I feel myself begin to blush so again I try to laugh it off.

"I think you are embarrassed to receive compliments?"

I feel even more awkward now. Hans really is very good looking. He's not my usual type but it doesn't mean that I don't like him.

"Nicole you are beautiful, you must have been told this?"

"You're doing this on purpose now…" I laugh. "…Hans, have you always been this confident?"

"Not always…" He drinks some beer. "…but when I was student back at home I got a job as a stripper and that helped a lot."

"A stripper?"

That was a shock, although now I know this I really can see him doing that for a living. He's got the looks, the confidence and I'm guessing the body to go with it.

Suddenly he stands up and before I know it, he's peeled off his T-shirt. I really don't know where to look but the rest of the bar certainly does as I hear a crowd of women whistling and cheering at his six-pack, or is it an eight pack? I really wasn't looking. Okay so maybe I was…

I rest my hand on my forehead as I laugh in complete disbelief at what he's just done. It's only a bit of fun as he pulls his T-shirt back on, and kisses me on the top of the head. Wow, I feel like I've just had my own personal strip tease, but in public. I can't stop laughing but inside…I'm mortified.

I look to the bar for Eva and Connor and I can't believe it, there at the bar facing this direction, is Jesé. He must've seen all of that. We look at each other and I don't know what to do. Should I go over and say hello? Whilst I'm wondering this, he holds his hand up in a quite a coy wave to me, before turning his back and his attention to the bar.

Chapter 17

A couple of days later, I take the bill to one of the tables in the corner of the restaurant and the customer hands me a €20 note and tells me to keep the change. That's almost €5 tip so I must be doing something right. Now the breakfast rush has quietened down I clear a couple of tables inside whilst chatting to Clara before turning my attention to the outside tables.

As I open the door to the restaurant and step onto the street I'm stunned for a second as sitting there at one of the tables outside, trolley case next to her, is my sister.

"Annie? What are you doing here?" I stand stuck to the spot, clutching my empty tray and bottle of cleaning spray. Seeing her in front of me brings up all kinds of emotions that I'm not sure I'm ready to deal with yet. I don't like the fact she's here, in my new life. With her at a distance back in the UK I felt almost protected from her.

She tentatively gets to her feet, she looks so different. Her long hair is scraped back into a ponytail, she's pale and her eyes look like she's spent the last few days crying.

"I had to come Nicole, I needed to see you, to speak to you…"

"Annie…" I hold my hand up. "I don't want to hear it, so I'm sorry but you've had a wasted journey."

"Please I'm begging you, just hear me out and then I'll go."

I stare at her case on the floor and she looks up at me.

"I… I didn't know how long it would take for you to speak to me so…" She looks down at the floor.

"I left Amelia with Mom and Dad."

"How did you even know where to find me?"

"Dad mentioned the name of the restaurant where you work, so I looked it up. I knew if I waited long enough I'd see you."

I decide to hear her out and get some more off my chest with her but I'm unsure of where to go. I don't want her in the restaurant where people can hear us.

"Let me finish my shift."

She smiles gratefully before sitting back down with what looks like her second cup of coffee, to wait.

I drop Laura a message to see if they're home and tell her the situation I'm in and she tells me to take her back to the apartment as they won't be back for a couple of hours anyway.

I try and get back to work but I can't concentrate knowing that she's sitting out there, so I ask Mio if I can leave an hour early and start earlier tomorrow to which he agrees.

We climb the stairs to the apartment in silence.

"Sit down." I gesture as I close the front door behind us.

"It's a nice place here…" She looks around before realising she won't be getting any pleasantries from me.

"I came to tell you Pete knows everything."

"He called me a couple of days ago."

"Oh…"

I sit down opposite her. "I'm not sure what you want me to say, Annie."

She breaks down into tears. "I just want you to know how sorry I am…but I've done the right thing now like you said, it's all out in the open. Everybody hates me but…"

I could scream. "It's like you're trying to put the blame on to me, 'you've done what I told you to do and everybody hates you'."

"No, that's not what I mean I know this is my fault I just want you to try to forgive me, I know it won't happen overnight."

I stand up in rage and begin to pace around the room.

"You can say that again. Annie what you've done, it's unforgivable. You slept with your sister's fiancé whilst your boyfriend was at home waiting for you and not just that, you got pregnant and tried to pass the baby off as your boyfriend's. Not to mention the fact that you convinced me that it was my fault James left me in the first place. What sort of person does that?"

She continues to cry. "I know, you'll never know how sorry I am…but she might be Pete's, I really want her to be Pete's…"

I look at her. "What was I doing whilst this was happening?"

"What?" She wipes her eyes.

"You know what I'm asking you, where was I? Or more to the point where were you? In mine and James' bed? Or did you pop away to swanky hotel for the night?"

"Please Nic…"

"Tell me!" I yell.

"It w-was at your f-f-flat…" she sniffles. "You were out, it wasn't planned. I called round after an argument with Pete and James offered me some wine whilst I waited…"

"Did you use the line you did a few weeks ago, on him?"

She looks at me puzzled.

"You know the one, what you said to Richard the night all of this came out…" I mimic her voice from that night. *"It's me you should have gone for if you wanted a good time, not the boring sister…'"*

She wipes her eyes. "You know I didn't mean that…I'm so sorry Nicole, please believe me. I'll do whatever it takes to put things right between us."

"Can you turn back the clock?"

She stares ahead. "Please… Amelia is still your niece."

"Amelia's the other innocent party here, I wonder what she'll think of how she came into the world."

Annie cries uncontrollably. I can't look at her so I turn my back to try and calm myself down. I pour myself some water.

I hear her take a breath. "I've done a DNA test, I contacted James t-t-to tell him… I really want her to be Pete's little girl. I think she is, I-I-I can feel it." She places her hand to her chest.

I try my hardest not to cry, wondering what will happen if she's James'. The family will be torn apart even more. I try not to think about that at the moment.

Just then the door opens and Laura walks in. She looks at me and nods her head, asking if I'm okay. I nod back as she puts her keys down on the bookcase.

"Annie…" Laura walks towards me and stands beside me.

"Laura…" Annie wipes her eyes. "Sorry…I…what must you think of me…"

"Probably best you don't know."

Annie stands up to leave. "I booked into a B&B just around the corner for one night. I'll head back there now. If you want to talk anymore later or tomorrow, let me know." She waits for an answer but all I can do is to nod my head.

I can't speak to her anymore today, I'm spent. As my sister closes the door I burst into tears. Tears of anger, hurt and humiliation.

Chapter 18

By the end of my shift at the restaurant on Wednesday, Laura has parked herself at a table in the corner with Mio who still seems to be a permanent fixture here, despite retiring. As I join them, I see Laura's marking classwork and Mio looks to be doing the restaurant books.

"Mio, why don't you relax?" I slide in next to him.

"*Chica*, you know that I find it hard to relax. I like to…to keep busy." Laura smiles in my direction and shakes her head.

The restaurant door opens and a couple of the regulars make their way inside, waving at Mio and myself. I love the fact that I'm getting to know people at the restaurant now, it's great to chat to the regulars. Mio excuses himself to get a drink with his friends, I sit down opposite Laura, who puts her pen down and seems to study me.

"What?"

"I could ask you the same Nic, you're just not yourself at the moment, I know you're struggling with the whole Annie situation…"

Hearing her name brings on a jumble of emotions.

"I'm okay, I just need some time." Hearing myself say this out loud even I think I sound like I'm trying to convince myself.

"But you look terrible, are you sleeping?"

"Thanks very much."

"… I'm just trying to help."

"I know you are… I'm sleeping same as normal, I can get off to sleep fine but when I wake up in the night my mind is just constantly whirling with so much. Questions, lists, songs and I just can't get back to sleep for ages."

Laura takes a deep breath. "Perhaps you should've met up again before she went back home?"

I shake my head. "I couldn't face it Laura, what can she say that could make things any better?"

"Maybe you should talk to someone again, Nic? To help you process what's happened and try to work a way around it?"

The thought has crossed my mind already. "I guess." I take a deep breath. "I don't want to have to keep turning to a professional to make sense of things in my head."

"But sometimes, we all need some help. You know how much it helped you last time and don't forget what she told you…you might need help from time to time in the future, it doesn't mean you've failed. Mental illness is something you're going through, it doesn't define you. Don't struggle with this on your own. Think about it."

I could get in touch with my counsellor and see if she'd be willing to give me some sessions over the phone. "I'll give it some thought."

Laura smiles. "How about we go and do something else on your list you want to do?

"Yeah okay, sounds good. We could do the cable car?"

"Let me just run these upstairs." She gestures to her books as she stands. "…and we'll head off."

We catch the metro to the Lago station to visit the cable car. We link arms as we do the 20 minutes' walk through the very green Casa de

Campo Park towards the entrance. The park feels forest like with its tree lined pathways. The trees are like giant parasols against the late afternoon sun.

"You seem more relaxed already." Laura says.

"How can you tell?"

"Your grip on my arm softened as soon as we started to walk through the trees." She pats my arm.

I always feel better around trees. I don't know why but I always have. I heard on the radio once about how it's proven that they're good for your mental health something about your nervous system and the relaxing effect that they have.

"Coleen and Lizzie might be coming over for a long weekend." Laura tells me.

"Oh wow, that'd be great wouldn't it?"

Coleen and Lizzie are Laura's sisters and as none of her family have yet met Diego they're getting pretty desperate to get a look him. The poor guy.

Laura fills me in on how much of her jewellery she has ready to start to sell at 'Mariella's'.

"I'm so excited Nic, it's just the pricing that I'm unsure of for each piece."

"Just make sure you don't under sell yourself Laura, your jewellery's stunning so your pricing has to reflect the high quality."

After a short wait in the queue for the cable car, we pay the entrance fee and are instructed to crouch down together in front of a wall with luscious green trees painted on it for a souvenir photo. That, we were not expecting…quite cheesy but good fun all the same. Unfortunately, as we are helped into our cabin as it is very slowly continues to move, the attendant doesn't ask what language we need the commentary in and so, off we go on our cable car ride….with French commentary.

"I have absolutely no idea what they're saying." I laugh.

"Oh well we'll just have to enjoy the view."

Our cabin glides above the parks as we see masses of trees which remind me of huge stalks of broccoli as we soar above them. We see the Royal Palace, the Almudena Cathedral and the Temple of Debod.

As we pass the Cathedral, the voice on our commentary suddenly seems to become excitable, if only we knew what they were saying. The Cathedral is next on my list to see.

I glance at Laura as she stares out of the window.

"What a view…"

We both fall silent as we take in the landscape around us. I feel tiny up here in our cable car compared to the vast size of the city below us. My mind starts to drift.

I think back to our conversation earlier when Laura said something about me looking unwell. I really need to start meditating again to see if it helps me to switch off my mind at night. Maybe I could start going for a walk through the park listening to relaxing music, which is something that I used to do following Gill's recommendation and I did find it helpful.

I do worry what I might be doing to myself, or might've already done, the way I'm anxious most of the time. Stress can have a negative impact on you physically and I tend to go through stages where I start to panic I could be starting up some type of cancer or illness in my body. The knots in my stomach… could I be causing an ulcer? I really have to stop myself from looking up illness online because no good can come of that, I'm just feeding the anxiety but sometimes it's not easy to stop myself.

When I split up with James, I completely lost my appetite for a couple of months. I was trying to eat but I felt like I physically couldn't get the food in, which then made me worry I had an illness because I'd lost my appetite when it's the anxiety taking away my desire for food. It's a vicious circle at times.

A few minutes later we climb out of our car and we're directed towards the shop to view the souvenir photograph. We look as though we've been 'suddenly surprised', but Laura decides to buy it.

"I can't believe you brought that it's hideous."

She studies it closely. "Yeahhh I know but I had to buy it, it reminded me of when I used to go to theme parks when I was a teenager." She smiles fondly.

"Ahh, when life was so much simpler…" I link her arm again as we walk.

"Did you like theme parks growing up?" Laura asks.

I think back to my parents taking us every summer to our local theme park.

"Loved them, we'd go every year for the same rides and we would always desperately hold onto each other with excitement on the rollercoasters…" I grin as the memories come flooding back to me but then the feeling of heaviness returns.

"She is still your sister you know, don't let your memories be ruined because of what's happening now."

I know she's right as I continue to listen.

"You told me so many stories about how you were made to feel second best growing up, invisible almost and that must've been really hard growing up feeling like that, but you've also told me how close the two of you were."

"Were being the word."

She smiles solemnly. "Come on, I fancy churros."

*

A few nights later it's the long awaited salsa night. Diego makes his annoyance clear that despite 'Calor' nightclub being just a seven minute walk away, Laura and I insist on getting a taxi.

"*Mujeres*, if you cannot walk very far in heels, why do you wear them? This I do not know…"

"It's not that we can't walk in them Diego, but we're saving ourselves to dance later…it's a salsa night."

The three of us pile into a taxi and arrive just a few minutes later outside the club which isn't far from the Plaza Major. We started earlier having a few drinks at the usual Mio's and now here we are, a little after 10 p.m. joining the queue to get in.

I can see Hans, Eva and Greg from my Spanish course a little further in front of us in the queue. Tonight's our salsa teacher Gael's DJ'ing night here at the club so we're all meeting up to see what he's made of and of course to practice what he's taught us. I won't lie, I've already had two vodka and tonics and a shot of some sort that Diego insisted we have.

I've really been looking forward to tonight, I feel it's just what I need to let go and take my mind off things. I had a call with my parents this afternoon and it seems now everything's out in the open, my Dad's convinced I need to go home so we can sort things out. It was something along the lines of…

"How can you sort things out if you are not even in the same country? You need to get yourself home this is ridiculous." Well I'm sure you can imagine my reaction to that.

Entering the club, we put our jackets in the cloakroom and I smooth my dress down. Tonight I decided to wear my ice blue asymmetric one shoulder dress and I just had to wear that turquoise ring of Laura's that I love. I finally managed to persuade her to let me buy this from her, now that she's selling them properly. I'm also taking a risk tonight in leaving my hair down loosely around my shoulders. It might frizz in a humid nightclub, but with my newly discovered frizz spray, I'm feeling quietly confident.

Laura looks gorgeous in her cap sleeved beige mesh dress, with little gold sequins, it really brings out her tan that she's kept topped up since the summer. Over to the left I see my course friends standing waiting for us.

Laura, Diego and I reach their side and I do all of the introductions. Eva hugs Laura and I excitedly.

"Oooh I can't wait to dance what we've been taught so far."

Us three girls admire each other's outfits. Petite Eva looks striking in a yellow strappy number which looks great next to her dark skin. Eva mutters something to me about Hans but I bat her comments away in jest.

Diego, Hans and Greg lead the way to the bar. We look over at the DJ booth to see Gael standing proudly wearing an extremely tight black T-shirt to show off his muscles, headphones on and bobbing his head along. The music is fantastic, he's playing songs I haven't heard in so long.

Tonight is going to be great I just have this feeling. Being here with my friends is really lifting me, giving me a quiet confidence.

Mirror balls hang from the ceiling and the strobe lighting brings a mix of red and green on to the dance floor. People are dancing already, some of them are so good they look professional standard. We watch them in admiration whilst the lads get the drinks. Even just watching them dance, we can't keep still, we're moving from foot to foot swinging and swaying our hips. I don't think anyone could keep themselves still with this music playing.

Greg turns around to face us with a silver tray with six shots and offers them around to us. The six of us raise our shot glasses '*Salud*' in the middle and knock back the potent tasting liquid. I can't help but pull a face of disgust. That was so strong... so I take a huge glug of my vodka and tonic to take away the taste.

Gael announces over the music. "I want to say a massive *Hola* to some of my students tonight who have come to support me and practice their Salsaaaaa. Vamos, practicamos."

This is met by cheers and roars from the six of us and is very well timed as Leon, Klaudia, Tymec and Nadia choose that moment to enter the club.

We all knock the rest of our drinks back and head to the dance floor to see if we can remember what Gael's taught us, as he changes the music to some of the salsa music that we hear during our lessons.

Diego being the only Spanish one of all of us is obviously a complete natural and he and Laura salsa dancing together is fantastic. I take a couple of sneaky photos of them before giving it a try myself with Hans. At first I feel self-conscious dancing with Hans after the other night but as he's so easy to be around, I soon get past it.

The music is infectious, the sound of the drums, the trumpets. It also helps that I've had quite a lot to drink by now which means that I actually have the guts to get up and give it a go in public in the first place. Hans and I don't do too badly at all and I really enjoy dancing with him.

After about half an hour of dancing, I'm desperate for some water so I head over to the bar to quench my thirst, as Hans takes Nadia for a spin. Laura appears at my side.

"How much fun is this?"

I turn to face her, leaning back on the bar.

"You two are terrific together." I reach into my bag to show her the photographic proof.

"How hot does Diego look?" She lusts as she flicks through the photos on my phone.

I look over Laura's shoulder and I can't believe what I'm seeing. It's Jesé.

He looks rugged in a black leather biker jacket, which really shows off his broad shoulders. His stubble looks heavier tonight too. Maybe it's just me? He's standing at the edge of the dance floor one hand in his pocket and just watching. I don't think he's seen me, I freeze. I don't know what to do.

"Earth to Nicole…"

"Sorry Laura, don't look now but Jesé is over there."

Laura stands completely still facing me, moving her eyes from side to side.

"Where? To my left?"

"Yep…forget the water, I need a proper drink now."

Laura buys us two shots and then we head back over to our friends and I do my best to put him out of my mind but can't resist taking a sneaky peek in his direction every now and again.

He's just standing, almost posing at the edge of the dance floor and then suddenly, as a blonde older lady approaches, he shrugs off his leather jacket and begins salsa dancing with her. The lady he dances with must be a professional dancer, she's so good.

My jaw drops to the floor, I would never have expected that. The way his hips move, the muscles in his arms straining on the sleeves of his white T-shirt. I need to get a grip…..on those arms…..but maybe I should get a grip on myself first and calm down.

The music changes to some more well-known salsa pop songs and Hans reappears at my side. I take his hands and we begin to dance next to Leon and Eva, Laura and Diego. We do various twists and turns and I note this time Hans seems to be getting more into the salsa, rotating his hips into me. His small blonde ponytail falling loose from its band, the sweat beading on his brow making him look like he belongs in a Cuban club. I see quite a lot of women casting their eye in his direction. I'm pretty sure he'll have a queue of women waiting to dance with him before the nights over, I almost feel guilty hogging him. A short time later, Laura and Diego decide to call it a night.

"We have classes tomorrow at 10." She tells me sadly.

I throw my arms around her. "Are you sure you can't stay longer?"

"I wish we could. Are you okay getting back with the others?"

Nadia steps in. "We'll get her home safely, don't worry."

I should probably call it a night myself I've had far too much to drink but I'm having such a great time and it is only one thirty in the morning…I can't believe I'm saying only.

Next its back to some genuine salsa songs that I recognise from a dance show on TV. Everyone seems to go wild as this one starts, the whole club seems to come alive even more. Hans moves his hands through his hair in one provocative move before reassembling his ponytail. He then takes me into a series of spins followed by a cross body lead. Lifted by the music, next we attempt a cross body lead step followed by a full 360 turn, which seems to be a bit too ambitious for us as we tread on each other's toes and stumble into each other which makes us both shriek with laughter.

Hans then decides to dramatically tilt me backwards and hold the pose at the end of the chorus just before the climax of the song kicks in. We're giddy with laughter as he pulls me back up to his eye line and it's then that I see Jesé over Hans' right shoulder on the other side of the dance floor, watching us. He raises his eyebrows to me suggestively as he takes a sip from his beer, I stop dancing for a brief second as our eyes lock. My heartbeat seems to become louder and louder in my ears. I feel a tug on my hand and my dance partner leans in close to my ear as he keeps a hold of my hand.

"Are you okay?" He asks.

Buoyed by the music and the copious amounts of drink and the fact that he's now watching me, I feel my inner dancer awaken even more.

"I'm fine…"

I take his hand as we start with some more salsa basic on the spot adding some 180 turns and then salsa basic. We step back before doing more twists and turns doing our best to add some intricate salsa arms. I feel my hips loosen further still, dancing more seductively as I feel Jesé's eyes burning into me.

Hans puts his hands on my hips and spins me around, doing my best to keep composed and not flail about with dizziness I reach out to put my hands onto his shoulders to steady myself before we return to safer salsa basic. My ambitious partner then leans in and suggests we try a body roll which drunkenly I seem only too happy to attempt. He then stands behind me, reaching an arm around on to my stomach as we body roll to the chorus. I don't know where this dancing person has come from, although I would that imagine the vodka has a lot to do with it. I'm having a fantastic time just really going for it, losing all of my inhibitions.

Out of breath and with the music now taking on a slightly slower pace, I break away from Hans and cast a glance in Jesé's direction. I see he's now talking to a couple of lads, one of which I recognise from the night I first bumped into him when I was out with Luís. I see his eyes flash over in my direction a couple of times but I pretend I don't notice and stroll off to the toilets with Nadia and Eva.

"Ladies we have to do this again." Eva says, as she teases her hair in the mirror.

I look in the mirror and add another layer of nude lipstick, rubbing my lips lightly together.

"We will definitely, let's make it a regular thing."

Nadia stands in the middle of us, linking her arms with ours.

Back out in the bustling club, I'm following the girls in the direction of the dancefloor when I notice Jesé leaning casually against the wall just up from the ladies toilets, seemingly waiting for me. We briefly catch each other's eye as he walks in my direction. I slow down, leaving my friends to continue without me as he reaches my side.

"So we meet again." He smiles.

"I'm beginning to think you're following me."

"I think you would like it if I was."

I can't help but laugh at his cockiness. "Hmmmm…"

Every time I'm around him, I hardly recognise the voice that I hear leaving my mouth. He makes me feel so much more confident, I feel lifted.

He slowly reaches his fingers to meet mine by my side and interlaces them. I look deep into his eyes. He's so hot I'm struggling to think straight. Just then more people pile into the club and we appear to be in their way as they bump into us. He gently pulls my fingers, nods his head towards the wall and slowly leads me away from the dancefloor.

I lean with my back against the wall as Jesé leans alongside me, facing my direction.

"You are here with Mr blonde pony-tail?"

I roll my eyes. "Yes, there's a group of us from my Spanish class." I look in Gael's direction in the DJ booth. "The DJ is actually our salsa teacher, the lessons are another part of my course".

"You have definitely picked up the dancing quickly." He raises his eyebrows once again and I feel myself blush but I attempt to laugh it off. Eva and Nadia are looking over at me, taking Jesé in and smiling excitedly.

I see him look over at Hans. "So you are not with him?" He looks back across at him as he continues.

"I think he would like you to be…in fact I know this."

"Are you jealous?" I ask

He takes a deep breath.

"Yes…" He steps closer and puts his hand lightly onto my hip and I turn to face him. I gulp, doing my best to ignore the fireworks I now feel in my stomach.

"He was taking off his clothes for you in the bar the other night."

I laugh. "He was just messing around…what about you, who are you here with?"

"Just a couple of friends, we come here each month."

"I never had you down as a salsa dancer…"

"There is a lot you do not know about me. I told you, you can get to know."

I nod my head slowly taking in what he's telling me, trying to give the opinion that I'm not too bothered. I don't want to give too much away about my feelings although I probably already have with the looks I've been giving him throughout the night. His hand on my hip slowly slides around to the small of my back and I feel him lightly pushing me towards him meaning we're now so close together my stomach is in knots with anticipation.

Gael chooses that moment to play a song that I requested a while ago. I take a step back from him before leaning in playfully, the confidence that the alcohol has given me makes me rest my hand on the side of his neck as I do so.

"So…let me get to know how good you can dance."

I walk steadily to the dance floor, praying I don't turn around to see he hasn't followed me. I'm just about to turn around when I feel him behind me, his hand on my hip once again before he slowly drags this down and on to my thigh. His breath on the back of my neck gives me goose bumps all over.

I turn around to face him and we start to dance the steps, only connected by our loosely held hands and our intense gaze on each other for a minute as we get into the music. Then it's as though we both crave to be closer to one another as we take on the closed frame position with his one hand on my back and he holds my right hand with his left, but not leaving much room in between us at all, other than when we part slightly to turn.

We are so close as we move it's like our bodies are completely in sync. The tension that we have is so powerful that I'm sure people in Antarctica can feel the heat between us. We're then next to each other doing a series of hip rotations as we spin and then he takes my hand and pulls me in towards him again as we resume our close position.

I cannot believe how well he can dance, he's amazing. At the end of the song I can't shake off the disappointment that the connection I felt dancing with him has finished, for now.

I no longer hear the music playing, I can't see the other people who are around us. It's just me and him. I feel like he's reading my mind as we look at each other, both out of breath yet still standing close together. I see him glance behind me before he leads me away from the crowds and into a deserted corner where he once again turns to look at me, neither of us speaking yet knowing exactly what the other is thinking. He plants his lips on mine, his hands are around my waist before travelling up and in my hair. I pull him even closer towards me as I passionately return his kiss.

I've wanted to do this all night, I've wanted to do this ever since he came to Mio's party and told me he'd finished with Lola. We stop kissing but he leaves his one hand on my neck and one on my waist as he looks at me breathlessly.

"*Eres increíble...*" He tells me.

I smile, my right hand on his bicep gently running my hand over his skin. I need more, so I return my lips to his as I wrap both of my arms around his neck, enjoying the feeling of him pressed up against me.

*

It's 4.20 a.m. when I leave the nightclub with Jesé. I pull my black jacket around me and Jesé throws his arm protectively around my shoulders, rubbing his hand up and down my arm in an attempt to keep me warm. I say goodnight to Nadia, Greg, Eva and Hans noticing that Jesé looks daggers at Hans as he hugs me, (even though Hans spent the last hour dancing with who I can only assume was a supermodel she was so beautiful) before joining the others in a taxi. I don't know why he felt the need to stare at Hans like that. It's him I'm with, it's him I've spent the last hour kissing like a couple of teenagers and it's him I'm going home with, or is it?

As soon as we reached the street outside, I started to sober up. Not that I'd need to be drunk to go home with him, believe me I can think of nothing more I'd like to do at this moment in time. I think it's obvious that we really like each other but the truth is, I still don't know if I can trust him and until I do know that I can, this is as far as things will go.

Jesé walks to the kerb to flag down a taxi and I reach for his waving arm.

"Let's walk, it's not far."

"Wouldn't you rather get back quickly?" He looks at me alluringly.

I shake my head, half smiling and I can tell by his expression he knows what that means.

"Understood." He smiles.

We slowly make our way back to Laura and Diego's neighbourhood. Now that we're outside, it feels awkward. Is it because now he knows he's not getting what he wants? I don't know.

"Sorry, I could have got in a taxi with my friends it would have saved you the job of getting me home."

He looks almost offended.

"I want to get you home. Yes I would rather it was my home you came to but not tonight, no?" He half smiles.

"Not tonight." I smile.

"I am not just interested in that…I am interested in you, Nicole." I smile timidly, my new found confidence now wavering it seems.

Even back on the main road it's quiet other than taxis and the odd car around. It's strange seeing the city this still.

"I can't remember the last time I was out this late."

"Maybe I am a bad influence?"

"Maybe you are."

I can still feel the effects of the drink and it would be so easy to throw caution to the wind and go home with him. We reach Laura's apartment and I look up at the window, hoping I don't wake them as I go in.

"Thanks for walking me home Jesé and thanks for a great night. I had no idea you would be such wicked dancer." I elbow him playfully.

He grins. "It's not the only thing I'm good at…"

I roll my eyes. "I'll take your word for it."

"Let's go out for dinner?" He walks closer to me, smoothing a stray strand of hair away from my face sending shivers down my neck and my arms.

"… Maybe."

He throws his hands up in mock annoyance. "Maybe? This is all you say…"

I giggle some more but say nothing.

"You still don't trust me do you?"

I look down at my feet and then back up at him, unsure of how to respond.

He sighs. "You will trust me, I will make you see who I really am."

Chapter 19

It's almost lunchtime the next day by the time I feel like climbing out of bed. I pull on the nearest clothes I can find which is a pair of jogging bottoms (complete with food stains on the leg), how did I not notice? And my *Mejores* hoodie and I scrape my lank morning after hair into a scruffy ponytail.

I sit on the sofa in the living room dissecting the night before in my head. I had so much fun, the most fun I've had in a long time. Now would be the kind of time I'd call my sister to tell her all about last night. I miss talking to her about things like this, and it's so sad to think that the way things are at the moment, I can't talk to her and I don't feel I could again about something like this, considering what she did. I can't help but get upset.

I sit crying, wondering how we'll ever fix this.

Suddenly I almost jump out of my skin as someone knocks the front door. I peer through the spy hole and I'm shocked to see its Jesé. I can't let him see me like this. I rapidly wipe under my eyes with the sleeves of my jumper and do my best to smooth my hair back neatly.

"Nicole it is me. One of your neighbours was leaving the building and let me in."

Now I've got to answer the door.

"Jesé, what a surprise." I open the door wider for him to come inside.

"You are crying?" He looks concerned as he moves to put his arm around me but I back away out of embarrassment. I sit down on the sofa, tucking my bare feet up underneath me. He sits down beside me and it's only then as he throws them onto the other chair that I notice the bunch of flowers. I desperately try to hide the food stain on my leg with a cushion but I see him look down and contort his face at the sight of my stained trousers before I manage to hide it.

"You are okay?" He asks.

I take a deep breath. "Sorry, I must look such a state."

He places a sympathetic hand on my leg and rubs it gently.

"Don't English people drink tea when they are upset?" He smiles.

I laugh at his stereotype. "We do…" I look towards the kitchen and Jesé takes this as his cue to make a drink.

He leaves me to my thoughts as he busies himself looking for cups and boiling the kettle and then a few minutes later he places two mugs down on the coffee table in front of us. I spend the next 20 minutes filling him in on the reasons why Annie and I aren't talking at the moment. The more I hear myself talking about it, the less important in a strange way it seems to be, as though it's no longer my life now. I feel that I've got used to it. I'm surprised at how attentive Jesé seems to be.

"The way I see it is yes, she has hurt you and it will be hard to forgive, it will not be easy at all but, eventually if you want to repair your relationship with her then you have to speak to her, but only when you are ready. She has to understand how she has hurt you and give you the time….the space that you need. It is terrible that she did this to you."

I look at him suspiciously.

He sips his tea. "Don't be so surprised that I give good advice."

"You have surprised me today actually, and last night with your dancing."

He reaches for the flowers which are strewn on the sofa. "…and again now." He gives me the bunch of yellow roses.

"Jesé I don't know what to say, they're stunning thank you."

He returns his cup to the table and stands up. I stand up next to him.

"I just wanted to say thank you for last night and even though I would love to have had breakfast together this morning…"

I smirk, shaking my head as he carries on.

"I am glad you have told me what happened, it makes sense to me now why you cannot trust easily…"

I smile sadly at his realisation.

"… Maybe we can have tapas instead of breakfast?"

I look down at my scruffs and back at him. "erm…."

"*Vale,* I know you don't want to…even though you do really." He grins.

"It's not that I don't want to…" I stop myself from finishing the sentence as I don't know what to say.

He walks towards the door and I follow him. How does he look this good after last night?

"So…you go for coffee with Luís." He starts.

"… As friends."

"So we can go for coffee too?" He's trying, just like he said he would.

I shrug my shoulders nonchalantly. "Sure…why not?"

He opens the front door.

I lightly touch his arm. "Thanks again for the flowers, and for listening."

"*De nada.*" He leans down to kiss me on the cheek and part of me feels really disappointed that he doesn't try to kiss me again properly. He turns to leave before pausing and turning back around to face me.

"By the way Nicole…" He looks me up and down. "Even dressed like that, you still look…" he nods his head in approval and gives me a thumbs up.

*

I'm pushing the trolley along in the supermarket as Laura grabs what we need from the shelves.

"I have to say Nic, I really didn't expect to hear you coming in last night…well, really it was this morning."

"I'm so sorry did I wake you two?"

She throws some ready-made tortilla into the trolley, giving me a look that tells me not to worry.

"So now you've told me about what happened with Jesé after I left, were you not tempted even a little to just go for it?"

My stomach sinks. "I was tempted, very tempted…but I just…"

"Well that's just it Nic, if you don't know and if you're not sure, you did the right thing."

Into the trolley goes the red wine and the bottled water.

"We've had Diego's Mom asking if we'll get married in Spain or back at home."

"Ooh could the tension be starting?"

She narrows her eyes at me.

I shrug my shoulders. "Fair question though, I'm intrigued myself…"

"I would love to do it here, but I just think I'll upset too many people. You know what my lot are like."

I picture Laura's large family of two sisters, two brothers her parents and numerous aunts and uncles.

"Hmmm, good point."

We dash from the supermarket laden down with carrier bags out into the November rain shower. By the time we've done the short walk home we're drenched. Diego unpacks the shopping whilst Laura dries off and I get ready for work. My mobile beeps with an email alert and to my surprise, James has replied to last week's email.

"Hi Nicole.

Firstly, I'm sorry for taking a week to reply to this, I wasn't really sure what to say, other than the obvious.

So now you know exactly what an idiot I was, I can't apologise enough. I wanted to tell you straight away but Annie begged me not to. I really struggled to carry on as normal with you after that and I couldn't face spending any time around your sister as I was so disgusted at what we'd done. Even now I feel sick to think of what happened. Annie told me that there was no way that the baby would be mine…dates didn't match she said. I was a fool maybe for believing her, maybe I should've pushed more but it was the easy option for me to leave, which is what I hear that you've done too now. I'm glad you followed your dream, even though the way you got there wasn't as you'd planned.

I want you to know that if Amelia is mine I will do the right thing by her. I can't bear the thought that I've come between two people so close, you and your sister. Believe me when I say just how sorry we both were and how sorry we still are. I know I don't have any right to ask you to, but, I really hope that you can find it in your heart to forgive her somehow and to forgive me? I know that I threw everything away that we had. There is no way in this world that your problems pushed me away, so please don't think that was the case. I was weak and I'll always regret it.

You are a great girl Nic, and you deserve a better boyfriend than I ever was.

James"

I exhale a sigh of what, of relief? I don't know. At least he replied, he didn't have to.

Tears run down my face, I'm seeing them in my head together…in mine and James' bed.
This is too much. I type a text to Gill my Counsellor, asking her if she'd be willing to help me over the phone now I've moved out of the country. Just a few sessions as Laura said to make some sort of sense of things and to help me cope with it rather than allowing myself to go back to the negative state of mind.

I lie down on my single bed and look up at the ceiling, hearing Laura and Diego cooking and laughing together in the kitchen. My thoughts turn to Jesé. I feel really confused about him.

I pick up my phone again and decide to drop him a text thanking him again for listening this morning. He really did surprise me. He replies straight away *saying "I'd happily listen to you every morning, after the night before*…" To which I laugh and throw my phone back onto the bed. He always makes me laugh with his cheekiness. Do I really think that he could do something to hurt me like James did, like they both did? After the past couple of months I'd say anything is possible.

Chapter 20

The next few weeks pass by quickly with my Spanish course and salsa lesson Saturdays and my four or five shifts a week at the restaurant. It's now December and my Spanish is really improving day by day and I've been out for lunch and coffee a couple of times with Luís which has also helped with practising.

Laura's jewellery has been on sale at 'Mariella's' for a couple of weeks now and after a slow start, the sales are really starting to pick up. Mariella has been spreading the word amongst her friends and I've been telling the regulars at the restaurant how beautiful her jewellery is. I've even seen one of the ladies wearing a bracelet of Laura's a few days later.

Jesé and I have text each other a few times, well quite a lot actually. We even bumped into each other in the street when he was on duty. We still haven't been for that coffee. He hasn't asked and neither have I, I feel it's safer that way, less to deal with in my head.

Maybe I should just throw caution to the wind and suggest meeting up like we talked about but something keeps on stopping me - fear.

If someone like my sister that I trusted so much could do that to me with my own fiancé, how can I trust Jesé? Or anyone really for that matter. I blame her for making me like this.

Things haven't changed much with my sister, but I've had a couple of sessions of counselling and talking things through with someone completely impartial is such a big help.

Mom and Dad are desperate for me to go home for Christmas but I've decided to stay here, not because of her but because this is my home now and I'd love to see what that time of year is like here. Laura and Diego have told me that I'm more than welcome to spend Christmas with them, they've been brilliant to me.

The festive lights here in Madrid have been on since the end of November. The weekend they were switched on a few of us from my course did the lights walk which started at the Serrano Metro Station and finished over an hour later at the Plaza Mayor markets which had also just opened. I loved it.

I've brought my parents' presents already as I need to post these next week at the latest so I know they'll definitely be there in time. I just need to buy something for Laura and Diego and I'll probably buy Luís a little something too.

*

One night Laura and I decide to go to the Cinema. On the way there she fills me in about her day and the fact that her Mom is desperate to start wedding planning already which is exciting.

"So do you think the wedding will be soon?"
We round the corner onto Calle de Atocha.

"We have talked about maybe, possibly next year around February. We don't want to wait, but I think I need to get meeting his parents out of the way first…" She smiles nervously. "Also when he meets my family…he might run for the hills."

I laugh. "Laura his parents will love you."

She squeezes my arm as we walk. "I really hope they do. Not long until we find out now anyway."

I'm surprised how beautiful the cinema building is. It houses stained-glass windows which are lit naturally by the sun as the rays reflect off the glass. I stand, staring up to take it all in.

The inside at first reminds me of an indoor shopping centre with its shiny floor tiles, it's really modern. We buy our tickets, standing in line at the 'Taquilla Entrada'.

Once we have our tickets, we head over to buy a large popcorn to share, but we accidentally on purpose end up buying a large popcorn each.

We follow the signs for screen three passing the fast food area and Laura nudges me.

"I know I've only seen him a couple of times but, isn't that Jesé over there?" she points subtly.

"Ah, he seems to be everywhere I turn at the moment." Not that I'm complaining.

"Are you saying hi, or…"

We stand on the spot, me wondering what to do as he chats to the young guy behind the counter and then I realise that standing next to him, is Lola.

"That's Lola." I feel disheartened.

Laura does her best to look without being noticed as I pretend to be looking the opposite way.

"He's at the cinema with Lola, are you sure?"

"Well unless I'm imagining her being there, which means you are too." I whisper loudly.

"Jesé doesn't look like he's having much fun to be honest."

Lola is laughing and joking with the staff as she pushes her chest outwards toward Jesé, once again her top barely covering her modesty. Jesé actually looks pretty annoyed. They suddenly walk towards us.

"Ahhh, they're coming this way." I mutter under my breath. "Act like we haven't seen them."

They head outside so maybe they've already watched a film. Who knows where they're off to next?

So he's at the cinema with Lola, after everything he said to me at Mio's party about her and after that night at the salsa club and how kind he was the next day when he popped round. Was he just telling me what he thought I wanted to hear? Is there still something between them? I was clearly right to be cautious.

Annie's words echo in my head from my last night back in the UK about me being the boring sister. Maybe because I didn't go home with him after the nightclub. Is that all he wanted? I'm questioning absolutely everything now, I really don't like being like this. I have to stop, but I don't feel in control of my own mind.

I snap myself out of it as we wander through to the screen whispering as we go, attempting to find our seats. We sit down four rows from the back, making ourselves comfortable as my phone starts to ring. I cringe as people begin to look and I can't find my phone quickly enough to switch it off. Typically as I find it, the ringing stops so I immediately switch it on to silent, noticing it was my sister.

"Annie?" Laura murmurs.

"Yeah it was her."

I struggle to concentrate on the film at first. I'm fed up of this whole thing, and I make the decision there and then that I will do something tomorrow to take my mind off it all like I am now. I do my best to sit back, relax and enjoy the English film with Spanish subtitles, remembering why I'm here in this wonderful city.

*

The next day I'm clearing some tables in the restaurant as I notice Mio deep in conversation in the corner with a man in a suit. I do my best not to listen in but I'm sure I heard him say something about a deposit. The suited man stands up and they shake hands across the table before he turns to leave.

"Mio....?" I hold up an espresso cup toward him offering him another.

He gives me a thumbs up. "Una mas, Chica."

I pour his coffee and prepare him a small tapa of patatas bravas and deliver it to his table where he's reading some paperwork. He looks up as I put his cup and plate down.

"*Gracias.*"

I go to walk away but he calls me back, beckoning me to sit down.

"Everything okay?" I check.

He looks ecstatic, I haven't seen him smile this much since his birthday party.

"The shop next door."

I'm confused. "The shop?" For a second I can't think what he means. "The empty shop, the old *carnicero*?"

He nods his head. "Juan and I…we have brought this."

I'm taken aback. "You have?"

He laughs at me before scurrying through his paperwork, apparently looking for something.

"Not for this, not a *carnicero*, not a….a butchers."

He hands me two sheets of paper.

"We want to make into function room for our restaurant…" He extends his arms outward. "…to hold more *fiestas*."

"Ohh that would be great."

He eyes me warily. "You not sure…you not, erm...convinced?"

"It's not that, honestly I just worry about you. You are supposed to be retired."

"Juan will be taking on most of the work, I might need another waiter *sí*… but…"

I lean in closely, placing my hand on his and rubbing it gently.

"Just don't do too much. *Vale?*"

He brings my hand to his mouth and kisses it gently.

"*Chica*….Juan and I we want more functions, to see the place full of life just like my birthday. So that means I need some young life injected into it."

I smile, understanding what he's saying.

He continues. "We would like if you would help us to get the shop turned into our fiesta function area?"

I feel a smile creeping across my lips. "I'd love to."

"We want to keep the old…traditional theme like here in restaurant, use old wood and….materials for tables. There is lots of work to be done to get the old shop ready…we will need builders, there will be painting…"

"Hold on…" I have to interrupt. "… I just happen to know a really good builder who only works three days a week now so he has time…" I think of Luís.

"You know good builder?" He doesn't look so sure.

"Yes, my friend Luís, I actually met him the first day I got here. He's really trustworthy, hard-working and I've seen pictures of his work."

Mio places his hand on mine as he smiles. "Then if you are recommending him *chica*, I know he will be good."

He gives me the paperwork of rough designs that Juan has sketched out to show Luís.

Chapter 21

I promised to treat Luís to a late lunch to fill him in on the possible work at the restaurant, if he will come with me to the Almudena Cathedral afterward and so, a few days later that's exactly what we do.

We've finished eating our huge paella for two and I've told him all about what Mio and Juan are looking for in the function room. I've shown him the plans they've sketched out and Luís loves them.

"Nicole, thank you so much for thinking of me. This project it looks really exciting. They are really interested in hiring me?"

"Definitely, I told them how hard-working you are and Mio was happy to take my word."

He stands up, walking around the table and hugs me. "I am so grateful to you."

I can see in his eyes just how touched he is which makes me even happier I could do this for him.

"If I can do this, this could lead to more work of making the furniture… I would be so happy, Nicole."

"Luís, not if you can, of course you can do it."

He expels a breath of air, seemingly still in shock at the offer.

"Shall we head over there now so you can get a feel for the place?" I ask.

We stand up, tucking our chairs underneath the table. Luís pulls on his bomber jacket.

"We will go to the Almudena first, I keep my side of the deal…" He nods. "Then we can go."

We follow the Calle Mayor passing souvenir shops as we chat aimlessly. One of the shops has a couple of manikins outside, one wears a red flamenco dress with black spots, and ruffled sleeves and skirt, proudly showing the tourists the traditions of Spain. The other displays an apron in the same red and black flamenco style which I'd actually really like to buy…

We come to the junction with Calle de Bailén and we see the Cathedral in front of us.

Crossing the street, I'm in awe, the Cathedral is absolutely beautiful. The sky above us is turning the most wonderful dark blue as night beckons and the colour of the Cathedral itself stands out against the sky. Lights are lit in the bell towers and the whole place is bathed in the most stunning glow.

We walk towards the entrance and a feeling of complete calmness takes over my body and mind. It's a simply beautiful atmosphere made even better by a woman playing the harp close to the entrance. The soothing music is so serene. We stand still taking it all in and I feel as though I'm floating I'm so relaxed.

"I can't believe this place, it's just… so peaceful."

Luís agrees. "It is very tranquil… I think more so today because of the music."

Without speaking, we then both drift away from each other needing to drink in more of the atmosphere. I walk through the people scattered around and cast a glance away from the Cathedral and out into the distance through the railings to the side to see the sun has set over the city rooftops.

The music is indescribable, almost like it sparkles. Every string of the harp is heard, as clear as crystal, I get really emotional, like I could just sit and cry. There's something so wonderful here and I'm suddenly choked up. It's like I'm being cleansed, I can't describe it.

I stroll towards Luís as he rests against the balustrades and as I get closer I can see he's got his eyes closed. I stand next to him and I don't know why but I rest my head on his shoulder, it just feels like the right thing to do. He throws his arm around my shoulder and there we stand, together. He's the first one of us to speak a few minutes later.

"You are okay?" I think he can sense that I'm not, or maybe I am? I don't know.

I wipe my eyes. "I think so."

He releases his arm from around me and leans to look at my face.

"You are sad about things, you are thinking of your sister?"

I take a deep breath. "You know what Luís? I'm tired of feeling anything about her so I'm letting it go now, I need to move on." I realise that I actually mean it, I'm exhausted.

He smiles. "This is good, here…it is a magic place I think."

"This country is like a magic place for me…" I laugh. "… But you're right it is, it's special here. I feel I don't know, like I'm free."

I look around us. If only we could bottle this feeling…

"Maybe you have had a…what is the word?" He gestures with his hands. "An epiphany?"

I giggle. "Maybe I have." I look down at the floor. "We will see what the results of the DNA test tell us and take it from there but, I can't do this to myself anymore. I've spent enough of my life letting fear and doubt hold me back."

"You did not do this to you…"

"I mean I can't let this rule my life."

"You need to trust the people around you."

"I do trust you, Luís." And I mean it, he's become a true friend to me.

He squeezes my hand. "I am glad, but I am not the only person around you, I was talking about J.."

"… I know who you meant."

We laugh before falling silent once again.

"I don't know Luís, Laura and I saw him with Lola a few days ago, at the cinema. There's clearly still something there with them so why did he tell me there wasn't? I can't take any more of being lied to."

Luís turns to look at me. "The cinema?"

"Yeah… I don't know maybe they'd watched a film together. They were talking to someone behind the counter when we saw them and then they left."

"I know that Lola's younger cousin, he works at a cinema…behind the counter…did he have brown hair, and…maybe in ponytail?"

I think back. "Yes…I think so."

He moves to stand in front of me. "That is him. Jesé always got on well with Davíd. Just after he and Lola finished, Jesé promised to help him as he wants to join *la políca*. Is it possible that it was about that?"

I shrug my shoulders. "I don't know… maybe?" I think back to the comment that Laura made about him looking annoyed, or something along those lines.

Luís nudges me. "He is a good man…"

"Come on…" I start to walk. "I want you to see the function room."

*

Mio stands outside talking to a couple of customers as we approach the restaurant. He sees us heading in his direction and walks towards us, his hand stretched out waiting for the introduction.

"Mio, esta es Luís. Luís…Mio." They shake hands as Luís tells him how grateful he is for the opportunity to be considered for the work.

Leading the way, Mio takes us through to the old shop which was left pretty much as an empty space. He runs through the intention of having the wall knocked down which used to divide the shop front from the storage space out the back, and then he'd like a generous bar area to the rear. A raised area for the DJ or entertainment is to sit in the far corner, then tables will then be around the outer edges.

Mio closes the door behind him leaving us to it so that we can take some measurements. Luís stands hands on hips, the excitement clear on his face.

"This place, it will be so good."

"I have no doubt." I smile.

I take a seat on the window ledge whilst Luís uses his laser measure and makes some sketches of his own. He looks so upbeat as he goes about his work.

Staring out of the window I watch as people walk past, the sound of laughter echoing through from the street and next door. This feels such a fresh start for me, being here.

"I am finished." He startles me. "When I get home I will do prices, do..erm...the calculations?" He asks me unsure of the word.

I lock up the shop behind us and take the key back to Mio.

"Gracias chica, you are to have a drink with me to celebrate?" He gestures to Juan, who brings over three small glasses of sherry and sits down to join us.

Juan tells me he's sorry he couldn't pop in to meet Luís earlier.

"I want to ask you...Nicole..." Mio starts. "...We have a....a proposition for you. When the work it is finished if you decide to stay here in Spain, I give you more work. I want you to take on...to be the manager... alongside the greeting customers and the waitressing that you do now?"

Am I hearing this right?

"Really?" My voice becomes high-pitched in enthusiasm.

"Really." Juan smiles, raising his glass to me before throwing back the contents in one.

I can't believe this, in a few months' time I could actually have a full-time job here, I'm thrilled. I leap up from my seat and throw my arms around Mio which I think takes him by surprise.

"You are saying yes?" He wonders as he laughs.

"Yes, definitely yes. Thank you so much."

I pull Juan into a hug and as I release him, he nods his head in the direction of the door where I see Jesé is standing next to the bar. I feel a lustful tug in my stomach as I stroll towards him. Tread carefully, I tell myself.

"Hola Señor…"

He laughs. "It seems that every time I see you, you are how do you say….erm...fondling a different man?" He jokes, looking in Mio and Juan's direction and referring to my gratitude hugs.

"Mio just offered me pretty much a full-time job as the manager in a couple of months' time…how amazing is that…" I just can't wipe the smile off my face.

He looks genuinely pleased for me.

"Que Bueno…" He nods his head in approval.

"Well, can I get you a table?" I motion towards an empty table in the window. "…although I'm not actually working this evening."

"Erm…, perhaps, only if you join me?"

"Oh, I..erm…" I glance around me, unsure of what to do.

"Have you been to the Christmas markets?" He asks.

"Yes, a couple of weeks ago."

I don't think he was expecting that to be my answer.

"You have?"

I can't help but smile at the look of defeat on his face. I ignore the warnings going around in my head and listen to my heart.

"I'd love to go again though."

*

I admire the beautiful Christmas flowers that seem to have cropped up everywhere around the city for December.

"I love poinsettia's…" I touch some of the bold red petals on display as we enter the markets of the Plaza Mayor.

We walk along slowly, taking in the sights around us. I can smell freshly baked cookies, the sugary scent lingering in the air. A stall advertises caramelised nuts and I see people walking away looking very satisfied with little white paper cones filled with the sweet almonds. I feel my taste buds start to awaken.

"So other than… flowers, what did you like last time at the markets?" Jesé asks.

I pause to pull the zip up on my red padded jacket.

"Mmmm, the smell of cinnamon, the Christmas lights…" I smile to myself "…the gifts, just the whole atmosphere of the place. It's so cheerful."

Jesé stops at one of the stalls selling what look to be Christmas biscuits.

"*Polverones?*"

"You have not tried them? They are delicious, you have to try them in Madrid at Christmas." He orders two bags, one for each of us.

"Taste them." He passes a bag to me and I immediately open it. He takes a bite from one of the biscuits. "They are…erm…crumbly shortbread with almonds."

"Mmm…" I nod.

We walk further through into the markets. As its midweek it seems quieter than the last time I came.

"So when you're not working but you're walking around the city, do you forget you're not on duty?"

"Maybe sometimes. It's hard to not be aware of what's going on around you."

"I can understand that."

From the corner of my eye I see him looking at me.

"If I saw a beautiful woman who was lost for example, looking at her map…"

I smirk, instantly knowing what he's referring to. "That would be a tough one."

"Even if I wasn't working, I would have to stop and help her." He carries on walking but turns to face me, putting his hand on his chest. "…I would have to, it would be wrong if I did not offer her directions."

"Oh I'm sure it would be."

I mention seeing him with Lola at the cinema.

"I actually went there to speak with her cousin, he wants to become a policeman. I was taking him some application forms and suddenly… there she is." He shakes his head. "I finally managed to get away from her outside…she is…too much."

"She sounds it."

We continue to stroll around together. It looks like Luís was right in what he'd predicted, him being there for her cousin. But I can't help but wonder, do I want to get involved in something like this? With a man who has only just split up with someone and she keeps appearing everywhere. I don't want to end up in the middle of an 'ex' situation.

I change the subject. "It seems like such a long time ago now, the day I arrived."

I start to think back to the first time I laid eyes on him. I never imagined I'd see him again, but now here we are, getting to know each other.

"This is true… but is maybe two months ago?"

"Just over two months, that's all. It seems longer, to me anyway."

"For me it does too." He smiles.

"A lot has happened since then…"

He stops walking and cocks his head to one side.

"It has…you have a job, you speak good Spanish, you have made friends, learnt salsa and now, and now you are here with the good-looking man."

I shriek with laughter at his take on the last couple of months, particularly with that last comment. "¿Sidra de Manzana? Apple Cider?" He takes his wallet from his jacket pocket.

"I love cider…" I go to unzip my bag "… But let me get these."

He looks almost insulted. "No, no…. I will buy these."

He holds his hand up to stop me taking out my purse and I feel a little awkward for a second. He hands me a bottle and I take a welcome gulp, enjoying the fizzy apple as it hits my taste buds. We walk over to the main building of the square the Casa de la Panaderia and take a few minutes away from the other people, leaning against the wall as we drink our cider. It's nice to just stand and people watch, to enjoy the surroundings and to take it all in. As I sense him looking at me, the anticipation in my stomach returns like it does whenever we're together.

I turn to face him. "Will you go to your parents' house in Alicante for Christmas?"

He takes a drink. "I am not sure yet. I may have to work on *Nochebuena*, Christmas Eve so… I should know in a couple of weeks."

I see him watching me for a few seconds, I think he's wondering whether to ask given the situation with Annie.

"You are going home?"

"No, I'm staying with Laura and Diego, I'm really looking forward to spending it here. It will be weird not being at home, but good weird." And I mean it.

"Oh no, I feel so bad to have told you that there is a chance that I will be at my parents for *Navidad*, I have just ruined your first Christmas in Spain if I am not around."

I push him playfully, he does make me laugh with his cockiness, but I'm starting to believe that he's not as self-assured as he makes believe.

"You are finished?" He points to my empty bottle.

"Yep…thanks." He puts the bottles in a nearby bin, coming back to my side.

We still have that chemistry between us, I'm trying not to think about it but every time we look at each other I can feel something inside of me, an excitement building.

He stops to watch an artist who sits on the plaza sketching an elderly lady. As we stand vaguely behind him, we see that the drawing is so precise. The way the artist has captured every blemish on her face, her smile lines and even the exact colour of her hair as it catches the light. I note the look of deep concentration on the artists face as he sketches. The lady looks to us and I can almost feel her asking us if it looks like her. Jesé tells her in Spanish that she will be very happy with the result, to which the sketcher turns around to thank him.

We walk on. "I loved to draw…in my school days."

I turn towards him in surprise. "Really, are you good?"

He looks quite coy as he tells me how he used to sketch and how much he enjoyed it but hasn't done anything like that for years.

"Maybe I am not so good at this now?" He laughs.

"It's not something you ever lose is it? A natural talent."

"Hmmm…perhaps not."

I think of Diego's art classes that start this week.

"Laura's boyfriend teaches art, he's starting some evening classes. He's been trying to get me to go along."

"You draw?"

I burst out laughing. "Not at all…other than when I used to doodle on a notepad whilst on the phone working in offices…" I think back to my repertoire of scribbling stars, boxes and palm trees… "I don't think that can really be classed as drawing."

"Maybe we should try these classes?" He looks really enthusiastic.

"I guess we could…it's just a taster class they start weekly in January."

"We should go then, what is stopping us?"

I really hope I don't embarrass myself with my lack of drawing ability. If all else fails, at least I get to spend more time with him which is something that makes me light up inside.

We stop to look at some of the gifts on offer at the next row of stalls. I see Christmas baubles, red with Madrid written on them in white. Jesé makes me jump as he leans in to my ear from behind me.

"If you want me to look the other way whilst you choose my present, I do not mind."

"Oh I already have your present…."

"How do you know what I would like?" He asks, looking into my eyes intently. "Actually I think you know exactly what I want…"

I feel my cheeks begin to redden and I suddenly have absolutely no idea why I'm taking this amount of time looking at Christmas baubles so I just buy the two.

I clear my throat. "Do you have all of your presents?" I ask.

"You tell me, am I getting all of my presents?" He asks suggestively. Boy am I getting hot, I try to laugh it off. "Jesé…stop…" I nudge him playfully with my elbow.

"You see, you cannot help yourself. Any excuse to touch me, or nudge me."

As we go to the stalls in the middle of the square I start to hear even clearer, the Spanish carols playing in the background. I smile to myself and take a deep breath, as though I'm absorbing it all into my system. God I love it here.

Chapter 22

The following afternoon out shopping, I'm wondering how Laura's managing to stay standing when she's holding so many hangers full of clothes.

"So for my Mom I have this gorgeous green scarf and chiffon dress, clothes for my sisters..." She starts to look through the pile in her arms.

I hold my arms out towards her. "Here let me take some of those so you know you have everything you need."

She piles various items of clothing across my arms, chuntering to herself as she does so.

"Thanks Nic, that should be everything now, I just need to buy Diego's which I'll buy when we get back from his parents and I'll just give my brothers some cash. Phew." She laughs. "The good thing is that with Colleen and Lizzie flying in this afternoon, they can take some of these back with them for me."

"Ah yes, the sister reunion weekend."

"Now don't forget tonight, once they've given Diego the onceover we're off out."

"About that… I don't want to intrude."

She looks at me furiously. "Nicole you're part of the family, my sister's love you. You're coming out with us."

"Thanks Laura…" it's lovely to hear her say that. "What else do you have planned whilst they're here?"

"Tomorrow they want me to take them to 'Mariella's', then they want to get hot chocolate so maybe the *mercado*."

"Good choice." My mouth starts watering at the thought of that delicious thick hot chocolate…it's clearly been too long since I had some.

"Do you have all your presents?" She asks.

"Actually…" I tell her. "… I need your help. I want to get Luís just something small, any ideas?"

She bites her lip as she thinks. "Aftershave?"

I shake my head. "Too personal, don't you think?"

"Hmmm, maybe." She looks around the store. "I know, maybe a gift experience?"

I follow her to the other side of the shop, she clearly spends far too much time here given that she knows where everything is. I begin to look through the selection on the shelf.

"Ah, this is the one."

I hold out a gift experience which is a short flight on almost like a zip wire across the river in Toledo. I remember him telling me the last time he went there he really wanted to try it.

"Toledo isn't far really is it?"

Laura shakes her head. "Less than an hour away, you should go, maybe go there with you know whooooooo." She sings. "Maybe you should buy him one of those too."

I laugh. "I'm not buying you know who anything, we're just friends Laura."

She turns around sharply. "You and Luís are just friends…"

I sigh. "Well, yes, but that's different…you know what I mean."

She giggles. "You're blushing again…I do know what you mean, but Jesé clearly wants more than just friends, and come to think of it you do too."

"We're just friends, okay?" I raise my eyebrows to get my point across.

We join the queue at the tills, Laura's arms looking more and more like a walking wardrobe by the second.

"So how were things with Jesé last night? I can't believe I still haven't even met the fella properly."

"Well he's coming to Diego's class…maybe you can meet him then?"

"Oh great, at last."

I cast my mind back. "Yeah last night was good. We chatted, we laughed…it was great."

She studies my expression. "You have that faraway look in your eyes again, you seem to get it every time you speak about him. Well that and the blushing…"

I interrupt her. "Yeesss I know I blush when I talk about him…but there's no pressure, we're just taking each day as it comes."

"As amigos?"

"Exactly."

*

Diego seems to have been a hit with Laura's sisters, he's won them over. I can tell.

He's spent much of the evening laughing at the stories they've been telling him about 'little Laura' but then, so have I.

As he heads back upstairs to the apartment from Mio's, Laura decides to walk him out, clearly so she can ask him what he thinks of them.

"Quickly, whilst Laura isn't here." Colleen starts. "We want to make this into a bit of a hen night, just in case there isn't time for one back at home before the big day."

"Sounds good." I agree.

Clara appears to clear the table as Lizzie proudly produces a tiara with L plates from her bag.

"We need to give our little sis a good send off into married life, even if it does end up being one of about three send-off's."

"We should have got her a stripper." Colleen groans.

"It's a bit late now…"

"A stripper?" I ask. "You think Laura would go for that?"

"Ah, why not?" Lizzie asks. "She would probably hate us for it but she would secretly be enjoying it at the time."

"I seem to remember her enjoying the one she arranged for my hen night." Lizzie adds.

I glance around to check she isn't on her way back. "If you are serious about this, I might know someone who could help us at the last minute?"

The girls look at each other before saying in unison. "Do it!"

I step outside to make the call to Hans who is only too happy to help us out at short notice. He agrees to meet us in an hour at 'Bar Alba' where his friend works, so he knows he can get in wearing his 'fancy dress'. That should leave us enough time to get Laura suitably drunk first, especially as she's already half way there. I cross over the street to use the cash point before I go back inside to the others.

There's a woman using the machine so I wait patiently behind her, taking my purse from my bag. As she turns around, I realise it's Lola.

"Oh…Nicole?" She questions, the recognition clear on her face.

Well this is uncomfortable. I turn around to check there's no one behind me in the queue that I'm holding up, there isn't.

"Lola…" I say half smiling, half grimacing.

She takes a deep breath. "You liked my boyfriend…well my ex-boyfriend, I remember. I could tell that you liked each other that night at the bar, Raul's birthday?"

"Nothing hap…"

She interrupts, stepping closer to me. "…I will just warn you…HE is trouble. He cheated on me, many times. He always came back to me. Even now, we still see each other."

She looks so smug. I think back to seeing them together the other day. I really don't need this hassle.

I gesture with my purse. "Sorry Lola, I need to get cash. I have friends waiting for me."

She steps aside so I can use the machine and I assume she's gone, that is until I turn around and she's waiting to the side.

"You like him?" she demands to know.

"I…I…we're friends that's all."

She huffs. "Do not say that I did not give you the warning."

I watch as she walks away, her words echoing in my ears. This is just too much at the moment, I feel so confused by it all. I cross back over towards the restaurant and take a deep breath before going inside.

Colleen grins. "Sorted?"

I sit back down opposite the girls.

"Yep, Hans will do it." I smile, getting myself back into the moment.

"Here she is…" Lizzie cries seeing Laura walk back through the door.

"What's all this?"

Colleen places the tiara on Laura's head with care, much to her resistance.

I hear Mio laughing from the bar as she looks to him for reassurance, other customers look on laughing along with us.

We lead Laura outside onto the street and jump into a taxi and just a few minutes later we arrive at 'Bar Alba'.

We can hardly get through the door as we make our way through to get drinks, it's absolutely heaving. Rock music plays loudly as a compere gets the crowd going by announcing that happy hour has been extended. There's a noticeable smell in the air that I didn't notice the last time I was here, almost like a stale smell but it certainly adds to the atmosphere.

Coleen buys us two shots of tequila each as Laura gives me a look of terror. We all knock the drinks back and head to the dance floor each with a bottle of beer.

For the next half an hour, I keep one eye on my phone waiting for Hans to let me know that he's on his way in. Laura seems to be getting drunker by the second as she's now telling anyone within ear shot she's getting married – as if they couldn't tell.

Hans lets me know he's just walked in and that his friend behind the bar has organised with the DJ to change the music, although what to I'm not sure. I'm hoping to something more suitable for a strip tease as at the moment the heavy metal music that's playing probably won't quite 'go'.

Suddenly the music changes to something raunchier, which isn't very well received by many of the clientele, as some of them start to shout and boo at the DJ. That is, until the crowd separates and Hans comes into view in his fireman outfit and walks slowly towards us. His hands clutching onto his braces. The men on the dance floor mostly disappear and the women get louder and louder, the loudest being Lizzie and Coleen.

I have to say that Hans looks…well, let's just say that my jaw has well and truly dropped open, as has Laura's, now she realises he's here for her.

He wears a helmet, navy blue baggy trousers, has a bare chest and his red braces sit perfectly over his pecs. He heads straight for Laura and twirls her around slowly on the dancefloor. Next, he takes off his fireman's helmet, removes her tiara and places the helmet on her head. Laura is laughing partly with embarrassment I think, but I can tell she's having the time of her life.

Hans shows off some on his best dance moves as he grinds against the bride to be before teasing the crowd by slowly sliding off his braces one by one leaving them hanging by his sides. Next he produces a bottle of oil and pours it down his chest before grabbing Laura's hand for her to rub it in. Laura's sisters snap away with their phones taking photos. Laura seems to be taking it all in her stride as she gets involved laughing as she does.

As much as I'm enjoying watching, I can't help but feel almost too afraid to look it's so embarrassing. Its great fun though and Hans is a hit - he could certainly make a career out of this.

Next, the trousers are ripped away to reveal a bright red thong and of course, he ensures he turns around enough times to give everyone a clear view of his bum. He dances a little more with Laura before calling it a night.

"Who organised that?" Laura yells over the music.

Lizzie and Coleen blame me and Laura looks at me in shock.

"Nicole you did this?" She grins.

I laugh. "Hey, don't blame me. I may have called him but it was their idea."

"Was that Hans from your course?"

"I wasn't sure if you'd remember him."

Hans decides to reappear just at that moment, although now his trousers have been reassembled and his chest is hidden by a T-shirt.

"Hans that was brilliant…" Laura tells him before introducing him to her sisters.

He looks really pleased with himself. "Thank you, I thought I might be rusty…it has been some time since I did this."

Coleen almost spits her drink out. "I thought you did this for a living…you should do."

He grins, clearly grateful for the compliment, before insisting on buying the four of us a drink and asks me to help him at the bar.

"Thank you so much for doing that, that's exactly what the girls wanted." I tell him.

He orders our drinks before turning towards me. "And what did you think?"

"You were brilliant."

"Good, thank you." He smiles, passing me a beer. "You looked a little, awkward?"

"Oh… I not awkward as such, I…"

He laughs. "I am joking with you."

I take a drink of beer, the condensation from the bottle dripping onto my top. I wipe it away, feeling glad I've had a lot to drink myself to make me able to relax more, and not to just think about everything all night.

"It was good last time we came here?" Hans asks.
I think back to that night when Eva set us up, we did have fun.

"Yeah we had a great night didn't we?"

"You are seeing that guy you went home with after the salsa?" He takes a drink.

Oh that night…an image of Jesé pops into my head and it suddenly seems so long since I saw him, despite it only being last night.

"I didn't go home with him, he took me home in a taxi and he went home, to his home." I exaggerate.

We snigger, the drink making me realise how I sound.

"Then come out with me, I will take you for drink."

I wasn't expecting him to say that, I don't know what to say. Again, Jesé springs into my mind.

Hans is very good looking and easy to chat to but I just don't really feel a spark with him. I feel like we're very different too, I'm more a blend into the background kind of girl where as he's more of a show off. Not that that's a problem, he's a lovely guy but I just don't think we would be very well matched and I tell him so the best way that I can.

"Okay, I do understand, but…"

I can't help but laugh. "But what?"

He tilts his head to one side as though he is considering what to say.

"Let's go for one drink. Give me a chance and if nothing else we become good friends, yes?"

I hear again in my head, Lola's words of warning about Jesé as I think through Hans' offer.

"I…" What harm can it do, I've been honest with him. "… Okay."

Chapter 23

The classroom's set up with eight easels spaced out evenly around the room, a selection of objects sit on a table at the front allowing each person a direct view. Diego starts to strategically place pieces of fruit into a bowl, laying them out artistically, not like you'd just throw them in at home. Next to the fruit stands a vase of beautiful sunflowers.

"I think we are ready..." Diego stands back to check on the view point that his students will have.

The high ceilings of the classroom mean that even though it's now dark outside, with the numerous lights switched on, the room is bathed perfectly in light.

Laura peers around at the door. "Just in time, people are starting to arrive."

She takes a step back, allowing Diego to welcome his students as she watches on proudly. Diego motions to her to flick the switch on the music player, which brings soft relaxing music into the room.

I look to Laura. "Are you sure you don't fancy embarrassing yourself with me?" I ask her, taking my position behind one of the easels...trying my hardest not to look back at the door to see if Jesé has walked in.

She shakes her head. "No, I'm just here to support Diego...and to finally meet..."

I grimace. "That's if he turns up..." I half turnaround to see him almost next to me.

"Oh, h-hi..." I stutter. Laura presses her lips together to stop herself from smirking.

"*Hola.*" He grins, removing his black leather jacket. He looks to Laura and then back to me.

I clear my throat. "Jesé…this is Laura you haven't met each other properly. Laura this is Jesé."

I watch on nervously as he reaches out his hand and Laura meets hers to his as they kiss on the cheek in greeting.

"Jesé, it's good to meet you at last."

The students start to take their places at an easel. Jesé looks around to see the others heading towards us and he swiftly moves into position at the stand next to me. I glance at Laura who raises her eyebrows and subtly nods her head in approval, now it's me struggling to stop myself from smirking.

I look around at the six other people in the class. There's who I'm guessing to be a married couple in their 60's, two women I presume maybe late 40's or early 50's and two guys who, from the family resemblance look like they're father and son.

I take a couple of sly glances in Jesé's direction as Diego talks to the class telling us that this lesson is for beginners and that we should just enjoy and draw as we see.

"Do not be…critical of yourselves whilst drawing, this is about trying something that perhaps is new to you, or maybe you have not done this for a while, no? It is about the…the clearing of the mind, focus on what you see here on the table in front of you."

Diego tells us to start with the sunflowers, luckily for me they're my favourite flower.

"We will draw only one flower from the bunch. If you feel unsure of where to start, focus on the centre of the flower. Note the…the multiple…uneven circular shapes in the middle."

Diego begins to stroll around the class, offering tips or suggestions as he goes. He pauses to help the father and son.

I take my pencil in my hand, I don't even know where on the page I should begin. I laugh to myself which makes Jesé look over at me briefly, before turning his attention back to his drawing pad. I put pencil to paper leaving what I think is enough room at the top of the page for the petals and enough at the bottom for the stem. I giggle to myself again, how do artists make drawing look so easy?

Jesé moves slightly into my eye line and we look to each other, grinning. It's good to be in his company again. He pretends to shield his work from me but I can still see. His sunflower is really taking shape. His brow furrows as he looks over to the vase and then back to the page in front of him.

I start to really immerse myself as I move on to the petals. I sketch them slowly, using very light strokes with the pencil as our teacher suggests. The first couple that I draw seem to be too small for the size of the centre of the flower so I rub those out and try again, making them bigger and more open. I sort of 'come to' for a moment and notice how much clearer my head seems to feel. I take in the gentle jazz music that plays in the background, Diego was right, this is really relaxing.

I sneak a look at Jesé's work and I'm really impressed. The flower is now drawn in its entirety and he's adding shading to some of the petals showing the darker areas on the flower. It's obvious he knows what he's doing and he clearly has a talent for this.

Diego passes by, also impressed at Jesé's work as they shake hands, Diego realising who he must be. I take a look at my sketch and then back to his.

"Jesé you've made my picture look worse with yours being so good." The three of us laugh.

Diego turns his attention to my work. "Nicole, you have captured the shapes well…notice that some of the petals they are slightly bent underneath…" he motions to the vase. "…I think you have done better than you thought, yes?"

He catches me off guard. "Erm…mayyyy-be…" I'm not really convinced but I'm really enjoying this, more than I thought I would.

After adding the thick green stem with the leaves on each side onto my picture, we're encouraged to walk around to each other's stations.

"I am not asking you to do this to compare your work, I want you to see what you have all achieved and this then inspires each of you." Diego is very encouraging. "*Todos*, there is coffee or juice at the back of the room, let us take a break before we move onto sketching the fruit."

Jesé and I make our way to the drinks.

"Coffee?" He offers as he holds the pot.

"Thanks."

He pours each of us a drink before we move away from the table and take a seat on a couple of the chairs around the room.

"What do you think?" I ask.

"Nicole thank you so much for telling me about this class. It has been so many years since I did this I had forgotten how much I enjoy it." He takes a drink from his cup.

That makes me smile. "I'm glad…you're really good."

He gives a short embarrassed laugh. "Thank you. You are enjoying also?"

I sip my coffee. "I really am, I know I'm not very good but that's okay, Diego was right, it's very good for the mind." I look away, afraid I've said too much. I hope I don't have to elaborate on that statement.

He agrees with me. "I have an old school friend who I think would like this." He takes his phone from his pocket. "… I will tell him about the class." He types out a quick message.

I look at the bowl of fruit on the table. "I'm not really sure how drawing pears and bananas is going to go." I grimace.

Jesé follows my line of sight. "You will surprise yourself…" He stands up. "… Perhaps if you get fed up of the drawing you could be a…how you say…a life model for next time?"

I burst out laughing, lost for words and feeling my face heat up.

He rubs my shoulder. "I am joking of course…I would want that to be private for me, not for the class."

He walks back to his easel with a cheeky smile.

*

Laura's busy writing the guest list for the wedding as she sits at the table and I'm trying out new hair styles in the mirror next to my bedroom door. I try a couple of 'up do's' but feel a bit fed up, I feel like I need a change.

"I tell you what Nic, there's no way we could have a small wedding. With family alone I'm on almost 60 people and that's just my side."

I make us both some tea and take her a cup, sitting next to her at the table as she writes.

"Does Diego have a big family?"

"Just his parents and a couple of Auntie's really. He has a few old friends that live near his parents so they'll come over with their families too." She sips her tea.

Laura continues to write her list. As I watch her, I think of how much she has accomplished since we met little over five months ago and of how close we've become since then. I'll be forever grateful that we met when we did.

"Your parents will come won't they?" She asks.

"I'm sure they'd love to come if they're invited but don't feel like you have to invite them."

She cuts me a look. "Of course they're invited."

I can tell she's wondering whether to mention Annie by the look on her face, but I think she can read my mind and thinks better of it.

"I can't wait to see you walking down the aisle." I picture her in a beautiful dress and beaming smile.

She relaxes back into her chair. "Ahh, I know I can't wait to do it. I'd do it tomorrow if I could."

Laura leans her arms on the table and looks at me with intent. "You will be my bridesmaid won't you?"

"Huhh?" I'm in shock.

"I want you up there with my sisters."

I throw my arms around her with excitement.

"I would love to, thank you so much for asking me."

I sit back down in my seat.

"You're welcome. It's just I realised when we were all out together the other night how much I want you up there with me when I'm nervous as hell."

"Well thank you, it means a lot that you've asked me."

Laura rubs my hand. "Also out of the three of you, I know I can trust you the most to help me to the toilet in my dress."

"What are you thinking for us to wear?"

We're interrupted by the sound of my mobile ringing. Grabbing it from the kitchen, I see that it's my sister and I cancel the call. I don't feel like speaking to her at the moment, I'm doing it on my terms now.

"Was that her?"

"Yep." I put my phone back down.

Laura fires up her laptop to show me some bridesmaid's dresses that she's spotted, and as we start to look through the hundreds of different styles and colours my phone rings again. We look at each other before I reach over to see that this time, it's my Mom.

"Hi Mom."

"Nicole love, how are you?"

I move around into the kitchen leaning against the work surface.

"I'm okay. How's things there?"

She takes a deep breath. "Annie has tried to call you, she wanted you to know that the results are back from the test."

My chest tightens at the thought of what I'm about to find out.

"Oh...well, what..."

"Amelia is Pete's, Nicole."

I do feel some relief to hear that, but then I get a sudden thought in my head. What if she's lying...again?

"Is that definite Mom, have you seen the results for yourself?"

"Yes I have, I've seen them."

I know it doesn't change what happened but, if she had been James's daughter it's as though there would always be that wedge there, not that I'm saying there won't be now...oh I don't know, I feel so confused.

"Are you still there?"

"Sorry Mom, I'm here. I just don't know what to say."

I can hear my Dad talking in the background telling her that I need to get back home to sort things out with Annie now. I feel the frustration begin to start.

I clear my throat. "Have you spoken to Pete?"

"We saw him earlier, he's obviously over the moon that Amelia's his but it doesn't change anything between him and Annie. I'm sure you're feeling the same?"

I nod my head and realise that she can't see me nodding.

"Something like that."

"I'll tell Annie I've told you now and to give you some time."

My Dad repeats himself in the background. I get the impression my Mom is doing her best to stop him whilst trying to stay calm as she speaks to me, which I'm grateful for.

"I'll call you in a couple of days Mom, thanks for letting me know." Laura tentatively walks towards me. "Are you okay?"

I exhale a breath that I feel like I've been holding onto for months.

"Amelia's not James's…thankfully."

"That's something I suppose."

"It's all just such a mess, I just don't…" I don't know what to say, or how to feel.

Laura puts an arm around me. "You don't need to say anything, just take each day as it comes."

I smile, grateful of her support as she carries on.

"What happened still happened, but at least the outcome isn't as bad as it could've been. Just do what you feel's right when it feels right."

I stifle a sob, pressing my lips together tightly.

"I could hear my Dad shouting 'get yourself home to sort things out with your sister.'" I wipe my tears. "If only it was that simple. Do my parents think that it makes everything okay between us now with the results? She still slept with my fiancé and lied to me about it for months."

We stand in silence for a couple of minutes, Laura now rubbing my shoulder in support as I carry on unloading my thoughts.

"I think the worst part of all of this is the fact that she let me believe that this was my fault. It was my fault that James wanted to end things…" I wipe my eyes. "… She said James wasn't worth it because he clearly couldn't cope with my mental health problems anymore. I can hear her now... *He needs to help you through the good and bad times but clearly he got sick of doing it.*' I was so low after that Laura." I shake my head in exasperation.

She takes a deep breath. "I just can't begin to imagine what on earth she was thinking...how could she do that?"

"That's a question I've asked myself a million times since I found out."

"I guess your Dad's just thinking of how he wants things to be back to normal, don't let his reaction get to you especially as he still doesn't know the full story."

"Why should I go back there? Why should I bow down to Annie? Nothing changes does it?"

"Everything changes..."Laura starts with enthusiasm. "Just look at us, me and you...in the past five months we've changed our lives completely. Nothing is unchangeable..."

I take a breath. "Should I be forgiving her now? Because I still feel a long way from being able to do that."

"That's completely understandable and you know that." She pulls me closer to her. "Now..." She looks at her watch. "How about we have a glass of wine whilst you get ready for your night out with Hans."

I smile sadly. "I'm not sure I should be going anyway..."

"No, don't say that, you are going it will do you good." She's right.

"But I don't want anything to happen like that, Hans..."

Laura finishes my sentence. "… Is just a friend I know, and you've been honest with him and told him that and he still wants to take you out. What's wrong with going out with a friend?"

*

A couple of hours later I meet Hans outside a cocktail bar not far from the Gran Via. His face lights up with a smile as he sees me approach before kissing me on the cheek. To be honest, it feels good to be out tonight, keeping busy and having the attentions of a good looking man is also a very welcome ego boost.

As we enter the bar it feels like an average Saturday night, despite it being Tuesday. We make our way to the only available bar table and I jump up onto the stool. House music plays in the background alongside the loud hum of people talking.

I look at Hans as he studies the cocktail menu. He wears his chin length sandy blonde hair down tonight with the first few buttons on his grey shirt open, revealing most of his muscular chest. The silver dog tags I've noticed he always wears are more noticeable. He dresses with such confidence and seems to be completely comfortable in his own skin, which I'm quite envious of. I cast my eyes back to the menu.

"Cuba Libre I think." I tell him. "How about you?"

"A Margherita for me…I will order." Off he goes to the bar returning a few minutes later.

"They will bring the drinks over."

I try to relax back, before remembering that I'm sitting on a stool and as the seat rocks back Hans grabs a hold of me, steadying me as we both burst out laughing. Well that got rid of any awkwardness at least.

The waitress delivers our cocktails and we waste no time in trying them, also trying each other's.

"Mmm, these are good." Hans says.

"Strong…." I declare, wincing as I swallow. "But good."

"You look different tonight." He comments as he moves back slightly, making me feel a little self-conscious.

"Laura and I had wine earlier, so I probably have rosy cheeks…" I reach a hand to my face.

"Your lips?" He motions towards me.

I'd completely forgotten Laura persuaded me to try her red lipstick tonight after I told her that I felt like I needed to try something different. It's amazing what a couple of pre 'drink' drinks can do for your confidence.

I never wear red lippy, always felt like it was too brave for me, and of course my OCD always used to tell me that if I wore red because it's the colour of the devil something bad would happen. I feel proud at the fact that when I put the lipstick on before leaving the house not one negative thought even crossed my mind.

I was the same when I tried to buy my red coat. I absolutely loved it in the shop, but my anxiety did its best to put me off buying it, but I fought against it and now whenever I wear it, I relish the fact I'm wearing the bold bright colour, its another step towards taking back control of my mind.

"Any more stripper gigs booked?" I ask, changing the subject back to him.

He laughs. "Not yet, but… maybe I could get some work at the restaurant where you work now you are manager?"

"I'm not the manager yet, not until the work next door's done."

"Will that be long time?"

"Luís, a friend of mine is doing the work, he's started this week so…"

Hans drains the last of his drink. "Well if there are any parties that need the entertainment?"

I laugh. "I'll keep you in mind."

Drinking from my glass I see Hans gesture to the waiter to ask for two more drinks. It seems I'm quite slow in the drinking tonight so I drink the remainder in one.

"How are you finding the course?" I ask.

He runs his hand through his hair. "It is good I especially like the dancing…" He wiggles his eyebrows making me laugh and I fear, redden my cheeks even more.

"I think we're really lucky, it's a good crowd too."

"It is, the guys are great. We should arrange to go to salsa club again, maybe this time you will dance with me?"

"I seem to remember dancing with you last time Hans, a lot." I say, grinning as I know exactly what he's talking about and who he's referring to.

Our second drinks arrive and the waiter takes our empties, I'm feeling really quite drunk now.

"What is the deal with him?"

My stomach jolts as it always does when I think of Jesé.

"What do you mean?" I ask.

He smirks and waits for me to answer his question.

"There is no deal, yes we kissed that night but that was it."

"His loss then?"

"Hmmm…" And mine too…

My eyes are once again drawn to his dog tags that he wears, and he catches me looking at them.

"You are looking at my chest?" he asks, looking pleased with himself.

I gasp in shock. "No…no…your necklace." I gesture, feeling embarrassed.

He unbuttons his shirt further, giving me a clearer view.

"They are designer…a gift from my parents." He holds them towards me.

Two more drinks later, we're chatting about our lives here in Madrid and Hans tells me about his upbringing in Germany.

"You have been to Germany?" He rolls up the sleeves of his shirt.

"I went once when I was really young, I don't really remember it."

"Now you have an excuse to go there once I am back at home, you can visit." He places his hand on my arm just for a second before removing it.

"You don't have a girlfriend waiting for you back there then I take it?"

He drinks some more of his cocktail. "No, I think that because I like to look good, this puts most women off."

"How do you mean?" I ask.

"Well, my last girlfriend, she got so fed up of waiting for me each time we went out – she said that I took too long to prep to go out."

I picture him in the mirror styling his hair and making his girlfriend wait. There's nothing wrong with wanting to look good, but I think I'd find that difficult having a boyfriend who took longer than me to get ready.

Hans excuses himself to the toilets so I take my phone from my bag. I see from the corner of my eye, someone standing directly in front of me. I look up expecting it to be Hans, but to my surprise, it's Jesé.

"Ohh…"

Jesé laughs, standing with his hands in the pockets of his jeans. He dressed smart casual, it's a good look, but then I doubt that there's a bad look on him.

"I saw your date disappear so I thought that I would come to say hello."

"It's Hans from my course, it's not a date."

"You do not have to explain to me Nicole. I…he is lucky man." He nods his head.

Where's my drink? I take a sip to distract me from the awkwardness.

"It's… we're friends…" I feel stupid at keep protesting to him.

"I'm here with friends…"He motions to the corner so I glance around at a group of three guys and two girls, one of them looks very much like Lola but to my relief, it isn't her.

"How've you been?" I ask.

"Good, I saw Luís yesterday. He is so glad to be working at the restaurant so thank you for getting him the work."

"I was happy to recommend him."

Hans returns to the table, standing beside Jesé who turns and sees him.

"Sorry, Hans?" he asks holding out his hand in greeting.

"Yes, hello again." They shake hands before standing in silence, looking at me. I feel like shouting *"Don't look at me…"*

Hans sits back down next to me pulling his stool closer to mine, on purpose I assume?

Jesé breaks the awkward silence. "It was good to see you both…I will get back to my friends."

He looks me in the eyes as he walks away and I want to run after him to tell him this is completely innocent. Does it even matter anyway?

"How strange to see him here, we were just talking about him." Hans looks over to where Jesé sits with his back to us.

*

Before my shift a couple of days later, I decide to take a look around a few shops to treat myself.

Annie called me yesterday so we've spoken about the test results now albeit rather frostily. She's still living in her and Pete's house but Pete is staying with a friend at the moment. She tried to call me again this morning but I need space, surely she can understand that?

The air feels quite crisp this morning and I felt the need to wear a warm scarf which feels really cosy against my skin. The sun still shines brightly, bringing its glow onto the wintry looking trees.

I round the corner and without realising it, I'm on Jesé's street. I only recognise it's his street when I see him standing outside of his apartment building...and he's not alone. I freeze on the spot before crossing over the road so he doesn't see me. Walking at a steady pace I cast a glance every now and again.

He's standing outside of his building with a woman, is he seeing her out after a night together? So what if he is? He's a free agent after all. He might have just bumped into her outside. I think it might actually be one of the women he was with when I saw him the other night, I don't know. I notice he has a carrier bag from one of the local art supply shops which makes me think back to Diego's art class.

Suddenly I see him pull the woman towards him for a hug. I try not to look, I keep striding ahead but I glance across the street again to see them kissing.

I should have gone out with him properly when I had the chance. After the Christmas markets and the art class, we got on so well again but...just something stops me taking it further every time. Trust is a big thing and it's not something I feel easy to do anymore, especially considering how things started with him. Plus my anxiety is also a big part of me and I need to feel comfortable being the real me around him without hiding anything. That might be a bit of a turn off.

Going by Jesé's reaction the other night, he clearly believes something is going on between me and Hans anyway. This is ridiculous, I feel so frustrated with myself. Too late now though it seems.

I cross the road, leaving his street behind and I suddenly get a waft of a familiar scent filling the air around me. It smells like a hairdressers and as I look to my right, sure enough there's a salon. My gut instincts kick in as I come to a standstill. I see my reflection in the window and I see her, I see Annie. I'm going to do it, it's time for something different. I pull the door open and in I go.

Chapter 24

I'm slowly getting used to my new hairdo. To think I wanted a bob cut for so long, but was always too scared to take the plunge, imagining what people's comments might have been and the self-conscious feelings that would bring. I'm so glad I did it…finally.

Last week I went for a long graduated bob which has a lovely shape at the sides, so I had about four inches off the length. I felt so liberated afterwards…I should have done it a long time ago. The stylist also suggested that I have my hair coloured to 'lift it' as she put it. I found myself agreeing and I'm really pleased with the mahogany brown result, which is perfect for winter.

I spoke to Luís yesterday and he let it slip that Jesé has been on a couple of dates with someone he met through his brother. Luís said he really thought Jesé and I would've got together - if only things were easier in that sense.

I once again felt so deflated, but that's my problem I know that. I'm trying not to think about it and I'm avoiding his street now – I really don't want to see any more public displays of affection between him and another woman.

When Hans asked me to go out with him again just yesterday, this was the reasoning why I found myself saying 'yes'. I know I have to draw a line underneath things now so tonight, Hans and I are off to the cinema.

Mio raises his arm to get my attention.

"*Chica*, please take these drinks to the workers next door and then, could you clear the tables at the back?"

I turn to see a tray laden with three mugs and a couple of plates of tapas.

"Mio, all of this is for next door?"

"*Sí*, we need to look after them…"

I leave my order pad and pen at the bar and carry the tray around to next door. I see Luís sawing in the corner so I put the tray down and call out to him. I can see how much work Luís has done just since yesterday when I came in to see how things were going.

He stops working, wiping his brow. "*Gracias…*"

"I'll bring you more later." I tell him to which he gives me a thumbs up and I head back to the main restaurant.

I clear the tables waving hello to Laura and Diego who have just walked in, I assume for lunch. After loading the dishwasher I see Clara has taken their order, and their drinks are ready so I take them over and sit with them.

"Did you have your video call with your parents last night?" Laura asks.

"Yessss."

"So, did they like your hair?"

I laugh. "They did actually, I wasn't sure they'd notice to be honest." Maybe it's a lifetime of feeling un-noticed and blurring into the background.

"Not notice? How could they not, you look so different Nic, it really suits you."

"Well thank you."

I leave them to eat and between serving, Mio and I go through some paperwork before I finish for the day. I take off my apron and pop into next door with Mio so we can see how the work is progressing.

The sound of drilling and banging greets us as we open the door, making me wince. I start to collect up the numerous cups and plates from their drinks throughout the day and pile them on to the tray. Mio spreads his paperwork with sketches onto the small table by the door and then we chat for a couple of minutes with Luís as the building noise continues around us. Even Luís is finding it distracting as we talk so he whistles loudly asking them to stop for a second. The thing is, I didn't realise that the 'them' making the noise was his builder friend Sergi and his other friend… Jesé.

Downing tools they come round to join us and Jesé nods in my direction, the corners of his mouth crinkling into a slow grin. I'm so shocked to see him here and surprised at the reaction my body is having to being around him, all I manage is a smile. It doesn't help that more of him is on show than I normally see with him wearing a white vest top, giving me a clearer view of his arms and chest which seem to glisten with sweat. He's covered in dust, there's even dust in his hair. I feel myself becoming flustered.

As the guys talk 'building work' I listen in, well I pretend to anyway but I'm struggling to concentrate. Jesé and I make eye contact every now and then, the spark very much still there it seems. Mio and I go to leave, telling the others we'll see them later in the week, Luís and Sergi only being able to work on the project the two days per week they aren't working for their employers. They're also working weekends too though, as they're so grateful of the opportunity. Jesé has been drafted in just for today so we're told. They're making brilliant progress and everything is on track to be finished on time in mid-January.

As I go to close the door I hear Jesé shouting me. I feel a buzz at hearing his voice calling my name. Mio takes the tray from me as I momentarily reopen the door and there he is.

"Nicole, you look…I like your hair." He grins, making my stomach flip, my hand flying up towards my hair. "…it was good to see you." He gives me a lingering look, before backing away and picking up some sort of power saw so I step back outside, closing the door behind me.

*

Hans and I have just watched an action film at the cinema. It wasn't really my thing, but Hans insisted I'd enjoy it. I prefer to watch feel good or comedy films enjoying the upbeat distraction that they bring. I also find them easier to concentrate on.

Walking down the steps from the cinema out onto the street I pull my jacket closer around me to keep the nip that hangs in the night air from setting in. I can even see my breath in front of me, that's something that's a first for me in Spain. Hans sees me tugging at my jacket and he puts his arm around my shoulders.

"This is better?"

I feel like he's telling me rather than asking me, so I simply smile at him as we walk.

The air outside feels calm despite the honking of car horns in a traffic jam. We stroll along chatting about our favourite films, his arm still around my shoulder and I wonder what would it feel like to put my arm around him, and so I do it.

Immediately it doesn't feel right but if I move it away now, Hans might wonder why and so I leave it be.

Seeing Jesé again yesterday has complicated things in my head even more. The more time we were spending with each other weeks ago, the more convinced I was that we were meant to meet but, Lola's warning only fired up my issues even more. I feel so torn. Could I walk away from him for good?

Hans rubs my shoulder which brings my attention back to the now.

"You would like to go for a drink?" He asks, stopping and guiding me away from the crowds.

I shouldn't be thinking about someone else so much whilst being out with another guy. His touch now running down my arm and clasping my hand.

"I…"

"Or you could come back to my place?"

I try to laugh his suggestion off but the look on his face grows cheekier by the second. I don't answer him.

"You are thinking of him?" He asks.

I look away, what do I say to that? "No… it's just…"

"Nicole I know that you have told me before you want to be friends but, I like you and I think you like me even if just a little…" He gestures with his fingers.

I laugh, throwing my head back. I can't help it.

He lightly tugs at my hand. "We could just have some fun together, I can help you."

"Help me?"

"Yes. To forget about him with, no strings. We will be helping each other."

I listen to what he's saying, maybe that's what I need to get Jesé out of my system - just some 'fun' with no complications. No need to worry about trust and what's going on with other people behind my back because it would be honest and open from the start. That's the beauty of that that kind of arrangement, but it's something I've never done before in my life.

He can tell I'm thinking about his proposition and so he takes a step closer to me looking me in the eye before pausing. I look at his lips, then and I meet his eyes and that's when he kisses me, just once on the lips before backing away, giving me a chance to stop him, but I don't. There we stand in the street, kissing. His hands are under my jacket and it's good to feel wanted again, good to feel something other than hurt.

Hans stops kissing me, our arms still around each other.

"Shall we get a taxi?" He lowers his head and starts to kiss my neck.

It would be so easy to go home with Hans and just enjoy myself but I can't. All I can think about is Jesé, still only Jesé.

I bite my lip. "Hans I do like you, but it wouldn't be fair."

His arms remain around me and my arms around him.

"I'd be lying if I said I wasn't tempted to go home with you, but I've got so much going on with my family and I'm confused about…"

"About him?" He smirks.

"Yes about him…I'm sorry."

"No, please do not apologise, you have always been honest with me."

"Thank you for being so understanding." I give him a long kiss on the cheek, as we break apart.

"If you change your mind, just let me know."

We both laugh awkwardly.

"He is messing you around?" He asks.

"No, I…I don't know, his ex keeps reappearing and I just don't want something that will be hard work."

"Your heart is still broken?"

I look at him, shocked by his question. "No, not anymore, not in that sense. But…I don't want it to happen again."

He squeezes my hand.

"So…" I start.

"We could get coffee?"

I eye him suspiciously.

"I do mean coffee…" He points to the café across the street.

"That would be good."

Chapter 25

That Saturday in class, we practice the use of reflexive verbs which are verbs that we use to describe an action we do to, or for ourselves. I find this difficult at first, but gradually it starts to come back to me the more we practice with each other. We're put into pairs to practice and soon Klaudia and I are going through our daily routines in an attempt to make it easier to remember how to use.

Every now and then we break off and whisper in English and it's like being back at school as we catch up with each other's news. It's so nice to have made some real friends here in Madrid as well as having Laura and Diego, especially as they jetted off to Gran Canaria this morning.

I'm filling Klaudia in on the fact that out of the blue, Jesé text me last night asking how I was. Again, very mixed signals. He asked about 'Mr Blonde-ponytail' but why is he so bothered now?

It took me a while to come up with a text telling him very casually in a roundabout way that there's nothing between Hans and I. I wondered if I should ask about the woman that Luís told me he's dating and eventually I did.

My exact words were "I hear from Luís that you've met somebody, I'm pleased for you."

After I sent the text, I spent the rest of the night wishing I hadn't, especially as he didn't reply. I worried I'd given him the wrong signals from that message. I replayed it over and over in my mind all night…but at least it was something different on my mind keeping me awake.

Back to class and Inés tells us more about a typical Spanish Christmas before going on to teach us some Spanish Christmas carols.

Using her laptop she plays a selection of songs. The wording is quite difficult to get the hang of and to say it's sung fast is an understatement.

Inés makes us stand up as we all attempt to sing together, the verses seem to be the hardest to grasp and with all of us getting tong tied as we try to keep up with the pace, we fall around in fits of laughter. It is a really lovely Christmassy sounding song and it sounds familiar, maybe I've heard it at the Christmas markets.

After lunch, Gael teaches us more salsa steps. He pulls off his jumper and throws it in the corner of the room as he hits play and the sounds of lively salsa music fills the air.

"*Chicos, Chicas*, these steps are now at intermediate level, you should be very proud of yourselves." Proud? I don't know if I can do it yet.

He claps once loudly to get our attention to begin, which makes me jump. He beckons Inés to join him as they demonstrate a 'passing behind the back' step which they make look really easy and fluid.

My old faithful partner, Hans and I give it a try. He's certainly picking this up quicker than me but he's very patient, helping me along. Things are comfortable between us despite recent events, I feel like we have a really good understanding of each other now. Gael moves around the class offering us advice.

"When he's next to you and he puts the hand on your waist..." He demonstrates on me. "Allow him to push you through but keep a hold of his left hand, it will look cleaner, smoother...."

I nod my head as he gestures for us to try again, which we do and slowly it starts to sink in. Sometime later, we each take it in turns to watch the other couples to see if we can pick up some tips from each other. Klaudia and Greg are really good which spurs me on to keep at it to perfect the steps. Eva and Tymec are next and they're going really well until Eva suddenly forgets the steps and bashes into her partner. Hans and I are next up and it actually feels like we do pretty well, I feel really excited and I do feel proud of myself for grasping the steps. Nadia and Leon are the last to show the class and they are definitely the best.

"*Todos,* that is the end of our lesson today, well done, *bien hecho.*"

As I try to catch my breath, the lads crowd over to us enthusiastically.

"We're going to Retiro Park tomorrow to have a kick around, what do you say?" Greg asks.

Nadia looks on confused. "A kick around, what is this?"

A few of us snigger, finding humour in the confusion that surrounds each of our countries slang words. Tymec gently drapes his arm around Nadia shoulders.

"A kick around is with football…" He demonstrates some kicks and flicks with a make-believe ball. Nadia looks mortified.

I laugh. "We don't have to do that, we can…drink coffee and just watch."

We all agree to meet early afternoon outside of the Retiro metro station.

I have a text from Laura telling me they've arrived safely at Diego's parents' house and warning me 'not to have any wild parties whilst they're away'. I decide to pick up some dinner on my way in so I stop off at the

Mexican takeaway on the corner of our street and choose some spicy chicken tacos.

As soon as I'm inside the apartment I throw my coat on to the chair, grab myself a plate and take a seat at the table. The chicken is delicious and every now and then I get the tang of a small piece of pineapple which really compliments the flavours.

Once I'm finished eating, I sit back and take in the quiet apartment. It'll be strange this week without Laura and Diego here. I feel a slight pang of homesickness and so I decide to video call my parents. I text my Mom who replies almost straight away agreeing that we need to catch up.

I wait at my laptop for my parents to answer the call. Mom's face appears on the screen as she answers.

"Nicole, how are you?" She sounds a little strained as though she's trying to put on a chirpy voice.

"I'm good thanks Mom, are you okay?"

I lean into the laptop a little more in an attempt to put my finger on what it is that makes her seem different. She's definitely distracted as she looks around the room.

"Yes, yes fine thank you sweetheart."

"Are you sure? Is Dad okay?"

She sighs. "Yes we're okay don't worry."

With Annie and I not speaking at the moment, every time I speak to my parents it always feels odd. I don't mention the elephant in the room but they always end up mentioning her in some way, in an attempt to put things right.

"Hopefully you'll get your Christmas presents soon, I posted them on Monday."

"Oh that's good, I'll let you know…" She breaks off.

"… Mom I know you're annoyed at me for not coming home for Christmas but I just really want to experience it here."

"I know you do don't worry. I'm just a little concerned about Annie, she's really not herself still."

Here we go. "That might not be a bad thing."

"You two need to discuss now love, surely? Somehow."

"Maybe in time Mom, but can't you understand at the moment it just isn't that easy?" I snap. Mom doesn't say anything, she just looks at me. I take a deep breath before I continue.

"My relationship with my fiancé broke down and the whole time she was there for me, a shoulder to cry on, day and night and the whole time, she knew the reasons behind it all - she *was* the reason behind it all. She let me beat myself up for months thinking it was my fault…" My voice begins to break. "…Do you think that's alright what she did to me?" I immediately feel lighter for telling my Mom exactly how I feel.

"Of course I don't Nicole. What she did was despicable and believe me your father and I have told her exactly what we think numerous times since we found out…she used your illness to cover her tracks and we're disgusted with her."

She looks really emotional, which shocks me. The way they've reacted to the whole thing so far, I really thought they were playing things down for Annie. I exhale, feeling as though I've got a weight off my shoulders just voicing how I feel. Perhaps I'm relieved to have my parents onside, I know they're only trying to make peace in the family.

"I've spoken to Pete a couple of times, we've sent messages." I tell her.

"I know when you're ready you'll speak to Annie sweetheart. But you know what your father's like, his two little princesses have fallen out and one of them is what seems like thousands of miles away. He worries that you'll never talk again." To me, right now, that seems very possible.

I smile sadly, thinking of how when we were younger he'd have one of us on each knee and call us his two little princesses.

September 1997 – Age Six - before glasses were fashionable…

That morning as Mom drops us off at school, I have the most horrendous feeling inside of me. As I watch her walk away across the playground and through the gates I'm terrified of the images that invade my mind. What if something bad happens to her? What if we don't see her again? I run through the open classroom door with tears streaming down my face, my hair in long pig tails with blue ribbons tied in flailing behind me, just desperate to get to my Mom, to feel her soothing arms around me.

It wasn't the first time I'd done this. By this time it was probably a once or twice a week fear that had somehow eaten its way into my mind. Mom tried all sorts to console me, asking me why I felt this way but I just couldn't explain why this overwhelming fear had somehow attached itself to me. Maybe this is simply something I was born with? Considering I had these problems from such a young age it's very possible.

Eventually I was calm enough to go back inside and Annie vowed to look after me that day.

A few hours later Annie and I run out into the playground, my mind distracted enough for now. That lunch break we agreed to play a game of kiss chase with some of the others from our class.

Five minutes into the game, the troublemaker, Daniel Warren starts to tease me.

"You can't play kiss chase in your glasses."

"Yes I can…" I continue to run around with the others, giggling without a care in the world.

I stop, receiving a peck on the lips from one of the boys. Annie jumps around with excitement - this is always her favourite game. Suddenly, Daniel barges over to me snatching my glasses from my face and starts to run away.

Without my glasses I can see a little, but everything is blurry.

"Give them back!" I shout, close to tears.

I run in the general direction that I can just about see him in, the tears clouding my view. He throws them right into the middle of the huge raised flowerbed at the corner of the playground and walks away laughing.

Annie comes sprinting over, smacking Daniel on the arm continuously until he backs away apologising over and over again. I, meanwhile attempt to climb up onto the flowerbed and try desperately to reach my glasses. My sister however comes to the rescue with her no-nonsense attitude, and climbs up and walks across in between the plants to retrieve my specs.

My tears are in full flow by this point as she puts her arm protectively around my shoulders, comforting me as I am reunited with my vision.

"Do not touch my sister." She shouts fiercely.

I felt so safe after that day, I don't think anyone ever said a cross word to either of us after that. From that day onward we were known as a sort of suit of armour for each other, well Annie more so for me than I was for her, purely down to my nature. I of course tried my best to protect her too, but she rarely needed my help. I was always scared of my own shadow.

What happened to that bond, did it disappear overnight? I would never in my wildest dreams have thought she would do anything to hurt me, ever. Where did things go so wrong?

Present Day

Sunday morning brings another beautiful sunny day here in Madrid. To look from inside you'd think it was boiling hot out there – a cloudless sky, the sun shining but as I step outside I can tell you that it isn't, there's a definite nip in the air, but it's still mild in comparison to back home.

I'm leaving Mio's after finishing my shift and just about to put my phone away when it starts to ring. I'm surprised to see it's Jesé.

"*Hola*…again." I answer, walking towards the metro station.

"Hola, guapa…." He calls me beautiful, the flirting starts straight away and so does the smile on my face. Very mixed signals again.

"So I see you have finished work?"

I stop in my tracks and turn around to see him standing outside Laura's apartment, he holds up his hand and waves at me. I wasn't expecting this, but I'm certainly not complaining.

"Are you following me?"

He laughs, his shoulders moving up and down. "Maybe I should."

Slowly he walks towards me, still talking on the phone as we watch each other. I take in every detail. His jeans, trainers, black jumper, his charcoal grey woollen coat left open with his grey scarf hanging loosely around his neck.

"I knew it was you...your red coat, it stands out." He reaches my side and we both hang up the call on our phones.

"It's my fault then. I'll have to start wearing different coats, just to throw you off."

"I haven't seen you for a while."

"That's not really true, I saw you covered in dust last week, playing builder." I still can't forget that image…

"You did yes, but I mean properly." He looks down at the floor, as though he's sad about that.

"Ohhh…." Should I say something? I have to. "…I did see you last week with, sorry I don't know her name…"

He takes a deep breath, the awkwardness written all over his face.

"Oh, you should have…"

I interrupt. "…You were busy, so I…" I glance around the street to pass the uncomfortable silence.

He looks down at the floor again before looking back at me. He puts his hands into his pockets.

"We went for coffee a couple of times, but…it is not to be."

I smile self-consciously, not knowing what to say without it being obvious that I'm pleased about what he's just told me.

. "You have plans today?" He asks.

"Actually I'm just on the way to meet my friends…you can come along if you like?" I surprise myself by offering.

"Nicole, you want me to meet your friends already? I am touched." I shake my head in jest before he answers.

"I have to go into work for a meeting but I want to know, can we meet for coffee later?"

"Yeah sure, where shall we meet? I'm going to Retiro Park."

"*Bien*, I can meet you there."

I check my watch. "Shall we say three thirty?"

He nods his head. "*Hasta lluego.*" I carry on walking to the station when he shouts me.

"Nicole…" I turn back to see him looking in my direction as he shouts again. "…*es una cita….*"

Una cita…. That's a word I don't know. I walk on and as soon as I'm inside the station I take my phone from my bag to look it up. *Una cita* means a date. I stand giggling to myself, typing out a reply to him "*No, es una cita.*" It's not a date and send it, with a smile on my face.

*

I catch the metro from Gran Via, changing at Sol onto the red line and then it's just three stops to Retiro. As I walk outside I see my friends sitting to my right on the steps.

"Here she is." Shouts Leon.

It seems I'm the last to arrive. I do the rounds hugging everyone, as seems to be our usual greeting nowadays.

Tymec and Hans are practising their 'keepie uppies' as Greg watches on with one foot on his electric scooter as he clutches the handlebars. Nadia, Eva and Klaudia look on in boredom before we all continue over to the park.

We cross the busy Calle de Atocha and walk through the iron gates into the park. This is the first time I've been here and I'm surprised at just how big it actually is. There's so many people here yet because of its size, it doesn't feel crowded at all.

Various pathways lead through it and once you're in the thick of the park and can't hear the traffic, it's hard to believe you're in a big city. People are walking, biking and roller skating. It's got a really lovely peaceful feel to it, reminding me of happy Sunday afternoons in the park back at home when I was a kid.

We walk through along the pathways lined with different varieties of trees. Even the colours of the trees are so different from one to the next. With autumn well underway and winter just around the corner, it's like the park has its own colour pallet with the rusty reds, the golden leaves that remind me of the sun as it warms the sky. There's greens so light in colour they're almost bordering towards yellow, darker evergreens that look heavy and dense.

The lads head for a patch of open grass just a stone's throw away from one of the many cafés that seem to be in the park. As they play football, the girls and I decide to get takeaway coffees which we sit on the grass to drink, close enough to them to pretend we're watching, but not too close so that we risk getting hit with the ball.

The air feels really fresh here similar to how it felt at the Temple of Debod, its being around the trees I guess.

We chat about our plans for Christmas that is until Nadia changes the subject.

"…. I don't know if you've noticed that Leon and I have been getting on well…"

Eva starts to squeal like a pig with excitement which gets the lads attention.

"Sssssh…" Nadia hushes Eva. "Nothing has happened but I'm not sure how to make it happen."

"Even after all of that salsa dancing you've done together?" I ask.

"Well you and Hans have been the same, dancing together, and nothing happened."

I feel my face change and I struggle to disguise the truth.

"What? When did this happen?" Nadia asks.

I shake my head "We went for a drink and to the cinema and we kissed that's all. There's really nothing going on. He's a great guy but…anyway…Nadia for the two of you, you can see that there's something there when you dance together."

"You can?" She asks.

"Definitely…" Eva tells her. "Just you leave it with me, Auntie Eva will get you together today." She giggles with a naughty glint in her eye.

Football finished for the day, the lads appear to be each taking turns on Greg's scooter. Hans is first as he whizzes off down the nearby pathways and back around to us. Gradually we each have a go. Standing to the side, Eva and I look on as Leon attempts to show Nadia how to work the minimal controls on the scooter. She scoots off for the first attempt on her own, playfully screaming as she does so. Leon jogs after her and climbs on behind her. A few minutes later they're whizzing off together standing closely. For a second I think Eva will explode with excitement as she sees them getting friendlier.

I prod her in the shoulder. "Enough of watching them…let's give this a try."

We wait for them to come back around and then its our turn.

Eva grabs the handlebars and leans the scooter towards me. "You go first."
I take hold of the handlebars and climb on, gently moving the control on the right-hand side and pushing myself off with my leg before quickly returning it to the scooter, and I'm moving.

When it comes to stopping, it's not as easy as it looks for me. Only I could over complicate something so simple. Rather than using the brake on the left-hand side of the handlebars, for some reason the natural thing for me to do seems to be to just keep on jumping off to the side, whilst holding onto the handlebars. Realising that's what I used to do as a kid with my little blue and pink push along scooter…obviously a long time before electric ones were invented.

"What's with the jumping off?" Eva asks.

"No idea..." I giggle "...it seems more natural to me to get my feet back on the ground. Here, you try..."

Eva glances around to see where the others are before climbing aboard and heading in their direction. I can hear her laughing to herself as she picks up speed but then starts to wobble around before re-gaining her balance and pulling up to the side of the pathway.

"Climb on behind me Nic, let's see if we can do it."

As I climb on behind Eva, I take the controls and we veer off.

"Faster...come on." She encourages me to push the controller to make us go faster which I do, gradually.

We pull up alongside the others and Hans and Tymec decide to race each other with Hans running and Tymec on the scooter. They look like kids giddy with enthusiasm as they zoom alongside each other, doing their best to overtake one another - until Tymec is declared the winner by Klaudia. We take photos of each other as we take turns to scoot along and eventually, I get the hang of using the brake on the left-hand side of the handle.

As I take my turn zipping along with the sun in the sky and my hair blowing in the breeze it feels really refreshing and in some way cleansing even. I switch with Nadia and Leon and they are soon videoing themselves as they zip along laughing. It looks like they're getting closer and closer by the second. They head back in my direction and then they pull up just a few metres away.

Klaudia watches them. "I think something's happening....." She throws her head in Nadia and Leon's direction discreetly as they reach our side.

"Nadia and I are going on a rowing boat on the lake." Leon tells us, as Nadia stands almost timidly beside him.

"That's a great idea… I will come along too…Nicole, Klaudia?" Hans offers.

Klaudia moves her foot sharply in his direction to which he grunts, it appears he got the message.

"Actually, no, I think I will head back anyway."

They walk off in the direction of the lake as Eva arrives back next to me, Klaudia and Hans.

"I've lost track of the others." She glances around. "Well other than the lovebirds who I can see are developing nicely."

I can't help but laugh at her as she stands there, all four feet six of her with her hands on hips, looking on proudly.

Hans leans in and kisses us both on the cheek. "Ladies, I will go now, we will meet before Christmas though?"

"Of course." I tell him. Klaudia decides make her way home too so they leave together.

Greg leaves his scooter with us as he goes off in search of the toilets. I check my phone in my bag to see it's just past 3 p.m. and I have a message from Jesé asking me to meet him at the cafe just a couple of minutes' walk from here near the park exit.

"Come on, let's enjoy a last few minutes on here."

We jump back onto the scooter doing another couple of laps around the same area. We climb off and Eva takes another turn on her own, going faster and faster before turning and coming back towards me and then we swap.

I'm happily zipping along increasing my confidence along with my speed. I glance down along the pathway for a split second, and I feel like I'm edging towards the curb. As I look back up to the path in front of me, I do my best to steer away slightly but with people coming towards me, I panic. I don't know what happens exactly, but the next minute I'm flying through the air trying desperately to slow myself down before I land on the floor in a heap.

I land on my left side, and can immediately feel a graze on my knee and left shoulder. I think I'm in shock for a couple of seconds and then I hear Eva shouting and see her running towards me.

"Oh my God Nic, are you okay?" She leans down to me. "Let's get you up."

"Just leave me for a second…" I tell her, feeling the need to stay still for a minute before gradually sitting upright.

An older couple suddenly appear next to us.

"*¿Ambulancia, Ambulancia?*" They ask, looking concerned.

Eva crouches down next to me, placing her hand on my arm.

"Do you need an ambulance? Let me check you over."

"No, I'll be okay…*gracias*." I tell them.

With the help of Eva, I gingerly get myself to my feet as I see Jesé almost next to us. Oh no. I'm mortified, he must have seen what happened.

Eva looks concerned. "Are you sure you're okay?"

Jesé reaches my side. "Nicole you are okay? I saw you fall, but I did not know this was you until I am closer." He puts his hand on my left shoulder which makes me wince slightly.

"I'm okay, just a bit bruised I think."

I begin to brush myself down with my hands, knocking the dust and grass off my clothes as Eva helps me. I look at my hand which is grazed and covered in dirt. Jesé and Eva look at each other.

Eva gently lifts my hand with her own. "We should get your hand cleaned up." She looks around us. "Maybe going home might be best, a public toilet might not be that clean and we need to clean this properly…"

Greg arrives back next to us as Eva tells him whats happened and that we're making a move home.

"Nicole, are you okay?" Greg asks?

"I'll be fine, sorry I hope I haven't scratched your scooter?"

"Don't be silly…as long as you are alright?"

I walk slowly towards the exit gates with Jesé and Eva either side of me. I can feel Jesé gently putting his hand on my back as we walk along, which feels nice. I suddenly find myself wishing he'd pull me in for a hug, it must be the shock of the whole situation. I take it we won't be getting that coffee now, I think to myself. Is the universe trying to tell me something? The fact that this has happened today when we would be sitting down together at last. I put a positive spin on it…maybe the universe is telling me something…I've fallen for him - literally.

We're almost at the gates, and my knee begins to throb slightly but my shoulder feels worse.

"Can we stop for a second?" I beckon towards a bench.

"Of course, you are okay?" Jesé asks.

I lower myself down and I notice a scuff on the material of my jacket at the shoulder. I shrug off my jacket and pull my top-down to check my shoulder.

"Ouch…" Winces Eva. "That will be one hell of a bruise."

Jesé kneels at my side as rubs his thumb very gently around the redness that's appearing which sends tingling down my arm, making me look up at him. I see Eva take a step back and wink at me as her mobile starts to ring.

"It's Connor." She tells me as she looks at the screen.

"Answer it." I tell her.

She moves away to talk to her boyfriend, keeping a watchful eye on the two of us.

"I can't believe you saw me fall." I shake my head.

"It was actually quite funny until I realised it was you, and you were still on the floor."

"I don't know what happened, I tried to step off rather than braking, which is what I've been doing all afternoon. It's my own fault…why didn't I just hit the brake…it's what it's there for. If I had just pressed the brake I would have stopped and I wouldn't have fallen…"

He sits next to me on the bench. "Do not worry about that, it was your natural reaction. We need to clean your hand…you have something…erm...some antiseptic at home?"

"No I don't think so, unless Laura has any."

"*Venga* I have some, we will go to my place." He stands up, holding out his hand to help me.

"Eva is coming too?" He asks.

I look over to my friend who is finishing her call and heading back towards us.

"I will take Nicole back to my place…" He tells her. "…I have first aid kit."

I see Eva attempting to hide a smirk as she presses her lips together.

"Of course…that would be great thank you Jesé." She turns to me. "Are you sure you're okay with Jesé looking after you?"

I give her a look that tells her to be careful what she says in front of him.

"Yes thank you, Eva."

She loosely hangs her arm around me and leans into whisper.

"Every cloud…I'll call you later…but maybe don't tell him I'm a nurse."

Chapter 26

I check my reflection in the mirror in Jesé's bathroom as I wash my hands, before joining him back in the living room. I still can't believe he saw me fall over, I'm so embarrassed.

"I made you tea." He tells me as I sit beside him on the sofa, his coat now removed to reveal his smart black jumper.

"Thanks." I remember the last time I was here and what we almost did. In some ways, that seems a lifetime ago.

He reaches for some cotton wool before dipping it into a dish on the table full of what looks like water.

"We need to wash your hand." He holds his hand out towards me to receive mine. He starts to dab gently at the broken skin.

"It's just a graze, honestly its fine." I reassure him as I watch him taking charge of the situation, feeling the warmth from his hand as it holds my own.

This is the first time I've seen his caring side. I like it, I really like it.

"I know… but it needs to be clean." He throws the cotton wool back into the dish. "Done. You will need some…how you say…*una tirita*." He searches for the right word in his head as he holds a box of plasters.

"A plaster?"

He smiles at me. "A plaster, *gracias*." He carefully squeezes what I'm assuming is some sort of antiseptic onto my hand before lightly pressing a plaster over it.

"I think you should have been a paramedic."

"I have many talents." He holds eye contact for a second before turning his attention to my leg.

"Do you need anything on your knee? I do not mind doing that for you too." He flirts which makes me laugh, as always.

"It's okay thanks, it's just red and a bit swollen but it'll be fine." I pass my hand over my knee, feeling the lump that's appeared over the last hour.

Before I can say anything else he's up, back in the kitchen and returning with a bag of frozen peas for my knee. He sits next to me and taps his thigh with his hand telling me to put my leg on his lap, which I do. He holds the bag of frozen peas on as he wedges a cushion underneath my knee for support. I can't help but think that I need to take off my jeans for this to work properly, but I definitely won't be doing that.

I allow myself to relax, resting my head back onto the sofa. A vaguely awkward silence hangs in the air between us. I look up at Jesé, who starts to laugh.

"What?" I ask.

He shakes his head before answering.

"I was just thinking that you have entertained everyone in the park today. Maybe you have a new job?"

"A new job?"

"As stunt woman." He laughs again.

"It's very risky poking fun at me considering that my foot is in your lap, one swift kick." I threaten him.

"I know that you would not do that." He lays his hand on my foot, which immediately gets hot under his touch.

"Hmmm…. Maybe you know me too well already?"

He considers my answer. "This is true, maybe."

We sit, just looking at each other in the eye with no words between us, the tension mounting only for a minute until I make a move to go home.

"Well thanks for looking after me, I'd better get back." I pull my brown knee high boots back on as I stand, and pick up my jacket from the arm of the chair.

He pulls up the sleeves on his jumper almost as though he's preparing for something.

"I will walk you home."

I pull my jacket on, feeling a couple of twinges as I move my arm back to slip it into the sleeve. I expect I'll feel like I've been hit by a bus tomorrow morning from the jolt of falling over.

"Jesé, it's fine honestly. You've done enough for me this afternoon and I'm really grateful."

"It is no problem, Nicole." He walks me to the front door. "I will see you soon?"

"You will. Thanks again."

I lean in to kiss him on each cheek as he places his arm around me. The arm stays there as we look at each other. I lightly touch his arm, feeling the solidity of his bicep beneath his jumper.

"Thanks."

I open the door and head out onto the stairs and make my way home.

*

The next morning I'm woken by a text from Annie. I feel fine until I reach from my bed for my phone and get a sharp pain that makes me gasp. The pain seems to be coming from underneath my boobs. I lay myself back down and read the short message of three words. *"Miss you, sis xx"*

Reading that makes me realise how much I miss her too, so I type a reply to tell her that I do. My finger hovers over the send button but I delete it instead. I feel like the anger is starting to dissolve towards her, but I'm not ready to forgive her.

I climb out of bed, checking my knee and shoulder as I go. The bruises are coming out more now but I feel like it could have been a lot worse.

After breakfast I take a shower and wash my hair and as I'm stretching up to wash my hair, I find I'm in more pain down my left hand side. By the time I've dried and straightened my hair, I'm in quite a lot of pain so I take a couple of paracetamol and have a rest on the sofa. I was expecting to feel worse this morning after lying down all night. I use Diego's frozen sweetcorn to try to bring the lump on my knee down some more.

The message alert on my phone sounds and I fully expect it to be Annie again, but it's Jesé, asking how 'his favourite stunt woman' is feeling this morning which perks me up.

I don't have a shift at the restaurant until late afternoon so I decide to check the cinema listings to see if I can catch a film. Sitting at the table, I bend down to plug the laptop charger in, and the pain is excruciating. I immediately sit straight back in the chair. Feeling like I need to catch my breath, I take a deep breath in which hurts even more. A feeling of dread washes over me, this can't be right.

I head to my bedroom and lift my top to take a look in the mirror. There's no bruising around my rib area but the underwire on my bra is feeling more and more uncomfortable by the second. As I look little further down, I seem to be swollen towards the bottom of my ribs. I really don't know what to do, should I go to hospital? The thought of going to hospital on my own fills me with dread.

I decide to wait it out and see if I feel better later. Maybe I'll just get some rest this morning so I dig out my book that I started a few weeks ago and do my best to relax. I really can't get comfortable, my jeans are digging into me just underneath where I'm swollen so I change back into my joggers.

Ten minutes later, unable to concentrate reading, I realise I don't even know where the hospital is. Checking my phone I see it's around a 20 minute journey on the metro to the hospital or a 25 minute walk. I start to panic. Feeling short of breath I steady myself against the kitchen counter and concentrate on breathing in and out slowly in a bid to calm myself down as the palpitations start.

Yes, I can speak and understand a lot of Spanish now but I'm by no means fluent. What if I don't understand everything they're saying to me? What if they don't understand me? I call Eva to ask her for advice with her being a trained nurse, but her phone just rings out. I leave a voicemail asking her to give me a call as soon as she can. I make myself some tea whilst I wait for her to call back. Half an hour passes but still nothing and despite it being an hour since I took paracetamol, they haven't even taken the edge off the pain. I think of calling Jesé, I could call Luís but for some reason, it's Jesé I want to turn to.

"Hola bonita." He answers.

"Jesé, *hola*."

"How are you feeling?"

"Not good, I think I need to go to hospital. Do you think you could come?"

"You are worse?" He sounds concerned.

"I'm in a lot of pain around my ribs, it hurts when I breathe in…." I start to feel emotional which irritates me but I manage to keep myself together.

"Nicole, stay there I am on the way." Just like that he's hung up.

It's less than five minutes later when he presses the intercom and I tell him to come up. As I open the door, his face appears to be full of concern.

"You are okay?" He puts his arm around my shoulders.

"I'm sorry to ask you."

"Ssshhh." He pulls me gently to him and holds me for a couple of seconds which is comforting. I feel like I could stay like this for hours, in his embrace.

I pull away. "Let me change back into my jeans and we'll go."

"Don't forget your health card for the hospital." He calls after me. I walk from my bedroom holding it out in his direction.

"Thanks, I would've forgotten it." I drop it into my bag, pick up my keys and off we go.

As we get out onto the street, Jesé hails a taxi which pulls up alongside us.

"Oh, I… I thought we would walk." I stutter, hoping to prolong the inevitable.

"Nicole, we are going to hospital, it is urgent…" He holds open the taxi door. "…You are not walking."

Jesé tells the driver where we're going as he sits down next to me in the back of the taxi. He looks to me and gives me a reassuring smile which I do my best to return.

I notice my breathing begin to change as the realisation sets in that we're on our way to the Hospital. Now don't get me wrong I know that no one likes being in those places but for me this is something that is likely to start my head off down a particularly scary pathway for me. Knowing that there are people there who are ill starts off the fear. I have to tell myself to just focus on why I am going…my ribs, and to do my best to stay grounded and just concentrate on what is going on now for me and not let my head project myself into all of these horrible scenarios.

Jesé then surprises me with a really sweet gesture by reaching for my hand, which he then holds for the duration of the journey, making me feel comforted.

*

I'm so glad I swallowed my pride and asked Jesé to come with me to the hospital. After seeing a nurse who spoke very little English, I did my best to tell her my symptoms in Spanish but it wasn't that easy. Jesé did a lot of interpreting for me. By the time we saw the doctor, I realised it was best that he did most of the talking. He even tried to leave the room for the doctor to examine me but I asked him to stay.

Apparently no one x-rays ribs anymore because cracks, breaks and sprains all have the same treatment - rest and painkillers. The doctor said he thought that it was more along the lines of a sprain, but he couldn't rule out it being a cracked rib given how much pain I'm in. He told me how important it is to make sure I'm taking deep breaths, even though it'll hurt as I need to keep my lungs clear or I could pick up a chest infection too.

Arriving back at Laura's that afternoon, I'm so glad to be home. I see from my phone I have two missed calls from Eva. Jesé takes off my jacket and steers me in the direction of the sofa.

"Sit down, I will make us tea." He throws his jacket on the back of the sofa.

"Are you sure you're not English?" I frown as he fills up the kettle. "All of this tea you keep making."

He laughs. "I'm just trying to make you feel at home."

I type a quick text to Eva and tell her I'll call her later.

Jesé's phone starts to ring from his jacket pocket. He looks to his jacket, then at me before continuing to make the drink.

"Are you not going to answer that?"

I remember the last time he was ignoring calls when he was with me, because it was Lola. I think he realises that himself as he suddenly makes a dash to answer the phone before it stops ringing.

"It is work." He tells me before he answers the call.

The whole of the phone call is in Spanish. I absolutely love hearing him speak Spanish, it really does something to me. I sit watching him and pretending not to listen in on his private conversation, as he puts the teabags in the cups and makes our drink.

As far as I can make out, he was supposed to be working this afternoon but had called to tell them he couldn't work today. As he finishes the call he brings the two cups over to the coffee table.

"I hope I haven't got you into trouble at work?"

"Stop worrying, this is fine." He sits down beside me on the sofa.

"I can't thank you enough for coming with me today, I'm so grateful."

"I know a way you can thank me, but with your injury you cannot do this at the moment."

I smack his arm, trying to hide the smirk on my face.

He looks around the room. "When is Laura home?"

"Thursday, I think they land late afternoon."

"You need to rest…maybe I should sleep on the sofa whilst they are away, I can look after you."

I wasn't expecting that. "You don't need to do that…"

"You are saying I can sleep in with you?"

I tut at him, despite the fact that I would like nothing more than for him to share my bed.

His smile fades. "I am being serious, you need someone to look after you."

"You want to look after me?" I ask.

He shrugs his shoulders. "Why not?"

"Jesé, that's really sweet but honestly I'll be fine. I'll call Mio and tell him I can't work this week, I'll rest I promise. You'll be at work yourself anyway."

*

It's only been one full day of sitting around and "resting" but I'm so bored already.

I started to watch a box set of Laura's about a Women's Spanish prison which is really good and about the only thing that's kept me sane today. Late afternoon I decide to go for a walk and I drop Luís a quick message to see if he's working this afternoon. I thought maybe he might fancy a coffee at Mio's as I want to pop in and see how the works going anyway. Luís is working at his day job today, but promises he'll call tomorrow to arrange a time to meet up.

Mio throws his arms around me as I walk into the restaurant, making me grimace as he hugs me quite tightly.

"*Chica*, no, you are not working…"

"I could say the same about you."

He throws his arms up in the air admitting defeat.

"Look, I am sitting drinking coffee." He gestures to his favourite table in the corner.

"Sit…I will get you a drink."

Clara, one of the waitresses appears next to us and insists on getting both of us a drink, telling me to sit down.

I sit with Mio sipping coffee as he talks some more about the restaurant plans. Juan also joins us for a while and he seems equally excited about the whole thing.

"I want you to rest this week, but maybe next week if you feel a little more…rested, like you need something to do, you could stay at home and read through all of the plans for advertising the room and erm…the different ideas and tell us what you think?"

"I'd love to, thanks."

I stay in the restaurant chatting for a while until I start to feel really uncomfortable sitting in the booth and guilty for not helping as the restaurant begins to get busy. I head out into the darkness, holding my rib as it now feels really sore and as I'm just about to put my key in the front door to the building, Jesé arrives alongside me laden down with carrier bags.

"Nicole, you should be resting."

"I have been resting, but I was so bored. I just had to get out for a while."

He gives me a look of authority.

"Don't give me that look, I promise I've only been to Mio's. I've been sitting down the whole time."

"It is okay, Doctor Jesé is here now…" He holds up the carrier bags with a smug look on his face.

I can't help but burst out laughing. "Jesé don't, it hurts me to laugh."

He rolls his eyes at me. "Just open the door."

Once we're inside, Jesé unpacks the bags to reveal fruit, milk, chocolate, fresh orange juice, magazines and all of the ingredients to make a chicken and chorizo paella.

"I can't believe you did this for me, you're actually going to cook paella too?"

"I told you I will look after you. But the best part is, tonight I am here and we will order pizza."

I look down at the ingredients on the worktop and back at him.

"Oh they are for tomorrow night... I'm too tired to cook tonight, work was busy today."

Next he produces a pizza menu from his back pocket and throws it on to the kitchen worktop in front of me before piling his ingredients into the fridge.

"Decide what you would like..." He holds the fridge door open as he leans across the worktop to pick up the chicken, brushing his hand against mine. "... Other than me."

I feign annoyance before turning my attention back to the menu, trying to hide the fact that I've been looking at his backside for the last couple of minutes.

I clear my throat. "I'll go for the regina I think, how about you?" I spin the menu around in his direction as he closes the fridge and stands next to me.

"Pizza carbonara."

I pick up the phone to place the order.

"Just so you know, these are on me..."

He opens his mouth to protest but I cut him short.

"... No arguments." I hold my hand up to stop him. "It's the least I can do after you came with me to the hospital yesterday and now..." I motion to the empty supermarket bags lying on the counter top.

I carry on dialling the number and I order our food in Spanish. Now it's Jesé's turn to pretend not to listen to me as he leans against the table, apparently reading one of the magazines he picked up for me, not realising its upside down.

"You are doing really good with your Spanish." He seems taken aback.

"Don't look so surprised, I've been trying to learn it for long enough." I sit down on the sofa, positioning two cushions behind me to keep me sitting upright and supported.

"Plus I do live with a fluent speaker and a native speaker, that kind of helps." I smile sarcastically.

He pulls the coffee table closer to me and indicates for me to put my feet up.

"I can see you are practising…" He brings his knees up, taking off his trainers and making himself comfortable on the sofa, turning in to face me. "What made you want to learn?"

I lean my head back momentarily on the sofa before answering him.

"I'm not really sure. There was just something that I loved that very first time I came to Spain when I was…" I think back. "…nine years old." I adjust my position, turning so that my back is against the corner of the sofa so I can see him better as we talk, my feet now touching his knees

"So you just knew… you loved this country, even back then." He smiles, almost proudly.

"I've always wanted to live in Spain, always and now I actually am, I can't believe it, even now."

"It is a dream come true for you?" He wonders.

"Definitely."

He clasps my foot with his hand. I've noticed he's being quite affectionate with me the past couple of days, not that I'm complaining. I suddenly switch to Spanish and ask him if he'd like a beer, red wine or some tea as I go to move from the sofa. I know it sounds silly but hearing myself speaking Spanish and Jesé replying to me makes me feel so proud at how much I've achieved since I came here three months ago. Jesé tells me not to get up and he'll have a beer. He opens his bottle, pours me some orange juice and sits back down in the same position.

I take a sip of juice and then rest the glass on the table, flinching at a sharp pain in my ribs as I stretch forward.

"So what made you want to be a policeman?"

He shuffles in his seat and I wonder if maybe he's uncomfortable talking about it, but once he starts to talk, he opens up.

"I just remember being in the city, me and my brother Ramon when we were also maybe nine years old...out with *Papá*. We saw policemen running after two guys through the streets and I was so fascinated that I ran after them, desperate to see what happened next."

"I bet your Dad was terrified when you ran after them?"

He nods. "He was not happy...but I did not think of this at the time. He ran after me with Ramon."

"So what happened?"

He sips his beer. "The police, they caught up with them, they were arrested. I thought it was the best thing I had ever seen." He rests his head against the back of the sofa as he continues. "After that, it was all I could think about for weeks. *Papá* brought me a *policía* costume and for months when I got home from school, I would wear it." He laughs before looking down into his lap and shaking his head. It's the first time I've seen him look embarrassed.

Without thinking I rub my foot against his knee.

"Aw, I bet you were adorable."

I smile, seeing him cast his eyes down to my foot briefly as he takes another drink from his beer. This feels so relaxing, I'm really enjoying his company.

"I know that you and Ramon are twins but do you look alike, are you identical?"

He leans forward to take his phone from his back pocket and as he does so, the scent of his aftershave hits me. It's different to the one he normally wears, I don't know how I didn't notice it earlier. It smells really fresh and yet again it does something to my insides.

Apparently finding some photos, he then moves closer to me and leans, almost as though he is lying next to me, so that I don't need to move to look at the pictures. I can hear my heart begin to beat faster and that scent, I swear it's put me under some kind of spell. I look down at him as he proudly shows the pictures of his brother and I can't help but focus on Jesé's lips and his stubble and what it would feel like to kiss him again, right now.

"You are okay?" He questions, looking up at me.

That snaps me out of it. "Sorry, I..." I can't think of anything to say so I throw myself back into the subject. "... Do you have a picture of you together?"

He scrolls further through his picture gallery. "Here, this is a few months ago."

"You definitely have the same eyes." I say. "I'd say that Ramon definitely got the looks though."

He sits back up and playfully throws his phone to the other end of the sofa. Without warning he grabs my leg with both hands.

"You will pay for that…" He warns me with a look of lust in his eyes. The anticipation building by the second. With my leg locked down by his hands, he dives to my foot and begins to tickle my feet as he sniggers, which makes me laugh as I desperately try to throw him off but keep my torso still to protect my ribs which is virtually impossible. I gasp in pain, which makes him stop.

"Nicole, I am so sorry…"

He moves closer to me resting one hand high up on my thigh and taking hold of my arm with his other hand, wondering what he should do. He grits his teeth together and I can tell he feels guilty. "*Idiota…*" He calls himself an idiot.

I pull myself up in my seat a little more. "It's fine, don't worry."

His hand does not move from my thigh, nor do I want it to. He has a look of such gentleness on his face. I look into his dark brown eyes and he looks right back at me. Just then, the intercom buzzes completely startling me.

"Ah, the pizza." I say.

He groans, walking to the door to let the delivery man up. As we wait for him to reach our floor with the pizza neither of us speak. We look at each other and then Jesé seems to pace up and down in frustration.

"You must be hungry?" I laugh and he joins in and before we know it, we're both laughing hysterically at the comedy of the situation.

I flick on the TV for some background noise as we eat and once we've finished eating I take some more painkillers.

"Do you need to go to bed? I can go home?" He checks.

I shake my head. "No, don't worry." That's the last thing that I want. He looks pleased at my reply.

"It is your turn now, show me some pictures of you and your twin…if you want to that is…"

A knot appears in my stomach. "No, it's okay…"

I retrieve a photo album from my bedroom full of pictures of the family that I grabbed in haste whilst packing. I sit down next to him.

"You'll be sorry you asked." I laugh in a bid to distract myself from the photos I'm about to look at.

The first one is of Annie and I on our 21st birthday at our party above the local pub. It's the photo I had on my bedroom wall for years and it's one of my favourites. Then there's a few of us together with my parents on holidays over the years and a couple of Annie and I on nights out.

It feels weird looking at these pictures as I haven't done so in a while. Even now as I look at these, I can't believe how she deceived me like she did.

"Wow, it is obvious you are twins."

"Really, you think so?" I'm surprised.

"You look more alike than me and Ramon."

I lean in closely. "Mmm, maybe…but we're not that much alike I don't think."

I flick back to the photo of our 21st and tell him the story of how Annie got so drunk that she was dancing out of control on the dancefloor, screaming and shouting. The toilets were downstairs from the function room and she couldn't even get down the stairs. I virtually had to carry her and help her go to the toilet.

I close the album and see him looking at me with such softness. I tilt my head, wondering what that look is about.

"Wh-what?" Smiling nervously.

He takes a deep breath.

"Just something I have noticed, the things you have told me about your sister."

"Oh, what do you mean?"

"It is like…" He looks around, seemingly searching for the words. "…It is like you have been in your sister's shadow…I obviously do not know her but, she likes the attention to be on her?"

His words are so precise, how can he see all of this the same way that I do, the way that I feel. He carries on…

"Now you are here in Spain, and not with your sister you are following your heart and you are…. you are living the life that you want for you."

I don't respond, I just think about his words.

"Sorry, I have upset you?" He places a hand on my back.

"No of course you haven't. It's just that, you're right."

I look at him apprehensively. "That's exactly how it's always been…well most of the time anyway."

Feeling so comfortable around Jesé, I take a deep breath and tell him about my past. My OCD, the anxieties that I've had ever since I can remember and the vital help I've had from my counsellor to desperately work through some of my fears and difficult to understand thought patterns. He, in turn, tells me how his old school friend has struggled with his mental health.

"Your sister… she helped you?"

I think back to the day I tried to talk to her, the first time I tried to talk to anyone about the way I'd been feeling.

"She noticed I'd been really distracted and she'd been around me enough times when I was doing the things I felt I needed to do to stay safe. The constant checking the doors were locked at night, that the gas on the oven hadn't been left on…but when I got to that point that I knew I needed help, I told her I thought I had OCD, she told me not to be ridiculous and of course I didn't have it. *There's nothing wrong with checking things…we all do it*' she said, but I tried to tell her how I felt when I was doing it and the thoughts that were going through my mind. It was a constant battle every day."

Jesé reaches for my hand as I carry on, and I can see the compassion in his eyes.

"I felt like I'd been shut down, I tried so hard after that to stop doing what I was doing but it was impossible, if anything, trying not to do it made me worse." I catch my breath for a second, remembering how I felt that day.

"…About a week later I finally rang a counselling centre and they offered me an appointment a couple of days later."

He rubs my hand. "It is so good that you were able to ask for help, I know how difficult it must have been."

"It was hard, but…getting myself to the appointment…" I fight back the tears. "…by then I'd told James, and I was so scared about going, I even convinced myself that they weren't going to help me and that I'd get there and they would be some sort of cult and they'd keep me there and not let me out or something... I pictured all sorts of things. James came with me to make me feel safer and he sat outside in the car." I shake my head thinking about it now. I start to feel breathless, realising just how bad things had got at that point.

I look at my hand as it sits in his, noticing him doing the same. He smiles at me.

"You have to be very strong to admit you need the help, it is good you have told me this Nicole..."

"Well I appreciate you listening, it's not something I tell people lightly."

"I know this of course, it is deeply personal, but you can speak to me...any time." He rests his hand on my leg. "...It has not been easy to beat this, but you are doing so well."

"I don't think it's something that ever completely goes away, OCD but the help I've had... I don't know what I would have done without it."

"Did your parents know?" he asks.

"I told them just after I started counselling, they were so supportive, but it is really difficult when you have people telling you that you just 'need to stop worrying about things' because it isn't just worrying. Anxiety runs way deeper than worry. It's all-consuming and it takes over so much of your life that you start to wonder who you are exactly.

After I was officially diagnosed, Annie tried her best to help me, she tried to keep getting me to talk about it but it was difficult because unless you have experience of mental health yourself, it's really hard to understand and for me to try and explain it to her..."

"It is exhausting…" Jesé agrees.

"Over the years with my counselling, somehow I gradually stopped the compulsions…a lot of the obsessions were still there and they still are at times, but its more generalised anxiety that I get now and at times health anxiety. It's still a struggle, but…it's more manageable now most of the time."

"Well you are doing fantastic so do not forget this Nicole, and you are having help again now that you need it too."

"Thank you." I smile gratefully. "… So now you know my darkest secrets…you sure you don't want run away?" I laugh self-consciously, looking down at the ground.

"Nicole, you are you…and the more that I learn about you, the more I like."

He leans forward and lightly presses his lips against mine. I wasn't expecting him to do that after telling him my most personal secrets, for him to react like that… I feel a sense of renewed strength.

We spend the next hour or so chatting about his school friend and the help that he's had from his employers for his mental health. I tell him how I've been trying to make sense of the way things with my sister have affected me, particularly how I felt so low after my split with James, with Annie convincing me it was my own fault.

I feel so much better for opening up to him and grateful for his support. What is it about Jesé? He certainly continues to surprise me the closer that we get.

Chapter 27

The following day, Luís has a few hours off and so, we walk around the perfume shop at one of the shopping centres. The front of the centre itself has a display of Christmas lights and with the carols being played instore, the atmosphere is wonderful. There are streams of lights everywhere I look with that tell-tale glow and sense of Christmas excitement.

The store's busy and I start to feel a little weary that someone might bump into me but I try and relax and enjoy being out of the house. It's great to see Luís too and hear his news.

"I'm glad to hear things are going well with Ana." I tell him.

"It is early days. We only have had three dates, but it is good."

A sales assistant offers me a sample of a new perfume on a testing strip and I have to say it smells so good and I'm tempted to buy some, well, that is until I see the price.

"You should buy it." He tells me.

I inhale the perfume on the strip once again, closing my eyes and taking it in.

"… Maybe after Christmas." We walk away from the counter. "I'll just enjoy this freebie until then."

Luís buys a small bottle of a different perfume for Ana and pays extra for it to be gift wrapped. As we walk out of the shop we notice that the centre seems to be getting busier.

Luís checks his watch. "You are hungry?"

"Hungry and in need of a seat..." I smile through gritted teeth.

He places his hand on my shoulder protectively. "We will sit down and eat. There are some good restaurants upstairs, you have been here before?" He leads the way to the escalator.

"Not to eat, no."

"There are brilliant views across the city from the top floor."

With all of the tables outside close to the view already taken, we take a seat in the middle of the indoor area, both ordering a sandwich and coffee.

"You and Jesé have seen each other?"

I pull my seat closer to the table as a distraction. "Is that a question, or do you already know we have?"

Luís throws his head back laughing. "Yes... I already know. Jesé and I do speak, you know this..."

"I assume you know about the salsa club? Although that seems like ages ago now."

He smirks knowingly, nodding his head.

"We went to the markets a few weeks ago and then, the art class together."

"He helped you at the hospital?"

"Thankfully, yes."

The waitress brings our coffees to the table and we thank her, both taking a sip from our cups. The hot milky coffee distracts me from the conversation as I think about what I'm about to say.

"The more I'm getting to know Jesé I'm definitely seeing a different side to him, a side that I really didn't expect to see from someone like him."

Luís looks pleased to hear me say that.

"It is good you are spending time together, I don't think the hospital was your best date though, no?"

I shake my head as I swallow my coffee. "They haven't been dates Luís, we've just been out."

He looks at me sceptically over his cup.

I sit back in my seat as I look at him. "What's wrong with that, me and you are friends."

"I just know there is something between you, I know that there is and so do you."

"I'm not denying that, but until I know I can trust him." I shrug my shoulders and even that hurts my rib. Luís accepts defeat, knowing that no matter how much he tells me about him, I still need to find out for myself.

Once we've eaten, we go outside onto the viewing platform to look across the city. Some dark clouds are creeping in but that doesn't detract from the view of the Royal Palace in the distance. Beyond that I can see the sweeping greenery of the parks and gardens. It's a wonderful view and it makes me realise again, just how lucky I am to be living here which is something I remind myself of everyday.

I leave Luís to the rest of his Christmas shopping and make the short walk home, where I take some painkillers, change into my scruffs and lie on my bed. I think I must fall asleep as soon as my head hits the pillow as the next thing I'm aware of is banging on the front door.

I look around my bedroom feeling confused thinking that it must be the middle of the night until I remember that I came straight in from lunch and lay on the bed. The tapping on the door continues and then my mobile starts to ring and I see Jesé's name across my phone's screen. Realising it must be him, I dawdle half asleep to the front door.

There he stands with his phone held to his ear.

"At last… I thought you were out learning more stunts."

I smile sarcastically, holding the door open for him to come in. I yawn as I take in his new look of black framed glasses which really suit him. In fact they more than suit him, he looks hotter than ever.

"Sorry I must have fallen asleep." I tell him as I close the door, clearing my throat. It's then that I wonder what sort of a state I look and discreetly try to tidy up my hair.

"I can see that."

I gasp, pretending to be offended. It feels good that we are this comfortable around each other again.

Jesé leans against the worktop. "How are you feeling today?"
I'm suddenly feeling much better now, I think to myself.

"Not too bad, I was in pain earlier which is why I went to bed."

He walks towards me and steers me onto the sofa. "You need to rest, sit down."

I do as I'm told. "I erm…I like the glasses." I'm glad I'm not wearing mine as I think they'd be steamed up by now.

"*Gracias.*" he adjusts them dramatically looking down at me on the sofa.

"I normally wear lenses but..."

I interrupt. "... But as you are only seeing me you thought you'd dress down?"

"I think we are good enough friends now that I can be myself with you."

Hearing him describe us as friends makes me disappointed, even though I spent most of my lunch with Luís trying to convince him we were just that – friends.

I fold my arms. "Be yourself? So you're not being Doctor Jesé anymore then?"

He tries to come back with a witty reply but he struggles to hold the laughter in.

"Well yes, I am still to look after you..." He smirks. "So until you are better..." He holds his hands out and shrugs his shoulders in smugness "... I am Doctor Jesé."

He backs away into the kitchen.

"And when I'm better?" I goad him on.

He opens the fridge and pauses looking at me intently.

"When you are better... I will be whatever you would like me to be."

"Well, there's an offer..." All this flirting, he makes me feel so alive.

He reaches into the fridge for the chicken.

"You are hungry? Tonight I am also your personal chef."

"I am actually, what time is it?" I've no idea how long I was asleep.

He takes the ingredients out from the fridge. "It is almost eight. I will make you paella."

Jesé gets to work chopping up the chicken, chorizo and onion and before too long there are the most wonderful smells of the smoky chorizo coming out of the kitchen. I watch him as he works without following a recipe, stirring the ingredients in the pan.

I stand up to stretch my legs, walking towards him and inhaling the delicious aromas.

"I take it this isn't the first time you've cooked this?"

"Believe it or not no, but I hate cooking." He throws in a carefully measured teaspoon of the deep yellow turmeric into the pan, the gingery earthy smell fills the air.

"Oh?" This surprises me.

"I will only cook paella or tortilla fresh, anything else just is too much work…"

I laugh. "Paella isn't exactly quick to make though…"

He tells me how his *Mamá* made paella every Saturday night for years and finally he persuaded her to teach him how to cook it just before he turned 18.

Sometime later, reaching for the plates he divides the food expertly between them and carries them to the table. I sit next to him as we tuck into our food.

The rice is cooked perfectly and thanks to the chorizo it has a delicious spicy kick. The tender chunks of chicken with the flavouring from the chorizo spices and turmeric is just so flavoursome.

"Jesé this is really good, you should definitely cook more often."

He swallows his food. "I am glad that you like it, but cooking more often…" He shakes his head. Jesé starts to tell me how when he's working night shifts that's when he turns to ready meals. If he goes for a drink with friends he will eat tapas so he doesn't cook very often at all.

"How about you, you like to cook?" He asks.

"I don't mind cooking, I can cook but after I moved back in with my parents I just got into the routine of not doing it very often."

Now that we've finished eating, Jesé takes our plates to the kitchen, pours us each a glass of water and sits back down next to me.

"You should try to cook paella."

"I have done once, years ago. Maybe I will again."

He relaxes back in his seat turning towards me and hooking his arm over the back of the chair.

"Anytime you want to cook for me…"

I snigger. "The only thing I want to do right now is lie down after all that food."

His eyes light up. "Nicole I thought you would never ask."

I feign irritation as I make my way to the sofa. He takes his usual position at the other end of the sofa, turned in to face me.

"Laura and Diego are back tomorrow?" He asks.

"Yes, I can't believe how fast those few days have gone, even though I've been bored out of my mind sitting around."

"You think that you will stay here, living with Laura and Diego?"

I sigh. "No. I've been thinking about this the last few days, I can't stay here indefinitely it's not fair on them."

"I can help you look for something…or you could move in with me?" He offers suggestively.

I roll my eyes. "Jesé, are you ever serious?"

"I am serious now but I only have one bed, we would have to share."

I feel myself begin to blush. "Ha, ha…" I nudge him with my foot. "In January I will start to look, but I imagine I would have to share with someone. I doubt I could afford it on my own."

Jesé goes to speak but I interrupt him. "Don't say anything."

*

Eva comes round the next day to help me tidy the place up before Laura and Diego get home. It's not that the apartment's a mess but I'd like to give it a clean so they can see I looked after the place whilst they've been away.

We get to work cleaning, although Eva has to do most of it, and then I make us some lunch. Next we head out to the supermarket so Eva can carry the majority of the shopping for me. I don't need to buy much just the essentials, but what Eva lacks in height, she certainly makes up for in strength.

She carries three bulging shopping bags back home for me with ease and just in time, as Laura lets me know they've landed back in Madrid.

I didn't tell Laura what happened in the park as I didn't want it to be on her mind while she was with Diego's parents, she was already nervous. We've exchanged a couple of texts while she's been away but I've tried to just leave them be.

When they finally walk through the door it's so good to see them. Laura throws her arms around me and squeezes me a little too tightly which makes me flinch in pain, but I do my best not to let her know.

Laura takes off her jacket exposing her sun kissed arms.

"It's so good to see you both." I tell them as I spot their tans. "How hot was it?"

They look to each other. "Around 23 degrees most days…" Laura recalls with a huge grin, clearly missing the temperature already.

"Ah…" I feel jealous. ".. Let me make you a drink and you can tell me all about it."

Diego takes the suitcases into their bedroom.

"No drink for me thanks Nicole, I need a siesta." He laughs.

Laura pulls her jacket back on. "In that case, Nic, we've got some catching up to do let's head off to Mio's, I want to check in on him too."

We sit at our usual booth in the restaurant and before too long, Mio's walking in our direction holding his arms out to Laura as they embrace.

"How did I guess you'd be here?" She tells him off for working.

"I am chatting, that is not working…" He tells her. "Nicole, how are you feeling?"

Laura looks at me.

"I'm okay thanks Mio. If you want, I can take some of the paperwork away when we go later?"

He gives me the thumbs up. "*Perfecto*. There are some drawings also of…tables your friend has designed…"

Mio returns to his seat at the other side of the restaurant with his friend Sebastián, as Clara holds her hand up in greeting from the bar asking us if we want our usual drinks.

"Is this the paperwork with all the plans?" Laura asks excitedly.

"Yes, I'm really looking forward to getting myself stuck into this. But come on, tell me all about your trip, what were his parents like?"

"First I want to know what's been going on, Mio asked you how you were feeling…"

"I didn't say anything whilst you were away but I sort of…fell off a scooter last Sunday…"

Laura gasps.

"…and I've sprained my rib."

I tell her all about what happened and my trip to the hospital with Jesé.

"Aw, that's so sweet that he went with you."

"I don't think I gave him much choice." I laugh. "But he has been really sweet, you're right."

Laura leans in towards me with excitement. "Oh yeah, come on spill the beans."

Clara delivers my café con leche and Laura's cortado.

"He said he wanted to look after me. He brought me some shopping round, we had pizza and just watched TV and then last night he cooked me paella."

As I hear myself saying it out loud I realise all over again just how much he's done for me and how attentive he's been. Laura sits upright looking at me wearily.

"Yet there's nothing going on?"

"I…no…" I hesitate.

"Does he realise this?"

"Of course he does."

"Are you sure about that? He seems to be doing an awful lot for you." She looks at me suggestively.

This starts me thinking. "We do like each other, neither of us have made a secret of that and... I even opened up to him, I told him about my anxiety…"

Laura leans forward towards me. "Well that's great you felt comfortable enough to do that…"

"I know, I didn't even give it much thought it was just natural as we were talking and it felt right to tell him..." I think for a second before telling her that he kissed me.

Laura puts her hand to her chest, to her heart. "You weren't expecting that?"

I laugh. "Well, no. It was the last thing I imagined he'd do."

"Don't leave the poor fella hanging too long Nic, he sounds more than decent enough to me. It shows you the type of guy he is, the way he's supporting you. Sometimes you have to take risks in life….and of course in love, but please don't let what your sister and your ex did to you ruin the amazing things that could happen if you find the right man. Not everyone is like them you know, remember that." She smiles, taking a sip of her coffee.

I feel my mind begin to analyse that statement and I know she's right, but I purposely push it aside for now.

"Come on tell me all about your trip."

A smile creeps onto her face. "To be honest I don't think it could have gone any better. His parents were lovely, very welcoming and I feel like they really accepted me." She looks really emotional.

I rub her hand as it sits on the table. "How could they not accept you?"

She smiles through her almost tears. "I'm being silly aren't I? I was just so relieved, I pictured all sorts of scenarios before we went."

"Did you give Diego's mom the necklace you made for her?"

"I did, but not until a couple of days into our stay…I felt a bit awkward at first, but she loved it."

"I told you she would. Full steam ahead now then with the wedding planning?"

"We've actually set a date…."

I gasp, my hand flying to my mouth. "When???"

She giggles. "16 February."

"That's about…." I attempt to count the weeks in my head.

"Eight weeks….ish." She tells me.

"You couldn't have chosen a warmer month for us to go back to the UK?"

"You know what, I thought that myself….but we don't have to be there for long." she raises her coffee in praise.

"Very true."

I'm so thrilled to hear they've set a date and it's so soon. Laura tells me how whilst they were with Diego's parents, they discussed everything they want and decided on a traditional church wedding followed by the reception in a beautiful hotel in the countryside. They called to see what dates they had available and they had 16 February free which was one of only two weekend dates that they had available until the following January. As they had discussed February already, they took it as a sign and booked it there and then on the phone.

"So we need to get booking our flights Nic but first, Christmas and then I need your help in buying a wedding dress."

I conjure up images of us shopping together for her beautiful wedding dress.

"Diego's parents have never been to the UK and they seemed quite excited at a trip there."

"Maybe you could have another celebration when you get back home, back here?"

"Great minds think alike. We're thinking of doing something small here at Mio's when we get back as I hear there's a new function room opening soon..."

*

The following afternoon, Laura decorates the Christmas tree as we sing along to our favourite Christmas songs. I help to decorate the lower branches, as she and Diego do the top.

Now they're back home I feel like I should go out more often to give them some space alone together, I don't want them to get fed up of me being around. Jesé called me earlier, asking if I'd like to go over to his place tonight for a few drinks. I started to think about what Laura said yesterday about mine and Jesé's situation and about how I shouldn't leave him hanging around too long. Maybe the next time he makes one of his suggestive comments I should see how the land lies a bit more with him, maybe by suggesting we go out properly? I just don't know if I'm ready for this.

I remind myself again of his supportive reaction just a couple of days ago when I bared all to him. He genuinely seemed to care.

With the Christmas tree fully decorated, I pop downstairs to return Mio's paperwork.

"*Chica*, what did you think?" Mio asks.

"Everything looks great, you and Juan have some really good ideas and the furniture that Luís has designed looks just right for the place, don't you think?"

"The tables, the…the benches, the detail that he will use…I feel like he has read my mind. It is exactly what I want."

He takes me in to see how the new function room's looking since I last saw it. I have to say it's amazing so far and it feels like an extension of the restaurant with the familiarity that I feel as I walk through the door. It's keeping the traditional theme, with a touch of love that Mio is famous for.

*

That night as I'm getting ready to go to Jesé's, I start to think yet again about how much he's done for me lately.

I then replay in my head, the short conversation with Lola when I saw her at the cashpoint. Do I really believe what she said about him? Do I believe someone who I don't even know, who I do know blatantly lied making out she was pregnant in an attempt to trap him?

I sit down on my bed and force aside the whole thing with James and Annie and accept that as a completely different situation and firmly in the past. I focus on Jesé who, maybe, possibly could be my future. Could I leave the hurt that they left me with out of any future relationships?

I've got to know Jesé a lot better over the last few weeks and although he can be quite cocky and overconfident I think some of that is just an act he puts on. I know some of it isn't an act, but I actually find that quite endearing about him. It isn't something that I've ever found attractive in a man in the past, but he's certainly won me over. I realise that I don't believe a word Lola says, I know she's poisonous.

I take a deep breath, feeling positive. I dress casually in jeans and my pink off the shoulder jumper for our night in but I add just a touch of nude lipstick so I don't look like I've made too much effort, and a quick spritz of perfume. I leave Laura and Diego looking very cosy together on the sofa, glad I'm leaving them with some space for the night. Especially after they've spent the last few days holed up with his parents and had me with them for months before they went.

Tonight will be the perfect opportunity to broach the subject of Jesé and I. I just need to find the right words.

Jesé opens the door to me wearing dark jeans and a red t-shirt, his stubble looking heavier which is something I always like.

"*Hola* Nicole…" He holds the door open for me. "How are you feeling?"

"*Hola*, a little better thanks. How are you?"

I follow him down the hallway towards the living room.

"I always feel better when I see you…" He looks back at me, grinning widely. "… Always."

Me too…

As we reach the living room I'm shocked to see Luís, Raul and another of his friends who introduces himself as Carlos, lounging in front of the TV. I hadn't even given it a thought that anyone else would be here. I realise that Carlos is his old school friend that has struggled with his mental health at times.

Luís gets up from the sofa and kisses me in greeting, asking how I am and he tells Raul and Carlos about me falling off a scooter to which they both look horrified. Jesé busies himself in the kitchen and I realise I'm still standing around by the door and I must look more than a little awkward. I sit down on the other sofa and slip off my jacket, meaning that there's a seat free next to me for Jesé - unless anyone else is coming that is.

He reappears with a multitude of crisps and snacks as he leaves them on the table in front of us. He walks around the back of the sofa and he places his hand on my shoulder.

"Nic, you would like a beer or juice?"

I enjoy the weight of his comforting hand on my shoulder, trying my best not to let him see me notice it.

"Juice please."

I relax back, trying to get comfortable and Jesé returns with my drink.

We all start to chat about football and Raul asks me if I watch any English football. I tell him how I've never been able to get into it like I do with Spanish football and the playful banter then begins between the guys about their favourite teams.

The chat then changes to old stories of Carlos and Jesé's school days as I see him sink down with embarrassment into the sofa. I learn about the time that they were both kept back after school for falling asleep during a science lesson.

Jesé tells me. "We were to watch how do you say...a...a...I think a video you would call it?" he looks to me and I nod my head.

"...it was about science and..." he laughs "...It was so boring but when our *maestro*, our teacher saw us he was so angry."

Carlos laughs hysterically as Luís and Raul begin to chuckle and I too listen to the story and I find myself wondering what school was like for them here in Spain.

"Other than that..." Carlos continues. "...We worked hard and got the good grades. Especially Jesé with his drawing and sports..."

Jesé holds his hands out in defeat. "Well I knew that I needed to be fit to do the job that I wanted and I have always enjoyed playing the sports."

I sip my drink. "So did you learn your good level of English at school?"

Carlos reaches for his drink. "In Spain we begin to learn English in early school, in *primaria* and we are encouraged to practice this."

They go on to tell me how they are taught English all the way through their school years and they are told of the importance of speaking this to help them in the future.

Jesé turns his head toward me. "We have some friends who live in less…erm…tourist areas of Spain who as they have not spoken the English for many years, it would be difficult for them to communicate in English now."

"Much like me with my Spanish I did this for a while at school but then, I didn't do any for a long time and it just disappears from your head if you don't practice."

Luís brings the boys yet more beers back from the kitchen and I have another orange juice as we start to watch a Spanish comedy show.

I struggle to concentrate on the programme with all of the thoughts that going around in my head. Jesé invited me here for a drink with a few of his closest friends, surely he wouldn't do that if he wasn't interested anymore? I need to know how the land lies between us but obviously it's not the right time now with other people here for me to start bringing these things up.

We're all in good spirits as we sit chatting in between and it's been a really good night. As 11 p.m. creeps closer, the guys make their excuses and get ready to leave. I pick up my jacket and follow them to the door.

They do their manly hugs goodbye and Jesé seems to do a double take as he sees me pulling my jacket on.

"Nicole, you are leaving too?"

I don't know what to say. "I…erm." I laugh awkwardly, looking at the others who are hovering. They come back to the door to say goodnight and then Jesé and I go back inside. He leans against the front door.

"Is this your way of keeping me here? Throwing yourself against the front door." I ask.

He sniggers looking down at the floor before looking back into my eyes.

"Another drink? I have hot chocolate if you want to change from juice?"

"Hot chocolate would be good."

I slip off my jacket again, and I begin to feel nervous at the fact he wanted me to stay after his friends had left. He joins me on the sofa with my hot chocolate and another beer for himself.

"You look cosy. You are comfortable?" He asks.

I'm sitting up diagonally on the sofa with my legs stretched out, my feet almost touching his legs.

"Mmmm, really cosy thanks". I drink some hot chocolate. "Especially now I have this." I clutch my mug with both hands.

He looks pleased with himself. I decide to broach the subject of Lola.

"I saw Lola a few weeks ago…" I take another drink from my delicious thick hot chocolate.

He drops his head back in irritation at the sound of her name.

"*El veneno…*" he calls her poison. "Did she know you?"

I rest my cup in my lap. "Oh she knew me, she accused me of…of liking you…"

We look at each other.

"She also told me not to trust you and that you used to cheat on her all the time."

Jesé gasps. "…The woman is crazy, Nicole, you know that she is lying…" He looks so angry. "…I am sorry. I am sorry that you saw her and that she spoke to you like this."

I hold my hand up to get my point across. "Jesé, I don't believe her."

He smiles appreciatively at me as I carry on.

"What I can't quite believe though is how the two of you got together in the first place?"

He bursts out laughing, maybe in relief.

"We met a little over a year ago in a bar, I was waiting to be served and she approached me. She seemed very forward and quite pushy but at the time I quite liked that because I was maybe still getting over my ex-girlfriend."

"Oh…" I don't really know what to say here it's the first time he's spoken about any of his past girlfriends and he kind of looks uncomfortable."

He shuffles in his seat. "We began to talk and she asked for my phone number. We went out a couple of times and then when I met her friends, she told them that we were moving in together."

I'm shocked. "What? That's weird…"

He smiles sadly. "I think that I should have known then that it was not right."

"So what happened?" I ask, eager to find out more.

He drinks from his beer bottle before resting it on the table.

"When we left her friends that night I asked her why did she lie? She said that she was trying to impress her friends and that I should not worry. But the look on her face, she was very annoyed, I could see. I did not see her for a couple of weeks and then when we went out the next time, she seemed okay."

"What changed?" This is painting a very strange picture.

"It was a few months later when I found out that she was looking through my phone, always wanting to know where I was."

"Very insecure then?"

"She had a clever way of covering everything up, at one point she even made problems with my brother. She made me and Ramon fall out for…maybe a few weeks. He could see what she was like, but then so could I, it sounds very…it is hard to believe that we were together as long as we were. But when things were good, they were really good but looking back that was not often enough."

I try to take it all in. The lies, the possessiveness and even her causing him to fall out with his family.

"That's the thing, it doesn't matter who tells you what about someone, sometimes you need to find out things for yourself."

He thinks about what I said.

"After I met you for the second time when you were out with Luís, it made me realise that me and Lola had to finish as I was looking at another woman in the way I did with you…"

This makes me want to dance on the coffee table, but I'm calm and collected and give nothing away.

"…I tried to finish with her but she begged for another chance. Then she just turned up at the bar for Ramon's birthday." He looks at me to see if I remember and I nod my head.

"…That's when she made up the story about being pregnant a few days later. She was obviously uncomfortable around you, she could see that we liked each other." Jesé grins.

I don't quite know how to take that.

"At least you got away from her eventually." I laugh, trying to make light of things.

He holds up his arms in victory.

A moment of quiet comes as we look to each other and it's then that I realise it's raining outside and I'd say quite heavily from the noise it's making on the windows.

Jesé gets up to look outside, I turn towards him as he pulls up the blinds and see the torrential rain beating against the glass.

He points at the window. "I think this will be here for the night."

I groan, wondering if it would be really lazy of me to get a taxi to travel two streets back home…

He pulls the blinds back down, further sheltering us from the downpour before sitting back on the sofa. I rest my head back, enjoying the sound of the rain on the glass.

Jesé's then the first to speak and to my surprise he changes the subject.

"You were glad to see Laura and Diego?"

"It was lovely to see them, I left them snuggled up on the sofa together so I was glad of the invite over tonight. Thank you."

"That is no problem."
We smile at each other.

"I should go soon, I don't want to wake them as I usually do if I come back late."

"They may not be sleeping." Jesé winks.

I'm horrified. "Oh please don't."

He bursts out laughing. "Why don't you stay here?" I'm suspicious.

He narrows his eyes at me. "I do not mean like that… Or maybe I do."

I look up at the ceiling in exasperation before making eye contact again. He leans a little closer, placing his hand on my leg. "Seriously, I will sleep here, on the sofa and you can have my bed."

I quietly consider his offer.

"…Think about it. You can go straight to bed, you don't have to go out in the rain and you won't disturb your friends."

Why do I feel so strongly that I should say yes? I want to say yes…

He continues to try to persuade me. "You can borrow a T-shirt to wear to sleep. It is up to you, unless you would prefer to sleep without one…"

I ignore that comment, but in my head I'm telling him that I would prefer no t-shirt and him lying beside me. I turn my head to the window hearing the rain still pouring down.

"Okay I will, thanks."

He nods his head once as he smiles.

We chat some more about team *Mejores* and he tells me there might be another game coming up that Ramon can't make, so I can have his ticket.

He reaches to take my mug. "You have finished?" I guess we're off to bed.

He takes his empty beer bottles and my mug to the kitchen.

"Shirt…" He remembers, walking out of the living room. He returns a couple of minutes later with a pillow and a blanket for himself.

"There is a shirt on the bed for you." He sits on the edge of the sofa.

"Thank you…" I suddenly realise I don't even know where his bedroom is so I have to ask him.

I stand up. "Which way am I going?"

"Let me show you to my bedroom." He holds his hand out confidently towards the door, gesturing that I should go first.

I walk with trepidation along the hallway passing the room that I know to be the bathroom, and as I approach the next two doors I stop and allow him to go first. My stomach fizzing with nerves, he opens the second door and I follow him into the bedroom.

"Your room for the night."

The room has mid grey walls and a darker grey Venetian blind hung at the window. The double bed in the centre of the room is covered with crisp white bed linen and I see a blue T-shirt flung onto the foot of the bed.

"I wasn't expecting it to be this nice." I admit.

Here comes the awkwardness. Jesé puts his hands into his pockets and takes a deep breath.

"You have everything you need?"

"I think so, thanks."

Slowly he backs away towards the door. "Goodnight, Nicole."

"Goodnight."

He closes the door and the bedroom falls silent, a scent that reminds me of fresh laundry fills the air around me.

I look around the room and see a bookcase in the corner holding what must be about 40 books. I move closer, running my fingers along the spines of the books, reading the titles. There's a few well known murder mystery novels, some biographies, a couple of books about football and even some very old looking drawing instruction books. Several trophies of different sizes sit on display which I assume are football related.

I get undressed and slip in to Jesé's t-shirt, feeling the material clinging to my body and it feels quite erotic that I'm wearing his shirt, and I can't help but wish he was staying in this room with me. I then realise I should've used the toilet before I got changed.

I look at myself in the mirror to check my backside is well covered and I sneak out into the hallway. I walk as quietly as I can to the bathroom and close the door gently behind me.

A few minutes later I open the bathroom door at the same time as Jesé opens the living room door and we startle each other.

"Ah…" I clutch my chest and wait a second for my heartbeat to return to normal, although standing here facing Jesé wearing just his tight black boxer shorts I think that might take a while.

"Sorry, Nicole." He gasps.

I see him look me up and down at the same time that I'm doing the same to him.

"Sorry." I tell him, swallowing heavily.

We both stand in our positions, me clutching the bathroom door and him clutching the living room door simultaneously. Oh my God I don't think I can actually move, I feel like some kind of force is pulling me towards him and I'm holding on to the door to restrain myself.

Jesé seems to open his mouth to say something but nothing comes out so I do the only thing I know I can do and I tell him goodnight again and walk slowly back towards his bedroom.

"Hasta mañana." He calls after me.

I turn back in his direction as I push open the door and he's watching me. I bite my lip and close the door before crawling straight into bed.

The sheets smell of him which only make matters worse. I'm lying in his bed knowing that he's a few feet away wearing just his boxers, I don't think I'll get much sleep tonight.

I hear him opening the bathroom door a few minutes later and he walks out into the hallway. Suddenly I'm filled with nerves as I wonder if maybe he will take his chances and come into his bedroom. For a second, I think I hear his footsteps coming towards the room, in fact I know I do, but then I hear his footsteps start again seemingly getting further away before hearing the living room door close behind him.

Lying there in his bed I close my eyes and picture that night he kissed me after we had 'that' talk. That night was really important to me, it was then that I realised just how comfortable I feel around Jesé and how I'm able to be myself when we're together.

Chapter 28

I wake up to sound of Jesé in the kitchen. Last night, it took me what felt like hours to get to sleep… I just kept picturing Jesé lying on the sofa.

If I'm honest I was silently willing him to come into the room because I know that there's no way I would have rejected him last night. Although it probably wouldn't have been the best time for anything like that to have happened anyway, given my injury, but I'm not entirely convinced that I would've let that stop me. I felt so close to him last night, but I wish we'd have been closer physically too.

I get dressed and open the blinds, pleased to see last night's rain is long gone, as sunlight floods into the room. I tidy my hair up the best I can before I join Jesé in the kitchen. He has the radio on low in the background as he pours his coffee and this morning he's wearing black jeans, nicely tight around his bum and a navy blue and red chequered shirt.

"*Buenas…*" I call to him.

"*Buenas.* Coffee or Tea?" He smiles.

"Mmm, tea please."

He gestures to a bar stool before pouring my drink. I see a sketch pad on the worktop but struggle to make out what the drawing is exactly. It looks like he might be drawing some eyes.

He sits on the stool next to me, half laughing as he slides the book away from sight.

"You slept okay?" He checks.

"Eventually I did. Did you? You look tired."

He clears his throat. "Maybe we would both have slept better together?"

I almost choke on my tea, tears start streaming from my eyes. Jesé stands up to pour me some water and as he hands it to me, he rubs my back in an attempt to soothe my choking.

"Sorry." He shrugs his shoulders. "You are okay?"

I nod my head before taking another drink of water and to my surprise, Jesé kisses me on top of my head before sitting back down beside me.

"I was awake for a while and I started to do a drawing of…of you…" he shakes his head as though he can't believe what he's just told me. I can hardly believe it either, as a smile sweeps across my face. I stand to try to look at the drawing, reaching across over to the pad but he slaps his hand on mine making us both laugh.

"…When it is finished, maybe."

We hold eye contact, neither of us moving our hands away. My throat feels dry. I take a deep breath, sliding my hand away before I start to talk again.

Change the subject, change the subject…"What time are you working today?"

He looks at his watch. "I have time to walk you home first."

I open my mouth to protest but he cuts me off with a look.

"Thanks for letting me stay last night."

He smirks. "I told you, it is no problem." He drinks some more coffee.

"I hope you will…stay again?" He looks at me longingly. A smile slowly creeps up on my face as I look him in the eye, my stomach now filling with joy.

"I hope so too."

*

Later that day Laura and Diego are out Christmas shopping together so I get stuck into my book on the sofa but every now and again I cast my mind back to last night. I think of what could've happened but didn't. Why didn't I bring up the subject of us? I had plenty of chances once the guys had gone home and it was just the two of us. Isn't it crazy how you can drive yourself mad by thinking about missed opportunities?

It's only four days until Christmas and I'm even thinking twice about the fact that I haven't got Jesé a present. I spoke to Laura this morning, I'm sure she thinks I'm lying when I say nothing happened last night.

Things feel really comfortable with Jesé, it's almost like we are together in some ways which is what's making me think that we should give things a try. Have we just been rubbing along together so well that we are actually together? I know I have no interest in getting to know any other man. I lie down on the sofa, and try to think things over logically.

My mobile begins to ring not long after, which abruptly wakes me up. It's Jesé.

"Jesé, what is it with you always waking me up?" I laugh.

"I would like to keep you awake…" I can hear the cheekiness in his voice. "…you are okay?"

I rub my eyes, realising what he means. "I'm fine." I clear my throat.

"Tonight you would like to come for drinks?" He asks.

Will it be a date? I wonder in my head before he goes on to add that he and his friends always go out every year a few days before Christmas. If I don't take any more painkillers now today maybe I could have a couple of drinks tonight to help me relax and not to overthink.

I put my Christmas presents for Laura and Diego underneath the tree. It feels really festive now here in Madrid, every time I step onto the main streets I'm reminded that Christmas is just around the corner.

I think of my family back at home and realise that I have the presents they sent me in a box in my room. When it arrived I opened the box and when I saw the wrapping paper I closed it straight away and hid it out of sight under my bed. I've always been worse than a kid where presents are concerned, shaking and poking everything with my name on it, so I knew I had to hide them away.

I take the box now from underneath my bed and pop the presents under the tree. There are four from my parents along with a bundle of cards I didn't realise were there and I'm surprised to see one present from Annie.

I hold that present in my hand taking in the white paper with the penguins in the snow on it and I swallow in an attempt to remove the lump that has now lodged itself in my throat.

Laura and Diego arrive home giving me a welcome distraction. They're laden down with bags from what seems like every shop in Madrid.

"It's so busy out there Nic." Laura complains as she dumps her bags on the kitchen worktop.

I look at the amount of bags they have and stare back up at them with my mouth hung open.

"I hope for the sake of your bank balance that you don't need to buy any more presents."

Diego laughs before throwing himself on the sofa. "I think she has a problem, Nicole."

I laugh. "You'll get no arguments from me there."

Laura narrows her eyes at him before doing the same to me.

"Surely it can't be a bad trait to have to enjoy buying people presents?"

Diego pipes up. "The bad thing is that none of them are for me as I saw everything."

Laura starts to hunt through her bags. "It doesn't mean that they aren't for you though."

*

When it's time to get ready for my night out I decide I need to pull out all the stops tonight to give me that confidence boost I need. I wear my leather look leggings and an emerald green strappy top. I decide on my black ankle boots, a very fine gold necklace and some gold leaf dangly earrings courtesy of Laura.

In the living room I see Laura strewn across the sofa wearing stripy pyjamas as Diego opens a bottle of wine in the kitchen.

Laura immediately sits upright and wolf whistles. "Wow... and I thought your jeans were tight."

"Too tight?" I question her.

"Absolutely not." She winks. "Are you staying out tonight? Actually let me rephrase that, looking at you in those…" She points. "… I'm guessing you won't be home tonight."

I look awkwardly in Diego's direction as he carries two glasses of wine back into the living room. He gives me a look that tells me not to worry that he's there.

"I'll see you later." I nod my head as I say it.

*

As I arrive at the bar just a couple of streets away off the Gran Via, I see Isabel standing outside smoking and seemingly lost in thought. She wears a beautiful burgundy bodycon dress with her dark hair down and styled in very light waves. As she sees me coming towards her she smiles warmly.

"Nicole…" She holds her arms out towards me and I step into them.

"It's good to see you." I tell her.

"It is good to see you too. You are recovered?" She asks.

"Almost, thanks. How are you?"

"*Bien, bien...*" She holds up her cigarette. "…Can you believe this is my first in three days?"

"Wow…you did well."

She shakes her head. "It is the drink. I drink and I want to smoke. Nicole, please do not let me have another tonight." Isabel's clearly annoyed with herself.

She stubs out her cigarette under foot. "*Venga*, let's go inside."

Loud music plays behind the sound of chatter and the light air that the ceiling fans give out makes my hair start to blow, just gently. Now I'm here it feels so good to be out, and hearing music brings excitement about the night ahead. I feel confident tonight and that's a good start. I hesitate as I walk through the crowds not knowing where the others are and then Isabel gestures towards the far side of the bar area as she walks in front of me.

I see the others standing enjoying their drinks. Raul, Carlos, Luís and as I lock eyes with Jesé, I feel a pang of nervous excitement fill my body. I greet everyone, saving the best for last as his hand immediately snakes around my waist as I step in his direction for my kiss hello on each cheek.

"Let me get you a drink…"

"White wine please." I tell him.

He leaves his hand on my waist as he slides closer to the bar to order my drink. I then move to stand behind him taking in his fitted white long sleeved shirt and the way that it grips the muscles in his back. I'm so tempted to touch him, to give him some signals that I'm ready…to just put my hand on his hip as I wait behind him. My hand hovers there, but, something stops me. Feeling suddenly flustered I take off my jacket and Isabel takes it straight from me, piling it on to their jackets on a stool. I smile my thanks to her.

Jesé turns around with my drink and raises his beer bottle to meet my glass.

"*Salud.*"

"*Salud.*" I take a welcome drink of the crisp white wine from my glass.

He leans in closer to me as he runs his fingers down my forearm.

"You look gorgeous." He tells me.

"So do you." I reply. "I think you are hoping to pull tonight?"

He smirks. "I am hoping that I already have."

A woman with short cropped dark brown hair arrives not long after and greets Luís with a kiss on the lips I realise that this must be Ana. Luís introduces us but before Ana buys a drink, we all decide to move on to bar 'La Musica' just one street away.

I'd forgotten how cold it was until we go back outside and I'm glad I brought my teddy jacket with me. Jesé and I walk together at the back of our group.

Outside it seems that everyone's in the festive spirit and having a good time. A group of friends are singing at the tops of their voices as they stand arm in arm. Passers-by begin to join in, some stop to watch the impromptu performance of the Christmas melodies.

I look up to see the blue icicle Christmas lights hanging in the darkness above us as we turn onto the Calle de Barco.

"I love Christmas lights…." I tell him.

Jesé looks at me and then up towards the lights. "You like them?"

"I do." I smile to myself.

"You are like Christmas lights for me."

I frown, thinking that I've misheard him. "I'm what?" I smirk.

He places his arm loosely around me as we continue on.

"You, it is like you light up every room for me, with your smile…"

I can't help but burst out laughing. So much so that Luís and Raul turn back to look at us.

"I'm sorry it's just that…that was so cheesy."

Jesé laughs for a second, temporarily removing his hand from my back and placing his hands in his pockets. "I am serious." He stares at me.

I stop laughing. "Sorry…"

His arm comes back around me as we turn the corner into the next street. I see him look at the others and then back to me and then he pulls me to one side to a standstill.

"Last night, knowing that you were in my bed but I was not….."

I take a deep breath as subtly as I can. "I know, I…"

Just then Raul chooses that moment to interrupt as he throws his arms around both of us.

"Come, they are only letting a few more people into 'La Musica'"

Jesé rolls his eyes at me in amusement before taking my hand in his as we walk the few steps more to join the end of the short queue with his friends.

As soon as we reach the others, Ana makes conversation with me asking me where in the UK I'm from and how long I've been in Madrid. We get talking and I find out that her Mother is English but has lived in Madrid for 30 years. Ana seems lovely and I'm glad she and Luís are getting on so well.

Ana, Isabel and I scour the cocktail menu whilst the lads catch up. A few minutes later I notice Jesé is talking to a blonde woman that I haven't seen before. Luís comes over to join us at the bar and I'm tempted to ask him who that woman is but I think better of it.

The blonde woman is quite openly flirting with Jesé, flicking her hair back and forth and leaning down far too frequently to display her cleavage. Jesé doesn't look like he's bothered by her flirting in the slightest.

He looks like he's listening to her half-heartedly and every few seconds, I see him look at me as though he's trying to read my mind or he's waiting for a sign.

Ana and Isabel head off in search of the ladies toilets leaving me with Luís. We begin to talk, but I just can't shake off how much that woman is bothering me. Just a few minutes ago outside, we had a moment and we even held hands for rest of the walk here. I have to speak to him about us, to know if there is an 'us'.

I order a strawberry mojito for myself and two original mojito's for Ana and Isabel. As I speak to the bar man he grins at me before leaning across the bar to hear me, getting closer.

Next, whilst he makes our cocktails he shows off to the best of his abilities, shaking the cocktail maker expertly. I can't help but smile my appreciation at him. Every couple of seconds, the barman looks up at me and grins back in my direction.

My eyes flit back to Jesé and I see him staring. He makes a break away from the chatty girl as she continues to talk at him even as he walks away.

I return to the others drinks in hand, passing the cocktails to the girls and I begin to chat with Ana and Luís. I make eye contact with Jesé as he moves around next to me.

He leans into me and his lips lightly graze my ear lobe as he speaks.

"I think you are trying to make me jealous?"

I immediately get the scent of that delicious aftershave that he wears mixed in with the scent of the beer from the night. I get goose bumps.

I slowly turn my head to face him, frowning as I do so. "What?"

"I thought that it was Mr blonde ponytail."

I see him turn to look at the bar man. "Actually he does look like Hans now you mention it."

I drink some of my cocktail through the straw before he leans back in towards me.

"I know that you prefer dark haired men…"

I snigger. "Is that so?"

He holds his hands out and shrugs his shoulders. "It is true?" he goads me, digging for a response as he nudges my arm teasingly. I give him my best smouldering look but say nothing.

We each drink some of our drinks and then I slowly lean in towards him.

"What about your blonde friend?" I look in her direction as she stands at the bar.

"I only have eyes for one woman."

We gaze at each other as he slips his arm around my waist, our hips now touching. I feel so attractive around him. He really does do something to me.

"Okay so, I think that…..maybe we need to…" I start, attempting to find the right words.

He interrupts. "… Maybe you were jealous that someone was flirting with me?" He grins.

I look up at the ceiling in surrender and then back at him.

"I was bothered…" I nod my head slightly.

He pulls me closer towards him still, and I run my hand up his arm before resting it on his bicep.

His breathing changes and I feel mine do the same.

"Tomorrow night, I am taking you for dinner."

It's impossible to hide my smile. "*Una cita?*" A date?

His smile matches my own. "At last…"

Chapter 29

It's been a great night but now, at the risk of sounding old, I'm in need of a serious lie down.

I let Jesé know I'm calling it a night as he waits at the bar to order another drink with Isabel. He insists on leaving with me to get me home safely.

"No I'll be fine honestly, it's still early stay with your friends."

He shakes his head furiously. "You are not walking alone."

I pull my jacket on. "I'll get a taxi outside."

Isabel finishes paying for the drinks and turns around to join our conversation, draping her arm around my shoulders.

"I need a cigarette so I will put you into a taxi." She scurries through her bag for her cigarettes.

We both gives her a look of infuriation, although I imagine for different reasons.

Isabel tuts at him before getting the hint and throwing her smokes back into her bag.

"Well *Feliz Navidad*, Nicole..." she hugs me. "... I will see you soon I hope?"

"I hope so too, *Feliz Navidad*..." I pull away and give her a serious look. "...and no more smoking, I know you can give up."

She nods, holding her crossed fingers in the air.

I see her take in that Jesé and I are holding hands, she nudges Jesé nodding her head in agreement telling him in Spanish that it's 'about time'.

I say goodnight to the others before reaching the fresh air on the pavement outside, with Jesé closely behind me.

The street outside's still full with people spilling out from bars and making their way onto their next stop - for more drinks no doubt. We walk slightly away from the bar in the hope of getting a taxi. As we come to a standstill Jesé puts his arms underneath my jacket around my waist, suddenly making me feel a lot warmer and certainly more awake.

"Come home with me?" He asks.

I laugh to myself, holding onto his arms and enjoying the feel of his muscles and his arms around me.

"Hmmm, tempting…"

He throws back his head in laughter, knowing that that it won't happen.

"You are sure you have to go?"

"I need my beauty sleep. You see I have a date tomorrow night and I want to look my best."

I run my hands down his arms, unlacing his hands from behind my back but keeping hold of his fingers, putting some space between us.

Jesé grins. "Well he is very lucky man, your date."

"Thank you, I'll tell him."

We turn around to see a white taxi heading in our direction which Jesé flags down. As it pulls up alongside us I step to get in the car and he pulls me back by my hand. Very slowly, he moves towards me smirking before he places his lips upon mine. I can't explain how it makes me feel, I just know that I don't want it to stop. But it does.

"I will pick you up tomorrow night, at eight."

I smile softly. "I'll be ready."

I climb into the taxi, letting the driver know my address with the biggest smile on my face.

*

It's Saturday morning and I've woken up feeling surprisingly fresh, I think I did the right thing calling it a night when I did. I lie in bed thinking of Jesé, I'm so looking forward to our date tonight, our long-awaited first date. I know it's my fault that it's long-awaited but I have a feeling it'll have been worth every second of the wait. I also can't stop my mind from wondering what will happen afterward.

My bedroom door slowly creaks open and Laura pops her head around it.

"Oh good you're awake." She smiles.

"Come in." I slowly sit up, readjusting my pillows behind my back as she sits herself at the end of my bed leaning against the wall.

"I hope I didn't wake you when I came in last night?"

"No you didn't, don't worry." She grins. "Tell me all…"

I fill her in on the escapades of the night out and she's chuffed to hear that tonight we're finally going out. Properly.

"What the hell are you going to wear?" She gasps. "Maybe we should go shopping?"

My mouth drops open. "On the Saturday before Christmas, are you mad?"

"You have a point there." She pauses. "Although I do know some shops that will probably be quiet at this time of year."

"Oh?"

She takes a deep breath. "Bridal shops."

I laugh out loud. "I'm assuming you mean for you now?"

She smiles widely. "What do you think? Do you fancy a couple of hours of watching your bestie try on some beautiful dresses before your big date tonight?"

I'm filled with excitement. "I'd love to."

"It's just that last night I had a dream and I saw the dress, my dress…"

Laura is so excited that she jumps up and hugs me, almost too tightly until she realises and releases her vice like grip.

I swing my legs out of the bed.

"Let me have a quick shower and I'll treat you to breakfast downstairs first."

"Done."

*

To say I'm nervous about tonight would be a massive understatement but I'm also extremely excited. I've had a long hot shower, washed my hair, shaved all of the necessaries and exfoliated and moisturised my skin. I'm wearing a navy blue long sleeved midi dress and I'm just putting my jewellery on when I hear the intercom buzz.

"Nicole, your hunky man's here." Laura calls excitedly.

I hear her tell Jesé over the intercom that I'll be out in two minutes. A twinge of nerves starts in my stomach, as I do a final check in the mirror.

I walk into the living room to see Diego sitting at the table using his laptop as Laura prepares their dinner in the kitchen. Laura stops cooking and walks towards me when she sees me leave my room.

"Let me see…" She looks me up and down. "… You're wearing your good bra." She stands hands on hips, giving me a knowing smile. Diego clears his throat as a reminder that he's here.

"Laura…" I look across at Diego who smirks.

"What?" She looks to Diego then back at me. "Oh Nic, Diego doesn't mind, do you?"

We both look at him as Laura reaches his side.

"*Madre Mia.*" He says.

I take a deep breath as I pick up my jacket from the chair.

"Right I'm off, see you later."

"Or tomorrow?" Laura calls out.

Chapter 30

I open the door to the building and step out onto the street into the crisp night air. There Jesé stands with his back to me, his hands casually in the pockets of his jacket giving me the sense that he's completely relaxed and calm. He turns around as he hears my heels on the pavement and gives me a lovely warm smile that meets his eyes.

"*Hola*..."

I meet his side and there it is, that delicious scent he wears.

"*Hola*, Jesé."

He kisses me on each cheek very slowly before giving me a lingering kiss on the lips too.

"You like to keep a man waiting, but I see that it has been worth the wait."

I smile my thanks to him. "So where're you taking me?"

"I'm taking you to a restaurant called 'Globo's', around a 10 minute walk. Shall we take a taxi?"

I look down at my heels and consider the taxi.

"Erm…a taxi would be good if you don't mind?"

"It is no problem."

He looks up and down the street and sure enough two taxis come along. I climb into the taxi first and make sure I sit more towards the middle of the back seat so as not to be too far away, so I don't have to move back towards him when he gets in.

The leather seats feel cold against my bare legs, but when Jesé climbs in, he sits closely beside me and surprises me by resting his hand on my thigh, which makes me instantly start to warm up.

We chat about his shift at work, but all I can think about is his hand on my bare leg, the heat and what feels like electricity prickling at my skin. Less than five minutes later we pull up outside the restaurant, pay the driver and head inside.

The atmosphere in the restaurant consumes me straight away, it has a kind of rustic charm. It's dimly lit with bare brick walls, red carpet and chunky red, brown and black furniture. Small white tea light candles sit on each table. Almost every seat in the restaurant is taken, it must be good here if it's this popular I think to myself.

We're shown to our table in the corner as we take off our jackets. Jesé's wearing a smart black long-sleeved fitted top with dark blue jeans. I take another look around the restaurant to compose myself.

"I like this place, it's really cosy." I smile, looking at Jesé to see that he's watching me.

For a second I feel quite nervous and I sit back in my chair.

"What is it?" I start to smooth my hair self-consciously.

He slowly begins to grin, keeping his eyes fixated on mine.

"You really look beautiful tonight, Nicole."

He makes me smile. "*Gracias.* I have to say, you're looking pretty good yourself."

"I had to make an effort, it is our first real date."

We look at each other, tension hanging in mid-air. Suddenly he begins to speak again as he runs his hand over his chin and cheeks.

"I did think about trimming my beard down but…"

"…I'm really glad you didn't."

As soon as I hear those words leave my mouth I can't quite believe I've said them out loud and I don't think that Jesé can believe it either, judging by the look of shock on his face. We both burst out laughing just as the waiter arrives back at our table to take our drinks order.

Jesé asks me if I'd like to share a bottle of white wine which I do, so he orders a bottle and not the cheapest I note. We begin to read the food menu, but every now and again we take a look at each other over our menus, each of us catching the other one out a couple of times. My stomach's doing that lovely happy dance over and over again.

The waiter returns just then with our bottle of wine and pours each of us a glass, before taking our food order. I decide on the Iberian pork stew and Jesé goes for the chicken in tomatoes with serrano ham.

He raises his glass to me. "To our first date, the first of many."

"To our first date…" We clink glasses before taking a sip of wine.

"I take it you've been here before?" I ask.

"Actually I have not, I wanted to bring you somewhere romantic so I asked Luís for advice."

"Well Luís has good taste…" I nod my head.

"I do have good taste too…" He gestures his hand towards me. "…Obviously."

"You could have taken all the credit for this place, I'd have been none the wiser."

He thinks to himself for a second. "This is true, no actually I researched and found this place myself. I lied earlier."

I laugh. "Nice try."

"So you have been in Madrid for how long now?"

"It will be three months at the end of December so…"

Jesé looks surprised.

I drink some more wine, a large gulp (as subtly as I can) to try to combat the nervous knot in my stomach.

"It seems longer than that, but maybe for me it's because I've wanted to do this for such a long time and, I guess I've actually been living it out in my head for years." I laugh, rather self-consciously.

He smiles, leaning forward in his seat and resting his elbow on the table, as though he's really listening to me as I keep talking.

"If I had come here with Laura, like I should have…" I wonder out loud.

Jesé tilts his head to one side as he thinks before smirking in his overconfident way.

"If you had done that, we could have been married by now."

I freeze mid sip of my wine before dissolving into laughter.

"Oh really?" I ask him sarcastically. "So me coming here a couple of months earlier would mean that we'd be married…now?"

Jesé sits looking at me, smiling proudly before laughing with me.

"So you want to get married one day do you?" I tease.

"Of course. Don't you?"

This is the first time I've really thought about getting married since what happened. Even when I was in the bridal shop today I refused to allow myself to picture it being me someday.

"Yeah, I think so…" I look down at the table. "I was engaged to my ex."

He gives me a look of surprise. "The ex that your sister…"

I interrupt. "… The one that my sister." I nod my head, smiling sadly.

"Ouch…"

Jesé takes a hold of my hand across the table. "He was very stupid…but that is good for me."

We smile at each other and suddenly I feel that I want to change the subject over to him.

"How about you, ever been engaged or lived with anyone?"

He ponders my question for a second.

"Lola I think wanted us engaged, married and living together after just two weeks." We both grimace.

"…Before her…" he drinks some wine. "…there was a woman at work that I was with for maybe two years, Camila. We did speak about moving in together but…she got promoted and moved to a different station, a different city and…she moved onto another guy."

I wonder, was he cheated on too? So I ask him…subtly.

"I think maybe…but I could not prove this so…"

I nod my head. "Sometimes things just aren't meant to be…"

"This is true. Like you were not meant to come to Madrid for some reason, until you did, you had to wait until this time."

Maybe he's right. "I do believe that things happen for a reason. Maybe if I'd come here in the summer with Laura, I would never have found out what Annie and James did? Who knows but…"

Suddenly I feel his leg brush up against mine under the table and I get a tingling feeling in my legs and in the pit of my stomach. I look into his eyes, those enticing eyes and I feel my breath catch in my throat.

The waiter then arrives with our food but I feel Jesé's gaze lingering on me. I feel like he's undressing me with his eyes. I reach for my glass to see it's empty so Jesé fills it up for me before refilling his own.

I clear my throat. "Thanks." I swallow some wine in a bid to moisten my suddenly dry throat.

He gives me a slow side smile as he raises his glass to his perfect lips. This man is so sexy it's untrue.

I start to tuck into my food and Jesé does the same.

"Do you have to work much over Christmas?" I ask.

I take my first mouthful of stew which is absolutely delicious. The pork is so tender, you can tell it's been cooked slowly and the aftertaste of the sweet honey lingers on my tongue.

He swallows some food. "I am working Christmas Eve, a 12 hour shift."

"That seems really harsh, it is Christmas."

He nods his head in agreement as he cuts up some more chicken on his plate.

"People still like to break the law, even at this time of the year."

I laugh at what seemed a silly comment to make. "That's true."

"Even the thought of *Papá Noel* is not enough to stop some people."

I bust out laughing, covering my mouth with embarrassment, which then makes him laugh.

"You would like to try some chicken?" He offers, holding out his fork toward me. "It is very good."

As I take the bite of food that he feeds me, we keep our eye contact the entire time.

"Mmm…" I swallow the chicken. "That's really good." I lick my lips slowly before using my napkin. Jesé simply stares at me before shifting uncomfortably in his seat. Somehow we manage to get the conversation back on track.

"What are your plans for Christmas?" He asks.

"Diego's cooking on Christmas Eve and I think Mio's joining us. Christmas Day we're all going to the restaurant."

"Mio's will be open?"

"No, officially it will be closed but Juan will be cooking for all of us, even some of my course friends are coming along which will be great."

Jesé finishes his food and sits back casually in his chair.

"What will you do for Christmas Day?" I ask.

"It will be afternoon when I am out of bed after working so…"

"Why don't you join us?"

He leans to one side in his seat. "This would be okay?"

"Of course it would." I smile.

"I would love to, thank you."

We clink glasses and each take a sip of wine, watching each other. The waiter reappears to take away our empty plates and asks if we would like to see the dessert menu. Jesé looks at me for a response.

"No dessert for me thanks."

He smirks cheekily. "That is a shame…"

I shake my head, laughing. "I wouldn't say no to another drink though?"

He grins. "Another bottle of wine? We could enjoy it in the bar?"

"Sounds good." I smile.

The waiter returns a few minutes later with the bill for our meal and another bottle of wine. Jesé very sweetly refuses to take any money from me for the meal. I stand up and take my coat from my chair as Jesé gestures for me to go first. I follow the waiter as he carries our wine and glasses on a tray over to a small alcove at the bar area. As I go to hang up my jacket, Jesé is very closely behind me. He puts his arm around me, resting his hand on my side as he whispers into my ear from behind me.

"You really do look incredible in that dress."

He moves around me into the alcove, taking a seat as he continues to look at me. Immediately I feel the colour building in my face.

"Jesé, you really don't give up do you."

He looks around the restaurant.

"Do not tell me you have not noticed…almost every other man in here is looking at you."

I shake my head and laugh to myself.

"I mean what I say…" He drapes his arm across the booth seating so I lean back into it and turn my body in towards him, very much enjoying being closer to him.

I take my now full glass from the table and take a sip as he refills his own glass.

"So you are 30 next year, in March?" Jesé he asks me.

I return my glass to the table. "Don't remind me…"

"What will you do to celebrate? You have to do something."

An image of Annie pops into my head.

"Erm… I'm not sure." I trail off.

I feel his arm around me becoming closer and he begins to trace his thumb in circles on my shoulder, perhaps out of comfort as he senses my unease.

"Maybe things will be easier by then?" He wonders.

I wrinkle my nose in uncertainty of his theory but I say nothing.

"I just…I think back to our 18th and our 21st, maybe my 30th will be the best?"

"You told me about your 21st, she wanted the attention on her…your 18th was like this too?"

"Well…you know what, maybe it's just me?" I laugh awkwardly.

He narrows his eyes. "You would like to talk about it?"

I take a drink of wine. "We were both at college so we didn't have much money but our parents threw us a party, same place as our 21st. We agreed, no new outfits, we would wear something we already had…sorry, is this really boring for you?"

"No it is not, I am happy to listen if you are happy to talk?"

I smile, grateful that he wants to hear. "Basically, Annie was out all afternoon and when she came back for us to get ready together, she had brought a new dress and had had a makeover at a salon in town. So there she was, hair professionally styled, make-up applied perfectly and with her new dress…" I shrug…needing a drink to distract me for just a second.

"…Of course I did my hair and my make-up, chose a nice dress I just felt…"

"You should not compare yourself to her…" He takes my hand again.

"It became a habit, I always became invisible next to her. We were always compared in some way growing up together. The comments all night, Annie you look amazing, look at your make up, did you do this yourself…"

As I hear myself telling him the story I realise just how much I have let her make me feel like this. It's as much my fault as hers, I have my issues I know that. I need to leave the comparing myself to her in the past now.

"You are amazing Nicole, I do not know how you put yourself down like this. I want you to see what I see…I know that you have…struggled but you have come so far. I can see a difference in you from when we first met…"

I smile at his lovely words, unsure of how to reply.

"For your birthday, you will do something to celebrate here with us."

"I will do something definitely. Anyway, your birthday is the same day so…a double celebration…well a triple with Ramon too."

He grins. "We will have private party maybe…just you and me though."

"What did you do for your big 3 0?"

"Ramon and I went to Barcelona with friends."

He sits for a second reminiscing before a naughty looking grin appears on his face. I can only imagine what he got up to. I shake my head as I feign disgust. He bursts out laughing, throwing his head back and leaning away from me for a second before putting his arm back around me and making me feel close to him again. I cross my leg towards him, meaning my foot now rests against his leg. I watch him as he takes a drink from his wine.

"Why doesn't this feel like our first date?"

He looks at me. "Perhaps because you already know how much you like me?"

He's hit the nail on the head there.

"...normally on the first date you are...wondering how much you find the person attractive? You already know this with me."

"I'm trying to be serious here."

"I told you, our first date should have been a long time ago..."

"It should have been and that's my fault...thanks for being so patient with me."

He rubs my leg. "We already know each other really well so maybe it feels like..." He thinks. "... date number five?"

I'm taken aback for a second. "Number five?"

He grins. "... Or six?"

"I didn't think there was such a thing as date number six? Normally by then you would know if you are interested in it being something more, surely."

He laughs. "Exactly."

I drink some wine, swallowing it slowly as I try to read his expression.

He leans closer to me. "If you don't know how I feel by now then maybe you have been walking around with your eyes closed."

I study his face as I take in what he said. I can't say anything but I slowly slide my hand onto his thigh, gently caressing it as I do so, needing him to know that he's right about the way I feel about him.

He looks at my hand and then back up at me before placing his hand on the back of my neck which sends tingles up and down my spine. He lightly pulls me towards him as he kisses me deeply. I reach my hand up to his face, feeling his stubble against my hand and against my face as we kiss each other with every fibre of our being. Tonight has been way too long in the making.

We pull away for a second and grin widely at each other. I keep my hand on his jaw and stroke it gently. Jesé looks at our wine on the table and knocks the last dregs in his glass straight back before gesturing that I do the same.

"I think we should go…" his voice sounds almost gravelly with lust. I say nothing. I jump up, grab my jacket, drink my wine and am out of the door before he's even left the table.

Chapter 31

For the whole taxi journey back to Jesé's apartment we sit as close to each other as we can get. His arm sits snugly around my shoulders, pulling me closer into him. Every now and again he kisses me and all I can think about is the fact that I can't wait to be out to be out of this taxi and alone with him.

He checks his watch as he whispers. "It is almost 11…It is a good thing you're not going home you would wake Laura."

The taxi pulls up outside his apartment. He releases his arm from around my shoulders as he fumbles in his pocket for money to pay the driver.

I smile sweetly. "I don't know what gave you the idea that I'm not going home?"

He turns his head in my direction with a shocked look on his face. I raise my eyebrows to him before climbing out of the taxi. I hardly recognise the person that Jesé seems to have turned me into, a confident version of me.

I stand on the pavement as I wait for Jesé to join me from the other back door of the taxi. The taxi pulls away and we look to each other as he stands at the kerb.

Slowly, he walks over to me, holding his hand out in my direction. The night air around us is quieter now and the anticipation of what is about to happen hangs between us. I look down at his hand before taking it with my own. We smile at each other, then we walk hand in hand through the front door of his building and we walk up the two flights of stairs to his front door. He opens his door and I follow him inside, through to the lounge, taking off my jacket and throwing it onto the chair in the corner with my bag. He turns around, and slowly begins walking towards me.

"I'll just…" I point towards the toilet "…if that's okay?" The look in his eyes, it's enough to melt me on the spot but that doesn't change the fact that I'm desperate for a wee.

I use the toilet in record time and as I open the bathroom door and walk down the hallway and back to the living room I hear the gentle hum of music playing. I stop for a second and smile to myself. Pushing the door open I'm surprised to see Jesé lighting candles on the coffee table with the lights dimmed.

"Oh wow…" I say softly to which he smiles.

"I almost forgot…" He dashes to the corner of the room. I take a seat on the edge of the sofa, crossing my legs as I watch him flick the switch on the Christmas tree lights.

"It's beautiful."

He sits next to me on the sofa, taking my hand in his. "So are you."

"I just knew you'd say that." I can read his mind it seems. He roars with laughter, making eye contact with me. I lace my fingers through his, needing that connection with him.

"How's the erm…the sketch coming along?"

He laughs, glancing up from his hand as it slides from my hand and slowly up towards my elbow.

"You will not let me forget that will you?"

I giggle. "I just want to see it…"

He looks shy. "You can see it, when it is finished."

I smile, understanding his feelings.

Jesé goes to stand up. "You would like more wine? I can open a bottle."

"Are you trying to get me drunk…again?" I pull him back down onto the sofa, keeping a hold of his hand.

He looks at me questioningly. "Again?"

"I seem to remember the second time I met you when I was out with Luís, you were plying me with drinks…" I bite my lip, moving my hand through his as he does the same.

Jesé grins. "Ah yes I remember." He seems faraway in thought for a couple of seconds.

"That is when I realised how much I liked you. I couldn't believe that I had been lucky enough to see you again."

I have to say I'm stunned to hear him speak like this, along with the fact that I felt exactly the same way.

"Really?"

He looks deeply into my eyes with such a genuine expression on his face. "Really."

I can't stop smiling.

"You know that I would never do anything to hurt you, Nicole. All I want is to make you happy, to take care of you."

As I sit here with him, hearing him say these words, I instantly know he wouldn't hurt me, he's such a respectable and honest guy, I'm only sorry it took me so long to realise.

The whole conversation just feels so genuine, like we're baring our souls to each other. No more games, no more hanging around or fighting our feelings for each other. I lean towards him and he meets me halfway as we kiss again. This time, now we're alone and in private I completely lose myself.

Jesé slowly leans into me pushing me backwards onto the sofa. I ignore the slight twinge in my ribs but he pulls away fleetingly, seemingly sensing my pain.

"You are okay, your ribs?"

I adjust my position underneath him slightly. "I'm fine, don't worry."

I kick off my shoes and they fall to the floor. He hears them drop and looks back at me, smirking as he copies me by slipping off his shoes. He hovers above me with such a tender look on his face that makes me crave for intimacy with this man. I pull him back towards me and kiss him with urgency as I tug at his jumper.

He stops for a second as the jumper comes off to reveal that very welcome sight of his gorgeous body. He lowers himself back down, keeping eye contact as he runs his hand up my leg and underneath my dress, pushing it up as he does so which sends shivers of pleasure all over my body.

The way he's looking at me it's as though he's asking permission to touch me, maybe he thinks that any second I will ask him to stop or that we'll get interrupted like the last time? There's absolutely nothing and no one that will stop this happening tonight.

He runs his hand gently over my chest which makes me want the barriers between us away so that I can feel his skin against my own. I wriggle beneath him, pulling at my dress and he leans to the side as he helps me to take it off. Jesé stands up as he slips off his jeans, looking down at me as I finish undressing. He blows the candles out and holds his hand out to me, and I know he's taking me to his bedroom.

We hold hands as we walk slowly to his room. He closes the door behind us and pushes me up against it, kissing me fervently before leading me to his bed.

*

Sometime later I wake up in the pitch dark bedroom and in Jesé's arms. I notice from the clock on the bedside table it's coming up to 3 a.m. and I smile to myself contentedly as I reminisce what happened in this bed just a few hours ago. Apparently knowing I'm awake, Jesé squeezes me gently before planting sleepy kisses along my bare shoulder, sending tingles down my spine. The next time I wake up I see Jesé putting a huge mug of tea next to me.

"What time is it?" I ask sleepily.

He props up his pillow next to me on the bed so I turn over to face him, seeing him leaning against the headboard. He's wearing grey jogging bottoms and a white polo shirt and looks very relaxed and in fact, he looks very refreshed.

"It is almost eight." He smooths my hair away from my face, leaning down and kissing me full on the lips. I pull myself up so I'm sitting next to him, making sure that the quilt covers me. Jesé playfully tries to tug the covers back down so I smack his hand away.

He dons a serious look. "Last night, it was amazing."

His hand rests on my arm and he traces his finger lightly up and down. I just can't wipe the smile off my face. It was an amazing night made even better by the fact that sleeping next to him was the best night's sleep I've had in a long time.

"When I stayed a few weeks ago…"I tell him. "…and you were on the sofa…"

He grins. "The night of the torture?" he squeezes my arm.

We both laugh as I continue. "I thought I heard you coming towards your bedroom after you'd used the toilet…"

"I wanted to be here with you..."he pats the bed. "…but I knew I could not be."

I turn onto my side, facing him. "If you'd have opened the door that night…I wouldn't have turned you down."

"Now she says this?" he asks dramatically, making me laugh.

"Sorry…but, it all worked out in the end."

He nods his head. "Eventually yes and it was worth waiting for..." He kisses me on the lips. "…after your tea you should go home and get changed, I am taking you out."

"Where are we going?"

"I am taking you to the park."

"Ah, the park. I'm still trying to recover from my last trip to the park."

"This time it will be pure relaxation, I promise."

*

Jesé walks me home around an hour later and he comes inside to wait for me to get changed.

Laura and Diego are out buying the Christmas food and drink according to the note she's left me on the table. Jesé peers over my shoulder as I read the note, but luckily I manage to screw it up before he reads what it says about me 'needing plenty of food now that I'll be getting all this exercise with Jesé every night.'

"What did that say?" He stands behind me one hand on each of my hips as he looks at me intently from the side.

"Oh, nothing." I fluster, holding the crumpled note close to my chest.

Jesé smirks. "I thought I saw my name on there?" He hovers in his position behind me.

Smiling I hold the note tightly in my grip and turn around to face him, throwing my arms around his neck.

"Laura just said that she hopes I had a good night with you."

He eyes me suspiciously as he drapes his arms around me in return.

"Hmmm…"

I kiss him longingly on the lips but after a few seconds he stops returning my kiss yet holds me close to him.

"You cannot just kiss me to stop me speaking you know."

I grin mischievously. "Can't I?"

"Okay maybe you can…"

"Do I have time for a shower before we go?" I ask.

His eyebrows shoot up in surprise. "I would love to take a shower with you…"

I burst out laughing.

"...but we don't have time." He tries to keep a serious expression but he struggles to hold his smile in.

Walking towards my bedroom I carry on talking to him.

"I'll just get changed, give me five minutes."

He pops his head around my bedroom door just as I'm taking off my dress.

"I can help you to undress?"

I throw my dress playfully at him and it smacks him in the face.

"Mmm…" He mumbles flirtatiously.

He holds his hands up in defeat. "*Vale, vale* I will wait on the sofa."

Dressed in jeans and a cream jumper, I stop on the doorstep to zip up my faux leather jacket. We decide to walk to the park as it's another lovely bright day.

Stopping to buy pastries for breakfast on the way, we eat them as we go. I swallow a bite of my delicious Ensaïmada pastry and look up at the beautiful blue almost cloudless sky.

"You know what, I can't believe tomorrow's Christmas Eve."

Jesé takes a bite of his pastry, wincing as the sugar lands onto his smart grey coat. He does his best to brush it off.

"It has come around fast."

"It certainly has." I smile. "So are you like most men in doing your Christmas shopping a couple of days before?"

He sniggers. "Well…" He takes his last bite of pastry, chewing slowly before replying. "… I sent in the post my parents presents last week, my brother collected his family's yesterday so I think…I am done."

I lick the sugar from my fingers before wiping my hands on a napkin. We wait at the traffic lights to cross over onto the Calle de Alcalá. Jesé rubs his hands together to knock off the last of the sugar before winding his arm around my waist. I look at him and he begins to chuckle to himself. I'm just about to ask him what he's laughing at when he gently places his thumb on my lips and I feel him brushing what must be the sugar from my pastry away.

The lights change and we cross over the street. Jesé takes my hand in his and something seems to happen to me. I feel so much closer to him after last night but it's the way he makes me feel, not just now but all the time, he seems to really lift me. I feel so happy when I'm with him and more balanced in my mind, like I'm the person I'm supposed to have been all my life, like some sort of fog has lifted. With Jesé, my new job and seeing the faith that the people around me have in me, I feel like a new woman. My anxiety doesn't feel so much like the heavy burden it has done ever since I can remember.

We approach the Banco de España building and I think back to when I came here with Laura couple of months ago when I'd still only seen Jesé just that one time when I first arrived. I was struggling to get him out of my head back then. Little did I know what the universe had in store for me.

We walk through the gates on the Plaza de Independencia and into the park. The sun is shining but even though it's a little chilly, people are enjoying themselves just walking through the park, playing football or out on their bikes and making the most of the outdoor lifestyle that they have here.

Passing a children's playground full of bright yellow and blue slides and climbing frames with safety sand on the ground underneath, I think how I could have done with some of that sand the day that I fell and I tell Jesé so.

He laughs. "I think that you enjoyed me taking care of you."

"As much as I enjoyed it… I'm glad to be feeling better now."

We stroll slowly up the pathways that lead us through greenery.

"Seriously though…" I get his attention. "… I can't thank you enough for how you helped me after that happened."

"You do not have to thank me…although I think you did last night."

I gasp in shock as he leads me to the edge of the lake, to the boating area.

"I thought we would go out on a boat." He gestures for me to pass through in front of him.

"What a lovely surprise… unless, I take it that you'll be doing the rowing?"

He shrugs. "Of course."

"…then yes, what a lovely surprise."

The attendant holds one of the blue boats steady for us to step into. I climb in first to the rear of and take a seat before Jesé climbs into the front and sits himself down facing me. He picks up the oars and begins to row us away and out into the centre of the lake. There are just three other boats out at the moment so it's blissfully quiet.

"This is so nice." I tell him, glancing around us at the trees and at the stillness of the beautiful clear sky.

The sun lightly shimmers on the lake making the monument of Alfonso XII reflect gently into the water. Jesé watches me, glancing behind him every now and again as he rows. We float out closer towards the statue which appears really tall now as we edge closer. I take in the boldness of the equestrian figurine at the top as it sits high above the park. The detail in the smaller sculptures underneath, one of them seeming to be an angel is so delicately portrayed.

Jesé rests the oars in the boat for a second as he slips off his coat before taking a hold of them again.

"So what were your Christmas's like growing up?" I ask.

"Each year was the same really. Christmas Eve, *Nochebuena* there would be the four of us and when we were very young our *Abuelos*, our grandparents would come too for the food. We lived in Cuatro Caminos until I was 23, then my parents brought the apartment in *el centro* and they moved to Denia permanently."

"So tell me how you and Luis came to be such good friends?"

"Luís moved in next door to us when I was I think 12, sometimes our families would get together for a drink on Christmas Eve before we ate with our own family. We would go out on our bikes together and of course with Ramon too."

I smile. "So were you as cheeky as a 12-year-old as you are now?"

"Oh well, of course…"

Jesé releases the oars again into the boat, relaxing back on his elbows, his smile broadening as he continues to talk. Our boat now bobbing along gently on the lake.

"*Mamá* always would make lamb for *Nochebuena,* we have usually prawns to start and for dessert we would have turrón or polverones. Sometimes we would go to mass, although usually only if *Abuela* wanted to."

"So did you not have your Christmas presents until January?"

"When we were very young I remember it being in January, but then times they changed and when we were older, we started to have some on Christmas Day and then more on the Three Kings Day. El dia de Navidad, we would open our presents in the mornings then we would go for a long walk before another big meal together as a family."

"You sound like you really enjoyed Christmas?"

"I did, of course. Ramon and I would argue about presents even though our parents brought us the same."

"Boys..."

"You will meet Ramon, maybe after Christmas?"

"I'd love to."

"I have told him about you."

A smile spreads across my lips. "Really?"

Jesé nods.

"Hopefully only good?" I ask.

"There is only good."

I look down at the ground for a second, before looking back at him.

"You are blushing, Nicole."

Very slowly he stands up, turns around and gingerly backs up towards me, taking a seat beside me. The boat rocks gently from side to side until he sits himself down and then it settles. I lean into him and kiss him passionately and when we pull away minutes later Jesé, looks around us.

"I wish we were alone." He flirts, running his hand up and down my arm.

I gaze into his eyes. "Me too."

Jesé stands up, adjusting his jeans awkwardly which makes me howl with laughter.

"This is your fault." He gestures.

I cover my face with my hands.

Chapter 32

Later that afternoon I do my first shift back at work. It feels really good to be getting back to normal working again, although I do need to be cautious with what I'm lifting. If the trays are too heavy, I'm just carrying two plates at a time and today, I'm only doing a couple of hours to help with the afternoon rush and then again tomorrow.

Serving a table at the back of the restaurant, I see Laura come through the door and she waves excitedly in my direction. I signal to her that I'll be two minutes so she takes a seat at a table in the middle and hangs her jacket on her chair.

Reaching the bar I give Juan the food order I've just taken, pour the drinks and take them over to the table. As I get to Laura, Clara has just delivered a hot chocolate to her.

"Sorry about that." I sit down opposite her, keeping an eye out for customers.

She waves her hand in dismissal. "Don't be silly, I can see you're busy." I see the look on her face develop into a grin and I start to smirk, knowing exactly what she's thinking.

Laura dissolves into fits of giggles. I shush her as best as I can.

"So how was it?" She whispers.

I sigh contentedly. "Where do I start?"

An image of Jesé returns to my mind from last night. The way he was looking at me when he told me how he felt stirs up all of my emotions once again. I can't hide my grin from her.

Laura holds her hands out in frustration. "Nicole I need details…but judging by the smile on your face it went very well?"

"We just had the best night together and afterwards…"

"Yeaaahhh….."She spurs me on, leaning in closer.

"… Well that was pretty amazing too."

Laura squeals excitedly and I feel the whole restaurant looking at us, including Mio who's now making his way over.

I roll my eyes at Mio in apology to which he sniggers. He kisses Laura hello.

"What is this excitement? For *Navidad*?"

Laura and I look at each other.

"Of course, we're excited for Christmas." Laura nods her head to get me to agree.

I stand up ready to get back to work and motion for Mio to take my seat, which he does.

Mio looks at each of us in turn. "You think I do not know?"

Laura freezes mid drink, eyeing me suspiciously.

I look down at him. "Know what?"

He laughs to himself, throwing his head back.

"It is….how you say… obvious…"

Laura grimaces. "What is?"

We both stare a Mio, somewhat confused.

"Just look at her…" He points at me.

Why do I suddenly feel uneasy at what he's about to say?

"She has the rosy cheeks, the big smile…"

I see Laura piecing her lips together desperately trying to hide the fact that she's desperate to laugh.

"...*Enamorado*... she is in love."

For a second there I really thought that Mio was going to say something extremely embarrassing, well more embarrassing than that anyway.

I'm rendered almost speechless. "I-I I'm not..."

Laura tilts her head to one side and watches me, but no matter how hard I try, I just can't stop smiling.

"I have to get back to work." I announce, walking back towards the bar taking a deep breath to compose myself. I consider Mio's words very carefully.

Once the lunchtime rush has descended, Mio tells me to call it a day so I take off my apron and grab my bag from the back room. Walking out to the restaurant I check my phone and see a message from Jesé. I read his text telling me he can't wait to see me.

I pour myself a coffee and join Laura where she still sits, marking classwork.

"You're finished?" She smiles.

"All done."

Laura bundles her paperwork into a folder. "Good, let me just get rid of this..."

She forces the folder into her bag under the table before checking that Mio is out of earshot.

"...now you can tell me properly all about last night, I want to know everything."

I give Laura the details about our meal together, how well we got on, how sweet Jesé was with the things he said and the fact that he was happy to sit and listen to me talk about Annie. I tell her how we got onto the subject of it not feeling like our first date.

"Nic, it sounds to me like you're besotted with each other."

Here it comes again, that grin. "Laura I just can't stop thinking about him. I'm pathetic aren't I..." Laura shakes her head. "You haven't be able to stop thinking about him since the day you got here, but now...just look at you." She sits back in her seat.

"He's so easy to be around, I can be myself and we have so much in common. I've been completely honest with him and he's been so supportive."

"I'm really happy for you Nic. It's grand to see you like this, you deserve it." She grips my hand on the table.

"Thank you."

I take a drink of coffee. "Did you get the envelope I left you on the worktop last night?"

Last night before I went out I snuck an envelope with some money towards the Christmas food into the kitchen.

"Yes we got it thanks but you shouldn't have done that."

"I wanted to."

I bite my lip as I think for a moment. "So I think I need to do some last minute present shopping."

"For Jesé?"

I nod. "I was thinking maybe some aftershave although that's quite predictable so maybe a watch?"

"Sounds like a good plan." Laura checks her watch. "Time is getting on though..." she jokes "...you may not want to leave it much longer unless you fancy braving the shops tomorrow on Christmas Eve?"

"Ugh..." That fills me with dread. "Maybe you could branch out and start making watches?"

"Make a watch? It would be very girly with the coloured stones I have..." She laughs. "...although, you might be onto something there."

I throw back the last of my coffee, pull my jacket on and wrap my cream chunky scarf around my neck.

"Fancy coming to help me choose? You might get some inspiration..." I smile sweetly at her.

"No way. I've already braved the shops once today, it's a free for all out there."

I groan. "Are you heading back upstairs or staying here?"

"You know what, Diego told me to stay out for a couple of hours whilst he wraps my presents so I'll stay and chat to Mio."

"Right well I'll see you later, wish me luck."

"Good luck..."

I check with Mio what time he wants me to start tomorrow before heading outside for my very last minute Christmas shopping. I decide to head for the nearest shopping centre 10 minutes away, but tell myself I'll check out a couple of jewellers on the way there too.

I'm almost at the corner of my street when I hear a really loud wolf whistle. An image appears briefly in my mind that it's Jesé, but I convince myself otherwise as I carry on walking. Then I hear my name being called and I know it's him.

I turn around and a smile, a very big smile creeps upon my lips as I see him walking towards me. He wears black jeans, a navy blue hoodie - the white *Mejores* football emblem clear to see as his smart grey coat hangs wide open with the hood from his jumper hanging over the back. He walks to meet me, hands in his pockets looking as attractive as ever.

"I should've known that was you."

He reaches my side. "You have many men whistling at you in the street I am sure but…."

He wraps his arms around me, making me feel protected from the world as he kisses me full on the lips.

"Mmmm…" I mumble. "But I only kiss some of them like that….I'm just off to pick up a couple of things."

"For *Navidad*?"

"Yesss, just a couple of things that Laura forgot I said I'd pick them up." A little white lie.

"The game tonight, you would like to go out, or….to stay in?" There's a naughty glint in his eye which makes my nerve endings begin to awaken.

I pretend to think and I'm very tempted to say let's stay in, but, it would be good to have the atmosphere of going out with it being a big game. He hooks his hands together behind my back and grins expectantly.

"Let me see, a second date with you?"

He sniggers.

"A third, we went on the lake earlier."

"That's true…"

"But do not forget, last night we said that it was more like maybe our fifth date so now it would be date number seven."

I toss my head back in laughter.

"Tonight we will go to 'Bar Gol'. A few friends may come too."

"Shall I meet you there, where is it?"

"It is not far to walk from here – Calle de las Veneras."

I shrug my shoulders, being none the wiser knowing the name of the street.

"We could get food first, just something fast?"

"Sounds good." I smile. "Just let me know what time."

As much as it pains me I pull away from him, knowing I need to get to the shops. He keeps a hold of the tips of my fingers which now feel like they are hooked up to the mains electric supply in his hands.

"7.30...I will meet you here." He casually points to where we stand.

I start to back away, laughing just as I always seem to when I'm with him.

"I'll see you later."

He releases his grip.

I walk away and glance over my shoulder to see him watching me with his smouldering gaze. I give him a playful look in return.

"What?" He holds his arms outward. "I am enjoying the view…"

I roll my eyes and continue on my way but I can't deny that knowing he's watching me makes me walk with a bit more of a strut.

Chapter 33

After a mad dash around a couple of shops I decided on a stylish chunky silver watch. I can really picture him wearing it, but I just hope he likes it.

I shower and change and then I'm back out into the Christmas scene of the outside. There's no sign of Jesé so I lean against the wall whilst I wait.

In the darkness I can see festive lights in apartment windows and shop fronts, there's even a couple of people out walking wearing novelty hats. I think of my family back home and I wonder what they're doing. In that moment just for a millisecond, I feel slightly homesick. I guess it's hardly surprising considering this is the first Christmas in 29 years I haven't spent with my family but, I remind myself of the life I've made for myself here and how glad I am I've done it which snaps me out of it.

"You are a million miles away."

I jump at the sound of Jesé's voice, hand on my heart as I wait for it to return back to normal.

"Sorry, you startled me." *His beautiful smile.*

"You are okay?"

His hand rests on my upper arm and I get a sudden need to be close to him. I move my body into his, allowing his arms and his scent to consume me. He squeezes me gently, and I can tell by the look on his face that he's contemplating my thoughts.

"You are thinking about your family?"

"How did you know that?"

"You have a look in your eyes."

He places his hand on the back of my neck and allows his thumb to gently stroke my cheek as he looks into my eyes.

"You are missing home?"

"No, I'm not missing home exactly, it's just because it's Christmas and I won't see my family and things with Annie are…" I shudder.

He smiles sadly giving me a tender kiss on the lips.

"You will speak to them tomorrow and on Christmas Day."

"I will, definitely."

"If you would like you can call them now, we can go to my place to watch the game if you would prefer this?"

"You're really sweet sometimes you know?"

He looks around us. "Ssshh…I do not want people to know this."

I prod him in the side. "No, I'm okay." I take his hand in mine. "Well, I am now anyway."

We take a walk to an Argentinian fast-food restaurant that Jesé tells me he loves. We eat smoky chicken burritos and share some fries before carrying on to the bar just a few streets away.

As we approach the door hand in hand, Jesé casually drops into conversation the fact that his brother, Ramon is here.

"So I get to meet your brother?" I notice that this is something that would normally put me on edge, but I feel comfortable about it.

Inside, football fans wait for the game to start. Two huge projector screens hang at either end of the bar showing the match build up. Jesé takes my hand and leads me through where immediately, I spot his twin brother Ramon as he stands at the bar chatting to Carlos. Ramon looks the spit of his brother, but he has maybe a slightly younger looking face as he's freshly shaven.

The brothers embrace each other and speak in Spanish each asking how the other is, before I see Ramon's eyes flick across to me and a welcoming smile appears on his face. Jesé takes a step towards me and places his hand on my shoulder.

"Ramon, this is Nicole. Nicole, this is my brother, Ramon."
Ramon places his bottle on the bar next to us and leans towards me.

"Nicole, it is a pleasure to meet you at last." He kisses me on each cheek.

"*Hola* Ramon, *encantada*."

"I think that you have, how would you say…….tamed my brother?" He laughs, making me look across at Jesé to see him smirking.

"Oh I don't know about that."

Jesé moves closer towards me next to the bar, placing his arm around my waist. He asks me in Spanish what I would like to drink.

"Erm…." I glance around the bar at the multitude of beers, and optics on display. "…*una cerveza*."

He asks Ramon and Carlos what they would like and he orders four beers from the bar, his arm doesn't move from around my waist and I revel in the feel of his touch. You'd think I'd be used to it by now but I just can't get enough of that feeling of being closer to him.

Checking my watch, I see it's just a few minutes before kick-off so I pop to the ladies before the game starts.

As I leave the toilet cubicle and wash my hands, I glance in the mirror above the sink and I see a woman with long dark hair just closing the door behind her as she goes into a cubicle. I do a double take as for a second,

I really thought she was Lola. Thinking nothing more of it, I check my hair in the mirror and dash back out to the bar just in time for kick-off.

During half time everyone dashes to the bar to order more drinks, it's getting really busy in here now. I feel my mobile vibrate in my back pocket and when I look at the screen its Annie calling.

Part of me really doesn't want to answer it, but maybe it's time to speak to her. I have an excuse to get away with being out, so I signal to Jesé that I'm going outside to answer my phone. He gives me the thumbs up as I slip through the throng of people and out into the cold night.

"Hi..." I answer. I notice how flat my voice sounds.

"Hi Nic. Are you watching the game?"

"Yeah, I've come outside to answer."

I glance around and I'm shocked to see Lola just standing, glaring in my direction. I turn my back to her and continue talking to Annie but I can feel her eyes burning into the back of my head. Feeling slightly uncomfortable I look back at her again before moving further away. She's actually making me feel quite weary of her now – the way she's staring at me. With Lola here and the frostiness I feel talking to Annie, I find it hard to concentrate on either of them. A feeling of being surrounded creeps in on me.

"How're things? Are you out with Jesé?" Annie asks.
As soon as she mentions Jesé I feel myself get defensive. I don't want to discuss him with her.

"With Jesé, his brother and a friend." I feel the need to change the subject as silence hangs between us. All I can think of is how I wish I hadn't answered the phone.

"Is everyone ready for Christmas there?" I glance over my shoulder to see that Lola, to my relief has disappeared. I turn to look through the window but I can't see her.

Annie talks about Christmas and then she tries again to bring up the subject of Jesé. I know that she just wants us to be back to normal and this is something that we would normally talk about but, I can't. She shouldn't be surprised that I don't want to talk about my love life with her. I ask how Pete is, to which she tells me they're talking more as he comes to see Amelia most days.

Ending the call feeling agitated, I go back inside and suddenly I'm stumped. I see Lola glancing around before she approaches Jesé who has his back to her. I stand still to the other side of the room, watching her.

She puts her arms around him from behind as he faces the projector screen. Ramon and Jorge stand facing the bar, oblivious to what's going on next to them. Jesé seems to relax back into her and takes a hold of her hand as it rests on his chest. I take a deep breath in to calm my annoyance.

Suddenly Jesé looks down at her hand on his chest and turns sharply to look over his shoulder. He's taken aback as he breaks away from Lola. She simply stands there smirking, hands on her hips. I've never seen Jesé look so annoyed as he asks her what she thinks she's doing. Carlos and Ramon turn around and are shocked to see Lola standing beside them. Ramon swiftly moves beside his brother as I make my way slowly towards them.

Arriving at Jesé's side, Lola pushes him as she shouts viciously before noticing me arrive alongside them.

"Oh here she is…" She waves her hands in my direction before proceeding to call me a few un-pleasantries in Spanish that she thinks I can't understand.

"I told you what he is like. He was….he was…all over me just two seconds ago, now do you see?"

I stare at Lola, unable to speak for a second as she's blatantly lying and trying to cause trouble.

Jesé tries to speak. "Nicole, I thought that it was you, she put her arms…"

I ignore Jesé and direct my annoyance straight at Lola.

"I saw exactly what you did…" The agitation from my call with Annie fuels my anger with Lola.

Apparently sensing Lola's aggressiveness, Ramon moves to my right-hand side as I hear Carlos asking the barman if they have security.

Lola lays into me. "You only see what you want to see…but YOU stole my boyfriend." People are starting to look now.

I roll my eyes which only seems to antagonise her as she lunges at me. Thankfully Ramon pulls her back just in time. Jesé steps in front of me and holds his hand out to tell me to stay behind him.

"Nothing happened between us when he was with you!"

"Your boyfriend he will cheat on you….and I hope that he does."

I don't know what I'm more surprised about - the fact that she's clearly out of control or the fact she just called Jesé my boyfriend.

At that point, two security guards arrive and take her from Ramon's grip and start to lead her away, but not before she manages to get one hand free enough to take a swipe at me.

She grabs a hold of my upper arm and as I try to shake her off, she grabs at the sleeve of my top and rips it leaving a nasty scratch on my arm as she does so. I gasp in shock. I think that's the closest I've ever come to being hit in my life. The security guards pretty much have to drag her outside.

"What the hell…" My legs feel like jelly as I try to process what just happened. I take a deep breath, resting against a bar stool.

Jesé puts his arm protectively around me. "You are okay?"

"I think so, I don't think my T-shirt is though." I gesture at my ripped sleeve.

I can only imagine what a state I look now standing in a bar with torn clothes. Jesé holds me closely to him and I can feel the frustration of the situation oozing from him.

Jesé looks to Ramon before turning back to me.

"I am taking you home."

We step out onto the street and begin to walk in the direction of home. My first thought is that Lola could still be around, I'll be glad to get home. The street is fairly busy so as subtly as I can, I scan around us in the hope I can't see her

"She will be gone now, she won't want to get into trouble with the police." Jesé assures me.

"It seems to me that is exactly what she wants…for you to arrest her, she would probably like that very much."

"You are sure that you are fine? We can sit down for a while…" He nods to the wall next to the community garden.

I pull my jacket around me. "I'm fine, I was just shocked that's all."

He places his arm around my shoulders.

"I feel bad that she tried to hit you like that. It is my fault."

"How can this be your fault Jesé? You didn't ask her to keep showing up and causing trouble. She's obviously not over you."

"Well I am sorry. I am glad you saw what she is capable of with your own eyes tonight."

"Not the best first meeting for me and your brother."

"Ramon knows exactly what she is like…do not worry about this."

We walk on, a few seconds of calm silence between us.

"Nicole…" Jesé starts. "…you know that I am not interested in anyone else….not since I met you."

Hearing him say these words puts the biggest smile on my face and certainly takes my mind off things.

"That's good to know." I grin.

He looks at me in disbelief before breaking into laughter and before long, I'm laughing along with him.

"I am serious." He stops walking and turns to face me, now with his arms around me.

As we are now on the busy Gran Via, all I can hear are people huffing and puffing at us. People are bashing into us as we stand in the middle of the bustling street, looking into each other's eyes.

"Even when I went for coffee with Sara, the woman that you saw me with…all I could think about was you and how it felt wrong to be with someone else…."

A group of joggers round the corner and almost bash into us.

With my hand on his arm I gesture for us to move back towards the shops. "I think we might be slightly in the way here."

"I do not care." He smiles. "I mean what I said. Since the first time that I saw you, I could not get you out of my mind. I do not want anyone but you, Nicole."

"I feel the same."

All I seem to do is smile when I'm with him, it's like he's switched on a light inside of me and now my whole life is lit up ahead of me whereas before, I struggled to find my way, to find my place in the world.

He continues. "Before I met you I was with Lola but it was wrong, it was not a good... relationship. Before Lola I was very hurt by Camila and I just needed to feel wanted again. I will probably never know if Camila cheated on me but the thought that it was possible...it made me doubt that I am good enough."

"You are more than good enough..." I tell him, cupping his face in my hands.

"You have made me see this Nicole...now how about we... I..." He struggles to get his words out. "*Citas*...dates, no more." He shakes his head. "Just...you and me are together?"

I realise what he's just asked me and I can think of nothing I'd like more. I make him sweat for a few seconds before replying.

"I'd like that."

He grins before kissing me tenderly on the lips. I do my best to ignore the fireworks that I can feel exploding in my body.

"Now I think we'd better make a move before we become the most hated couple in Madrid." I motion around us.

Jesé sniggers. "*Venga.*"

We walk on, hand in hand.

Jesé raises his eyebrows. "It is a shame for the night to finish now, it is not even 10."

"Mmmm…" I smirk.

We're about to turn the corner into Calle de la Salud, my street and I feel Jesé hesitate. I keep a hold of his hand and walk past my street and on towards his.

"Maybe we should go back to your place…as its still early." I smile playfully.

Jesé then picks up the pace as we continue onto his street, and I do my best to keep up with him.

Before I know it we're through the door and up the two flights of stairs to Jesé's front door, both giggling as he slams and locks the door before we race through to his bedroom. He lifts me onto his bed as we begin to undress each other.

"Eres tan hermosa Nicole, quiero besarte y estar conmigo para siempre." He whispers and all I can say is, it's a good job I'm not standing up as I go completely weak at the knees.

Chapter 34

It's very much Christmas Eve as I walk back into the apartment at around 6 p.m. the next day, after working a few hours at the restaurant and helping to close up early for the evening. Spanish Christmas carols are playing loudly as Laura and Diego prepare the food in the kitchen.

They don't hear me as they have their backs to the door, I stand and watch them for a second enjoying seeing them singing along together, until Diego spots me.

"Nicole, Merry Christmas…come and join the *fiesta*…"

Laura runs towards me her arms open wide. "*Feliz Navidad*…"
I laugh at her excitement but I have to admit it's infectious.

"*Feliz Navidad*." I hug my friend in return before hanging up my coat on the rack. "Are you drunk?"

Diego bursts out laughing. "She has had one glass of the fizz and she has the excitement like a child."

"Diego, pour Nicole a glass." She pulls me towards the kitchen as Diego hands me a glass.
I raise my glass to them both. "*Salud*."

"*Salud*." They repeat as we clink glasses.

I roll my sleeves up. "Right what can I do to help?"
In Spanish, Diego asks me to help Laura chop the mushrooms whilst he prepares the shrimp. I get straight to work alongside Laura.

Diego really seems to know his way around a kitchen as he instructs us both in what to do next.

"I told you that I am to cook tonight ladies, there is no need for you to help me to do this."

I'd feel awful just sitting back whilst Diego does all the work and I tell him so, much to Laura's annoyance judging by the look on her face.

"Pah…I'm not sure I'd feel so bad." She jokes, taking another drink from her glass.

Diego laughs, creeping up behind her holding the fresh shrimp in his hands and dangles them in front of Laura's face making her scream loudly before running out of the kitchen and diving onto the sofa.

"Diego, you know I hate them."

"How can you hate them?" I ask her. "I've seen you eat those loads of times."

Diego shakes his head in an attempt to stop laughing.

"She will eat them yes but to touch them…not cooked, for Laura, she cannot."

An hour or so later Mio arrives with two bottles and the biggest smile on his face.

"*Nochebuena*….I cannot believe it is *Navidad* again already."

"Mio you always say this every year." Diego recalls as he takes Mio's jacket from him.

When Mio is in the room he always brings so much love with him, he has such a kind heart that it makes you want to look out for him. No wonder he has so many friends that he counts as his family.

Diego forces us out of the kitchen so Laura and I sit with Mio on the sofa, relaxing back and enjoying his tales of Christmases when he was younger.

When we finally sit down to eat at a little after 8 p.m. the whole apartment looks and smells perfect. The aromas of mixed herbs and garlic with the delicious looking sherry sauce to go with the mushrooms that Diego has made makes me remember just how hungry I am.

We sit at the beautifully decorated table with the lights aglow on the Christmas tree. Laura's really made an effort with a red tablecloth, gold place settings and red and green candles dotted down the middle of the table.

Laura and Diego sit next to each other as Mio and I sit opposite them. To start, Diego serves up beautifully tender mushrooms in the garlic and sherry sauce and that wonderful fresh shrimp that he terrified Laura with earlier. She's enjoying tucking into it now that it's cooked and Diego teases her once again about that as he drapes his arm around her shoulders.

Mio places his cutlery down onto the table as he turns to me.

"*Chica*, I hope that he will make you this happy." He nods his head towards Laura and Diego.

"Jesé?"

He nods.

I feel slightly self-conscious but as I look at Mio, I can see how much he cares about not just Laura and Diego, but me too. He's genuinely so proud of them and that's clear to see.

"Do you know what Mio…I think he will." I squeeze his hand as it rests on the table next to me.

Mio looks really happy. "Where is he tonight?"

Laura gives me a knowing smile from the other side of the table as she hears Mio's probing questions.

"He's working but once he's had some sleep tomorrow…"

Mio interrupts. "… He will come to the restaurant?"

"Yes he'll be there."

"Good, I speak to him then."

Diego stands up to clear the table and as he does so he tells me in jest that Jesé had better watch out.

*

Christmas morning was quite a different scene to back at home, but in a good way of course. I woke up to a text from Jesé that he sent me at a little after 7 a.m.

"*Feliz Navidad, bonita.* Can't wait to see you later so you can unwrap your present :)"

That immediately put a smile on my face.

I spent around half an hour talking to my parents on video on my laptop. Annie and Amelia were there too which was sort of strained in way with Annie. I won't have to see her very often is how I'm trying to think of it. I can't believe how quickly Amelia has grown, she loved the presents I brought for her, well she seemed to, it's not like she could actually tell me she did.

Usually, Annie and I go a bit crazy at Christmas buying each other quite a few gifts, but this year, it just felt really odd. I couldn't bring myself to buy her anything. I feel even weirder about that in the fact that she did buy me something but I still haven't been able to bring myself to open it.

We've had a lovely lazy morning together, the three of us. Laura and I devoured a box of chocolates before we even got dressed. I spoke to Laura's family for a few minutes too before leaving her and Diego to chat to them whilst I got ready for the lunchtime feast.

*

Christmas lunch downstairs at the restaurant was absolutely delicious. Juan certainly surpassed himself by cooking a wonderful seafood soup and he decided to cook delicious turkey and all the trimmings. He even cooked a mixture of prawns, mussels and lobster in a bid to cater for all of us.

Here we sit around the long line of tables we pushed together this morning, now tastefully decorated with candles and the remnants of the multiple Christmas crackers that Laura spent weeks hunting around the shops to buy especially.

There's been such a lovely atmosphere all day. Everyone has got on so well we've laughed and sang and obviously eaten enough food to last for the month as is always the case on this day every year. I couldn't have wished for a better Christmas day so far but as I see Jesé walking through the door, I know that it's about to get even better.

There are lots of jovial cheers being shouted over the gentle hum of the background music as he makes his way through the restaurant towards the empty seat beside me at the end of the table.

He and Diego shake hands on his way past and Laura kisses him hello, which then makes everyone stand up in greeting as he walks past. He receives kisses from Eva and Nadia and hugs and handshakes from Greg, Leon, Tymec and Hans as he continuously casts his eyes in my direction in between the pleasantries. Next there's Juan and his partner Javier and then Mio stands up to be introduced to him as Jesé finally reaches my side.

Almost as though Jesé can't wait a second longer to be in contact with me he slides his arm around me as I introduce him properly to Mio and his oldest friend Sebastián and they shake hands. As everyone retakes their seats and chats amongst themselves, Jesé pulls me in to his embrace kissing me firmly on the lips.

"I thought I would never get to you…" He whispers in my ear, laughing at the amount of people he's just encountered on his way in.

We stand together with my arms around his neck and his around my waist and I notice how tired he looks. I suddenly realise he hasn't really been properly introduced to all of my friends from my course.

"Guys…" I look to them at the other end of the table. "I should introduce you properly, this in case you haven't already guessed…is Jesé." Then begins another chorus of hellos and raised glasses.

Jesé hangs his jacket on the back of the chair revealing a beige fitted chunky knit jumper.

Juan stands up. "Jesé, you have been working I will get you food, there is more than enough left over."

Seconds later, a plate of food arrives in front of him. There's turkey, lamb and all manner of vegetables followed by a large glass of white wine of which he takes a huge gulp.

As Jesé eats, he asks me about our *Nochebuena* last night. I regale him with details of how entertaining Mio was as we ate and how he even played us a few songs on Diego's guitar. I warn him about the promises he made to speak to him about making me happy to which he laughs, taking a glance at the man himself. Jesé puts down his cutlery taking my hand, before looking in Mio's direction to put his mind at rest. In Spanish he tells him I'm the best thing thats ever happened to him. I try to hide the shocked but delighted look on my face but I'm finding that hard to do. Mio looks elated as he raises his glass to me

Once suitably filled with food, Jesé relaxes back in his chair retaking a hold of my hand on the table.

"You have spoken to your family?"

I sip my wine. "Mmm, this morning for about half an hour."

"Your sister?"

"She was there too with Amelia." I nod. "She brought me a present, it actually arrived with my parents presents weeks ago but I haven't been able to open it yet. Does that sound stupid?"

"Of course not, I understand." He moves my hand to his lips and plants a kiss. "Maybe you could open it later."

I smile at him, grateful for his understanding.

There's more hustle and bustle as various plates and bowls are placed in the middle of the table.

"Dessert." Juan declares "Please…eat, *comer*."

In the middle of the table sit two traditional Christmas puddings, two jugs of custard, home baked polvorones, mazapan cookies and mantecados. I always love Christmas pudding and custard but in a change from tradition a little more this year, I decide to go for the mazapan cookies followed by a few polvorones too.

As Jesé has never tried Christmas pud and custard, he decides to go for it.

"Do you like fruitcake?" I ask as he puts himself a slice of pudding before passing the spoon onto Greg as he eagerly awaits a few seats down.

"I think so." He smirks as he pours some custard. "I just thought that as it is my girlfriends Christmas tradition…" He grins, taking a glance at me. "….that I should try some."

I love hearing him call me that.

"*Chica*…."Mio calls out, bringing his seat closer to the table opposite me. "I have your first job, as my manager and….my organiser of the events."

"Ohh…" I turn myself back around to face him to listen keenly. "*Digame*." I ask him to tell me the details, feeling the excitement rise in my stomach.

"*La Noche Vieja*…we are to have party here, at the restaurant. You will arrange it, yes? For New Year's Eve."

"I'd love to." I tell him. "So I only have six days to organise?"

Jesé laughs. "You can do this, easy."

My enthusiasm kicks back in. "Oh thanks Mio, I'm really looking forward to it."

"Just remember, a party…I want people to dance, to drink. I want the atmosphere in here to be *perfecto*. It is practice for the new room."

My head starts to spin with ideas of decorations, food, music and the like, until Jesé snaps me out of my planning.

"Do you think we could go for half an hour, maybe we could go for a walk?"

"Sure."

Having some time alone together sounds good to me. We pull our coats on as I tell Laura we won't be long, to which she kisses me on the cheek.

It's starting to get dark as we head outside and there's a stillness to the air that tells me that most people are tucked up indoors with their family and friends and making the most of the day.

Jesé places his arm protectively around my shoulders as we casually stroll along and I in turn, put my arm around his waist feeling the warmth that his body radiates.

"How was work last night?" I ask.

"It was okay… I was thinking of you, wishing I did not have to work."

I squeeze him against me. "I wish you hadn't had to work either."

We round the corner onto the Plaza del Carmen and take a seat on the steps that lead into the square. It's nice to be outside and I take a couple of deep breaths, enjoying how refreshing the air feels tonight. Although if the truth be told, I don't enjoy that as much as I'm enjoying Jesé's arms around me. We snuggle next to each other and I put my head on his shoulder, letting the calmness of outside relax me even further.

"Do you want to open your Christmas present?" He asks me.

I take in the look on his face and cast my eyes downward to which he laughs loudly.

"No, really, I have brought your present with me." He reaches into the inside pocket of his coat and produces a wrapped box.

"Oooh…" I beam excitedly. "When you said open my Christmas present I thought you meant…." I raise an eyebrow suggestively which makes us both laugh.

"You can open that later." he suggests.

I suddenly feel quite alert. "No puedo esperar…" I tell him I can't wait, rather flirtatiously to which he takes a deep breath before exhaling with a whistle.

I clear my throat. "Sorry."

Jesé moves my hair away from my face and looks at me meaningfully.

"*Feliz Navidad*, Nicole." He hands me my gift. I tear off the wrapping paper to reveal the perfume that I tried whilst out shopping with Luís.

"Oh Jesé, thank you so much, I love it." I open the box to reveal the gorgeous deep purple coloured bottle and waste no time in spritzing the perfume on to my neck.

"Let me see…." Jesé leans in to my neck to take in the scent before planting a couple of kisses there making me squirm with delight. He then reaches into his coat pocket and produces another present in a small red gift bag.

"Another one?"

He laughs. "Of course…it is Christmas."

Inside the bag sits a small box and when I open it, I see a beautiful pair of stud earrings in the shape of daisies.

"Jesé, they're just…they're exactly the sort I would choose myself. Thank you."

I remove the studs I chose earlier today from my ears and in go my new daisy earrings. As I don't have a mirror, I lightly touch my finger to my ears to feel them in pride of place.

"Here…" Jesé retrieves his phone from his pocket and puts his camera on selfie mode for me to admire them properly.

"They look perfect. Thanks so much." I kiss him on the lips.

"De nada."

He takes a photo of us together with his phone and I admire it with the biggest smile on my face, happy to see the picture of us as a couple.

"I actually have a present for you too but it's at Laura's…*venga*…" I stand up holding out my hand towards him. He laughs, kind of self-consciously I note before pulling himself up onto his feet and joining his hand to mine.

We walk back to Laura's apartment and as we go through the door he notices my present from Annie with the gift tag clearly visible, still in its wrapping paper on the kitchen worktop. He picks it up and gives it to me.

"Maybe you feel like opening it now?" He wonders out loud.

I look at the package in his hands and back at him before looking back at the present again.

"I want you to open your present first." I reach under the Christmas tree and hand it to him. He looks really chuffed and he hasn't even opened it yet. I think I hold my breath in anticipation as I wait for his reaction.

He unwraps the present slowly and when he opens the box to reveal the watch, a look of surprise registers on his face.

"Nicole, I love it thank you so much. *Gracias*." Phew.

He removes it from the packaging, taking off his old watch with the scratched clock face and he puts his new one onto his left wrist, admiring it again.

"It is a perfect fit too." He pulls me towards him, pressing his lips against mine.

"Now it is your turn." He tells me, sliding the box from my sister across the kitchen counter towards me.

Part of me wants to leave it, a way of not 'letting her in' to anymore of my Christmas day. I decide to open it so that it's done then, rather than leaving it to haunt me until I do it.

As I tear the paper off and lift the lid I'm taken aback by what I see. There sits a stunning silver bracelet with the words *'your dreams are now your reality'* inscribed onto it, it's such a thoughtful gift.

I take the bracelet out to look at it closely, and at the words and the sentiment. The words ring so true - it took me 13 years to get here but my dreams are definitely now my reality.

"This gift, it means very much to you?" Jesé asks.

I nod. "She's trying I guess…" I still can't bring myself to put the bracelet on.

He takes my hand. "She is right, just look at what you have achieved coming here on your own."

"But I knew Laura…"

"But you did this for you, for yourself. You didn't follow Annie, you didn't wonder what if…"

I interrupt him. "Actually I did wonder what if for a long time before I…" He shoots me a look of annoyance which makes me purse my lips together.

"The point is that you did what you wanted, you came here to Spain to live a life you always dreamed of. You did not stay in your sister's shadow, you did not let your anxiety hold you back anymore. You are living your life, you have found yourself."

My breath catches in my throat and it's almost as though in that second just then, I realise that he's right.

"…and I met you." I smile, feeling emotional.

He places his hands either side of my face. "I am so glad that you did." I rub his arm affectionately, being unable to wipe the smile away.

"I know that you won't forget what happened but life is too short. Do not waste it by being angry with her - that will only affect you more. Maybe it will make her realise too, if she has not already done this that she needs to treat people differently. To treat them with love and compassion like I know that you do."

I stand in silent thought for a moment, he gives me time to get my head around things.

"…maybe if you had not fallen out with your sister, maybe you would not…..have had the…" he stands, frustrated to which I giggle at the look on his face.

"What am I tying to say?" he grimaces. "Without contact with Annie, constantly asking her for her opinion you have succeeded, you have done this yourself. You do not need her to protect you or to control you. You do not need to feel invisible, you should never feel like this, Nicole. You are your own person too and I think you now know this? You have the confidence to be you, perhaps more than you have ever had?"

Wow, he's good. The realisation sets in further. I feel like I can start to try and put this behind me. I certainly won't forget what she did and things won't go back to how they were, I don't think they ever will and I'm not sure that I'd want them to.

Chapter 35

"I'm so glad you like your present, sis." Annie tells me as I call her to thank her, which I felt was the right thing to do.

"I do, so thank you." There's still a frostiness there, I can hear it oozing from my voice and right now that feels impossible to remove.

"I'm so proud of you, I….I have no idea if I have the right to be proud of you anymore?" She half laughs, seeking my permission.

I make a promise to myself there and then to live my life for me. Not to be second best and wonder what could have been. From now on, I will always go for what I want, I owe myself that.

Back down at the restaurant, the atmosphere's still relaxed, although people look as though they are starting to wind down for the evening.

"Where have you two love birds been?" Eva sings as we walk back in, her arms firmly around Connor's shoulders.

Jesé pours each of us a glass of white wine as we take a seat next to Hans and Tymec. I notice Hans looking intently at Jesé as he leans closer to us.

"Does this mean that I have lost my salsa partner?" He gestures to the two of us.

Jesé looks at me as I laugh light-heartedly.

"Well Jesé won't be there at our lessons each week so I guess I'll just have to keep getting better with you Hans." I raise my glass towards him to which he lifts his bottle of beer.

"That sounds good to me." Hans agrees.

Jesé joins in. "As long as you don't teach her to be better than me, then I do not mind."

Hans holds out his fist towards him to fist pump. It's great to see Jesé getting along with my friends.

That night, I stay at Jesé's apartment. After walking back the long route much to his insistence (he wanted me to see the Christmas lights on Christmas day again as he knows how much I love them) we then couldn't wait to be alone again.

We're now curled up on the sofa together watching TV. It feels so right just sitting together with candles glowing on the coffee table, creating a sense of calm as we sit with a mug of tea on our laps. It's the perfect end to a perfect day.

"You are happy?" Jesé asks.

I place my hand on his thigh leaning towards him, towards those lips.

"Very."

He smiles, leaning in to kiss me to which I playfully move back slowly, bit by bit, giggling until I surrender.

"You look happy." He notices.

"Well, I guess maybe, some of that might be because of you." I shrug my shoulders nonchalantly, taking a drink of tea. "Although I have drunk a lot of wine today."

He nudges me playfully. "Well you make me very happy, Nicole."

I have a sudden thought. "You're not working New Year's Eve are you?"

"No, I am not so I will be there. I might even let you…how you say…boss me around? If you need any help."

"Ooh, tempting…"

My phone on the coffee table beeps with a message. Annie has sent me a picture of Mom and Dad asleep on the sofa next to each other with their obligatory glass of Christmas cream liqueur in their hands.

"Do you have New Year's resolutions? I know that is what English people do."

I think for a moment. "Well, to be honest I can't wait to get stuck into the event planning side of things at the restaurant, so just to do a good job of that and, I'd like to find a room to rent to give Laura and Diego their home back." I finish my drink and return my glass to the table. "How about you?"

Jesé swirls his drink around his glass.

"Maybe to play football more often again, and I would also like to do more exercise in general."

I nod in support, lifting my feet up onto his lap. His expression then becomes serious.

"I would also like for my girlfriend to move in with me…"

"Really?" I look at him in shock. He rubs my feet as they sit on his knee, turning to face me.

"Yes really. I know that it maybe is soon?" I don't know what to say. "…but I have known you for four months now and…" He shrugs his shoulders and seems to be lost for words but then so am I.

I'm pretty sure I'm in love with him which is something that I've known for weeks now, but here I was thinking it's too soon to tell him that, and now he's suggesting that I move in with him. I have to say that the thought of moving in with Jesé fills me with nothing but joy but could it be too soon?

He carries on. "… I wouldn't mind doing this every night with you, when I am not working. Amongst other things of course." He smirks.

"I wouldn't mind doing any of those things either, but I just don't want things to move too quickly and then…I don't know."

"There is no pressure of course." He smiles at me reassuringly. "Just take some time to think about this."

I give him a long kiss on the lips. "I will."
I nestle in beside him on the sofa, thinking that this Christmas can't possibly get any better.

*

Waking up on Boxing Day morning, I'm really eager to get the planning started for our New Year's Eve party at the restaurant. After leaving Jesé in bed which wasn't easy, I'm showered and changed and sitting at the table at Laura's making lists of my ideas.

The first thing I think of is entertainment. I wonder if Gael would be interested in DJ'ing for a few hours for us so I decide to drop him an email to see if that's something he'd be interested in. Next, decorations.

I have visions of little red lanterns all along the window sills and across the bar to give a lovely ambience to the place along with some tasteful balloons dotted around. I make a separate list of things I need to buy, adding red lanterns and battery tea light candles to the list which means we don't have to worry if someone accidentally knocks a candle over. I figure that they'll be a good little investment for our future events too. I also have visions of some sort of confetti dropping from ceiling at midnight but that's something I'll look into once I get downstairs later as I can't really remember what the ceiling looks like in terms of lights etc. Ah, fairy lights too I remember, adding them to the bottom of my list.

I can hear movement from Laura and Diego's bedroom as Laura gingerly creeps out from behind the bedroom door still in her pyjamas with her hair scraped back from her face.

"Morning." I say, which seems to be a bit of a shock to her system judging by the look on her face.

She holds her head. "Nic, I didn't hear you come back."

I laugh. "I haven't been back long."

I take a sip from my glass of juice on the table before making my way into the kitchen.

"Why don't you sit down?"

She makes her way to the sofa and lies down exhaustively.

"… Or lie down." I continue. "You look like you need a coffee?"

"Oh you're a lifesaver." She groans.

I make us both some coffee and sit on the armchair. Laura pulls herself up into a sitting position to face me.

"How come you look so….perky this morning? Or is that a stupid question considering where you spent the night?"

"Well there is that…" I blush. "…Mio asked me last night to plan an event for New Year's Eve at the restaurant, he wants a party."

"Oh wow that'll be great." she smiles. "Hopefully my hangover will have disappeared by then."

"There is something else actually Lau…."

She drinks some coffee. "Go on…"

I take a deep breath. "Jesé asked me to move in with him last night." Her mouth falls open.

"That was pretty much the same response I had."

"You're joking?"

I move forward in my seat. "I know…I couldn't believe it either."

"Did you say yes?" she asks.

"I told him I'd think about it."

She leans her head to one side. "You don't want to yet?"

"That's the thing, I think I really do…" I grin. "I don't want to rush things though, I had images of me renting a room somewhere, so I'd be out of your hair."

"Nic we told you there's no rush, stay as long as you want."

"It was just so unexpected. He was great about it though, told me there's no pressure and to think about it, but now it's all I can do to *not* to think about it…"

We both squeal with excitement before remembering that Diego is still asleep in the next room.

*

Later I'm strolling around one of the stores at the shopping centre with a basket full of items thinking that I really should have gone for a trolley, when my phone starts ringing. I pause in a corner, gently placing my bulging basket down on the floor. As I see my phone screen I once again get that pang of pleasure as I see it's Jesé. I feel my smile grow bigger as I answer.

"*Hola…*"

"I don't mind admitting that I am already missing you, Nicole."

"Well I would have invited you shopping with me but…" I glance around at the now huge queue at the tills.

"… *vale*, I am glad that you did not."

"You see I'm always thinking of you, I just couldn't put you through shopping with me. I don't think you're quite ready for that yet."

He laughs loudly.

"What are you doing with your day off?" I ask.

"Well I was thinking about our new years' resolutions, me playing more football and I decided why wait until January?"

"Mmmm…" I agree.

"But can you believe that no one wants to play football today? I think, from yesterday…"

"Yeah maybe it's just a little too much after all that food and drink."

"So I have been for a, how you say, a jog?"

"Oooh, I'm impressed." I nod my head as an image of Jesé in shorts appears in my mind.

"Only because you are thinking of my legs."

I gasp quietly, he has literally just read my mind.

"Well, I won't deny it." I glance around, feeling like people around me can tell what I'm thinking too.

"Hmmm, I thought so. I will let you see them later…perhaps."

I smile in anticipation. "I'll go straight to Mio's from here, I can't wait to show him what I've brought. Fancy meeting me there later?"

"Yes of course, I'll see you there."

Chapter 36

At Mio's a bit later, I'm giving him the lowdown for our big night.

"Juan has decided on his menu for the evening..." I count on my fingers. "...my salsa teacher has agreed to DJ, all of the decorations are sorted so I think we're nearly there." I smile with excitement, wondering if Mio has taken all of this in. He smiles and shakes his head in disbelief.

"*Chica*, you have arranged this so quickly, I know it will be a fantastic night. I have been telling the customers and they cannot wait."

"You don't think the regulars will be put off with the DJ?"

Mio holds up his hand in protest. "No, no. People here, we love to dance and that is what this place needs..." He points at the air enthusiastically. "It is practice for our new events room."

"Maybe Sebastián can play his guitar so it's something people are familiar with?" I offer.

Mio laughs. "Nicole, do not worry...people they love this."

I grin excitedly, pushing my paperwork back into my folder before tidying the lanterns back into the bags.

"Actually Mio, I had another idea, for when the room is up and ready."

Mio knocks back his espresso. "More ideas?"

He holds the bags steady on the table as I repack them with my decorations.

"Maybe we could offer flamenco classes? Maybe Spanish lessons too, and I thought maybe meditation classes?"

"*Buenas ideas*..." He pulls me into a hug. "With all of these plans...the room, it could be used most days."

I just feel so elated at how my new job and project is coming together.

"You have someone waiting for you Nicole, no more work talking." he nods his head in the direction of the bar.

I see Jesé sitting at a table, happily sipping from a mug of what looks suspiciously like tea. I stroll over to him and am met with a huge smile before he stands and kisses me fully on the lips.

"That was a welcome…how long have you been sitting here? You should have joined us."

He retakes his seat and I sit down opposite him.

"I have enjoyed sitting and watching you…" He does that eyebrow raise again that makes me feel giddy.

"Hmmm…"

"I love to see you like this, so…enthusiastic…." he leans closer and whispers. "…so *passionado*."

I start to blush, but only slightly, feeling boosted after hearing that.

"I feel so passionate about it." I can hardly keep still I'm buzzing so much.

"You do not feel as passionate as you do about me though." He sits smug, to which I playfully tut. He knows he's right.

We move over to one of the booths by the window that has just freed up and Jesé slides in on the seat beside me, draping his arm across the back of the seat behind.

"Are you hungry?" I take a look at the menu on the table.

"You work here, you do not know the menu?" He teases.

"That doesn't mean I can't read it though."

Clara approaches the table and asks if we want to order any food. We're just about to order when Laura and Diego stroll through the door hand in hand and head for our table.

"Hey you two, mind if we join you?" Laura asks.

"Of course not." Jesé gestures to the opposite side of the booth.

Clara smiles, telling us she'll come back to us for our order.

"You look better now." I tell Laura.

She breathes a sigh of relief. "Diego made me one of his hangover cures."

"Oh?"

"It is only some tortilla, it is the eggs, very good for you." Diego tells us.

Laura eyes the menu in front of me and slides it across the table.

"However, it's now made me famished."

"Famished?" Jesé looks at her, furrowing his brow.

"Starving, hungry…" She tells him.

The restaurant is fairly busy now as I look around us and I start to wonder if I should offer to help out. Jesé looks at me suddenly.

"No, no, no…you have been working this morning."

I roll my eyes. "Shopping is hardly working Jesé."

Laura joins in. "Actually…it was."

Jesé points to the mound of shopping bags in the corner next to the bar.

"It is your time off now."

"Okay you win." I give in. I put my hand on his thigh. "Let me just squeeze past you for the toilet though."

As I leave the toilets, a few minutes later I catch sight of myself in the mirror and I do a double take. My hair is just in a simple half up half down style as I pulled it back for shopping earlier, but it's shinier than it's looked in a long time and despite hardly having any make up on, my skin is glowing, the shadows under my eyes barely visible now I'm finally starting to sleep better. Living here is definitely agreeing with me.

I walk back to the others at the table, and is it me or do they all stop talking when I get back? Jesé slides over to the other side of the seat so I'm now sitting opposite Laura.

"Jesé was just telling us about how he will teach you to cook paella." Diego offers, sensing my suspiciousness.

"Was he now?"

Jesé nods in agreement.

"Maybe you should teach me something else? If I make paella better than you did, it could get quite awkward." I tell him.

Laura joins in. "Nicole makes a mean Sunday roast, Jesé."

"I look forward to trying that." He rubs my leg. I love the fact that we can't keep our hands off each other.

We spend the rest of the evening sharing some tapas and we try a couple of Juan's new rustic pizzas that he plans to cook for the party. We talk about what we'd normally do to see the New Year in if we were back at home and we even talk about their wedding plans. Laura and Diego decide to call it a night quite early on, leaving the two of us alone.

I nestle against Jesé's arm until he wraps his arm around me.

I look up at him. "You will come to the wedding won't you?"

"Of course."

"You will have to meet my family though."

"Well, I will be my charming self."

Back at Jesé's we spend the rest of the night talking about anything and everything. We even book our flights back to the UK for Laura's wedding, deciding on staying for just three nights. We book into a hotel not far from the venue. I know we could stay with my parents but with Annie being there a lot as my parents are helping with Amelia, it would be too much too soon. Plus I want me and Jesé to have our own space.

We listen to music and it's gone 1 a.m. by the time we call it a night. As we climb into bed, he pulls me close to him, looking me in the eyes. I close the gap between us as we kiss lovingly. He pulls away, still looking at me. I trace the line of his beard with my thumb feeling so contented.

"I love you, Nicole, *Ti amo*."

I don't even have to think about my response. "I love you too, Jesé." He grins, before chortling timidly. He strokes the side of my face and I hold his hand as it passes my lips, planting kisses upon it.

Chapter 37

The next few days are filled with shifts at Mio's, more party planning and I even have time for a catch up with Luís over lunch. I'm so pleased to hear that he and Ana are coming to the big party. Klaudia will also be back here in Madrid after spending Christmas back at home, so all of my course friends will be there too, I can't wait.

I'm in the kitchen at the restaurant with Juan, discussing the food for the party (which is tomorrow night) as Juan prepares an order of gambas for a customer.

"I will start to prepare tonight a lot of this food, Nicole." he then switches to Spanish and lists the items he will prep tonight, the items that will have to wait until tomorrow and then the food which he can't prepare until the very last minute.

The plates of gambas and patatas bravas are then ready for service. I pick them up and walk back around onto the restaurant floor announcing it to the two regulars, Pablo and Mía. As they tuck into their tapas they ask me about the party and they tell me how much they're looking forward to it.

As I turn around and walk back towards the kitchen, the bell tinkles above the door signalling more customers are coming in. I change direction and as I meet their side, I gasp out loud my hand flying to my mouth.

"Mom? Dad?" Are they actually here in front of me or am I imagining it?

They walk towards me, arms held wide open and pull me in for a hug.

"It's so good to see you, Nicole…" Mom says.

Dad steps back and watches on for a second, grinning like a maniac. I surprise myself by almost getting choked up. Mom switches positions with Dad as he takes me into a hug.

"I can't actually believe you're here." I'm in shock.

Mom stands beside me clutching at my hand. "This place is just as I imagined, it's so Spanish."

I giggle at her words, throwing my arm around her shoulder and pulling her towards me. It's then that I realise I'm taller than my Mom, how did I not notice this before?

Seconds later Laura creeps through the door with a guilty look on her face which soon changes to self-satisfied smile as she sees the three of us in deep animated conversation.

"Laura, I can't believe you did this." I walk towards her, my arms enfolding her petite frame.

"Actually, I really wish I could take the credit for this."

I release her from my hold as she glances at my parents, all three of them are now all smiles.

"It was Jesé's idea." Now I'm shocked.

She continues "Jesé wanted to surprise you but he didn't know how to get in contact with them so he came to me for help."

I stare at the three of them in disbelief.

"So when did you all cook this up?"

"Erm… Christmas Eve?" Laura asks them to which they both nod in agreement.

Mom retakes my hand. "Jesé even booked our flights but he wouldn't take any money from us. He helped us find somewhere to stay…" She pauses in thought. "… One of your other friends I think works in a hotel?"

I wrack my brains and then it suddenly comes to me, Isabel is the general manager in a local hotel. My mind is spinning.

My Dad steps closer. "I think I like your new young man already, Nicole. Although…I'm having some trouble pronouncing his name."

Mom, Laura and I all burst out laughing. I rub my Dad's arm affectionately.

"Don't worry Dad, I'm sure you'll get the hang of it."

Just then, Juan presses the service bell. Laura steers my parents over to a free table in the middle of the restaurant.

"I finish at five so I won't be long." I call out to them.

Juan sees my look of surprise as I take the next batch of food out. He asks me if my parents have arrived, it seems like I'm the only person that didn't know about this. I can't believe how much trouble they've all gone through to keep the secret.

It hits me what Jesé has done for me. Arranging all of this, paying for my parents' flights, and helping them to get a hotel.

I take the next plates over to table two and when I come back, I see Mio has introduced himself to my family. My Dad is patting him on the back as they stand next to the table.

"*Chica*…" he calls out to me, I head in his direction. "…your family are here, come…" He tugs at my apron "… take this off."

I do as I'm told and sit myself down next to my Mom who hugs me yet again, filling me once more with that familiar scent of home. Mio then brings over a tray filled with glasses of sherry for everyone.

"Jesé is at work until six but hopefully you can meet him tonight."

Mom sips her drink, marvelling at the taste. "Oh yes I know, he told me."

I look at her in bewilderment.

"He wanted to meet us at the airport but he couldn't change his shift."

"I... I don't know what to say." I lean back in my seat.

Mom prods me mischievously, with that playful glint in her eye that I haven't seen for a long time.

"Tell me Nicole, is he as gorgeous as I've been picturing?"

*

A couple more drinks and an hour or so later, Mom, Dad and I decide to take a stroll. Not wanting to head too far out, I take them to the Puerta del Sol.

"Nicole love, Annie thought about coming with Amelia but she thought, well *we* also thought..." she gestures to her and my Dad. "...that it might be too much."

I smile sadly. "It would've been..."

Mom rubs my back, tears glistening in her eyes.

"We do understand why you feel like you do, please don't think that we don't."

"Thanks Mom."

Dad puts his arm around me. "I'm sorry if I tried to force you to speak but…I know we need to leave you girls to it now. It's not our business…" He rubs my back gently. "…We're so proud of you for doing this, coming here…dealing with…with your worries. We know how hard it's been for you throughout all of this, but what you've achieved here…."

I can't believe I'm hearing him say this.

"…I know it hasn't been easy…but we're so proud of you." He kisses me on my forehead before sliding over to my Mom and leaving me for a second with my thoughts.

The temperature seems to have dropped a little and I spy my Mom linking arms with my Dad to keep warm as they take in the atmosphere. It's bustling with people walking in every direction around us. I explain to my parents how at midnight on New Year's Eve, it is Spanish tradition to eat 12 grapes, one for each strike of the bell on the famous clock. They believe that it will bring them good luck for the year ahead.

To my surprise, my Dad seems to be really taking everything in. From the lighting on the beautiful buildings, to the chatter of the people around us, even though it's not exactly quiet here you can just tell that people are less tense and are enjoying the laid-back pace of life.

We come to a standstill next to the statue of King Carlos III.

"What do you think?" I ask them.

Mom breathes in loudly, smiling to herself. "I just want to take it all in Nicole, it's wonderful."

I'm so pleased to hear her say that. "Dad?"

"Huh?" He asks, seemingly coming out of his daydream.

"I take it you like it?"

"Yes I certainly do, it seems very…cultural."

Mom and I take a sneaky glance at each other in amazement. We continue to meander along the Puerta del Sol, starring up at the Christmas Tree sitting proudly in the square as it glows with its silvery blue lights.

"Do the Royal family live here in Madrid?" Moms asks.

"Apparently they live just outside of the city. The Royal Palace in *el centro* is so beautiful though, Mom…" I suddenly have an idea. "…. we could do the tour of the inside whilst you are here?"

"That would be superb."

My mobile starts to ring and I realise that it must be Jesé.

"Hi…" I say, glancing at my parents who give me a knowing look. "You're too good at keeping secrets…" I walk ever so slightly away from them.

Jesé tells me that he's just finished work and wants to come and meet us straight away so we arrange to meet in a bar close by.

My parents look at me expectantly. "Yeeessss that was Jesé." I link arms with my Mom.

"I think it's about time you met him." Suddenly I have a knot of nerves in my stomach as I lead the way.

As we open the door to 'Bar Suerte' I see Jesé leaning casually against the bar. From behind I see he's wearing his smart grey woollen coat over black jeans with brown shoes.

The moment he turns around, I completely forget about the nerves that I'd been feeling. His smile and those kind eyes completely engulf me and I can't wait for my parents to meet him.

Jesé extends his hand out towards my Dad and they shake hands.

"Clive, it is a pleasure to meet you."

"It's good to finally meet you too, erm…Jes…"

I cut in, to rescue Dad. "…Jesé." I smile, gently nodding my head towards Dad who looks at me in relief. Jesé sees the funny side and attempts to stifle a laugh. I see my Mom tidying her hair as she watches on before Jesé turns his attention to her.

"Maggie…" Jesé again holds out his hand in greeting but he also embraces my Mom, giving her the kiss on each cheek to which I note she looks absolutely thrilled. Mom keeps a hold of Jesé's hand, she looks absolutely enthralled by him and who can blame her?

Mom manages to find her voice. "At last we can put a face to the name."

"I can see where Nicole gets her beauty from." He really is using every line on them which makes me laugh.

Jesé gestures towards an empty table. "We should sit down."

My parents lead the way and as we follow them, Jesé puts his hand on the small of my back rubbing lightly which sends a tingle up and down my spine.

"You are okay?" He asks.

I smile back at him. "I'm more than okay, thank you so much for this."

He stops walking and plants a kiss on my lips.

Mom asks Jesé about Christmas as I sneakily try to teach my Dad to say my boyfriend's name.

"So Dad…" I subtly lean across the table towards him. "…Just remember that a J is pronounced as a H…"

"Hezzie…"

I burst out laughing, I just can't help myself and before long Dad is joining in. Jesé and my Mom turn to look at us and I can tell by the look on Mom's face that she knows what we're doing.

The waiter arrives with our drinks. An orange juice for me, Mom has a gin and tonic, Dad a whiskey and Jesé a beer. Mom briefly touches her hand to Jesé's as it sits on the table.

"Please don't think that Clive is being rude Jesé…" She has the perfect pronunciation. "…but he isn't the best at pronouncing certain words. The girls and I have spent years trying to tell him that the word finger begins with an F and not a T." She shakes her head.

"I'm not that bad." My Dad laughs along with us.

Jesé grins in response. "It is okay, if you are struggling, you can call me Jes?" But as he's still pronounces this with a J, my Dad still struggles which only entertains us more. In the end it sounds like my Dad is calling him Jess, but thankfully Jesé doesn't seem to mind.

I tell my parents more about my new job and about the party for tomorrow night. They then start to ask about how the two of us met which makes me blush.

Jesé smiles confidently as he tells the story of how he was on duty when he helped me with directions, literally as I first arrived here. My Mom starts 'ooh-ing and ahhh-ing.'

As he regales them about how we then met again a week later through Luís, he gives me the occasional side glance as he speaks, but I watch him intently. Somehow it feels really heartfelt as he talks and in some strange way I feel as though I'm hearing this for the first time. I delicately rest my hand on his leg as he talks, as I suddenly feel the need to touch him, to be closer to him, to let him know that he has come to mean so much to me.

My Mom looks emotional by the end as she places her hand on her chest.

"Well that's just so nice and you two make such a lovely couple."

My Dad raises his glass towards us.

Jesé takes my hand from his lap and kisses it as he looks at me and I surprise myself by feeling emotional too. I think he realises this as he moves closer and puts his arm around me.

"Maggie, I think Nicole is feeling…how would I say in English?" He looks to me for help.

"*Emocional?*" He says in Spanish.

"Emotional." I laugh. "Well it's your fault."

Chapter 38

I wake up the next morning to see the sunlight attempting to make its way through a tiny gap between the blinds. I turn to face Jesé who is still sleeping peacefully on his back. I watch him for a few minutes lying there and I think about the trouble he went to, getting my parents here to see the New Year in with me. I kiss him lightly on the cheek, that recognisable feel of his beard prickling my lips, before I climb carefully out of his bed. I pull on my jeans and jumper from the night before and creep out into the kitchen with the intention of making him breakfast.

Opening the fridge I remember a conversation we had a while ago about how he doesn't really cook very much, which explains the almost empty fridge. Luckily he has three eggs and I spot two slices of bread so I make him poached eggs on toast. I'm just pouring his coffee when he wanders out of the bedroom wearing just a pair of navy blue stripy pyjama bottoms and his glasses.

"This is for me?" He asks as he reaches my side, putting his arms around my waist from behind and squeezing me against him, making me almost spill the coffee.

The thin material of his bottoms does nothing to distract from what is clearly on his mind. He rests his head on my shoulder giving me a playful look. I know that look and he knows exactly what it does to me so I try to compose myself by making a joke.

"If you had enough eggs I would have made you some too."
He gasps, pulling away from me before realising that I'm joking with him.

"Of course it's for you…" I hold a plate out towards him and he kisses me on the lips before taking a seat on one of the stools and tucking in.

"Good?" I lean against the worktop, sipping my tea.

"*Sííí…*" He mumbles his appreciation.

I leave my cup in the sink and run the pan from the eggs underneath the cold tap. I look back at him to see he's watching me.

He smirks. "It is like…you live here already."

I lean my head to one side thinking about his words. "I guess it is." He looks me in the eye as he eats his last mouthful of his breakfast.

"I will not say anything more…" He holds his hand up as he walks towards me, placing his plate in the sink with my cup. "… I will just…*espere*…" he starts in Spanish. "I will wait…"

*

With just three hours to go until the party starts, I've placed the little red lanterns with the 'fake' candles in them along with the window sills and across the bar. I've hung gold fairy lights around the archway into the kitchen and wrapped them around a few of the pillars.

I managed to get hold of a few transparent large helium balloons, which are filled with gold confetti that I've just left to float up to the ceiling. Around midnight we'll burst these so that the confetti floats down onto everyone.

Directly opposite the door to the restaurant, I've strung a large '*Feliz Año Nuevo*' sign and draped gorgeous fairy lights down the whole of one of the walls in the restaurant. There, all done. I breathe a sigh of relief and sit myself down, taking a gulp from my bottle of water as I admire the decorations. I think I've done a good job, even if I do say so myself.

Juan comes out from the kitchen bringing yet another pile of plates loaded with napkins and placing them on the table ready for the buffet. He asks me in Spanish if I've finished decorating to which I tell him I have.

He flicks off the light switches next to the bar and I get a glimpse of what it will look like later on with the fairy lights sparkling and the candles glowing. I have to say, it looks so effective and once the guests are here and the music is playing, I think the atmosphere will be perfect. The lights go back on so I switch off the candles and fairy lights until later.

The next task is to move the tables and chairs around to create a huge area in the middle just like we had for Mio's birthday party a few months ago.

My phone vibrates in my back pocket and I see that my Dad has sent me a picture of my Mom eating *churros* at the Mercado de San Miguel. I love this. It's great to see my parents embracing some of what Spain has to offer. I would have loved to have gone out with them today but I was desperate to do a really good job in preparing for tonight. It will all be worthwhile later, and then I still have two days to spend with them before they go home.

Just as I'm finishing up decorating and I've helped Juan and Javier (who he's dragged in to help us for the evening) in the kitchen as much as I can, Laura walks in.

"This place looks amazing."

"Thanks Laura, I'm so excited now."

"I've just dropped some more jewellery over at the shop and now I've come to take you away. I've booked us both in to have our nails done for your special night." She tells me.

"Laura you're a star, let me just grab my jacket."

*

Tonight, I'm wearing black jeans and a shimmery grey one shoulder top with my new earrings from Jesé. Thanks to Laura's thoughtfulness, my nails are now a beautiful vibrant red.

Laura and Diego are having a pre-party drink in the kitchen before we leave. Laura wears her jeans and Royal blue halter neck top but it seems that as Diego is wearing a similar coloured shirt he's pleading with her to get changed.

"Do you think we look too much like we're matching?" Laura asks me.

"No of course not, it doesn't matter that you're wearing similar colours does it?"

Diego huffs loudly to which Laura rolls her eyes.

"Exactly. You see Diego, it doesn't matter."

She places both of her hands on his chest in an attempt to talk him around.

"Just remember that you look hot, and that's the main thing." She kisses him, she certainly knows how to win him around. As they stand smooching in the kitchen I think it's time that we made a move.

"Okay you two, that's enough we've a party to go to."

With the party due to start at 8.30 p.m. we arrive just before eight so I can make sure all of the fairy lights and candles are on for the full effect and that Gael is ready to start playing the music before everyone arrives.

Gael has just finished setting up his equipment as we walk in and Mio is sneakily stealing a few bits of food from the buffet table. I say hi to Gael, leaving him to start the music - he starts with some recent chart songs to get people in the mood straight away. Already the atmosphere is just what I had hoped for and the room is still virtually empty.

Mio's face lights up as he realises that we're there. He looks very handsome in a smart black shirt with grey trousers.

"Mis dos chicas favoritas." He calls us his two favourite girls as he pulls us into a hug before telling us how beautiful we look.

"Ahem…" Diego clears his throat jokingly to which Mio tells him that he looks muy guapo.

Diego starts to turn on the candles and fairy lights for me before buying the first round of drinks.

Mio gives me his verdict as he takes in the overall finished look.

"The room Nicole, it looks…*estupendo*."

"*Gracias* Mio." I'm so glad that he likes it.

A group of locals arrive first and are impressed with the room décor and they say how different the place looks. My parents are next to arrive.

Mom has on her special occasion black sparkly dress and Dad looks good in a smart shirt and jeans. I hug them both hello before getting them drinks from the bar.

Laura leaves Diego chatting to Gael as she brings me yet another drink.

"Another already?" I ask.

She touches our glasses together. "That's the beauty of New Year's Eve and we have a lot to celebrate this year."

I look around us, taking it all in realising that I'm suddenly nervous. I take a deep breath.

"You're nervous?" Laura asks, nudging the stem of my wine glass towards me.

I grit my teeth together. "I wasn't, but seeing people arrive…well I sort of am now."

Laura laughs, moving to stand next to me. "Don't be, you've done such a brilliant job in a short space of time."

"You think?"

She rolls her eyes. "Will you look around us?" She gestures. "… and I don't just mean tonight either."

"Laura, thank you." We continue to glance around, waving at another couple of regular's as they walk in.

She nudges me. "I've always loved New Year's Eve, there's always sort of…an anticipation, an excitement that anything can happen."

She turns back towards me. "I want you to remember that Nicole. This year coming, think of everything that the new you has achieved and think of the excitement of everything that lies ahead. Leave everything else in the past. Just keep doing what you've been doing and focusing on the positivity…your anxiety will get the message and one day, hopefully it will ease away so much you'll barely notice it's there"

"I don't know what to say Laura, so much of what I've achieved I have you to thank…"

"...No no...all I did was offer you a place to stay and you did the rest." She takes a hold of my hand. "... I want you to remember that too."

I start to feel emotional so I pull her in for a hug.

"...I'd say that a certain someone has had a massive positive effect on you too."

We pull apart as she nods her head towards the door and I turn to see Jesé arriving with Luís, Ana, Raul and Isabel. Jesé comes straight over to us as the others hang their coats on the rack near the door. He kisses me in greeting, smelling as divine as always, but it's a different scent to the one I'm used to him wearing, it seems more woody, a spicy scent.

"You would like drinks?" he asks us motioning to the bar.

Laura looks at her glass. "Not for me just yet thanks, Jesé." She winks, leaving us alone.

"Nicole, you are looking...." He looks slowly down my body before meeting my eyes. "....Wow."

I feel my face heat up. "Stop..." I giggle. "New shirt?"
He's wearing a crisp white short sleeved fitted shirt which shows off his masculine shape.

"Yes, I have dressed to impress you."

"Nicole..." Isabel sings as she reaches my side kissing me on each cheek.

"It's so good to see you, Isabel. I can't thank you enough for helping to get my parents in at your hotel."

She shakes her head. "It is no problem, I have just met your parents actually, they are so nice."

Raul appears next to me passing me another glass of white wine as he kisses me on the cheek.

I notice Isabel is drinking, I can't help but look at her suspiciously. "So you are drinking, does that mean that you will be smo…"

"…Nicole, I have not smoked since our night out last week. Can you believe this?" Isabel grins, excited to tell me the good news.

I look to Raul who nods his head. "It is true, I have not smelt any smoke, and she has not brought any cigarettes. Even El Dia di Navidad, no smoking and she had the wine."

The four of us get talking about our Christmases and eventually, once Luís and Ana have snuck away from Mio, they join us. The music then changes to Isabel's favourite song so she drags Raul away to dance. It's great to see so many people dancing this early on.

Luís leans in towards us. "Nicole, I have some good news for you."

"Oh?"

"My cousin Moya, her roommate is moving out in a couple of weeks if you are interested?"

I feel disappointment wash over me. I glance sideways at Jesé but his expression is unreadable.

Luís continues. "I have told her all about you and she wants to meet you, but I think the two of you would become friends."

Now I feel torn but I do my best not to show it. "Thanks, where does she live?"

"She is in Tetuán, where we grew up." He gestures to the two of them, making me look at Jesé again.

"It is a good area." Jesé assures me, nodding his head.

It had always been my plan to rent a room somewhere but then when Jesé asked me to move in with him I couldn't stop thinking about it. It does make me feel really excited to think about waking up next to him every morning, what more could a girl want? Tetuán feels so far away from Jesé, from work from Laura and the life that I have here.

Ana tells Luís that she wants to introduce him to a friend of hers who's just arrived so they excuse themselves, which then leaves the two of us alone again.

We both go to speak at the same time which makes us laugh.

"You are confused now?" He asks me.

I surprise him, and even myself by saying. "No." I shake my head in absolute certainty.

"You are not?"

I throw my head back in laughter, moving closer to him. He puts his hand on my hip.

"Jesé, since you asked me to move in with you it's all I can think about."

A slow smile creeps upon his lips. "Really?"

"Really." I nod my head. "So what, we've only known each other a few months, but I think I know you pretty well by now."

"I know you very well." He teases.

"I've wasted enough time in the past…so if you still want me to, then I'd love to move in with you."

He moves his hand to the back of my neck and pulls me towards him, kissing me passionately. When we break away from each other we both have huge smiles on our faces.

"Woah you two, you're in public you know..." Eva says.

"Eva, you're here..." I throw my arms around my friend.

"Sorry we would've been here sooner but we went to a bar for drinks first and we couldn't get taxis but we're here now."

I look over to the door to see Greg, Klaudia and Tymec strolling in. Hans follows with who I assume must be his date and Nadia and Leon are hand in hand behind them. Gael chooses this moment to start playing salsa music to which I hear my Mom cheering excitedly from the back of the room.

I look at my watch and think of the wise words that Laura said just a few minutes ago. There's something I need to do. I grab my bag and my jacket from the kitchen and head out onto the street before I change my mind.

Before midnight, before this year is over I want to speak to Annie so that I can leave the worst of things in the past before the New Year begins. I dial her number and she answers on the first ring.

"Nicole?"

"Hi, it's me."

"I didn't expect to hear from you, I'm so glad you've called."

I look up at the dark sky closing my eyes momentarily.

"Well to be honest I didn't expect to be calling you but..."

"I miss you." She tells me.

"I can't pretend that I don't miss you too because I do but...it's the 'you' that I thought that you were..."

Annie starts to cry.

"… I also can't tell you that I forgive you because I can't, not yet." I feel better just for saying how I feel.

"I understand…"

"In time maybe I will, but I don't want to keep holding onto this tension between us, it's not healthy. I want to be civil."

"I know I don't deserve your forgiveness but maybe one day…"

I wipe away the tears I didn't even realise had fallen.

Annie keeps talking. "I think that maybe you and I being apart is better for you."

I wasn't expecting that. "What do…"

She interrupts. "…I know that I've always made you feel like you can't be you…I know I've always tried to be the centre of attention. I made you feel like you had to hide away. I…I don't know why I'm like that, I just…." She gulps. "It's my fault, I'm the reason why you've been worse since James, I know that and I'm so sorry I'll never be able to tell you just how ashamed I am to have done that to you."

Hearing her admit that is a big step and it makes me realise yet again just how different we are as people, because I could just never imagine doing that to somebody. Using their vulnerabilities against them. I couldn't even do that to my worst enemy…if I had one that is.

"Annie, I know we're twins but we're different you and me. I never had the confidence to do what I wanted, to follow my dreams…"

"…Until now." She cuts in. "…I just want you to know that I'm so proud of you and that I love you. Maybe when you're here for Laura's wedding, we could meet up?"

I nod my head. "Maybe we could."

"I've decided to get some counselling Nicole, I don't want to be like this anymore and I know how much that helped you so I'm willing to try anything. I will make you be proud to be my sister again…"

I open the door back into the restaurant feeling relief. I wanted to speak to Annie to take back control of the situation. I know that we will never be as close as we were before. Too much has happened between us now but I surprise myself by realising that I feel okay about that, more than okay. I have a new life here with nothing but positivity and excitement around me.

Gael strolls onto the dancefloor to encourage people to salsa. Jesé takes my glass from my hand and leads the way onto the dancefloor as we are joined by Laura, Diego and my course friends. The atmosphere is fantastic as people sing along, clapping excitedly.

My Mom's jaw is almost on the floor as she sees us salsa dancing. As soon as the song is finished she rushes over to me, hugging me tightly as Jesé watches with a smile on his face. He tells us to stay still as he takes a photo of us together before my Dad comes running over insisting on another with him in it too.

The music changes to gentle background as the lights come up and people start to eat. Once I've had some food I start to clear away the plates and the rubbish into the kitchen and Juan follows me into the kitchen with a huge pile of plates too. I then dash around collecting empty glasses before unloading the dishwasher and re-stacking the shelves behind the bar with clean glasses.

As I pass my Dad who stands talking to Luís, I can't help but giggle to myself as Luís is trying to teach him how to say Jesé's name. I think he almost has it.

Back to the kitchen, Juan then reloads the dishwasher whilst I get the grapes ready for midnight. I can't believe how quickly the time has gone and just how well it's going. It's coming up to 11 p.m. already.

Juan dims the lights again and heads back out to the dancefloor as the music becomes louder. I pop a couple of grapes in my mouth and as I turn around I'm startled to see Jesé in the kitchen.

I put my hand to my chest. "You scared me…" I giggle.
He has a very determined look on his face as he saunters towards me. He lightly pushes me against the fridge, my breath becomes ragged with desire as he kisses me fervently.

"Sorry…" he smirks. "I just have wanted to do that all night, away from other people's eyes."

I swallow hard. "Wow…"

He laughs. "Sorry."

I hook my arms around his neck. "Don't ever apologise for doing that." He sees the grapes in bowls on the worktop beside me.

"You know that those are for midnight to bring you the good luck?"

"Well, maybe I don't need to eat those for good luck…"
He looks up in disbelief.

"I'm pretty sure that I have everything I've ever wanted."

He smiles widely. "Do you know something Nicole, I think that I do too."

Epilogue

"3, 2, 1 Happy New Year!"

I burst the confetti filled balloons with the broom handle as Jesé takes a photo of the confetti falling down much to everyone's delight. People are eating the grapes at each gong of the clock as played by the radio. What a fantastic sight it is.

The sound of the laughter in the room is so loud, it's wonderful. Jesé and I wish each other a Happy New Year and I have a sneaking suspicion that this will be my happiest yet.

Gael won't let anyone rest as he puts the music back on and people continue dancing. Sebastián leads the way, as the regulars follow him back to the dancefloor. Isabel joins him as he twirls her around over and over again. Raul shakes his head in laughter, glad to be sitting on the side-lines with his beer.

I decide to have a welcome couple of minutes sit down with Laura as we marvel at how much of a success the night has been.

"Just think you can say you're getting married this year, can you believe it?"

"I know, I can't wait." She tells me. She glances over at Diego as he chats to Mio and Jesé.

"You guys will have your place back to yourselves soon..."

Laura gasps. "You said you'd move in with him?"

I nod my head excitedly. "Can you believe it?"

Laura flies around to the other side of the table to squeeze me in excitement.

Gael is at the front once again providing an impromptu salsa lesson after plenty of pleading from my Mom. Salsa music is playing loudly, creating the perfect party atmosphere.

"Okay now remember, 1, step forward and replace into centre for 2. 3 step back and replace to centre for 4 and then we repeat…*vamo*s."

I stand at the side of the dancefloor with Jesé holding me, as we look on as regulars to the restaurant and my wonderful family and friends as they follow Gael in swinging their hips in time with the music. Everyone's smiling and laughing and having the time of their lives which makes me so happy to see. Even my Dad, Mio and Sebastián are trying out their best moves.

I can't believe my luck at how much I've achieved in just four months. I live in a country that I adore, I have a job that I really enjoy and have made some of the best friends, not to mention finding something that I really didn't expect to find. The love of my life. But this moment now, this is my best moment in Madrid.

Thank you!

Thank you so much for reading my book, I really hope that you have enjoyed reading it because it gave me a lot of joy writing it. If you have enjoyed it, I would be grateful if you could spare a few minutes to write a review on Amazon. If you are on twitter, please look me up at @JayneMay_Author.

I have been writing Hola Madrid for 5 years on and off, and during that time I was lucky enough to visit Madrid twice and it's a wonderful city. I hope that my passion for Spain is clear in my writing.

Travelling really inspires me and I have many more ideas for books that I'm excited to get started on writing in the near future.

I would like to thank Rufus for his editorial critique a few years ago, way back when my first draft was completed. I'd also like to thank my parents for their ongoing support of my writing. My Mom and my Auntie Yvonne for being my guinea pigs and for reading my book several times to give me their honest feedback. It was so lovely to know that you enjoyed it.

Special thanks to Pattie for the help, the patience and the understanding and guidance that you gave me years ago and that to this day, I am still so thankful for. You were also one of the few people that I trusted to read my first real attempt at writing a book all of that time ago, even though I didn't complete that book, you encouraged me to keep writing. I will be forever grateful to you for so many things.

My lovely friend Nicola, for always making me laugh, for cheering me on and listening to me talk about the characterisation of Jesé and about Spain in general.

Lastly but by no means least…thank you to my wonderful husband Paul and the best travel partner. Thank you for being with me every step of the way and not just in travelling with me to these beautiful places, but in life in general. I'm so glad to have seen so many inspirational places in the world with you and look forward to the many more that we will discover together. Thank you for listening and supporting me and for always being there and always being you.

Printed in Great Britain
by Amazon